CELL 8

CELL 8

Anders Roslund and Börge Hellström

SILVEROAK
New York / London

SILVEROAK
New York / London

An Imprint of Sterling Publishing Co., Inc. (New York)
and Quercus Publishing Plc (London)
387 Park Avenue South
New York, NY 10016

ISBN 978-1-4027-8715-7 (hardcover)
ISBN 978-1-4027-9016-4 (ebook)

Distributed in Canada by Sterling Publishing
c/o Canadian Manda Group, 165 Dufferin Street
Toronto, Ontario, Canada M6K 3H6

For information about custom editions, special sales, and premium and corporate purchases, please contact Sterling Special Sales at 800-805-5489 or specialsales@sterlingpublishing.com.

Manufactured in the United States of America

2 4 6 8 10 9 7 5 3 1

www.sterlingpublishing.com

IT'S NOT THE FACT THAT HE KNOWS HE'S GOING TO DIE. IT'S NOT THE FACT *that he's been sitting waiting for four and a half years. That's not it.*

The punishment, the real punishment, is knowing when.

Not "later." Not "when he's older." Not at some point in the distant future, so distant that he doesn't need to think about it.

But precisely *when.*

The year, the month, the day, the minute.

When he will stop breathing.

When he will feel no more, smell no more, see no more, hear no more.

Ever.

Only someone who has been condemned to die at an exact moment in time can understand how hellish that is.

The uncertainty makes death almost bearable, allows you not to think, because you can't possibly know—but he knows.

He knows that he will cease to exist in seven months, two weeks, one day, twenty-three hours, and forty-seven minutes.

Precisely.

then

HE LOOKED AROUND THE CELL. THAT DISTINCTIVE SMELL. HE SHOULD BE used to it by now. It should have become part of him.

He knew that he would never get used to it.

His name was John Meyer Frey and the floor he was staring at was piss yellow and unnaturally shiny. The walls that assailed him had probably once been white and the ceiling over his head screamed of damp, the round stains on the greenish background making the fifty-five square feet seem even smaller than they actually were.

He took a deep breath.

Worst of all were the clocks.

He could cope with the endless corridor of countless iron bars that kept anything that wanted to escape locked in; he could put up with the sound of rattling keys that bounced off the walls so your head felt like it would burst and your thoughts were shredded. He could even put up with the shouting of the Colombian in Cell 14, which got louder and louder as the night wore on.

But not the clocks.

The corrections officers wore huge fucking wristwatches in fake gold and it felt like the hands were taunting him whenever one of them passed his cell. At the far end of the corridor, on a water pipe that ran from the East Block through to the West Wing, was another one—he had never been able to fathom why, it seemed so out of place, hanging there, ticking away, unavoidable. Sometimes, he was certain of it, he also heard the church clock in Marcusville strike: the white stone church with the tall, thin steeple on the square that he knew so well. In the early morning in particular, when for a brief while it was almost silent and he lay still awake on his bunk, searching for something on the greenish ceiling, it pierced through the walls and counted the hour.

That's what they did. Counted. Counted down.

Hour by hour, minute by minute, second by second, and he hated knowing how much time was no longer left—that two hours ago his life had been longer.

It was one of those mornings.

He had lain awake nearly all night, twisting and turning and trying to sleep, sweating and feeling those minutes. The Colombian had shouted more than usual; he'd started around midnight and continued through the night until sometime after four, his fear ricocheting off the walls in the same way that the rattling keys did, his voice getting louder and louder by the hour, something in Spanish that John couldn't understand, the same thing, over and over again.

He'd dozed off around five, didn't look at a clock, just knew that it was around then; it was as if time was inside him, his body counting down even when he did everything he could to think about something else.

Half past six, no later. He woke up.

The smell of the cell assaulted him; the first breath made him gag and he hung over the dirty toilet bowl. It was more like a porcelain hole with no lid that was far too low even for someone who was five foot seven. He had gone down on his knees, waiting to spew, and then had to put his fingers down his throat when it didn't happen.

He had to empty himself.

Had to get rid of that first breath, had to get it out; difficult to get up otherwise, difficult to stand up.

He hadn't slept through a whole night since he came here, four years ago now, and he had stopped hoping that he ever would. But last night, this morning, had stolen more from him than any other morning or night.

It had been Marvin Williams's second-to-last night.

About lunchtime, the old man would be escorted down the secure corridor, over to the Death House and into one of the two cells there.

His last twenty-four hours.

Marv, who was his neighbor and friend. Marv, who had been on Death Row the longest now. Marv, so wise, so proud, so different from the other madmen.

Diazepam enema. Marv would be dribbling by the time they came to get him; he would be drugged and docile toward the end. He would slowly and drowsily consent to be escorted out by the men in uniform, and by the time they locked the door of East Block, he would have forgotten the smell.

"John?"

"Yes?"

"You awake?"

Marv hadn't slept either. John had heard him tossing and turning, walking around and around his tiny cell, singing something that sounded like children's songs.

"Yes, I'm awake."

"I didn't dare shut my eyes. D'you understand, John?"

"Marv . . ."

"Scared of falling asleep. Scared of sleeping."

"Marv . . ."

"You don't need to say anything."

The bars were off-white, sixteen ugly iron bars from one wall to the next. When John stood up and leaned forward, he did what he always did—he put his thumb and index finger around one of the bars, encircling the metal, holding on. Always the same, one hand, two digits, he enclosed what enclosed him.

Marv's voice again, one of those deep baritones, calm.

"It's just as well."

John waited in silence. They had spoken to each other ever since he came here. On the very first morning, Marv's friendly voice had helped him to get up, to be able to stand up without losing his balance. The conversation had continued ever since, and was still going on; staring straight ahead through the bars at the wall opposite, for several years, without being able to see each other. But now. His voice caught in his throat. He coughed. What do you say to someone who is only going to live for a day and a night more, then die?

Marv was breathing heavily.

"You know, John, I can't stand waiting any longer."

They read quite a bit. John had never read before. Not by choice. After a few months, Marv had forced *Huckleberry Finn* on him. A damn children's book. But he'd read it. Then another one. Now he read every day. So he didn't have to think.

"What will it be today, John?"

"Today, I want to talk to you."

"You have to read. You know that."

"Not today. Tomorrow. I'll read again tomorrow."

Marv. The only black man in town.

That was how he used to introduce himself. That was what he'd said that first morning when John's legs didn't want to work. A voice from the other side of the cell wall, and John had reacted in the way he always reacted: he told the voice to go to hell and eat shit. The only black man in town? John had seen for himself when the four guards had escorted him down the corridor and opened the door and then locked it for the first time. Not many other white men in East Block. He was on his own. Seventeen years old, and more terrified than he'd ever been in his life. He'd spat at the wall and kicked it until small chips of plaster powdered his shoes and he had shouted *fucking nigger, I'll get you* until his voice was hoarse.

And so it continued in the evening. "Hi, my name's Marv, the only black man in town." John didn't have the energy to shout anymore. And Marv had just carried on, told him about his childhood in some hole in Louisiana, how he had moved to a mining town in Colorado, that he'd visited a beautiful woman in Columbus, Ohio, when he was forty-four and gone into the wrong Chinese restaurant at the wrong time and seen two men die at his feet.

"Are you frightened?"

Death. The one thing they couldn't think about. The only thing they thought about.

"I don't know, John. I don't know anymore."

They'd talked without stopping all morning, so much to say when time would soon cease to be.

They'd watched others being escorted out; they knew the procedures that were written down in the Department of Rehabilitation and Correction's manuals and that hung on the walls all around, telling you how you would live, hour by hour, in your last twenty-four. A female doctor had been in earlier, put diazepam in a tube up his anus, and Marv was slowing down now as a result. He slurred as he tried to keep control of his words and it sounded like he was dribbling out of the corner of his mouth when he spoke.

John wished he could see him.

All this, to be standing beside someone and yet not, to be close to someone and yet not be able to touch him, not even put a hand on his shoulder.

The door at the end of the corridor opened.

Hard heels clacked on the piss yellow.

The peaked hats, like caps, the green-brown uniforms, the shiny black boots; four guards marching, two by two, down to Marv's cell. John followed every step, saw them stop a couple of yards away, their faces turned to what was on the other side of the wall.

"Put out your hands!"

Vernon Eriksen's voice was quite high, his accent typical of south Ohio, a local boy who'd come to work at the prison in Marcusville for a summer when he was nineteen and had stayed, and was then promoted to senior corrections officer on Death Row only a few years later.

John couldn't see what was happening anymore; the big uniforms were in the way.

But he knew.

Marv's hands were poking through the bars and Eriksen had put the handcuffs around his wrists.

"Open Cell Seven!"

Vernon Eriksen, a corrections officer whom John had slowly come to respect. The only one. The only one who got involved in the inmates' daily life, despite the fact that he didn't really need to or in fact shouldn't at all.

"Cell Seven open!"

The central security PA system crackled; the door to Marv's cell slid open. Vernon Eriksen waited, nodded to his colleagues, and stayed standing where he was while two officers entered the cell. John watched him. He knew that the senior officer hated doing this. Collecting a prisoner who he'd come to know, escorting him to the Death House, preparing him for death. It was not something he'd ever said, it was not something he could ever say, but John had understood and recognized it a long time ago; he just knew. He was tall, Eriksen, not muscular but solid, with thinning hair, an old-fashioned pudding-bowl haircut like an inverted gray halo under the rim of his uniform hat. He was looking into Marv's cell, watching the movements of his colleagues, his white gloves fiddling with the two sets of keys that hung from his belt.

"Stand up, Williams."

"It's time, Williams."

"I know that you can hear me, Williams, stand up, for God's sake, so I don't need to lift you."

John heard the two officers forcing his neighbor up from the bunk, feeble protests from a drugged sixty-five-year-old man. He looked at Vernon Eriksen again, who was still facing the cell. He wanted to scream, but not at the senior officer, who bizarrely was on their side, so to shout at him would be meaningless. Instead he turned around and pissed into the hole that was

7

supposed to be a toilet. No words anymore, no thoughts. As Marv was led out of his cell on the other side of the wall, John chased a piece of paper down into the water-filled hole. He forced the piece of paper back and forth with his jet stream until it finally stuck to the white porcelain.

"John."

Marv's voice, somewhere behind him. He buttoned up his orange prison coveralls, turned around.

"I want to talk to you, John."

John looked at the senior officer, who gave a curt nod, then approached the bars, the metal bars between the lock and the concrete walls. He leaned forward, as he always did, his thumb and index finger encircling one of the bars. Suddenly, he was face-to-face with a person he had seldom seen but had spoken to several times a day for the past four years.

"Hi."

That voice that he knew so well, friendly, safe. A proud man, straight backed, his black hair had long since turned gray, clean shaven as John had always imagined he would be.

"Hi."

Marv was dribbling. John could see that he was trying to concentrate, that the muscles in his face would not obey. A prisoner who is about to die has to be sedated, no unnecessary anxiety; John was certain it was in fact for the officers' sake, to quell *their* fear.

"This, this is yours."

John watched Marv lift his hand to his neck, how he fumbled for a while with deadened fingers, but finally got hold of what he was after.

"I would have to take it off later anyway."

A cross. It meant fuck-all to John. But everything to Marv. John knew that. Marv had found God a couple of years ago, like so many others who were kept in this corridor while they waited.

"No."

The older man bundled up the silver chain, wrapped it around the crucifix, and thrust it into John's hand.

"There's no one else. To give it to."

John looked at the chain he was now holding and then uneasily over at Vernon Eriksen again.

The senior corrections officer's face—John had never seen it like this before.

It was completely red. Like he was in spasm, like it was burning. And his voice, it was too forceful, too loud.

"Open Cell Eight!"

John's cell.

That wasn't right. John looked at Marv, who didn't seem to react, then at the three other officers, who stood still but glanced at each other, confused.

The cell door was still locked.

"Please repeat, sir."

A voice from central security over the PA system.

Vernon Eriksen lifted his chin in irritation, made sure he was looking straight at the officer at the other end of the corridor when he spoke: "I said, *open Cell Eight*. Now!"

Eriksen stared at the bars, waiting for the door to slide open.

"Sir—"

One of the three officers appealed to him by throwing open his hands, but he had barely opened his mouth before his boss interrupted.

"I am aware that I am now deviating from the set time schedule. If you have a problem with it, please file your complaint in writing. Later."

He looked over at central security again. A few more seconds of uncertainty.

They all stood in silence as the cell door slowly slid open.

Vernon Eriksen waited until it was fully open, then turned to Marv and nodded in the direction of the cell. "You can go in."

Marv didn't move. "You want me to . . . ?"

"Go in and say good-bye."

It got cold later, damp; there was a draft from the window in the corridor high up by the ceiling, a muted whistle that dropped to the floor. John buttoned his coveralls right up to the collar, orange cotton with no fit, and the letters *DR* printed in white on the back and thigh.

He was shivering.

Maybe it was the cold.

Or maybe it was the grief that he was already starting to fight.

now

HE STRUGGLED AGAINST THE STRONG WIND. NO ONE ELSE ON DECK. THEY were all inside, somewhere in the floating community of restaurants and dance floors and duty-free shops. He heard someone laugh, then the murmur of voices and the clinking of glasses, music pumping electronically from one of the lounges full of beautiful young things.

His name was John Schwarz and he was thinking of her. As he always did.

The first person he had really been close to. The first woman he'd ever touched; her skin, he could feel it, dream it, yearn for it.

It was eighteen years now since she died.

To the day.

He moved toward the door, one last deep breath of cold Baltic air, then into the boat that smelled of engine oil and drunkenness and cheap perfume.

Five minutes later, he was standing on a tiny stage in a huge lounge, looking out over the crowd who would be his audience for the evening, who were there to be entertained between drinks and cocktail umbrellas and bowls of peanuts.

Two couples. In the middle of the dance floor, which was otherwise empty.

He cocked his head. He wouldn't have spent his Thursday night on the Åbo ferry either, if he could help it. But the money—with Oscar at home, he needed it more than ever.

Three quick numbers with a swinging four-beat usually woke them up, and there were already more people on the floor; eight couples holding each other tight, leaning in toward each other, hoping that the next number would be the first slow dance, one that required body contact. John sang and searched among the dancing people and those standing around the edge of the floor waiting to be asked. There was a woman, so beautiful, with long dark hair, dressed in black, who bubbled with laughter when her partner stepped on her toes. John followed her with his eyes and thought of Elizabeth who was dead and of Helena who was waiting for him in an apartment in Nacka; this woman, both of them—Helena's body and Elizabeth's movements. He wondered what she was called.

They'd had a break and a drink of mineral water. His shirt, which was turquoise and blue with a black collar, was now soft and damp under the arms from the smoke and spotlights that harassed him. He was still trying to make eye contact with the woman, who had not left the floor for a moment; she had just switched partners a couple of times and was hot now too, her face and neck glistening.

He looked at his watch. One more hour.

One of the passengers, whom he recognized from a couple of trips around Christmas, approached the throng on the dance floor. He was the sort who got drunk and was calculating, accidently touching women's thighs whenever he could. He moved between the couples and had already brushed a young woman's breasts for a moment. John wasn't sure whether she'd noticed—they seldom did; what with the music and the passing bodies, a groping hand just vanished.

John hated him.

He'd seen men like him before: they were drawn to the band, dance music, and strong beer and sprayed their angst on anyone who got in the way. A woman who danced and laughed was also a woman who, in the dark, you could press against, grope, steal from.

And then he took something from her.

The one who was Elizabeth and Helena.

The one who was John's woman.

The man slid his hand onto her behind as she turned away; he came too close and ended up thrusting his crotch against her hip in what appeared to be a clumsy dance step. She was like all the others, enjoying herself too much and too nice to realize that he had just stolen something from her. John sang and he watched and he trembled, felt the anger that had once fired him up and made him fight. For a long time he had hit people; now he just hit walls and furniture. But this creep, this man who took what he could, he had rubbed against one woman too many.

then

HE LAY DOWN ON THE BUNK AND TRIED TO READ. IT DIDN'T WORK. THE words just swam on the page, thoughts that wouldn't focus. It was just like it had been when he first came here, when he was new, and after two weeks of kicking the walls and iron bars he'd realized that it was simply a matter of putting up with it, that he had to keep breathing while his appeals filled space, to find a way to pass the time without counting.

But today, today was different. Today he wasn't doing it for his own sake. He knew that. He was thinking of Marv. It was Marv he was reading for. *John,* every morning the same question, *what's it going to be today?* It was important to Marv. *Steinbeck? Dostoyevsky?*

Four uniformed officers had just escorted the sixty-five-year-old man down the long corridor of locked cells. He was dribbling, thanks to the sedatives they'd given him, and his legs had buckled under him several times, but he'd kept his composure; he hadn't screamed or cried, and the sharp barbed wire above their heads had twinkled dismally in the weak light that managed to force its way in through the small windows even farther up by the ceiling.

For John Meyer Frey, Marvin Williams was the closest to what other people called a true friend that he'd ever had. An elderly man who had eventually cajoled the aggressive and terrified seventeen-year-old boy into talking, thinking, longing. Perhaps that was what the senior officer had seen—a sense of family strong enough to make him grossly neglect security procedures. They had stood face-to-face in John's cell, talked quietly together, feeling Vernon Eriksen watching them from the corridor, allowing a few minutes of shared time.

Now he was going to die.

His choice, electric chair or lethal injection. Marv had never been like the others. He hadn't made the same choice as the others.

He was in the Death House, in one of the two death cells in the Southern Ohio Correctional Facility, in Marcusville—the final destination for your last twenty-four hours of life, Cell 4 or Cell 5. No other cell had

17

the same number, the number of death, not here, not in East Block, not anywhere else in the great prison. One, two, three, six, seven, eight. That's how they counted in all the units, all the corridors.

The only black man in town.

He had explained after a few months of nagging, once John started to read the books he recommended. Before the Chinese restaurant with the two dead men at his feet in Ohio, Marv had lived in the mountains of Colorado, in Telluride, an old mining community that had been deserted when the minerals were exhausted. It died out for a while until hippies from the city had moved there in the sixties and transformed it to suit their alternative lifestyle. A couple of hundred enlightened, young, white Americans who believed in what you believed in then: freedom, equality, brotherhood, and everyone's right to roll a joint.

Two hundred white people and one black man.

Marv really had been the only black man in town.

And some years later, whether it was to provoke people or to demonstrate brotherhood and all that, or due to his constant need for money, he had agreed to marry a woman from South Africa who needed a green card. He had regularly appeared in front of a panel of officials and explained that the only true love for the town's only black man was, of course, this white woman from the home of apartheid, and he had done this so successfully that she was an American citizen by the time they got divorced some years later.

It was also for her sake that he'd gone to Ohio and stepped into the wrong restaurant.

John sighed, gripped the book even harder, tried again.

Throughout the afternoon and evening, he managed to read only a few lines at a time. He kept picturing Marv in the death cell, which had no bunk—maybe he was sitting there now, on the blue stool that stood in the corner, or he was lying curled up on the floor, staring at the ceiling.

A few more lines, sometimes a whole page, then back to Marv.

The light slowly drained from the small windows and was swallowed by the night. It was hard to lie next to the empty cell and not listen out for Marv's heavy breathing. To his surprise, John managed to sleep for a couple of hours. The Colombian made less noise than usual, and he was tired from the night before. John woke around seven, with the book under him, then lay there for a few hours more, before rolling over and getting up, almost refreshed.

He could hear clearly that there were visitors.

It was easy to differentiate between the voices of people who were free and those who had been sentenced to death. It was easy to recognize the tone that you hear only in the voice of someone who doesn't know *precisely* when they're going to die, the uncertainty that allows them not to count.

John looked down toward central security. He counted fifteen people as they passed.

They were early—still three hours to go until the execution—and they filed slowly past, peering down the corridor with curious eyes. At the front, the prison warden, a man whom John had seen only once before. The witnesses followed him. John assumed that it was the usual: a few members of the victim's family, a friend of the person to be executed, some representatives of the press. They were all wearing overcoats and the snow still lay on their shoulders; their cheeks were red, due to the cold or in anticipation of watching someone die.

He spat in their direction through the bars. He was just about to turn around when he suddenly heard central security opening the door and letting someone into the corridor of East Block.

It was a short, stocky man with a mustache and dark, slicked-back hair. He was wearing a fur coat over his gray suit; the snow had melted and the fur was wet. He marched down the middle of the corridor, the black rubbers over his dress shoes slapping on the stone floor. There was no hesitation; he knew where he was going, to which cell he was headed.

John brushed his hair down with a nervous hand and tucked it behind his ears, as he always did, his ponytail hanging down his back. He'd had short hair when he came here but had let it grow ever since, every month another half inch, in case he ever lost the clock that ticked inside him.

He could see the visitor clearly now, as he had stopped squarely in front of his cell; the face that he fled from in the dreams that perpetually haunted him, a face that had once been full of acne and now carried the scars that time and good living had not erased. Edward Finnigan was standing outside in the corridor, his color leached by winter, his eyes tired.

"Murderer."

His lips were tight. He swallowed, raised his voice.

"Murderer!"

A fleeting glance over his shoulder to central security; he realized that he should keep his voice down if he wanted to stay.

"You took my daughter from me."

"Finnigan . . ."

"Seven months, one week, four days, and three hours. *Exactly*. You can appeal as much as you like. I'll make sure that your appeals are turned down. In exactly the same way that I'm able to stand in front of you now. You know it, Frey."

"Go away."

The man who was trying unsuccessfully to talk quietly raised his hand to his mouth, a finger to his lips.

"Shhh, don't interrupt. I don't like it when murderers interrupt me."

He moved his finger away. The forcefulness returned to his voice, a force that only hate can provoke.

"Today, Frey, I'm going to watch Williams die, courtesy of the governor. And in October, I'll be watching you. Do you understand? You only have one spring, only one summer left."

The man in the fur coat and rubbers was finding it hard to stand still. He hopped from one foot to the other, moved his arms in circles; the hate that he had stored in his belly was being released into his body, forcing his joints and muscles to jump forward. John stood silent, as he had when they met during the trial. The words were to much the same effect; at first he had tried to answer but had then given up. The man in front of him didn't want any answers, any explanations; he wasn't ready for that, never would be.

"Go away. You've nothing to say to me."

Edward Finnigan dug his hand into one of his coat pockets and took out something that looked like a book—red cover, gilded pages.

"You listen to this, Frey."

He leafed through the pages for a few seconds, looking for a bookmark, found it.

"Exodus, chapter twenty-one . . ."

"Leave me alone, Finnigan."

". . . twenty-third, twenty-fourth, and twenty-fifth verses."

He looked over toward central security again, tensed his jaw, gripped the Bible with white fingers.

"*But if there is serious injury, you are to take life for life, eye for eye, tooth for tooth . . .*"

Edward Finnigan read the text as if it were a sermon.

"*. . . hand for hand, foot for foot, burn for burn, wound for wound, bruise for bruise.*"

He smiled as he slammed the book shut. John turned around, lay down with his back to the bars and corridor, fixed his gaze on the dirty wall. He lay like this until the steps receded down the corridor and the door at the end was opened and then closed again.

Fifteen minutes to go.

John didn't need a clock.

He always knew exactly how long he'd been lying down.

He looked at the fluorescent tube on the ceiling, the glass covered with small black marks. Flies that had been attracted to the light that was always on, they had come too close and been fried by the heat. The first few nights he had to hold his hands over his eyes, fighting not only the fear and all the new noises, but also a light that would never be switched off; it had been hard to relax with a glare that constantly held the dark at bay.

He was going to look at it now, until it was over.

Sometimes he hoped there was something after.

Anything more than just a brief inglorious sense of death; more than just the knowledge that *right now I'm dying*, and then the next moment for it to be over.

The feeling was strongest at times like this, when someone else was about to die, someone who no longer needed to count.

John would lie down and bite the arm of his coveralls and feel his heart pounding; it was hard to breathe, hard to breathe, and then the shakes would rack his body until he spewed all over the floor.

As if he were dying, every time.

John gripped the sides of the bunk when the light seemed to briefly go out. Or had he just imagined it? It flickered again, vanished. While Marv Williams's body was cramped by electric shocks of between two thousand volts and twenty-five hundred volts, the lights in East Block and West Wing and all the other units in the prison flickered on and off. He had probably vomited after the first shock and then a little bit more with each subsequent shock, until he was completely empty.

It was as if the light came back on and John knew that his ravaged body had for a few seconds slumped forward in a heap on the chair, still alive. He bit the arm of his coverall and wondered what Marv was thinking, if thoughts were louder than pain.

21

The second shock always lasted for seven seconds, a thousand volts, and the saline water in the copper electrodes that were attached to the head and the right leg started to hiss.

John didn't bite the orange material anymore. He undid the two buttons closest to the collar and gripped the silver chain and cross that hung there. While he squeezed it, he was sure that the lights went on and off several times, the third and final shock.

Marv's eyeballs had burst out of the sockets now.

Urine and excrement everywhere.

His swollen body, blackened by third-degree burns where the electrodes had been secured, would be too hot to touch for some time.

He himself hated everything that religion stood for, but did what Marv would have done—he held the crucifix in one hand and with the other made the sign of the cross in the air in front of him.

now

THERE WAS ONLY AN HOUR LEFT, SO HE SHOULD JUST LOOK THE OTHER way. They had already turned at Åbo and were on their way home: just a couple more songs, upbeat numbers that got the drunkest people off the floor and then a slow song for those who didn't want the night to end, that was all; then a few hours in the cabin and Stockholm again.

But he couldn't. He couldn't look the other way, not again—the man who was stealing from the women on the dance floor, and who had done it before, had now thrust his crotch against her hip for the second time and she had been just as oblivious to it.

John had been watching her all night.

The dark hair, the delight in being able to dance herself into a sweat; she was beautiful. She was both Elizabeth and Helena at the same time.

His woman.

"What the hell are you doing?"

He had suddenly stopped singing, was hardly aware of it himself. Anger could not read music and the others behind him had continued for a few bars, then lowered their instruments, waited in silence.

He should look the other way.

He spoke from the stage again, looking at the man who was still standing too close to her.

"You leave her alone. Now."

The clink of glasses from somewhere over by the door. The strong wind was buffeting the large windows. Otherwise silence. The silence that is created by a sudden pause in the music, when the singer breaks off the chorus.

Thirteen couples froze on the dance floor.

They were all suspended midstep, dancing to something that they recognized as an eighties potpourri. They were still out of breath as it slowly dawned on them what was going on. They turned one by one in the direction John was pointing, toward the tall, fair man standing in their midst on the dance floor.

25

The microphone crackled when John spoke too loudly.

"Do you not understand? When you've gone, we'll go on playing."

The man took a step back, swayed a bit, his crotch no longer pushing against the woman's hip. He found his balance again, turned around to face the stage and John, his middle finger in the air. He just stood there, said nothing, didn't move.

Some people left the dance floor.

Others leaned toward their partners, whispered something in their ears.

Someone threw up his arms impatiently: "Come on, play! We're dancing."

The man still had his finger in the air as he pushed his way through the stationary couples, heading for the stage, for John.

Lenny's voice somewhere behind him: *Forget it, John, just leave it until security gets here*, and Gina sighing: *That's enough, just let the pisshead swear a bit*; even the bassist who hadn't said anything until now: *There's no point, there'll be another one here tomorrow.*

He heard them.

He didn't hear them.

The drunk man stood below him, laughing and sneering, his stinking breath and face roughly level with John's waist. His finger was still in the air, but now he lowered it, and formed a circle with his index finger and thumb on the other hand, looked John straight in the eye and then thrust the lowered finger into the circle, two times, three times.

"I'll dance with whoever I want."

Someone dropped a fork.

Maybe a loudspeaker snapped.

John noticed nothing. There was nothing that he could later explain. He was concentrating on counting out time. If anyone could, he could. *If I just keep counting, this fucking feeling will go, I'll calm down again.*

He'd learned how to do this.

To not hit.

Never to hit again.

He looked down at the man who was sneering at him and violating the air with his hand; he ran his own hands through the long hair that he no longer had, tried to tuck it behind his ears as he had always done when agitation and fear pushed aside what should have been control. He saw Elizabeth's sixteen-year-old face and he saw Helena's thirty-seven-year-old face, and he looked at the woman who had just been dancing herself dizzy and who was now standing stock-still some way off, and then at the drunken hands that had pushed against her and suddenly everything just exploded: all the fucking years of counting and all the fucking years of repressed anger that pushed against his chest from inside when he tried to sleep. And without being aware of it he pulled back his leg and kicked with all the might that only time can muster; he hit him somewhere in the middle of his laughing face and then heard nothing of the confusion and commotion as the people around surged toward him.

PART I

monday

IT WAS A RATHER BEAUTIFUL MORNING; STOCKHOLM IN THE MIST IN THE distance, the encroaching sun, vapors dancing on the water. Half an hour more, then dock, town, home.

John looked out of the plastic porthole. The enormous ferry glided slowly down the channel, at no more than a few knots—the waves formed by the metal prow as soft as from any small boat.

It had been a long night. He was tired, had gone to bed sometime after four, but hadn't been able to sleep. That's the way it was sometimes, when what was happening now became confused with what had happened back then. His eyes were aching, his head was aching, his whole damn body was aching. He was frightened. It was a long time since he'd been frightened; he'd found an everyday routine and settled down—Helena sleeping beside him and Oscar fast asleep in his bed next door. They had a life together. The apartment was small but it was theirs; sometimes it felt like there had never been anything else, as if he could forget everything else.

There was a draft from the porthole. The cabin was cold, as always in January. Two evenings onboard, a good wage, his own cabin and free food—that was enough and he could deal with it. Dance-band music and drunk conference delegates were something that he had gradually learned to cope with. After all, he was a father now, and a regular income almost compensated for the feeling that sometimes gripped him in the middle of a song, onstage with the others. A feeling of loneliness, despite all the sweaty, laughing couples on the dance floor, of not being able to talk to anyone, not being able to move.

He had kicked him in the middle of the face.

John closed his eyes, squeezed his eyelids shut until it hurt, and then he looked out again. Stockholm was getting closer; the skyline of Södermalm looked as if it was falling down into Stadsgård dock.

It shouldn't have happened.

He was never going to hit anyone again.

But that bastard had had his hand up her skirt, he had thrust himself

33

against her, and she had tried to get away, his hand on her behind. John had warned him, and people had stopped dancing, and when the man took his hand away and laughed at him, stood there right in front of him, it had felt like it was someone else, as if John was an onlooker, the raw energy, it wasn't his.

Someone knocked on the cabin door. He didn't hear it.

They had called it *low impulse control*. Back then, a long time ago. They had examined him and talked to him and given the diagnosis, a young teenager who fought everything he could fight against. Someone had of course talked about a mother who had died when he was young and someone else about the things that had happened later. But even back then he had scoffed at things like that. He didn't believe that the explanation lay in his childhood. It wasn't the result of difficult potty training or broken toys; he hit everyone he came into contact with because he had no choice, because he *wanted* to.

The noise by the open cabin door continued.

Stockholm grew outside the porthole, the skyline defined into buildings. It was the kind of winter day that he had grown to appreciate: Stockholm, a warm sun that brought color to your cheeks, and then the cold returned with the dark, a fight between the life that was waiting and the past that had to go. He gazed over at a jetty as they sailed by, a big villa that he always watched out for—it lay in such a good position, right down by the water, a well-maintained garden hidden beneath a thin layer of snow. He saw the ice around the abandoned jetty where an expensive yacht was normally moored in summer. *Stöpis.*

One of his favorite words in Swedish. Water that ran over the ice when the temperature rose, and then froze again during the cold nights. *Stöpis.* Several layers of thin ice with water in between. He didn't even know what it was called in English, had never got around to learning it, if it even existed.

There was another knock on the door.

This time he heard it. Far away, a knock that penetrated his thoughts. He turned around to face the cabin: a bed and a wardrobe and white walls, a door at the far end where the noise was coming from.

"Am I disturbing you?"

A man in a green uniform, tall, broad shouldered, red beard. John recognized him. One of the security guards.

"No."

"Can I come in?"

He pointed to the cabin. John didn't know what his name was.

"Of course."

The security guard came over to the round window and looked, distracted, at the city in the distance.

"The view. It's lovely."

"Yes."

"Will be nice to get ashore."

"Why are you here?"

The security guard pointed at the bed but didn't wait for an answer, just sat down.

"The incident last night."

John looked at him.

"Right . . ."

"I know who it is. The kind of guy who gets too close. He's done it before. But that's not the point. It's never a good idea to kick anyone in the face onboard."

There was pack of cigarettes on the shelf that doubled as a bedside table. John took one out, lit it. The security guard moved demonstratively away from the smoke.

"You've been reported. Around fifty witnesses is a few too many. The police are already at Stadsgård dock waiting."

Not that.

The fear he had not had to feel for so long. That he had nearly learned to forget.

"I'm sorry, buddy."

The green uniform on the bed. John looked at it, took a drag on his cigarette, couldn't move.

Not that.

"John—that is your name, isn't it? Just one thing. Personally I don't give a damn if some Finnish bastard who deserves it gets his head kicked in. But you've been reported. And the police will take you in for questioning."

John didn't scream.

He was convinced that that was what he was doing, but no sound came out.

A single silent scream until his lungs were empty. Then he sat down on the bed, lowered his head, his hands clasped to his cheeks.

He couldn't understand why, but he was for a moment in another place, in another time; he was fifteen years old and he had just hit a teacher from behind with a chair: a single blow to Mr. Coverson's face just as he turned around. He lost his hearing on one side as a result, Mr. Coverson, and John could still remember how he felt when he faced his victim in the courtroom, when he realized for the first time that every blow has a consequence. He had cried as he'd never cried before, not even at his mother's funeral. He had understood, truly understood that he'd robbed the man of something vital, forever, and he'd known that he'd hit someone for the last time. Three months in that shitty, awful juvenile detention center had not changed that.

"They'll stop the shuttle bus."

The security guard was still sitting down. He was taken aback by the intensity of John's reaction, the sudden terror that filled the simple cabin. To be questioned by the police. To risk being charged with assault. Sure, no one would want that. But this—his head was shaking violently, his chalk-white face that couldn't speak—the guard couldn't comprehend it.

"They'll be waiting for you there. When you drive off."

John could hear him somewhere above his head, a voice that dissolved and disappeared in cigarette smoke.

"But if you went down the ordinary gangway with the other passengers who don't have vehicles, you might be able to buy yourself a couple of hours more."

He left the ferry in a crowd of people with duty-free shopping bags and suitcases on wheels, as the morning rush hour built up in the city, and then hurried along the sidewalk away from the center, toward Nacka. There was moisture in the air and carbon dioxide and something else that carried him to Danvikstull, where he flagged down a taxi with a sweaty hand and said he wanted to go to Alphyddevägen 43. He had been dreading this day for more than six years but had long ago decided he would not run away. He wanted to get home. To Helena, to Oscar. He wanted to hold them and talk about the future and he wanted to eat rice pudding with blueberry jam, as if it were his last meal.

THE EARLY MORNING STUNG EWERT GRENS'S CHEEKS. HE DIDN'T LIKE THE long fucking winters; there was nothing about them that he liked, especially around now, at the beginning of January. He hated every day of the cold. He had problems moving his neck, and his left leg wouldn't do as it was told—defects that only seemed to get worse as the temperature plummeted. It made him feel old, older than his fifty-seven years. Every joint, every muscle that had lost its youth, shouted out for spring, for warmth.

He was standing outside the main door on Sveavägen. The same stair that led to the same apartment on the fourth floor where he had lived for nearly thirty years now. *Three decades in the same place, without getting to know even one of his neighbors.*

He snorted.

Because you don't want to. Because you don't have the time. The kind who just get in the way. The kind who hang up notices on the bulletin board by the main door asking people to stop feeding the birds on their balconies. Neighbors who only talked to each other when someone played their music too loud and too late, and who threatened to call in noise pollution officers or the police. *Don't fucking want to know people like that.*

Stuck at a complete standstill in traffic, he had been on his way to see Anni when he suddenly remembered that his visit this particular Monday had been postponed until lunch. Every Monday morning, for all these years, and then some junior nurse books her in for physio. Tired and irritated, he had pulled out of traffic, crossed the middle of the road, and driven back to park in the space that he'd just left, only to discover that it had been taken. He swore loudly and parked where he shouldn't.

He wasn't expected at Kronoberg for another couple of hours and had therefore started to walk up the stairs to his apartment when he suddenly stopped on the second floor. Not there. Too big. Too empty. He hadn't been home at all for a while. The sofa in his well-lived-in office at the far end of police headquarters was very narrow and he had difficulties fitting his large frame onto it, it was true, but he slept better there. And in fact he always had.

So he started to walk slowly along the sidewalk. Crossed Sveavägen, down Odengatan, past the Gustav Vasa Church, then turned into Dalagatan. The same route, twenty-five minutes, no matter what time of year. Thin gray hair, a furrowed face, an obvious limp because his left leg was lame—Detective Superintendent Ewert Grens was the sort of person other people moved away from on the sidewalk, the sort of man who is heard without having to say a word.

He was singing now.

Once he'd passed the old alkies who sat on the benches in Vasa Park and the forlorn entrance to Sabbatsberg Hospital, he normally picked up speed. His lungs needed that time to get going properly, and he sang, loud and out of tune, not bothered by the people who turned and stared, all the way to police headquarters while the blood pumped around his ungainly body. Always Siw Malmkvist, always a song from a time that no longer existed.

I know that I acted hastily
Yes my words were heartless and cruel.

This morning Siw's version of Patti Page's "Don't Read the Letter," 1961. He sang and remembered long days without loneliness, a life so far in the past that it was hard to keep track.

Thirty-four years in the police force. He had had everything. Thirty-four years. He had nothing.

In the middle of Barnhus Bridge, which linked Norrmalm with Kungsholmen, he sang even louder. Over the noise of the traffic, the strong wind that always lay in wait just there, he belted it out across Stockholm, suppressing the agitation and thoughts and feelings that at times nearly tipped into bitterness.

Is it too late to be sorry?
Forgive me for being a fool

He unbuttoned his coat, pulled off his scarf, let the old lyrics float freely between the cars that drove by in second gear, and the people who hunched up and hurried past on their way somewhere. Grens was just coming to the chorus when he felt an impatient vibration in the inner pocket of his jacket. Once. Twice. Three times.

"Hello."

He talked loudly into the electronic void of his mobile phone. A couple of seconds, then a voice that he detested.

"Ewert?"

"Yes."

"What are you up to?"

As if you cared, you little ass kisser. Ewert Grens loathed his boss. Just as he loathed, in principle, everyone in his workplace. It was not something he tried to hide. No one could avoid noticing. This little runt, a cocky superintendent, was too young and too self-important to even tie his own shoes.

"What do you want?"

He heard his boss taking a breath, bracing himself.

"Ewert, you and I have different roles to play. Different areas of responsibility. For example, it is me who decides who is employed here. And where."

"That's what you say."

"So I was wondering how it was that *you*, as I've just found out, have already given the vacant post in your section to someone. Someone who, by the way, has nowhere near the experience required to be a detective inspector."

He should hang up, he should sing what he had to sing. The sun had just risen and Stockholm was waking up on the right side of the bed, it was his time, his ritual, his fucking right not to have to deal with idiots.

"That's the way it goes. When you're not quick enough."

A train passed underneath him, the sound echoing off the bridge and drowning out the voice on the phone. He didn't mind.

"I can't hear you."

The voice tried again.

"You can't employ Hermansson. I've got another candidate. Someone who's qualified."

Ewert Grens was about to start singing again.

"There you go. Too late. I signed all the necessary papers yesterday evening. As I realized that you'd stick your oar in."

He snapped the phone shut and put it back in his inside pocket.

He continued on his way, cleared his throat—he would sing the whole song from the beginning again.

Ten minutes later he opened the heavy door at the main entrance on Kungsholmgatan.

The lunatics were already there.

A line waiting for the morning's reports. Every Monday the same, full house, the curse of the weekend. He looked at them, most of them tired; the apartment had been burgled while they were at the cabin, a car stolen from a parking lot, a shop window smashed and the display taken. He walked over toward the corridor and locked door, behind which lay the stairs to his office, a couple of floors up and a few doors down from the coffee machine. He was just about to punch in the code and go through when he saw a man lying on the sofa farthest away. A line number clutched in his hand, his face twisted and crooked, coagulated blood trailing from one ear. The sound of his voice unclear, as if slurring his words, a language that Grens was sure was Finnish.

Blood had been coming out of her ears.

A step closer. The prostrate man reeked of alcohol and the smell was so rank that Grens stopped abruptly.

It was his face. Something wasn't right.

Grens breathed through his mouth. Two steps forward and then he bent over him.

The man was heavily bruised.

His pupils were different sizes. One small, the other dilated.

The eyes, he saw them in front of him, her head in his lap.

He hadn't known, not then.

He went quickly over to the registration desk. A short exchange, Grens waved his arms around and the young policeman stood up, hurried behind the detective superintendent over to the drunk man who'd arrived half an hour earlier in a taxi and had just lain there on the sofa ever since.

"Get a patrol car to drive him to the ER—neurology—at the Karolinska Hospital! Now!"

Ewert Grens was furious as he jabbed the air with his finger.

"Severe head injuries. Different-sized pupils. Blood draining from the ears. Slurred speech."

He wondered if it was too late.

"Everything points to a brain hemorrhage."

He, if anyone, should know. That it might be too late. That you couldn't always ensure recovery from a serious head injury.

He had lived with that knowledge for more than twenty-five years.

"Have you registered his complaint?"

"Yes."

He was searching for the young policeman's name badge, made it obvious that he was looking straight at it; made eye contact again.

"Give it to me."

Ewert Grens opened the security door and walked down the corridor, past the rows of silent, waiting offices.

A person had just been bleeding from his ears, had looked at him with different-sized pupils.

That was all he had seen.

That was all he was able to see.

He could not possibly know that this single act of violence was linked to a murder and was the continuation of a process that had started many years ago, far away; it would prove to be the most extraordinary criminal investigation he had ever come across.

A BRIGHT LIGHT SHONE FROM ONE OF THE UPSTAIRS WINDOWS. IF ANYONE had been walking along Mern Riffe Drive just then and looked up at the exclusive twelve-room house, he or she would have seen a man in the window, stocky, around fifty, a mustache and dark, slicked-back hair. He or she would have seen his pale skin, his tired eyes, how he stood there, completely still, staring listlessly into the dark and had then started to cry, his tears rolling slowly down his round cheeks.

It was still night in Marcusville, Ohio. Several hours until dawn. The small, silent community was asleep.

Everyone except him.

Except the man who was crying with grief and hate and loss, who was standing in the window of what had once been his daughter's room.

Edward Finnigan had hoped that at some point it would pass. That he would be able to stop the hunt, that he would stop delving into the past, that he would be able to lie down next to his wife again, undress her, make love to her.

Eighteen years. And it just got worse. He grieved more; he missed her more and more—he hated more.

He shivered.

Pulled his bathrobe tighter around his body, moved his bare feet back a step from the dark wooden floor onto the thick carpet. He lifted his gaze from the town out there, the streets where he'd grown up, the people he knew so well, turned and looked around the room.

Her bed. Her desk. Her walls, floor, and ceiling.

She still lived here.

She was dead, but this room, it was still hers.

The body on the autopsy table is that of a naked woman. Weight 143 pounds. Length 67.7 inches.

Flesh not remarkable. Muscles not remarkable. Normal hair growth on body.

No sign of injury to face. Diffuse bleeding from right nostril.

He had shut the door. Alice woke up so easily and he wanted to be alone; here in Elizabeth's room he could cry, hate, and yearn without upsetting anyone. Sometimes he just stood at the window and stared at nothing. Sometimes he lay on the floor, or bent down over her bed, her teddy bear and the pink pillow, just as it had been back then. Tonight he would wait by her desk, sit in the new chair that she had never used.

He sat down.

Pens and erasers in a pile in front of him. A diary with a lock. Three books, which he leafed through absently; she had never really got past the horsey stage. A bulletin board on the wall; a yellowing sheet down in the left-hand corner: her schedule from Valley High School, one of Marcusville's two public high schools. They'd been clear about that, that she should go to an ordinary school. If the daughter of one of the governor's closest advisers didn't go to the local school, that would signal dissatisfaction, and that was what politics was all about, giving signals, giving the right signals. Above the schedule, another sheet of yellowed paper, some telephone numbers, doodles and scrawls in pencil around the edge. At the top, a message from the trainer of Marcusville Soccer Team about a series match against Otway, a reminder of a doctor's appointment at Pike County Hospital in Waverly, confirmation of a field trip to WPAY Radio Station, 104.1 FM in Portsmouth.

She had stopped midstep.

She had been on her way and he had taken all that away from her.

Livor mortis on the posterior of the body. Purplish in color, symmetrical spread with signs of contact pressure on lower back and buttocks.

Several numbered bullet holes on the anterior and posterior of body.

Edward Finnigan hated him. He had taken Elizabeth away forever, from the next day, from life, from this house.

The door handle moved. Finnigan turned his head quickly.

She looked at him with resignation in her eyes.

"Not tonight as well."

He sighed.

"Alice, go back to bed. I'll come soon."

"You'll sit here all night."

"Not this time."

"Always."

She came into the room. His wife. He should touch her, hold her. But he couldn't anymore. It was as if everything had died eighteen years ago. After a year or so they had had sex with each other twice a day, every day, so she would get pregnant, so they would have another child. But it hadn't worked. There was no way of knowing whether it was their shared grief or just the fact that she was older and the female body slowly becomes less fertile. Not that it mattered. They never held each other anymore.

She sat down on the bed. He shrugged.

"What do you want me to do? Forget?"

"Yes. Maybe."

Finnigan got up abruptly from what had once been his daughter's chair.

"Forget? Elizabeth?"

"The hate."

He cocked his head.

"I'll never forget. And I will never stop hating. Damn it, Alice, he murdered our daughter!"

She sat in silence for a while, resignation in her eyes; she found it difficult to look at him.

"You don't understand. It's not about Elizabeth anymore. You're shutting her out. You don't feel anything anymore."

She paused, took a deep breath, steeling herself to continue. "Your hate. Your hate is blocking everything out. You can't love and hate at the same time. That's just the way it is. And you've chosen, Edward. You made your choice a long time ago."

`4 pints of blood, partially coagulated, in the left pleural sac.`

`   2 wounds to the left lung: anterior site of entry and posterior`
`site of exit.`

"I never got to see him die."

He paced backward and forward across the floor, the anger pulsing through him, forcing him to move.

"We waited. Years we waited. Then he died! Before he was supposed to die. We never got to see it. *He* decided when it was over. Not us!"

Alice Finnigan sat on her daughter's bed. The only child she'd ever had. She would never stop grieving either. But this, Edward's hate, their marriage that was no longer a marriage—she was about to give up. She had forgotten what it was like to live, for real. A couple more years sullied by this bitterness and she would go, leave behind whatever this was that she no longer recognized.

"I'm going back to bed. And I want you to come with me."

He shook his head.

"I'll stay here, Alice."

She got up from the bed and was walking toward the door when he asked her to stop.

"It feels . . . it feels just like when someone breaks off a relationship. *Alice, listen to me, just for a minute.* You love someone, so you feel you've been abandoned. But that's not really it, that's not what really bothers you, that's not what's so painful that it makes your whole damn body burn. *Please listen to me, Alice.* It's the power. The power you no longer have. Being forced to be at the mercy of someone else's decision. Losing the power to decide yourself when your relationship is over. That's always what hurts, more than the loss of the love that is no longer there. *Do you understand?"*

He looked at her with pleading eyes. She said nothing.

51. Liver weighs approx. 3 lb 8 oz. There is a bullet path through the posterior wall that continues under the gall bladder.

"That's what it feels like. That's how I've felt since he died. If only I could have been there and seen him die, see him gradually lose the ability to breathe, if I'd been able to be there and have closure . . . then I could have moved on, I know it, Alice. But now. It was *him* who decided. It was *him* who finished it. Alice, of course you understand, you have to understand, my whole body is burning, burning!"

57. Left kidney weighs 4.6 oz. Right kidney has bullet path from left to right. Large crater in the upper pole, about the size of a golf ball, with hemorrhaging.

She said nothing.

She looked at him, turned around, and left the room. Edward Finnigan remained standing where he was in the middle of the floor. He heard her closing the door to their marital bedroom.

He listened to the silence, heard a light wind blowing outside, a branch tapping against the window. He went over and looked out into the dark. Marcusville was sleeping, would sleep for a while yet; it was three hours until dawn.

IT WAS ALREADY LUNCHTIME WHEN EWERT GRENS RANG FOR A TAXI AND then hurried down the corridors of the police headquarters. He was late and he hated that, she was waiting, she was sitting there, depending on him, they'd made her look nice, brushed her hair like they always did, helped her to put on one of the blue dresses. He asked the driver—a short thin man who laughed a lot and talked for the entire journey about Iran, his home country, how beautiful it was, the life he'd had there and would never have again—Grens asked him after a couple of endless quarter hours on Kungsholmen to drive slightly faster, showed him his ID, said it was a police job.

Fourteen minutes across town and seventy miles per hour over Lidingö Bridge.

He asked to get out of the car a short walk away from the big building. He needed to gather his thoughts. She was waiting for him.

He had been well and truly battered. First had to get rid of the man who had slurred in Finnish. Blood running out of his ear. A whole morning had passed and Grens hadn't been able to dislodge the image of the person lying on one of the police station sofas. *Mottled eyes, one pupil small, one pupil dilated.*

Aggravated assault. That wasn't enough. It was more than that.

Attempted murder.

He got out his mobile phone, rang Sven Sundkvist, the only person he could actually tolerate in the building where he'd worked all his adult life. He asked him to stop what he was doing, he wanted the identity of the person who kicked other people's heads in, then he wanted him brought in for questioning, because that sort of behavior should cost him time behind bars.

Slowly walked the last hundred yards to the nursing home.

He'd been coming here for twenty-five years, at least once a week, to the only person he'd ever really cared about, the only person who'd ever really cared about him.

He was about to walk into her room again. He would do it with dignity.

They'd had their whole lives ahead of them.

Until he had driven over her.

He had long since realized that the images from that day would never stop crowding his mind. Every thought, every moment, he could relive those seconds.

The big fucking tires.

He didn't make it.

He didn't make it!

The wind was blowing in off the water, freezing Baltic temperatures straight in the face. He kept his eyes on the ground—the gravel path was partially covered in ice and he knew that the excessive weight on his good leg made it difficult to hold his balance; he had nearly gone head over heels a couple of times now and cursed the pointless seasons and poorly maintained path loudly.

He had felt the van lurch when it hit her body.

Grens crossed the large parking lot at the front of the building, found the window where she normally sat, looking out into thin air.

He couldn't see her. He was late. She trusted him.

He hurried up the steps, nine in all, carefully salted. A woman of his own age was sitting at the slightly oversized reception desk, one of the ones who had been there when they first came in one of the police transport vans; he'd arranged it all, she had to feel safe.

"She's sitting in there."

"I didn't see her at the window."

"She's there. She's waiting. We've saved her lunch."

"I'm late."

"She knows you're coming."

He glanced in the mirror that hung outside the restrooms between reception and the patients' rooms. His hair, face, eyes, he was old, looked tired, sweaty from his skating on ice. He held back a short while, until his breathing had steadied.

He had sat with her bleeding head in his lap.

Grens walked the short distance down the corridor, past the closed doors, stopping in front of number fourteen, the numbers in red above her name on a sign by the handle.

She was sitting in the middle of the room. She looked at him.

"Anni."

She smiled. At the voice. Maybe the sound of the door opening. Or the light in the room, that now came from two sources.

"I'm late. Sorry."

She laughed. It was a high, bubbling laugh. He went over to her, kissed her on the forehead, took a handkerchief out of his pocket and wiped dry the saliva that was running down her chin.

A red dress with light stripes.

He was certain that he'd never seen it before.

"You look lovely. New dress. It makes you look so young."

She hadn't aged, not like him. Her cheeks were still smooth, her hair as thick as before. He was losing his energy out there, with every day that passed. She seemed to be conserving hers, days in a wheelchair in front of a window, it was as if she still had everything.

The bright blood just didn't stop running from her ears, nose, and mouth.

His hand on her cheek, he released the brake that locked one of the back wheels, rolled her out through the door, down the corridor to the empty dining room. He moved one of the chairs by the table nearest the large window with a view down over the water, and positioned her there, then got cutlery and a glass and a hard plastic bib; the food was standing in the fridge, some sort of meat stew with rice.

They sat opposite each other.

Grens knew that he should tell her. Only he had no idea how.

It didn't change anything.

He fed her at the same speed that he ate himself; the homemade stew had been reduced to a suitable brown and green and white mash on her plate. She ate well, she had a good appetite, she always had. He was sure that that was why she stayed so well, all these years in a wheelchair, far removed from other people's conversations, as long as she ate and got energy, she would be there, wanting to live and keep on living.

He was nervous. He had to tell her.

She swallowed and something got caught in her throat; a severe coughing fit, he got up, held her until her breathing was regular again. He sat down and took her hand.

"I've employed a woman."

It was hard to meet her eyes.

"A young woman, like you, back then. She's smart. I think that she'll be good."

He wondered if she understood. He wanted to know. He wished it were possible to know if she was listening, if she was really listening.

"It won't affect us. Not like that. She could have been our daughter."

She wanted more food. A couple more spoonfuls of the brown stuff, one of the white.

"I just wanted you to know."

By the time he was back out on the veranda by the entrance, it was blowing a mixture of snow and rain. He tied his scarf, buttoned his coat all the way up. He was down the steps and had started to walk across the parking lot when his mobile phone started to ring.

Sven Sundkvist.

"Ewert?"

"Yes?"

"We've found him."

"Bring him in for questioning."

"A foreigner."

"He kicked a person in the head."

"Canadian passport."

"I want you to bring him in."

The rain intensified, the drops mixed with snow seemed ever bigger, ever heavier.

Ewert Grens knew that it wouldn't help in the slightest, but he looked up at the sky and cursed the endless winter, damning it to hell.

IT WOULD SOON BE LIGHT IN THE SMALL TOWN IN SOUTHERN OHIO THAT
was dominated by the huge prison with high concrete walls. It was cold
out, snow falling as it did throughout the winter, and the inhabitants of
Marcusville would start their day by clearing the driveways to their
houses.

Vernon Eriksen did his last round through the corridors of locked-up
people.

It was half past five; one hour left, then he would finish his night shift,
change into ordinary clothes, walk to Sofio's on Main Street, a Mexican
restaurant that did a decent breakfast, double blueberry pancakes and
crispy fried bacon.

He'd left West Wing and was on his way to East Block, his footsteps
echoing on the walls that he still thought of as new, even though they'd
been there for more than thirty years now. He could clearly remember the
building at the edge of town that was to become high walls and cells that
would accommodate prisoners, and for that very reason divided the
inhabitants of Marcusville into two camps as it slowly grew: those who saw
it as new job opportunities and a second chance for a backwater town, and
those who saw it as a fall in property prices and a constant worry about the
criminal elements in their midst. He hadn't thought about it much himself.
He was nineteen and had applied for a job in the newly opened prison and
had then just stayed there. He'd therefore never had reason to leave
Marcusville; one of the leftovers, a bachelor who instead clung to the work
that had become his everyday as the years passed and now, now that he was
over fifty, it was too late to break out. He sometimes went to Columbus for
a dance, occasionally ate dinner with a woman some miles south in
Wheelersburg, but that's where it stopped, nothing more, no intimacy, he
always left before.

His life, it had somehow always been connected to death.

He mused on it every so often, that it had somehow always been present,
right from the start.

It wasn't that he was frightened of it, not at all; it was just that it had always been there, he'd lived with it, worked with it. As a child, he'd often sneaked down from their apartment upstairs and between the wooden banisters on the stairs watched his father receive clients in Marcusville's only funeral parlor. Then, as a teenager, he'd become part of the family business, another pair of hands to help with the cleaning, arranging, and dressing of bodies that lacked life. He'd learned to give it back, if only for a while—the undertaker's son knew that with makeup and a professional hand you could create the illusion of a living person, and the nearest and dearest, when they looked into the coffin, weeping, to say good-bye, that was what they wanted.

He looked around.

Walls that were more than thirty years old. The prison was starting to look worn.

Nearly fourteen hundred inmates who were to be punished, imprisoned, and occasionally freed. A little more than half as many employees, somewhere between seven and eight hundred. An operational budget of fifty-five million dollars, approximately forty thousand dollars in expenses per prisoner per year, one hundred and seven dollars and sixty-three cents per prisoner per day.

His world: he knew it, was secure in it.

Life, death, in here too, but in another way.

He passed central security and gave a brief nod to one of the new employees who'd been sitting reading some magazine but hastily put it to one side when Vernon approached, and now sat with a straight back studying the images on the various security cameras.

Vernon Eriksen opened the door to the corridor in East Block.

Death Row.

Twenty-two years as senior corrections officer among people who had been convicted and sentenced for capital murder, who were counting the days and would never live anywhere else.

There were one hundred and fifty-five prisoners in Ohio, sitting there waiting for death.

One hundred and fifty-four men and one woman.

Seventy-nine *African Americans*, sixty-nine *Caucasians*, four *Hispanics*, and three who until recently had a separate statistical column under *other*, but which now had been broken down into two *Arab Americans* and one *Native American*.

Sooner or later, most of them came here.

Either they were already serving their sentence in one of the cells along the corridor where he was standing, or they were transported here, with only twenty-four hours to live. It was here, in Marcusville, that those sentenced to death in Ohio were executed.

They're here with me, he thought.

I know them all, every single one. My life, the family I never had, every day, like any other marriage.

Until death do us part.

Vernon stretched his long body. He was still slim, in relatively good shape, short fair hair, thin face with deep creases in the middle of his cheeks. He was tired. It had been a long night. Trouble with the Colombian, who made more noise than usual, and the new guy in Cell 22, who hadn't been able to sleep, understandably, crying like a baby, like they usually did at the start. Then it had got cold. This damn winter was the hardest in south Ohio for many years and the radiators had never really gotten going before they broke down; the whole system was going to be replaced but the bureaucracy was slow, and, most important, it didn't work here, therefore it wasn't cold.

He walked slowly down the middle of the corridor. A kind of peace had fallen, regular breathing from some of the cells, deep sleep now just before the dark evaporated.

He passed cell after cell. A quick glance, left, right, quiet on both sides.

As he got closer, he moved away from the line that was painted down the center of the corridor and walked along the row of metal bars to the right, looked into Cell 12 and saw Brooks lying there on his back, into Cell 10 at Lewis with one arm under the pillow and his face right up against the wall.

Then he stopped.

Cell 8.

He looked in, as he had so many other times before.

Empty.

A prisoner had died there and they had chosen to keep it empty ever since. Superstition, really, that's all it was. But prisoners were not supposed to die in their cells before their time; they were to be kept healthy and alive until they were executed.

Vernon Eriksen searched the emptiness. *For better or for worse.* The light on the ceiling that was always on, the bunk without bedclothes.

Until death do us part. He rested his eyes on the dirty walls that no longer incarcerated anyone, heard sounds from the toilet that was no longer used.

He felt the energy return to his legs, his headache lifted.

He smiled.

HE HAD BEEN AT HOME ON HIS OWN AND SHOULD PERHAPS HAVE TIDIED up and cleaned the place and he should have made supper and he should have collected Oscar from day care only two buildings away.

He had tried to sleep. All morning he'd lain on their bed and tossed and turned with a cushion over his face, but the light from the bedroom window had forced its way in through the blinds and bounced off the pale-colored walls, and his headache was now so intense that he felt sick.

John sat up, his feet on the soft rug by Helena's side of the bed. He was sweating. *He had kicked him in the face.* He could feel his hands shaking, placed them firmly on his thighs and pressed his arms down, but they continued to shake, even when he increased the force.

Helena would be back any minute. She had sighed silently when he called and asked her to get Oscar, when he explained that he was tired, that it had been a long night and he needed a few hours' sleep on his own.

Whatever you do, John, no trouble with the police, ever, his dad had whispered, and then held him tight before turning around and disappearing forever.

He heard the elevator laboring out in the stairwell, someone on their way up. It stopped, two pairs of feet got out, the high voice that shouted and whipped up an echo outside and the small fingers that pressed insistently on the doorbell, while Mommy looked for her keys in a chaotic fabric bag.

"Daddy!"

Oscar ran down the hall, tripped over the doorframe into the bedroom, fell on the floor, and then a short silence reigned until he decided he wasn't going to cry, and got up instead, the final steps over to the bed with his arms stretched out in front of him.

"Daddy! You're home again!"

John looked at his son; his whole face was one big smile. He leaned forward, lifted him up, held him close until the thin body started to

55

wriggle, already tired of being still and wanting to break free. He followed the five-year-old, who continued to run through the apartment as if he was discovering it for the first time. He heard her steps too, looked toward the door, at Helena who was standing there.

"Hi."

She was beautiful, red hair, eyes that made him feel loved.

"Hi. Come over here."

He held out a hand, pulled her in toward him and hugged her, her cold coat against his cheek.

He had tried to do the normal things. He'd seen the way Helena looked at him when she thought he wasn't looking, she'd been able tell that he was different, not that she'd said anything, but he knew. If he just went on as normal there would be no reason for her to ask.

"What's wrong?"

"Nothing."

"John, I can tell something's wrong."

Oscar was at Hilda's on the fourth floor. Hilda was six and had the same amount of energy as her guest. As Oscar would be there for a while, he could talk.

"It's nothing. Maybe just a bit tired."

He was doing the dishes. Washing the dishes was normal.

She came and stood beside him. Some half-full glasses of milk in her hand, which she put down in front of him, under the running water.

"You've been away for three days. It's the middle of the day. Oscar isn't at home. You normally touch me, John. You normally can't get close fast enough. 'Nothing.' You can do better than that."

Helena waited beside him. Suddenly she took a step back, and out of the corner of his eye he saw the thick sweater going over her head, hands undoing her jeans, her camisole on the floor, bra, panties. She stood there, so beautiful, her skin cold, the fair springy pubic hair his fingers could always remember.

"I want you to touch me."

He couldn't bear to move.

"Look at me, John."

That damn pressure in his chest.

She stepped up to him, her naked body so close. He wanted to hold her. He needed her.

"I can't. I've got something I need to tell you first."

He'd gone to get his bathrobe, wrapped it around her chill. They sat down at the kitchen table—he asked if he could smoke and to his surprise she hadn't said anything, just shrugged. He went to get the pack from the top shelf of the cupboard full of bowls and glasses.

"There was a girl named Elizabeth. I was seventeen back then. The only person I've loved. Until I met you."

He lit a cigarette.

"I saw her yesterday. Not her. But someone like her. And you."

He inhaled the smoke, held it for a long time before releasing it. It was the first time he'd had a cigarette in this apartment.

"She danced and we played. She sweated, just like you. She was having fun, laughing. Then a drunk fucking Finn started to grope her. Harass her. He stood too close and wouldn't let go."

He was nervous. His American accent got stronger, clearer, as it normally did when he was agitated, angry, sad, happy.

"There was trouble. I kicked him in the face."

She sat in silence.

"I'm sorry, Helena."

Still she didn't move, just looked at him, for a long time, until she decided to speak.

"Elizabeth. Me. A sweaty woman. And someone you kicked in the face. I don't understand."

He wanted to tell her, he did. Everything. But he couldn't. The past was so well encapsulated that he couldn't reach it. He talked about the kick again, the person who sank unconscious to the floor in front of him. And she had reacted as he'd expected her to react. She shouted. That it wasn't right. That he risked going to prison, that it was assault, probably aggravated assault. Then she cried, she wanted to know who he was. This person who hit other people, she didn't know him, didn't know who he was.

"Helena, listen to me."

He held her, his hands searching inside the robe, her skin warm and safe and he was scared, more than he'd ever been before, of the loneliness that sat beside him.

"I *will* explain."

He took her hands, held them to his cheeks.

"There's more, so much that I haven't told you. But I'll tell you now."

John tried to breathe normally. The fear tore at him. He took a deep breath, was just about to tell the only truth he knew, when the doorbell rang.

He looked at her, waited, then another ring.

He got up and walked toward the noise.

SVEN SUNDKVIST PRESSED HARD ON THE DOORBELL THAT LOOKED NEW and was screwed to the white plastic that framed the door. A shrill sound that reminded him of early mornings on the bus from Gustavsberg to Stockholm, mobile telephones lying in wait in teenage hands, irritating games on their way in to school in the city.

He looked at the door. He didn't like being there.

A warrant had been issued by the duty prosecutor for the arrest of a dance-band singer, in his absence, who had kicked a patron in the head. He was now to be taken in for questioning, charged with attempted murder, and read his legal rights. Ewert had phoned several times, insistent, demanded that Sven and Hermansson should go and get him. Sven Sundkvist had protested; he was considered to be one of the best interviewers in City Police and didn't want to skip the first rule of questioning: never confront the accused in a negative environment.

It was that simple.

Build up trust between the interrogating officer and the person being questioned.

Maintain that trust.

Exploit it.

Sven had suggested sending out a patrol car. As they usually did. Ewert had interrupted him brusquely, asked him to stop talking rubbish and just get the guy, he didn't want any mistakes, he had no time for battered skulls on the Finland ferry.

Sven Sundkvist sighed loudly. To be standing here at the front door in a corridor on the fourteenth floor and meet the nut job for the first time.

He shook his head, looked at his colleague. A young woman with short, dark hair and a broad Skåne accent. She was calm, simply studying the locked door, prepared but not holding her breath.

"What do you think?" Sundkvist pointed at the mailbox and the nameplate. The surname. It was right.

"He's coming."

He liked her. They'd met for the first time the previous summer when she'd been on placement from Malmö and had ended up in one of the most bizarre investigations that Sven had ever been involved in. They had worked together with Ewert Grens, who was leading the investigation, and she had impressed him: she'd been smart, competent, assured.

And now she was a detective inspector already. After only three years.

Sven listened to the silence. They didn't have time for this. Three different murder inquiries on his desk was enough, but this, which was at most *attempted* murder, was precisely the sort of thing that easily became a tightness across your chest, one preliminary investigation too many.

He was starting to lose patience, pushed the doorbell again, a long ring.

"He's coming now."

She nodded at the door. Someone was approaching, reluctant footsteps getting closer.

He didn't look like much. Assault and kicking with pointed boots were not the first things that came to Sven Sundkvist's mind when their eyes met. He was short, no taller than five foot seven, thin, winter white, straggly hair. He'd been crying. Sven was sure of it.

"Sven Sundkvist and Mariana Hermansson, City Police. We're looking for a John Schwarz."

The man in the doorway looked at the two police ID cards that were held out, then turned around and looked anxiously into the apartment. There was someone else there.

"Is your name John Schwarz?"

He nodded. Still turned away from them, as if he wanted to run but couldn't.

"We'd like you to come with us. We've got a car downstairs. I think you know what it's about."

Whatever you do, John, no contact with the police, ever.

"Five minutes. Give me five minutes."

Canadian passport. That could fit. An obvious accent, similar to other native English speakers. Sven gave a short nod, of course, five minutes. They followed him into the hall, stayed there while John Schwarz disappeared into the next room, in the direction he'd been looking. Sven looked at Hermansson. Still just as calm. She smiled at him, he smiled back. They heard voices from somewhere farther in. Schwarz's voice and a woman's voice—they were talking quietly, but she was upset, you could make that much out, she was crying and raising her voice and Sven Sundkvist was getting ready to go in when the face with the unkempt hair came back. A leather jacket from a hanger under the hat shelf and a long scarf from a basket on the floor, then he came out with them, closing the door behind him.

John Schwarz sat in silence while they drove from Alphyddan in north Nacka to Bergsgatan on Kungsholmen in central Stockholm. Sven had checked him at regular intervals in the mirror, at first in case of an attack but then out of concern; he seemed to be completely unreachable, absent, like they sometimes were just before they collapsed and disappeared into another world.

Hermansson was driving and seemed to be just as competent as he was at finding her way around the city's busy road network. Sven recalled the conversation they'd had when they were on their own in the car, driving in the opposite direction, just before they'd stopped outside the block of apartments and taken the elevator up. She'd asked him, again and again, and she hadn't given in until she got an answer. She had demanded to know how she'd got her position. How she could jump the long line of officers who had served longer than her. How much did Detective Superintendent Grens have to do with it? Sven had told her the truth. That Ewert had decided. And that when Ewert had decided something, that was what happened. His informal power in the police headquarters was greater than anyone dared to admit. Decisions rarely had anything to do with hierarchy and formal channels; in reality it was people like Ewert Grens who ruled.

John Schwarz remained silent. He stared at nothing, heard nothing, wasn't there. Not when they stopped the car, not when they got out, not when the elevator doors opened into the Kronoberg detention center and they walked toward the debriefing room. Two officers met them and made sure that he took off his clothes. They searched his naked body and all the pockets in his clothes, then issued him with new ones, far too big and with the Prison and Probation Service logo on the shirt and pants. It wasn't until one of the officers opened the door to the holding cell that he suddenly stopped, looked around, and started to shake. The cramped room in front of him—the size of a small bathroom with a bare bunk—made him resist; he threw himself back and gave voice to his terror.

"No! Not in there!"

He lashed out so that the two officers had to grab hold of his arms and force him up against the wall. He continued to scream as Sven Sundkvist and Hermansson rushed forward.

"I can't breathe! Not in there! I need to breathe!"

John saw the policemen and saw the guards and perhaps it was the way they *I can't!* were holding him or the strong smell from the bare cell walls, he *I can't breathe!* could feel himself screaming and he couldn't do anything about it, that his legs *can't* wouldn't carry him, that what was light suddenly went dark.

Sven Sundkvist glanced briefly at Hermansson. She nodded. Both the officers, quick looks. They were all in agreement. The person they were holding and who, according to his papers, was named John Schwarz was losing it. They relaxed their grip around the resisting arms.

"Take it easy. That's where you have to go. But you can go in yourself. And the door, we'll leave it open."

The older of the two officers, in his sixties, silver hair that had once been dark, he'd seen this so many times before. They kick people in the face. But they can't face the horror of a cell. Before, he used to lock the door, just like they deserved, but now he didn't want the noise and fucking irritation of someone getting psychotic. And this one was pretty close. He looked at his younger colleague, asked him to accompany him into the cell and sit beside him with the unlocked door open. If the suspect was going to lie on the floor and go into spasms, he certainly wasn't going to do it on his shift.

John registered the pressure easing around his arms *someone gives me some air* and that those standing around him took a few steps back, that they pointed at *someone tells me to breathe* the door that was open and the cell that smelled *someone gives me some air through this sack* and he tried to move, his feet shuffled on the hard floor, he went in.

Sven Sundkvist was holding a passport with a dark blue cover that flashed in the light of the corridor's bright fluorescent tubes. *Schwarz, William*

John, nationality Canadian/Canadienne. He flicked through it, distracted: a photograph of the man crouching in the holding cell just a few yards in front of him, his date of birth looked about right, thirty-five years old, born in some hole that he'd never even heard of.

Sven gave it to Hermansson and asked her to take it to forensics for investigation.

"I will. In a while. When we're done here."

She smiled, *I may be new but I'm not your lackey. I'd be happy to do it but I work on an equal footing.* Sven smiled back, *Of course, you're making a stand, I would too.*

The prison doctor was young, thirty at most. Sven saw him coming down the long corridor and thought to himself that they always are, young, recently qualified, working in a detention center didn't give much status, somewhere to start and get some experience, nothing more than that. Schwarz stared down at the floor and mumbled something incomprehensible while the doctor held his arm and took a blood sample for a DNA analysis. The fear in the cramped cell seemed to diminish, Schwarz wasn't shaking anymore, wasn't breathing as heavily, until he suddenly sprang up and shouted again, convulsing like before.

"Not again!"

He pointed at the doctor's hands, at a diazepam enema that was going to be stuck up his rectum.

"Not again!"

The young prison doctor had taken the blood test that he'd come for and then tried to conclude his visit by giving the patient a sedative. The doctor looked at the officer who was sitting in the cell and then at Sven and Hermansson, shook his head, shrugged and threw up his hands, then put the tube of milky fluid back in his bag.

Someone gives me medicine. Someone puts me in a sack. Someone gives me oxygen, regular breaths every two minutes.

John Schwarz sat leaning forward on the bunk in the open holding cell. He wasn't shouting anymore, he didn't move. Sven Sundkvist and Hermansson had stayed until he sat down and the panic seemed to have ebbed, at least for a while. They waited a few minutes more, and took a call from Ewert Grens, who wanted them both to be present when Schwarz's apartment was searched in a couple of hours—a routine operation to secure any evidence a forensic investigation of his clothes and shoes might give; he'd managed to leave the scene of the crime and sometimes not even a plea of guilty and several witnesses were enough for the judge on duty.

One last look at the man who was now sitting quietly in the cell, then they left, took the lift down, and made their way to their own offices.

"Is that normal?"

"Schwarz?"

"Yes."

Sven sifted through images from his nearly twenty years in the police.

"No. Some seem to shrink when they get into the cell. But that—no. I don't think I've ever seen such a violent reaction."

They kept going, punched a code into a lock on the door that separated one corridor from the next, walking in silence and trying to understand how the past could spark such terror, what earlier experiences in a person's life would be strong enough to generate such a fear of small spaces.

"My son."

Sven turned to Hermansson as he spoke.

"He's named Jonas. He's seven, nearly eight years old. He's adopted. And the first few years, the first two years to be precise, we couldn't understand it, Anita and I, he was just like Schwarz was now."

They were nearly there, slowed down, wanted time to finish the conversation.

"He screamed just like that. In panic. If we held him too tight, if we hugged him for too long, if he was constricted and couldn't move freely. We talked to everyone we could at the time. We still don't know. But when he was a baby in the orphanage in Phnom Penh, they kept his whole body tightly bound in his blankets."

They had passed the photocopier, stopped outside Sven's office.

"I don't know. Just something I recognized in Schwarz."

He looked at her.

"I'm certain of it. He's been confined in some way before."

tuesday

MARIANA HERMANSSON HADN'T SLEPT WELL. A SOUND, MUCH LIKE THE one that John Schwarz had released in the hallway outside the holding cell the day before, had woken her on at least two occasions. She didn't know if it was her or someone else who'd passed her bedroom window. Maybe it hadn't been there at all, maybe it had been a dream, the workings of her tired mind.

She was twenty-five years old and had now been living in her apartment, a sublet on the west side of Kungsholmen, for six weeks. It was expensive and furnished with the owner's excessive number of chairs from his own workshop, but living only a short walk from police headquarters in Stockholm, city of apartment waiting lists, made paying out the extra thousands a little easier.

It was still cold when she locked her front door in the block of apartments by the north end of Västerbron and walked through Rålambshovsparken to the walkway along Norr Mälarstrand. Ten minutes of open park and the smell of water before she hit the asphalt again.

She was still caught in the sound that had kept her awake last night.

In the open holding cell with the shaking body on the bunk, who tried to hide himself from the people who were standing near and far away.

His fear had been so potent, you couldn't escape from it—as if it were contagious and she couldn't get rid of it.

She breathed in the air that felt almost clean, deep breaths as she looked out over the water, watched a boat pass and disappear into the snow-white trees that lined the Långholm canal. She was starting to get used to the capital. More lunatics, longer traffic jams, and the feeling of having moved here by chance, it was all still there, but with each day that passed it got easier to keep the loneliness at bay. The days were work, the evenings were work, she wanted it to stay that way, until her soul had arrived and moved in too. And she was happy in the old police headquarters at Kronoberg. Grens was who he was, intense and cantankerous, and with eyes that held a sadness, and she was starting to understand Sven better; what she had first thought was shyness was in fact thoughtfulness, he was wise and friendly, her biased view of a faithful husband—she could just picture him with his wife and adopted son at the kitchen table in a terraced house in Gustavsberg.

She was there, kicked the wall to dislodge the snow on her shoes and went in, door to the left, and upstairs to forensics. Nils Krantz, an elderly forensic scientist, the sort who had started out as an ordinary policeman and then got his training in the force, she was sure of it, had promised yesterday to have Schwarz's passport ready for pickup this morning. He had sighed, as they always did, but had then taken it, gone over to his desk, and started to look through it, without giving her another glance.

Krantz was already there when she opened the door.

Reading glasses on his forehead, hair just as unkempt as always.

She didn't need to say anything—the passport was lying on the table, ready for pickup. Krantz got up when she came in, pointed at it, and shook his head lightly, smiled that smile that she still couldn't work out, whether it was friendly or ironic.

"*John Doe.*"

She hadn't heard properly.

"What do you mean?"

"This. An unidentified man. A John Doe. Congratulations."

EWERT GRENS WASN'T THERE. NO MATTER HOW HARD SHE STARED AT his chair. And Hermansson was in a rush. She didn't know why, a tension somewhere in the middle of her stomach made her feel hounded, it gnawed at her and irritated her, made her breathing labored. Whether it was her recent conversation with the doctor who had given her an update on the battered Finn Ylikoski's critical condition, that their work might turn into a murder inquiry at any moment, whether it was Schwarz's reaction outside the holding cell, the terrified scream, or whether it was this, the false passport in her hand, she didn't know; all she knew was that she wanted rid of it, that it was stealing her energy so she had to go somewhere else, get away from Grens's empty office.

She went to Lars Ågestam instead, the public prosecutor who had been given responsibility for the preliminary investigation, to brief him on what Krantz had just told her. Then she went back to Kronoberg and her own office, read the report that had been filed twenty-four hours earlier, then her own reports on the arrest at Nacka and a police search at the same address.

She was worried. Which was rare.

This feeling, his face that had been so terrified and yet empty at the same time, it kept getting in the way—she wanted to move on, and fiddled with the tall pile of outstanding investigations.

But she had to do it.

On Ågestam's orders, she called the Canadian embassy and inquired about the passport that was lying on a table in front of her. The clerk answered. Gave precisely the answers that she didn't want to hear. She interrupted him, got up with the receiver still in her hand, told him that she was on her way over, that she would continue the conversation when she got there.

Hurried steps down the corridor, she was still buttoning her jacket when she passed Grens's office.

He was there now, she knew before she even got there—you could hear the music playing loudly out in the corridor, something from a time before she was even born, Siw Malmkvist singing and Ewert moving to the rhythm on his chair. She had seen him dancing around the room on a couple of occasions when he thought no one was looking, in the middle of the floor to that empty music. She should ask him sometime, who it was he was actually holding, there, next to the desk, dancing to a Siw Malmkvist chorus.

She knocked on the open door. He looked up, irritated, as if he'd been interrupted in the middle of something important.

"Yes?"

She didn't answer and instead walked in and sat down on the visitor's chair. Grens stared at her, astonished, unused to people just coming into his room without permission.

Hermansson looked at him.

"I—"

Ewert Grens lifted a finger, put it to his mouth.

"In a moment. When she's finished."

He closed his eyes and listened to the voice that filled the room, the voice of the sixties and youth and the future. A minute, maybe two, until first of all the voice and then the band were silent.

Ewert looked her in the eye.

"Yes?"

Hermansson considered telling him what she thought about having to wait so he could listen to some music.

She decided not to, not this time.

"I went up to see Krantz this morning. He worked very late last night."

Grens was impatient, indicated with his hands that he wanted to hear more. She continued, felt breathless without knowing why, as if she was hurrying more than she needed to.

"John Schwarz's passport. It's fake, Ewert. The photograph and the stamp, Krantz is convinced they've been manipulated."

Ewert Grens gave a loud sigh. He was suddenly tired.

A fucking awful day.

Right from the start, as soon as he'd come into the building just after six this morning, the investigation gloom had dominated in the corridors. Idiots who reported on pointless interviews, came back after disastrous investigations, handed out autopsy reports that said nothing. He had let a couple of hours pass, then taken a walk in the small park that had no name, before coming back to an office that was just as empty as when he left it.

John Doe.

An unidentified foreign man in custody.

That was all they fucking needed.

"Excuse me."

Grens stood up, left the room, and walked down the corridor. He stopped in front of the coffee machine, black with nothing in it, plastic cup burning the palm of his hand as he slowly walked back, and holding it steady as he walked over the carpet.

He blew on the liquid and put the cup down on his desk to cool.

"Thank you."

He looked at her, surprised.

"Sorry?"

"For getting me one as well."

"Did you want one?"

"Yes, please."

Ewert Grens lifted the hot cup demonstratively to his lips, tasted the first drops.

"An unidentified foreigner. Do you know what a pain in the ass that can be?"

He'd understood and dismissed her sarcasm. She swallowed her rage, then spoke.

"I am of course new here. But I'm certain. Schwarz's reaction. It stayed with me all of yesterday evening, all night, this morning. There's something wrong, that's all there is to it."

Grens listened.

"I called the Canadian embassy. I'm on my way over there now. You see, Ewert, the passport number, *that's genuine enough.*"

Hermansson held up her hand.

"And it *was* issued for a man by the name of John Schwarz."

The heavy breathing, forcing its way up.

"And even though both the photo and the stamp have been manipulated, which we've just had confirmed, *it's never been reported stolen.*"

She waved the passport she was holding between her fingers.

"Ewert, there's something that's not right."

THE DOOR TO THE HOLDING CELL IN KRONOBERG DETENTION CENTER WAS still open. John Schwarz was sitting on the bunk with his head in his hands, just as he'd been sitting the evening before, just as he'd been sitting all through the night. He counted each breath, terrified that he would suddenly stop, *have to make sure that I get air, that it goes down my throat and reaches my lungs, don't dare to sleep, can't sleep, sleeping means not knowing whether I'm breathing or not and not breathing means I'm dead.*

Now.

The officer beside him had taken over from his colleague a couple of minutes earlier. He'd tried to talk to the suspect, say hello to him, but the bent head hadn't heard, hadn't seen, he was somewhere deep, deep inside himself.

I'm going to die now.

Twice during the night he'd got up and banged his forehead hard against the bars until two arms had dragged him away. He'd shouted something incomprehensible, not so much words as a cry, a sound.

I'm *dead* now.

It was a long time since someone had demanded so much space in the holding cell. He wasn't violent, it wasn't that, but the guards on duty had called for the doctor and reinforcements, and there was a tangible feeling that something was about to go badly wrong, this man, he's going to go to pieces in front of our very eyes.

Dawn had brightened into morning, and it was now daylight.

It was probably around half past nine. Or just after. And John Schwarz suddenly got up, looked at the two guards, and spoke coherently for the first time since he came there.

"I smell."

The officer beside him in the cell had also stood up.

"You smell?"

"The smell, I have to get rid of it."

The officer turned to his colleague who was standing just outside the door, the silver-haired one who had come back for the next day's shift.

The older man nodded.

"You can have a shower. But we'll sit with you."

"I want to be alone."

"Under normal circumstances, we lock the door and the guard sits outside. But not in this case. We don't have time for assault suspects who commit suicide in our showers. So you shower. In our company."

He sat down on the wet drain, his knees pulled up, back against the wall that was hard. *Elizabeth's eyes, they laugh so.* The water pummeled his body, he increased the pressure and turned up the heat, hot drops on his skin. *Their hate, I don't understand it.* Face up, he closed his eyes, it burned, he tried to suppress the thoughts that refused to back down. *Dad crying, he's holding me, I've never seen him cry before.* He sat there for thirty minutes, didn't pay any attention to the officer who was sitting far too close. The water, the heat had helped him to be resilient, at least for a while.

John Schwarz now knew.

He had to get away from there.

He couldn't face dying again.

HERMANSSON HAD JUST LEFT EWERT GRENS, BUT EVEN BEFORE SHE turned out of the corridor she heard the music again, just as loud as a short while ago. She smiled. He had his own style. She liked people who had their own style.

In her hand she was holding a passport, one that didn't exist.

She still hadn't fully recognized that this was just the start of something that would become so much more, but she had a feeling. Schwarz had been with her for more than twenty-four hours now, refusing to leave her thoughts. So she hurried along Bergsgatan, Scheelegatan, Hantverkargatan, a few minutes' walk east along the road toward the center of Stockholm, and any moment now, a few hundred yards ahead, she would see the ugly building beside the Sheraton Hotel. She paused briefly, her eyes searching for the windows of the Canadian embassy a few floors up, when she was suddenly surprised by a voice, from behind, up close.

"Hey, bitch."

He was standing on the other side of the high iron fence, in the grassy churchyard around Kungsholmen Church, a middle-aged man staring at her with great intensity.

"Hey, bitch, look at this."

He'd undone the top button of his pants, was fiddling with the zipper now.

She didn't need to see any more.

She already knew.

"Get your dick out, you bastard."

She put her hand inside her jacket, for just a second, then held up her gun.

"Go on."

She looked at him as she spoke, her voice calm.

"And I'll blast it off. With the new police-issue hunting ammo. Then it's done."

For a long moment, he looked at the bitch who was holding a gun and said she was from the police. Then he bolted, ran away, tried to do up his fly, fell over one of the low gravestones with almost illegible writing and moss growing around the edges, kept on running without looking back.

She shook her head.

All these nut jobs.

The city bred them, fed them, hid them.

Mariana Hermansson watched him until he disappeared into some bushes, then kept on walking, past the city hall and under the railway bridge, a couple of minutes more, then an elevator up to the glass door that opened from the inside when she rang the bell; she was expected.

The Canadian embassy official introduced himself as Timothy D. Crouse; he was a tall young man with short blond hair. He had a friendly face and walked and talked like they usually did. Hermansson had met quite a few in connection with various investigations and had already been struck by how similar they were, embassy people, no matter what nationality or ethnicity, the way they walked and moved like diplomats, the way they talked like diplomats . . . she wondered if they were like that from the outset and that's why they were attracted to it, or whether they became like that along the way, fitting in so they wouldn't be noticed.

She handed him the passport that belonged to a man who was now sitting in custody in a holding cell, suspected of attempted murder. Crouse felt the dark blue cover with his fingers, the paper inside, he studied the passport number and personal details.

He didn't take particularly long and seemed to be certain when he spoke.

"This is genuine. I'm convinced of it. Everything's correct. I've already looked up the number. The personal details are identical to the ones that were entered when the passport was issued."

Hermansson looked at the embassy man. She took a couple of steps forward, pointed at the computer.

"Can I have a look?"

"There's no other information. I'm sorry. That's all we can get up."

"I want to see *him*."

Crouse considered her request.

"It's important."

He shrugged.

"Of course. Why not? You're here. And I've already given you all the other information."

He pulled over a chair and asked her to sit down beside him, poured a glass of water, and then apologized for the time it took for the computer to hook up to the system.

Two men in dark overcoats were now standing outside the glass door and were let in by a female employee. They passed by Crouse's desk, nodded in recognition, and continued on.

"Soon. We'll get there soon."

The screen started to come alive. Crouse typed in a password and then opened something that looked like a register. Two new screens, names in alphabetical order: a total of twenty-two Canadian citizens with the surname *Schwarz* and the first name *John*.

"The fifth from the top. See. He has this passport number."

Crouse nodded at the screen.

"You want to see what he looks like."

A new register, a new password.

A photograph of the John Schwarz who had ordered and received the passport that was now lying in front of them on the desk, the John Schwarz who, according to the Migration Board, also had permanent residency in Sweden, now filled the computer screen.

Crouse looked at it without saying anything.

He leaned forward, flicked through the passport, then pulled up the photograph and personal details.

Hermansson knew what he was thinking.

The man in the passport was white.

The man she had described who was suspected of attempted murder and who was now sitting in a holding cell was white.

But this man who was beaming at them from the Canadian authorities' computer, the man who had once been the legitimate owner of the passport that Crouse was holding, he was black.

EWERT GRENS WAS IRRITATED. THE DAY THAT HAD STARTED BADLY AT SIX in the morning when he opened the main door to the police headquarters had now, as the morning slid into lunch, got worse. He couldn't face any more idiots. He wanted to sit behind his closed door and play loud music and have the time to systematically go through at least one of the piles of investigations that should have been closed ages ago. He didn't get time to do more than start before someone knocked on the door. Pointless questions and unfounded reports that he snorted at as before, and people who came to say he should turn down the music, who he told to go to hell.

He longed for her.

He wanted to hold her, feel her steady breathing.

He had been there the day before and normally waited for a few days, but he felt compelled to go out there again this afternoon, a hamburger in the car and he should be able to squeeze in a short visit.

Grens waited until Siw had sung her last, then lifted his new cordless phone that he couldn't quite get his head around and phoned the nursing home. One of the younger female staff answered, one of the ones he had gotten to know. He said that he'd thought about coming out in a couple of hours and wanted to make sure that it wouldn't clash with a visit from the doctor or some group activity.

It felt better. The anger that always lurked in his chest shrank a little, didn't take up so much space, he had the energy to sing along again to Siw's "Seven Little Girls (Sitting in the Back Seat)."

Seven little girls sitting in the back seat
hugging and a-kissing with Fred

He even whistled, out of tune and with a sound that could peel the walls.

I said, why don't one of you
come and sit beside me

Ten minutes. That was all. Then the door again, someone feeling lonely. He sighed, put the report he was reading to one side.

Hermansson. He waved her in.

"Sit down."

He didn't know why. And was still unsure how he should deal with his reaction. But it made him happy whenever he saw her. A young woman . . . it wasn't that, and he was careful to keep it that way.

It was something else.

He'd considered sleeping at home in his large apartment more often, thought that he'd be able to cope.

He suddenly found himself reading the movie listings in *Dagens nyheter*, he who hadn't been to the movies since James Bond and *Moonraker* in 1979, when he'd fallen asleep watching it, all the boring, endless space voyages.

On a few occasions he'd even nearly gone to those fucking awful shopping streets in the center to try on some new clothes—he hadn't done it, but *nearly*.

She put a piece of paper down on his desk. A picture of a man's face, a passport photo.

"John Schwarz."

A man somewhere in his thirties. Short, dark hair, brown eyes, black skin.

"The original owner of the passport."

Grens looked at the picture, thought about the man who *called* himself John Schwarz and who, according to the reports he'd got from Sven, Hermansson, and the prison staff, was not doing well at all. He was a nobody now. The Swedish police authorities didn't even have a name for him anymore. His strange behavior, his fear, and the kick he'd given someone else in the head; he was carrying some baggage with him, he came from somewhere.

Who? Where? Why?

The investigation of an attempted murder had just become more complicated.

"I want you to set things up for questioning."

He paced restlessly around the room as he always did, from the desk to the worn sofa where he sometimes slept, back to the desk, back to the sofa.

"You'll get him to talk. I'm sure that you can do it better than Sven or me, that you can reach him."

Grens stopped, sat down on the sofa.

"You have to find out who he is. I want to know what the hell he's doing here. Why the singer in a dance band is running around hiding behind a false identity."

He leaned back; his body was used to the hard stuffing, he had lain there many a night.

"And this time, report directly to me, Hermansson. I don't want to have to get any information via Ågestam in the future."

"You weren't here this morning when I came in."

"I am your boss. Is that clear?"

"If you're here next time, or at least contactable next time, then I'll report to you in detail. If you're not, I'll report to the prosecutor who's heading the investigation."

She had left his room angrier than she cared to admit and was on her way to her own office. She hadn't got very far when she suddenly turned— she just had to do it.

She knocked on the door again, for the second time in twenty minutes.

"There was something else."

Grens was still sitting on the sofa. He sighed, sufficiently loudly to be sure that she heard, then waved his arms around in front of him and said that she should continue.

"I have to know, Grens."

Hermansson took a step into the room.

"Why did you promote me? How did I manage to bypass the officers with far longer service than I have?"

Ewert Grens heard her question. He wasn't sure whether she was joking.

"Is it important?"

"I know your views on policewomen."

She wasn't joking.

"Well?"

"So explain."

"City Police employs about sixty people a year. What the hell do you want to hear? How good you are?"

"I want to know why."

He shrugged.

"Because you are. Really fucking good."

"And policewomen?"

"The fact that *you're* good doesn't change anything. Policewomen aren't good enough."

Half an hour later he was sitting in the car on his way to the woman he'd longed for. A hamburger and a low-alcohol beer from the fast-food place on Valhallavägen just before he turned off for Lidingö. It was still cold outside, the thermometer hadn't managed to get above zero, not even at this time of day. He felt the chill, as he always did after he'd eaten, and the damn heater in the car wasn't working.

He phoned Ågestam, who answered, out of breath, in his shrill, almost falsetto voice. Grens really didn't like the young prosecutor, and the dislike was mutual. They'd met and worked with and against each other a couple of times too many in recent years, and with each investigation their differences became more pronounced.

But today he held his tongue. He was on his way to see Anni and wanted to keep hold of the feeling that the prospect of the visit had given him.

Instead he explained that he wanted information about the committal proceedings that Ågestam was going to instigate later that afternoon against a man who was still called "John Schwarz" in the court papers. They talked about Ylikoski's cerebral edema; he was in the neurosurgical ward at the Karolinska Hospital, still sedated so he could breathe with a respirator. They discussed how claustrophobia now dominated the holding cell corridor, then talked briefly about the details of a false identity, and "Schwarz," waiting to learn if his case would go to trial, and with what charge.

"Aggravated assault."

Ewert Grens started; the car swung into the middle of the road and was about to cross the continuous white line when he gripped the steering wheel, forced the veering vehicle back, and continued driving on the right side.

"Aggravated assault? Did I hear you right, Ågestam? This is attempted murder!"

"Schwarz did not intend to kill him."

"You have no idea what bleeding and swelling in the brain can do. You have no idea of the consequences. He fucking kicked his head with all his might!"

He was driving faster now, unconsciously pressing the accelerator to the floor while he waited for the young prosecutor to answer.

"I hear what you're saying, Grens. But *I* have the legal knowledge, *I* am heading the investigation, and *I* will decide what kind of charge is reasonable."

"It was—"

"And only *me*."

Ewert Grens didn't shout as he normally did when Ågestam tried to fill a suit that was too big. He just hung up in despair and dropped his speed as he came off the Lidingö Bridge, past the apartment buildings and expensive houses as the traffic thinned out. He knew. He was on his way to her and he knew.

The nursing home was beautifully lit, despite the fact that it was the middle of the day; floodlights angled across the facade of the old house—that was new, he hadn't seen it before.

A warmth surged through his body when he got out of the car. Every time the same feeling, as if all the tension was released. He didn't need to be on his guard, he didn't even need to be angry. This house meant trust and routine. And she was sitting inside waiting for him; he was the way he was and she had always put up with it.

She was sitting by the window, as usual. She must know that the life she was no longer part of was going on out there, so she took her place, as best she could, in her own way.

It was the young auxiliary nurse who met him out in the hall. White coat over her own clothes. Ewert Grens knew that she was studying to become a doctor, that this was extra money to pay off her student loan, and she was good, looked after Anni well, so he hoped that it would be a while until she passed her exams.

"She's waiting for you."

"I saw her. By the window. She looked happy."

"I'm sure she knows you're coming."

She didn't hear him open the door to her room. He stood on the threshold, looked at her back that stuck up from the wheelchair, her long blond hair that had recently been brushed.

I held you when you were bleeding from the head.

He went over, kissed her on the cheek, maybe she smiled, he thought she did. He moved the cardigan that was hanging on the chair beside her bed and sat down next to her. She continued to stare out the window, eyes unwavering. He tried to understand what it was she was looking at, followed her gaze, same direction. The open water. Boats sailing far below in the sound between west Lidingö and east Stockholm. He wondered whether she actually saw anything. And if she did, if she then knew what it was she was looking for out of the window all day.

If I had been quicker. If I had realized. You might still have been with me today.

He laid his hand on hers.

"You're beautiful."

She heard him talking. At least, she turned around.

"It's been crazy today. I had to come. I needed you."

Now she laughed. The loud, gurgling laughter that he loved so much.

"You and me."

They sat next to each other and looked out of the window for nearly half an hour. Silent, together. Ewert Grens breathed to her rhythm, he thought about another time when they had walked slowly side by side, days that could have been so different; he thought about yesterday and this morning and the unidentified suspect who was stealing time from other things, of Sven, whom he should appreciate more, of Hermansson, whom he didn't really understand.

"I said yesterday that I'd employed a young woman. That she's so like you. She doesn't take any nonsense. She knows who she is. It's as if you were back in the corridor again. Do you understand? It doesn't mean anything, not for us. But sometimes I forget that it isn't you."

He had stayed longer than he intended. They'd sat by the window some more, she had coughed and he'd got her some water, she had dribbled and he'd dried her chin.

It was then that it happened.

She had been sitting beside him and the boat was so clear as it passed below on the water.

She had waved.

He'd seen it, he was sure of it, she *had* waved.

When the big white ferry from Waxholmsbolaget had sounded its horn, she had laughed, lifted her hand, and waved it back and forth several times.

He had gone to pieces.

He knew that she couldn't do it. All the fucking neurologists had concluded that she would probably never be able to perform such a conscious action.

He had run out into the corridor, his heavy body lurching forward, shouting to the young woman who had let him in earlier.

The auxiliary nurse, whose name was Susann, had listened. One hand on his shoulder. The other on Anni's arm. Then she had slowly tried to help him understand that it hadn't happened. She explained that she understood that he loved her and missed her and so desperately wanted to see what he claimed he'd just seen, but that he had to accept that it wasn't possible, that it hadn't happened.

She had stroked her hand back and forth several times.

He knew exactly what the fuck he'd seen.

Ewert Grens had barely left before he started to feel stressed again. Anni was still with him as he approached central Stockholm and the rest of the day that was waiting for him. He hated the feeling of being behind and, in order to stifle it, reached for the mobile phone that was in his briefcase and dialed one of his few stored numbers.

Hermansson's broad Skåne accent after two rings.

"Hello."

"How's it going?"

"I've just read through everything we've got. I'm well prepared. I'll question him after the committal proceedings."

She had waved.

"Good."

She would wave again.

"Good."

"It was you who called, Ewert. Was there anything else?"

Grens focused on the car in front; he had to forget for a while—later, he could continue to think about Anni later. Right now there was a Finnish man lying in the Karolinska Hospital, someone else who risked becoming a person who would forever more watch life through a window.

"Yes. There was something else. I want to know who that bastard is."

"I've—"

"Interpol."

"Now?"

"I want to find his identity. He exists somewhere. The level of violence . . . he's done this before." Grens didn't wait for an answer. "Go up to Interpol in C Block and speak to Jens Klövje. Put out a blue notice for the bastard. Take the photographs and fingerprints with you."

Ågestam had wanted more. He would get more.

"He exists in some register somewhere. I'm sure of it. We'll know who John Schwarz is by tomorrow morning."

IT TOOK HERMANSSON EXACTLY FIVE MINUTES TO GET FROM HER OWN office to Jens Klövje's much larger office in C Block. It was her first visit to the Swedish Interpol, but she recognized him all the same, one of several guest lecturers for one of the courses at the Swedish National Police Academy. Klövje was Grens's age and he nodded at her absentmindedly when she opened the door, that uneasy feeling of disturbing someone again.

She put the false passport down on the desk in front of him, the fresh fingerprints beside it.

"John Doe."

Klövje sighed.

"Again?"

"He goes by the name of John Schwarz. Age, height, the details in the passport are all correct."

"Is there a rush?"

"His committal proceeding will be in a few hours."

Klövje looked through the passport, page by page, then studied the fingerprints. He hummed something that Hermansson didn't recognize.

"Is this all?"

"You can get a DNA profile tomorrow. But we don't want to wait until then. Grens is certain that he's registered somewhere, in the criminal records."

Jens Klövje put what he'd got in a plastic envelope, weighed it absently in his hand.

"How does he speak?"

"What do you mean?"

"Does he speak Swedish?"

Hermansson visualized John Schwarz sitting silent in the back of the car, his face hidden in his hands, screaming in English in the holding cell corridor with his arms waving in front of him.

"He hasn't said much. But from what I've heard, on the stairs when we went to get him . . . yes, he does."

"Accent?"

"British. Or American. The passport is Canadian."

Klövje smiled.

"Narrows the search down a bit."

He put the plastic folder in a tray by the computer.

"I'll send this out in fifteen minutes. I'll stick to English-speaking countries to begin with. It will take a few hours, time differences and all that, but I'll be in touch as soon as I hear anything."

She nodded to him, he nodded back. She turned around and moved to leave.

"By the way, I agree with Grens."

He kept on talking as she left.

"We've got him."

THE OLD STONE STAIRWELL ECHOED WITH THE SOUND OF THE GUARDS' hard heels, mixed with the monotonous sound that the man who called himself John Schwarz made as they went up into the courtroom on the second floor of Stockholm City Hall. He'd been making the noise ever since one of the guards had locked the handcuffs around one of his thin wrists—an irritating shrill sound that pierced through your head and got louder the closer they got.

The oversized clothes John wore were made from a fabric that scratched and was too thin. He was freezing; it was cold outside and almost as cold inside the vast, high-ceilinged building, and the radiators were few and far between. Same officers as yesterday afternoon, the older one with the silver hair and the younger one who was tall and had blue spectacle frames; they walked beside him, one step for every step he took, but he barely noticed them, just increased the force of the noise that locked his jaws shut and stared straight ahead.

The door was wooden; it was open and there were people inside.

Public prosecutor Lars Ågestam (LÅ): During a search of John Schwarz's apartment on Monday, these pants and these shoes were found.
For the defense, Kristina Björnsson (KB): Schwarz pleads guilty to kicking Ylikoski in the head.

Someone turned on the ceiling lights. It was still a long time until dusk, but it was one of those days when the light seems to have petered out by midmorning and a gloom held the capital in its great embrace. The silver-haired guard looked him in the eye and unlocked the handcuffs. The man who called himself John Schwarz kept making the grating noise as he looked out of the large window that flashed in the artificial light. It was a long way down to the ground—he'd considered it, of course he had—but he didn't dare jump.

LÅ: A forensic analysis has shown traces of Ylikoski's saliva on the
pants, and Ylikoski's hair and blood on the shoes.
KB: Schwarz pleads guilty but states that his intention was to force
Ylikoski to stop harassing a woman on the dance floor.

He sat beside his lawyer. She was stressed, he could feel it, but her smile
was friendly.

"That noise. I wish you'd stop it."

He didn't hear what she said, the sound was in the way and he didn't
dare stop, it kept his jaws together, if he let it stop then only the scream
would be left.

"It might not be to your advantage. Making that noise."

The sound. He wouldn't let it go.

"Don't you understand what I'm saying? Would you prefer me to speak
English? These are the committal proceedings. From experience, I know
that suspects get a more favorable hearing if they behave as normally as
possible."

He lowered the volume.

But it was still there.

The sound was his, the only thing in the room.

LÅ: Schwarz is not named Schwarz. He has no identity. I request that
he is held in custody on charges of aggravated assault, due to the
risk that he might further complicate the investigation by absconding.
KB: Schwarz had no intention to injure. Furthermore, he suffers from
acute claustrophobia. Being held in custody would therefore be
inhumane.

He was quiet then. When the court clerk explained to him the terms of
custody on the grounds of suspected aggravated assault, he instead sank to
the floor in a fetal position with his hands over his ears so he wouldn't have
to hear, while the clerk ran his hands through his red hair in agitation and
repeated his request that he stand up.

Both the officers held him by the arms, they pulled him to his feet.
Handcuffs around his wrists again. He was shaking when they pushed him
out of Court no. 10 and down the stone stairs.

The monotonous noise echoed like before, and the silver-haired guard
seemed to be exasperated. He walked beside him the whole way down,

alternately hissing quietly, then raising his voice.

"Had you planned your strategy with your lawyer, then?

"You're going to be here for a long time.

"Until they've IDed you. Until you've got a name."

He looked at the officer, shook his head.

He didn't want to.

Didn't want to listen, didn't want to talk.

Old Silverhair didn't give up, took a couple of steps forward, stopped directly below him on the last step and turned around. They were about the same height now, their breath mixing between them.

The guard punched the air.

"Don't you get it? Kronoberg detention center is full of foreigners like you, who don't have any ID. With no fixed custody period. Why don't you just say who you are instead? And get procedures moving again? They're waiting for you. It'll take the time it takes. You'll be the one who loses out, you'll be the one sitting here with full restrictions for longer than you need to, cut off from everyone you care about."

The prison clothes scratched, the thin man who had just been held in custody on reasonable grounds was tired; he looked at the silver hair, his voice weak.

"You don't understand."

He moved restlessly from one foot to the other on the hard step.

"My name."

He coughed, spoke louder.

"My name is John Schwarz."

IT WAS JUST AFTER THREE O'CLOCK WHEN JENS KLÖVJE FAXED OVER several documents regarding a man in his thirties who called himself John Schwarz and had been kept in custody. Klövje had for the present concentrated on countries where English was the official language—after all, Hermansson had been clear on that point, the suspect's accent was significant, his mother tongue easy to identify.

A couple of minutes later, various hands in various Interpol offices around the world picked up the inquiry from their Swedish colleagues from the fax machine.

Some sighed and put the paper to one side, some planned to do a search later in the day, others immediately started to look through the registers that were open on the screen.

Marc Brock in the Washington Interpol office was one of them. On the desk in front of him he had half a café latte, paper cup with a plastic lid every morning from Starbucks on Pennsylvania Avenue. He drank it slowly without really looking at the fax he'd just received.

That meant work and concentration at the computer, and he . . . he was tired. It was just one of those mornings.

He looked out of the window.

It was the eleventh of January, still cold, spring was a long way off.

Marc Brock yawned.

The fax, it was still lying on top, he pulled the pile over. A search request from Sweden.

Northern Europe. Scandinavia. He had actually been to Stockholm once, when he was young and in love and the woman was beautiful.

The summary was written in good English. A person who was probably not of Swedish origin had been held in custody for aggravated assault. A John Doe who called himself Schwarz, who had a false passport and now refused to give his correct identity.

Marc Brock studied the photo, a pale man with a stiff smile and uneasy eyes.

89

A face he might have seen before.

He turned on the computer, opened the registers he needed, searched using the information that the Swedish police had sent—the photo, known personal details, fingerprints—with a request that it be dealt with swiftly.

It didn't take particularly long, it actually never did, not even when he was tired.

He drank some more coffee, yawned again, and then realized he didn't really understand what he was looking at.

He shook his head.

It didn't make sense.

He sat quite still and stared at the screen until it became blurred. Then he got up, walked around the room, sat down again and decided to go through the whole procedure again, one more time. He logged off, turned off the computer, waited a few seconds, then turned the computer on again, logged on, opened all the registers and ran the search a second time, using the information he'd been given about a man who only a matter of hours ago had been kept in custody in a city in northern Europe, and who called himself John Schwarz.

He waited with his eyes glued to the top of the desk, then slowly looked up at the screen.

The same answer.

Marc Brock swallowed his discomfort.

It didn't make sense. Because it quite simply couldn't make sense.

The man in the photo, the man he only minutes ago thought he might have seen before, was dead.

EWERT GRENS KNEW WHAT HE HAD SEEN. HE HAD WAITED TWENTY-FIVE years for this. He didn't give a damn about whether it was possible or not. She had seen the boat, and she had waved her hand back and forth, several times. It *had* been a conscious action. He, if anyone, knew every single expression she used, each one she was capable of, as only people who have lived together closely for many years do.

It was one of the archipelago ferries. They all looked the same. Grens pushed the Schwarz investigation over into a corner of the desk, placed an empty notebook in front of him, and phoned Waxholmsbolaget, which operated ferries all through the Stockholm archipelago. He swore loudly at the electronic voice that asked him to press a number and then another number and he shouted, *I want to talk to a person*, at the receiver and then threw it down. He sat there with the empty notepad and receiver lying in front of him, then after a while turned around to the old cassette player and put on one of three mix tapes of all the songs that Siw Malmkvist ever recorded, in chronological order. He fast-forwarded to her version of "Ode to Billie Joe" from 1968—it was different, he liked it a lot. He listened to the whole song once, *time 4 minutes and 15 seconds*, calmed down, rewound it, turned down the volume, and listened to it again while he lifted the receiver. The same damn electronic voice, he pressed this number and that, and waited where he was supposed to wait until he eventually heard a real human being.

Ewert Grens explained the time and place, he wondered what the boat was called, the one that had passed along the water below the nursing home. He also wanted to book some tickets, three people, for sometime later in the week.

She was helpful, the woman with the real voice.

The boat, the one he *knew* she had waved at, was called the *Söderarm* and stopped at Gåshaga jetty on Lidingö and arrived at Vaxholm forty minutes later.

You told me.

You wanted to go.

He turned up the volume, the same song for the third time, he sang along and he stood up, danced alone around the room, holding her.

Someone knocked on his open door.

"Apologies. I'm probably a bit early."

Grens looked at Hermansson, nodded at her to come in and pointed to the visitor's chair, went on moving slowly over the carpet; there were still some bars left.

Then he sat down, with a sweaty forehead, out of breath.

Hermansson looked at him and smiled.

"Always the same music."

Ewert waited to get his breath back, it was more regular now.

"There is nothing else. Not in this room."

"If you open the window. Out there, Ewert. In the real world. It's a different time."

"You don't understand. You're so young, Hermansson. Memories. The only thing that's left when you've lived."

She shook her head.

"You're right. I don't understand. I don't think it has to be like that. But you're a good dancer."

Grens nearly laughed. And that didn't happen often.

"I used to dance quite a bit. Before."

"How long ago was that?"

"Twenty-five years. At least."

"Twenty-five years?"

"You can see how I look. With a limp and a neck that won't move."

They sat in silence for a while. Until Ewert leaned forward and pulled the telephone toward him.

"Do you mind waiting outside? Until the others come. There's a phone call I have to make."

She left the room and closed the door behind her. Grens dialed the number to the nursing home, asked to speak to the matron. He explained that he was going to take Anni on a boat trip and that he'd like one of the staff to go with them. The young woman, Susann, the one who was studying to become a doctor. He knew that she did extra shifts and so insisted on paying her himself, because it was important that it was her, and only her. Some protest, but he got what he wanted, and he was a happy man when he opened the door again and let in the three people who were standing waiting in the corridor by the coffee machine.

Sven was drinking some with that artificial milk substitute, Hermansson had something that looked like tea, Ågestam's smelled like hot chocolate. Grens asked them to sit down and then went out to get himself a cup of black coffee, nothing else.

He drank half of it, felt the warmth moving around his body.

"Schwarz."

He looked at them, they no doubt felt the same. Who could be bothered with this?

"Klövje has sent out an Interpol blue notice to search for the bastard. Every English-speaking country now has everything we have on him. If he's in any of the criminal records, we'll know about it in a few hours."

They were all sitting on the old sofa, the one he usually slept on. All in a row, Hermansson in the middle with Sven and Ågestam on either side.

"Have you got anything to say?"

Hermansson blew on her tea before speaking.

"There are twenty-two people called John Schwarz in Canada. I asked the official at the embassy in Tegelbacken to check them all, the same guy who helped us yesterday."

"And?"

"None of them matches the man who is now sitting locked up in Kronoberg detention center."

Ågestam had hot chocolate on his upper lip.

"We don't know who he is. Or where he comes from. What we do know, on the other hand, is that he's capable of kicking someone in the face, and yet is terrified of us connecting the dots. Yesterday in court it was horrible—he lay down on the floor shaking when it was announced that he'd continue to be held in custody. I've never experienced anything like it."

Ewert Grens snorted.

"I don't fucking doubt it. Chocolate on your face, like a child. What exactly *have* you experienced?"

Lars Ågestam stood up and strode around the room on his skinny legs, hand through his hair several times to check that his fringe was in the right place, as always when he was agitated.

"I *have not* experienced ongoing investigations being put to one side to prioritize a comparatively insignificant one. I *have not* experienced an investigating officer attempting to influence the prosecutor's choice of crime designation."

He ran his hand through his hair again.

"Grens, are your priorities being guided by personal issues in this case?"

Ewert Grens slammed his hand down hard on one of two desk drawers that were open.

"You can bet your ass they are! And if you knew as much as I do about extreme violence to the head, you might give it the same priority, my friend."

As he spoke, he grabbed hold of the open drawer, pulled himself toward it to gather momentum, and then let his chair spin around halfway until he was sitting with his back to the prosecutor, demonstrating his disgust.

Sven Sundkvist couldn't bear any more tension between the detective superintendent and the public prosecutor, the silence that invaded as Ågestam stared at Grens's neck, so he hurriedly interrupted.

"Schwarz's reaction. I don't think it's got anything to do with the assault that he's pleaded guilty to."

"Continue."

"Ewert, I think that the inertia he showed when we first took him in, his withdrawal interspersed with sudden, loud, horrible screams, it's shock we're dealing with. He's frightened. He's frightened of something that's happened before, that somehow has something to do with this. Being locked up. Controlled. He's experienced it before, he's been damaged by it."

Ewert Grens listened. *He's smart, Sven, I forget it every now and then, I must remember to tell him.* He looked at all three of them in silence, before starting to speak.

"I want him in for questioning. Now. As soon as we're done here."

Ågestam nodded, turned toward Sven.

"You do it. Your theory, Sven, I buy that."

Grens interrupted.

"So do I. But Hermansson will do the questioning."

Interrogating Officer Mariana Hermansson (MH): Hi.
John Schwarz (JS): (inaudible)
MH: My name's Mariana.
JS: (inaudible)
MH: I can't hear what you're saying. You'll have to speak up.

Lars Ågestam looked at Ewert Grens in surprise.

"Hermansson? Isn't Sundkvist better suited for this?"

"What the hell are you talking about, Ågestam? I'm sure that a smart young woman will get a lot further than a smart middle-aged man in this case."

MH: Are you sitting comfortably?
JS: Yes.
MH: I understand if you're nervous. Sitting here. It's a strange situation.

"Trust. Hermansson will win his trust. She'll help him with the small things first."

MH: Do you smoke, John?
JS: Yes.
MH: I've got some cigarettes. Would you like one?
JS: Thanks.

"She'll be friendly, continue to help him, she'll be completely different from the rest of us bastards."

MH: What's your name?
JS: John.
MH: What's your *real* name?
JS: That is my name. John.
MH: OK, so that's your name. John?
JS: Yes?
MH: Did you know that your wife was here a couple of hours ago?

"You see, Ågestam, it gets fucking tough after a while, even when you have to . . . to sit there lying to someone who only wants the best for you. And Hermansson—Schwarz will be convinced—Hermansson will only want what's best for him."

MH: You have full restrictions. And you will until you talk. So long as you obstruct the investigation, you won't be able to see your wife. Do you understand?

JS: Yes.
MH: She had a child with her too, a little boy, four, five years old. Your son, I guess? You won't be able to see him either.
JS: I have to . . .
MH: But I can arrange it.

"After a while, interviewing officer Hermansson will start to pop up outside the interview room. And she'll help him then too. She's kind. She understands."

MH: There's a small park outside this building. Do you know it?
JS: No.
MH: You can meet him there. If I come with you. I find it hard to believe that you meeting with a five-year-old might complicate the investigation. What do you think?

"He'll talk, Ågestam. They always do in the end. There will be a moment that crystallizes all Hermansson's friendliness, kindness, and understanding, and when Schwarz feels it, Hermansson will take the next step, then she'll make demands, she'll demand something back."

Ewert Grens stood up and walked to the door. He waited until the three people on the sofa had stood up as well.

"And then it will be his turn to give."

The meeting was over.

He was convinced. Schwarz would talk soon.

Soon they would know who he was, where he came from.

KEVIN HUTTON SAT WITH THE BLINDS DOWN IN ROOM 9000 AT 550 Main Street in Cincinnati. He always did—the daylight irritated his eyes when he had to read onscreen and he was doing it more and more, staying in the office and communicating via the Internet. He was thirty-six years old and had worked in the FBI office in western Ohio for ten of them. The work had changed following the explosion of information in the digital world, he was special agent in charge and that was as far as you could get in a local office, and yet the jobs were not really what he'd imagined when he'd first opened the door to what was still his office. He should be out there. In reality. All this, more and more office work, sometimes he just longed to be somewhere else.

He drank a lot of water. It was ten in the morning and he was already on his third bottle of expensive mineral water from the shop on the corner by the garage. He had put on weight with all this damn sitting, and water instead of morning coffee meant a lot of running to the toilet, but it worked.

He had just poured a glass when the call came from the head office in Washington.

They didn't say much. But he realized that he should put the water to one side, that today had just taken on another dimension.

He was given a phone number, a Marc Brock at Interpol, he was to call him, he had all the information there was.

Having searched through all the accessible databases, a procedure he repeated three times, Marc Brock had gradually come to understand over the past hour that whatever it was that wasn't right, was in fact right.

The man in the photo, the man who was wanted, was a dead man. Every single time. And yet, it couldn't be right. Not if you took into consideration *where* he died.

Brock had phoned the person who had sent the information, the officer who had requested help: someone called Klövje in Sweden. He had had time to reminisce about Stockholm again, the woman whose name he still remembered, and he had envisaged the beautiful city built on islands with water everywhere while he waited for an answer—they had walked around hand in hand for several days—with the receiver to his ear, and he had wondered who he would have been now, if it had worked out, if he had stayed with her.

The Swedish voice had been formal and spoken correct English with a Swedish accent. Brock had apologized, realized that he had no idea what time it was—the afternoon, he had suddenly remembered when Klövje answered the phone, six hours' difference, that was it.

The stiff smile, the uneasy eyes.

Brock had insisted. He wanted to check the photo he had of a man who called himself John Schwarz. He wanted to compare, not with the photo stuck in a Canadian passport, but with the real thing.

Klövje had confirmed the picture's veracity twenty minutes later. He had been to the jail, the cell where the suspect was being held, and he had with his own eyes seen that both faces, the one in the passport and the real one, were one and the same.

Marc Brock had thanked him, asked if he could get back to him, and lifted the receiver again as soon as he had put it down, convinced that his colleagues over at the FBI head office would think he was completely crazy.

Kevin Hutton had been ordered to call Interpol, someone called Brock.

He would do it in a moment.

He swung around in his chair and looked out over Cincinnati, where he'd lived since he applied for and got the job in the local Ohio office. The tall buildings, the busy main roads.

A few more deep breaths—he was still shaking.

Because if the first summarized details from the FBI head office were correct, he should open the window and scream out across the noisy city. Because it just wasn't possible.

And he, if anyone, should know.

Marc Brock confirmed everything.

Hutton heard the anxiety in his voice and he realized that Brock also found it hard to believe, that he would happily forward what he had because then he wouldn't need to deal with this shit anymore.

You're dead, for fuck's sake.

Kevin Hutton had immediately recognized the man in the picture.

His face was twenty years older. His hair shorter, skin paler.

But it was him. He was sure of it.

He opened the window, leaned out into the cold January air, closed his eyes, and shivered. He closed his eyes in the way you do when you just don't want to understand.

SHE HAD MOVED HER HAND.

He should sing, laugh, maybe even cry.

Ewert Grens couldn't face it.

All these years, he had somehow given up hope. And now, he didn't know, it was sorrow, guilt, loss. Like a curse. The more she waved, the clearer everything else became. What she wasn't doing. The damn guilt that he'd learned to suppress, it was hounding him again, he couldn't escape it, it knew where he was and smeared him with its terrible fucking blackness.

They had had each other. And he had driven over her head. A split second, then they had ceased to be, midstep.

He loved her.

He had no one else.

He wasn't going to go home this evening. He would sit here with the Schwarz investigation in front of him until his eyes couldn't see any longer, then he would lie down on the sofa, sleep, get up again when it was still dark; he needed the dawn.

Grens ate a sandwich with some cheese from the vending machine out in the corridor by the coffee machine, the plastic packaging was greasy, butter or something else.

She had done a good interview, Hermansson. Schwarz would trust her, it wouldn't be long now. Strange guy. As if he was trying to hide from them, despite the fact that they were sitting on the chairs directly opposite him, looking at him.

There was silence in the room. He looked at the shelf on the wall and the cassettes and the photograph of Siw, but it didn't work. Anni had waved and there was no room for music in the room. Just wasn't. Just fucking wasn't.

He had never felt like this before.

It was her voice that comforted him, that filled the room with what had once been.

Not today. Not now.

Jens Klövje knocked and pushed open the door that was standing ajar. He was red in the face, having just walked fast along the corridor and down the steps from C Block. He was carrying a bundle of papers in his hand, still warm from the fax machine, and explained that Ewert might want to see what was written there, that he was leaving it with Grens and was going back to his desk to wait and see if any more had come.

Grens finished his cheese sandwich, brushed some crumbs from his desk into the greasy wrapper in the bin.

Friday 25 September 1988 at 1623 hours PV 903 with Inspector Kowalski, Officer Larrigan, and Officer Smith were called to 31 Mern Riffe Drive in Marcusville in connection with a shooting.

He looked at the thin pile of documents, counted five pages and picked them up.

We discovered immediately that the front door to the villa, half a step up, was unlocked. There was a curtain hanging just inside the door that was pulled shut. The lights were on and it was silent inside the house.

He had read several thousand reports written by overzealous policemen before. This one was obviously American and had different names and different addresses, but was just as detailed, just as fearful of making formal errors as all the others.

Grens stood up. He was restless. There were other thoughts inside him, far more interesting than Schwarz and his past. A couple of times around the room, he could feel the silence now, he wasn't used to it and it was louder than either Siw or chatty investigators.

She had done something the bastards had claimed was impossible.

It had taken twenty-five years, but she had done it, and he had seen it.

He knew that he was pushing it, but he couldn't help it. He sat down again and dialed the number of the nursing home.

"It's Grens. I know it's late to be calling."

A brief hesitation.

"I'm sorry, but you really can't talk to her at this hour."

He recognized the voice that had answered and that continued, "You know she needs her sleep. And that she's in bed by now."

Susann, the young woman who wanted to be a doctor, who was going to accompany them out onto the water. He tried to be friendly.

"It was you that I wanted to speak to. About our little trip later on in the week. I just wanted to make sure that you'd been informed."

It was hard to make out whether she sighed or not.

"I've been told. And I'll be coming with you."

He apologized again, then hung up, maybe she sighed again, he didn't know, quite simply chose not to listen.

According to the nameplate on the front door, the house is occupied by Edward and Alice Finnigan. The house, which comprises a total of twelve rooms, was scanned using the S-method.

He picked up the American fax again. More focused now—he'd rung and checked, and she was asleep, she was comfortable. He might as well work, continue searching for the man who had once been John Schwarz.

The door to the bedroom, which is to the right of the front door, was ajar. When Officer Larrigan tried to open the bedroom door he discovered that a woman was lying on the floor just inside the door.

Grens leaned forward.

That feeling. When it's the start of something.

He read on and it slowly dawned on him what Klövje had meant, why he had been so out of breath, why his swollen face that had popped around the door a while ago had been so red.

Having entered the room and confirmed that the woman, the injured party, did not have a weapon in her hand or on her person, Larrigan called for a doctor and ambulance to come to the house immediately. Larrigan had time to confirm that the woman was lying in a position that indicated that she had fallen sideways, with her right side to the floor. Her eyes were half open and she moved her head slightly.

A person had died. She had been lying on the floor in a house in some goddamn hole called Marcusville and she had gradually ceased to be.

The ambulance personnel from ambulance A 915 and Dr. Rudenski, who entered the house a few seconds later, immediately lifted the woman and laid her on her back in the hall. Then they began to administer first aid, and at the same time confirmed that the woman's pulse was weak. After a few minutes, the woman was transported to Pike County Hospital, where they arrived at 1716 hours. The woman was given no. 1994-25-6880.

Jens Klövje had said that there was more to come. Other documents from an investigation carried out eighteen years ago in connection with the man who now called himself John Schwarz and who was sitting in a locked cell in the detention center a few hundred yards away.

Suddenly Ewert Grens was in a hurry.

STILL JUST AS COLD.

Vernon Eriksen stared in anger at the heater that hung dead on one of the institution's concrete walls. He was freezing—he would give them to the end of the week, that was long enough, then the heating in the prison had to go back on. They weren't animals, the inmates, even though the world out there sometimes expressed views that were to the contrary.

It was worst in the East Block that housed Death Row. The prisoners there froze like dogs at night and there was a damned racket in the cells because they couldn't sleep—the Colombian who always made such a noise and the new guy in Cell 22 who was crying for the second night in a row was enough in itself, but now, with the damned cold, the others were worked up, even those who normally never made a sound.

Vernon looked over at the long row of metal cages.

Everyone who was in there knew.

They were counting down. What else could they do? They waited, sometimes asked for clemency, sometimes had their date postponed, but they got nowhere, they stayed where they were and waited; days, months, years.

He should have gone home. He'd clocked off four hours ago. Normally at this time of day he'd walked from the prison to Sofio's for his blueberry pancakes, taken a detour along Mern Riffe Drive and as he passed looked into the kitchen, felt the warmth he always did when he caught a glimpse. In fact, by this time he would normally have reached his house on the outskirts of the town, maybe he'd already fallen asleep, at least gone to bed with the morning paper lying unread on the empty pillow beside him.

He was putting it off on purpose.

Soon.

He'd go soon.

He hadn't been prepared when the warden had suddenly called him to his office. They seldom talked, although they knew each other well, but as long as everything was working they had no reason to meet.

That was how it felt, even when he first called.

That this was something else.

The warden's voice had been tense and excessively clear, as if he was anxious and therefore had to hide it by pretending to be anything but.

The warden had smiled at him and shown him into his spacious office: leather sofas and a meeting table and a window twice the normal size that looked out to the main entrance. He had offered him fruit and after-dinner mints and not looked him in the eye, had managed to pull himself together and asked how long Vernon had actually worked as senior corrections officer at the prison in Marcusville, on Death Row.

Twenty-two years, Vernon had replied.

Twenty-two years, the warden had repeated, that's a long time.

Yes, it sure is long.

Do you remember them all, Vernon?

Them all, who?

The people who've done time here. In your section.

Yes. I remember them.

The warden had played with a piece of paper that was lying in front of him on the desk. There was something written on it. The reason why he had asked Vernon to come. His fingers along the edge of the paper—Vernon had tried to see, but the letters were too small and impossible to read upside down.

More than a hundred in your time, Vernon. Some released, some executed, most just waiting. And you remember them all?

Yes.

Why?

Why?

I'm curious.

That piece of paper. Vernon had leaned forward, wanted to see but hadn't managed, the warden's arm had been in the way.

I remember them because I'm a corrections officer here. My job is to look after them and rehabilitate people. I care about them. I don't have many others to care for.

The warden had offered him more fruit. Vernon had declined but took another mint, which he let melt in his mouth, and he started to realize, just then, after the fruit and the second mint, what the conversation was about.

He hadn't been prepared.

Even though he should have been.

So, you remember . . . the warden had started . . . so you possibly remember an inmate called John Meyer Frey?

Vernon had perhaps gasped, he had perhaps changed position on the leather sofa, he wasn't sure, the question had been so sudden and he had heard it and responded and tried to tackle it, and that was precisely why it had been so hard to see himself from the outside—with all that was going on inside, he had enough on his plate trying not to suffocate.

Of course. Clearly. I remember John Meyer Frey clearly.

Good.

Why?

Vernon, how many of the inmates have actually died here in prison *before* they were executed?

Not many. But it does happen. But not many.

John Meyer Frey. When he died—do you remember anything in particular from that time?

Anything in particular?

Anything.

While Vernon pretended to think, he had tried to use the pause to pull himself together, find the thoughts, the answers that he had practiced.

No. I don't think so. Nothing in particular.

No?

Well, he was young, of course. There's always something special about people who die young. But no more than that.

Nothing more?

No.

You see, Vernon, I think we have a slight problem here. I was talking to someone called Kevin Hutton a short while ago. He works for the FBI in Cincinnati. He had some questions.

Right.

He wondered, for example, who had declared Frey dead.

Why?

He also wondered where the records of Frey's autopsy are.

Why?

I'll explain, Vernon. In a minute. Once we have established who might have declared him dead and where the autopsy records might be today. Because the FBI can't find that information anywhere.

Vernon Eriksen should perhaps have taken another mint. He should perhaps have looked out of the large window for a while. But as soon as they were done, once the warden had explained the reason for the FBI's interest, he had said a polite thank-you and asked if he could get back to him if he remembered anything else, and then slowly walked down the stairs to Death Row.

The row of metal bars was still there.

And at least he hadn't let anything slip.

The cold air from the crappy heater that wasn't working.

He looked at it in anger again, kicked it hard with his black boots. He would go home soon.

Just those few extra steps. Past Cell 8.

Do you remember them all, Vernon?

Them all, who?

The people who've done time here. In your section.

Yes. I remember them.

He stood facing the metal bars, as he often did, looked in at the empty bunk.

But he didn't smile, not today.

IT WAS GOING TO BE A LONG NIGHT.

Ewert Grens had realized this somewhere in the middle of the patrol report by the American police officer. The feeling was just there, the feeling that he got a couple of times a year when yet another shitty routine investigation suddenly became something else; most recently last summer when a prostitute from Lithuania had taken hostages and tried to blow up a morgue, the summer before that when a father had taken the law into his own hands and shot and killed his daughter's murderer.

Now he felt it again.

Because Schwarz's background had a dark underside that he hadn't registered at first.

And what until recently had been aggravated assault was suddenly, he was sure of it, going to mean a lot of fucking frustration, difficulties, for all of them.

The woman was dead on arrival at Pike County Hospital. Resuscitation was attempted but without success. The woman was declared dead at 1735 hours.

Klövje had gotten back to him three times in the course of the evening at about thirty-minute intervals, with new reports from the fax each time.

The corpse of Elizabeth Finnigan had five bullet holes. Two (2) on the left-hand side of the chest in the region of the heart. One (I) in the liver. One (I) in the right kidney. One (I) about 3 inches down from the Adam's apple in the middle of the throat.

Grens had been there far too long now, he had realized, and knew that he was preparing himself.

He would not be sleeping tonight.

Following a conversation with D/Supt Harrison it was decided that the woman's body would be kept in Pike County Hospital morgue until transport arrived for forensics in Columbus.

Two plastic cups of coffee. The machine that was squeezed in between the newly acquired photocopier and an ancient fax machine spluttered as it occasionally did at night, irritated at not being allowed to get the rest that even a coffee machine needs. He drank one of them straightaway, the heat tearing at his chest, making his heart pound, as it sometimes did when it tried to escape the caffeine.

He picked up page after page from Klövje's pile, which had grown considerably through the evening. Patrol reports, some more police officers with much the same story. The autopsy record, nearly absurd in its vocabulary and precision. The forensic team's descriptions, details from the crime scene, a dead body on the floor.

Ewert Grens sat on his chair by the desk, the dark pressing in against his windows, and tried to understand.

He gripped the final document, the one from a prison called Southern Ohio Correctional Facility. In Marcusville. The town where the woman had been found dead.

Ewert Grens read it.

Again.

And again.

This, this, he realized, was the start of something that would make people cower far beyond the country's borders. And therefore some idiot would soon put on the pressure and sound off and say that the matter should be moved from an investigator's desk to a politician's.

No fucking way.

He picked up the phone and dialed a number in Gustavsberg, on the south side of Stockholm. He knew that it was late. But he didn't care.

No answer.

He let the phone ring until someone answered.

"Hello?"

"It's Ewert."

The sound of someone swallowing, clearing his throat, trying to wake his voice that had just been asleep.

"Ewert?"

"I want you here at seven o'clock tomorrow morning."

"But I was going to come in late tomorrow morning. You knew that. Jonas's school, I—"

"Seven o'clock."

Grens thought it sounded like Sven had sat up in bed.

"What's it about, Ewert?"

He didn't hear the yawning that filled Detective Inspector Sven Sundkvist's bedroom, didn't feel that he was freezing, naked on the edge of the bed.

"Schwarz."

"Has something happened?"

"There's going to be one hell of a noise. You put all other investigations to one side. The Schwarz case is now top priority."

Sundkvist was whispering; he presumably had Anita beside him.

"Ewert, explain."

"Tomorrow."

"I'm awake now."

"Seven o'clock."

Grens didn't say good night. He just put the phone down, then picked it up again as soon as he got a dial tone.

Hermansson was awake. It wasn't easy to make out whether she was on her own or not; he hoped she wasn't.

Ågestam was just about to go to bed. He sounded surprised—he knew what the detective superintendent thought of him and certainly didn't expect to get a phone call from him at home.

They both asked what it was about, without getting an answer, but promised to be sitting in Ewert Grens's office at seven o'clock sharp.

He read for a while longer.

Half an hour, then he stood up, the bulky body pacing back and forth across the room.

Half an hour more, then he lay down on the worn sofa, scoured the ceiling.

Suddenly he laughed.

Not surprising you were so fucking terrified.

Ewert Grens's loud laugh was given free rein only here, alone. With other people, in other places, he couldn't remember if he'd ever laughed.

Schwarz, you've got nowhere to fucking go now.

He thought about a document from the prison in Marcusville that he'd just read, several times, about a great country that still perpetuated the threat of the death sentence as a way of life, and he thought about the fact that it felt good to lie there and laugh and know that all hell was waiting only a few yards away on his desk, and he was about to let it loose.

IT WAS PAST TEN IN THE EVENING, U.S. TIME, WHEN THE REQUEST FOR legal assistance came through from Sweden. Kevin Hutton had hung around in the office on Main Street, with a view over Cincinnati: he had been waiting for it to come. A strange afternoon, a strange evening. He'd chain-smoked and downed mineral water until his stomach complained. For the past hour he'd alternated filterless cigarettes with some old crackers that he'd found in the staff kitchen. He was tired but didn't want to go home. The information from Brock at Interpol had made him flustered at first, and then angry, and then this awful emptiness that clung to him until he had no idea what he needed to do to stand up.

But you're dead.

All these years in the FBI and he'd never experienced anything like it. So near, so big. This was the sort of thing you lived for, longed for, wasn't it? The day you could always remember later, that stood out from all the rest. The case that no one else had experienced, when there were no answers because no one had even contemplated the questions. That was when you left your mark. That was when you got noticed in a large organization. All of that, and yet the only thing he had was this bottomless emptiness.

An hour later he was in his car heading south, his colleague and subordinate Assistant Special Agent in Charge Benjamin Clark sitting beside him. Hutton had explained, and realized as he did how implausible the whole thing sounded, but Clark had understood and he'd come to the office as soon as they'd got off the phone.

It was dark outside; the road was covered in black ice.

Kevin Hutton should perhaps have driven more slowly, but now that they were on the way he couldn't get there fast enough. It was a long time since he'd been to Marcusville. He'd lived there for nearly twenty years, but it meant nothing. Another life, another time. Sometimes when he came across photos from back then, it was as if it was someone else, not him, it wasn't him. He'd cut all contact with his parents many years ago, and when his brothers then later moved away there was nothing left that he needed, his childhood territory had become that picture he'd left on a shelf somewhere to gather dust.

And now he was about to wipe some of it away.

They had driven there in under an hour and a half. He tried to see as far as he could through the windshield, into the dark—it was all so familiar, and yet not. He hadn't realized back then how different Marcusville was. A small town with fewer than two thousand inhabitants spread over two and a half square miles. So small. So without a future. You often had to get away, break all ties, in order to see things as they really were. He didn't even need to compare it with the rest of the States, it was enough to compare it with the rest of Ohio. Income per household was lower than average. Assets per household lower than average. Number of African Americans well below average. Number of Latin Americans well below average. Number of people born abroad well below average. Number of college students well below average. Number of inhabitants with university degrees well below average . . . he could continue for as long as he liked, and he didn't miss it at all, the memories gone.

The streets were nearly empty at this time of night. Nowhere to go, nowhere to long for. He recognized every single house. There were lights on in several windows, behind the potted plants and flowery curtains, and he saw people moving about inside, Marcusvillites, like he would have been if he hadn't gone looking for a new life.

They passed Mern Riffe Drive and he looked over at the house that had once been Elizabeth Finnigan's. He knew that her parents still lived there, that they still grieved. She had been sixteen years old.

Ruben Frey lived just around the corner, the short distance that was a street called Indian Drive. Same house, everything was the same. Kevin Hutton stopped the car and glanced at his colleague. He wanted to talk about how he felt, because he felt something in his stomach when he sat in his car by the tiny lawn and looked at the front door and the windows that fronted the road. He had stayed here so many times. Ruben was short and fat and a bit odd sometimes, but he had understood everything that Kevin's parents didn't. Ruben hadn't pitched a fit when they managed to smash the light out front and he hadn't made a fuss when they occasionally forgot both time and space and went in with muddy shoes all over the parquet floor. That hadn't been important to Ruben.

He'd asked them to take off their shoes, he'd asked them to clean up after themselves, but never raised his voice, never with that sharp edge that continued to ring in your head.

Such a good man. It wasn't fair.

Now he was going to get out of the car, knock on the door and explain that he needed to ask some questions.

Kevin was cold—he had his coat on, but he was cold.

Ruben Frey opened the door almost immediately. He hadn't changed a bit. Perhaps his hair was a bit thinner, perhaps he was a bit thinner, but otherwise it was as if he'd been asleep for twenty years. They looked at each other, the dark that surrounded them and the cold that gave away the fact that they were both breathing deeply.

"Can I help you?"

"I'm sorry to disturb you so late. Do you recognize me?"

They looked at each other again.

"I recognize you, Kevin. You're older. But it's you."

"Ruben, this is Benjamin Clark, my colleague at the FBI in Cincinnati."

They shook hands, the shorter, older man and the tall, young man.

"The thing is, Ruben, we have to ask you some questions. Or rather, a lot of questions."

Ruben Frey listened, looked Kevin in the eye.

"It's nearly midnight. I'm tired. What's this about? Can it wait until the morning?"

"No."

"So what's it about?"

"Can we come in?"

It was as if the house embraced him as soon as he walked in. Kevin studied the wallpaper, the wall-to-wall carpets, the small pine staircase that went up to the second floor, the copper tubs that stood lined up in every corner of the hall. But most of all, it was the smell. It smelled the same as it had back then: slightly stuffy, pipe tobacco, fresh bread.

They sat down at the kitchen table, a red Christmas runner in the middle that would probably lie there until summer took over.

"It's exactly the same."

"You know how it is. You're happy enough. And you don't really see what it looks like anymore."

"It's great, Ruben. I was always happy here too."

Ruben Frey sat at the end of the table, the same place as back then.

Benjamin Clark and Kevin sat on either side. They both looked at him, and maybe Ruben shrank a little.

"What do you actually want, boys?"

Clark put his hand into the inner pocket of his jacket; he held out a photograph, put it down on the pine table in front of Ruben Frey.

"It's about this man. We think you know who he is."

Frey stared at the photograph. The face of a thirty-five-year-old man, pale complexion, thin, short dark hair.

The cannula is dripping, I can see that. I also see the doctor sticking the needle in and emptying the antidote somewhere in his thigh, he has to wake up, the morphine will slow his breathing, and I try to hold the boy's legs still whenever the car swings. I see his eyes, the fear of a person who has no idea of what's going on.

"What is this, Kevin?"

"I want *you* to answer that."

Ruben Frey continued to stare at the picture. He put out a hand, lifted it up, held it in front of his eyes.

"I have no idea what this is all about. You, of all people, should know that."

Kevin Hutton looked at the man whom he liked so much. He tried to read the round face, the eyes looking down at the image. He wasn't sure whether it was surprise, whether it was consternation, or acting.

"Surely you recognize him, Ruben?"

Ruben Frey shook his head.

"My son is dead."

I look at him. For the last time. I know that. This is how it has to be. He looks frightened. When he boards that airplane it's over. I don't like the fact that he's so frightened. It will get easier. It has to.

"Ruben, look at the photograph again."

"I don't need to. The hair is shorter. The complexion paler. This person is like him. With the exception that he's alive."

Hutton leaned forward; it would perhaps be easier to say if he was closer.

"Ruben, I want you to listen to me. This photograph was taken twenty-eight hours ago. In Stockholm, the capital of Sweden. The man in the picture says that his name is John Schwarz."

"John Schwarz?"

"That's not his real name. We have his fingerprints and DNA from the Swedish police. Identical to those we have ourselves, but that were taken earlier."

Hutton paused briefly, wanted to be sure that their eyes met when he said it.

"Identical to those we have from your son."

Ruben Frey sighed, or did he snort? It wasn't easy to tell.

"You know that he's dead."

"The face in that picture there belongs to John Meyer Frey."

"You yourself were at the funeral."

Kevin Hutton put his hand on Ruben's arm, the shirt folded up to the elbow, as always.

"Ruben, we want you to come with us to Cincinnati. We need to question you there. Tonight. Then you can sleep there. I'll get a good bed for you. And tomorrow, we'll probably do a second interview."

Kevin Hutton and Benjamin Clark waited in the car while Ruben Frey slowly packed a few toiletries and a change of clothes in a far-too-large overnight bag.

They let him take his time.

He had just seen his dead son in a recently taken photo.

PART II

seven years earlier

january

THE NEW YEAR FELT OLD ALREADY, NO MORE THAN A DAY SINCE New Year's Eve, but Vernon Eriksen was relieved, finally it was over: the constant nagging and expectation, everyone preparing themselves for the party of a lifetime, putting all their glad rags on, only to be as disappointed as they always were when dreams were put to the test and proved to be just that, dreams.

Always that reluctance.

The hours that dragged and stuck to your skin, the last day of the year was a time to remember and he hated it, was almost frightened; everyone who had left him, the loneliness became so acute.

His mother had died suddenly of cancer when he was growing out of his teens, and he remembered his father making her pretty in the funeral parlor—Vernon had stood there and watched as his hands gently washed her white skin, as he cried while he brushed her hair.

Six weeks later his father was hanging from one of the beams in the cellar.

Sometimes Vernon fled from the feet that hadn't been standing on anything, from the eyes that shone red. *I am the one who decides over life and death*, his father had always said with a twinkle in his eye, always as he attended to the dead, filled them with life again before the family took their farewell. *You see, Vernon, it's not God, it's not anybody else, I am the one who decides.* He had always seemed lighter after that, and Vernon had loved him; they had looked at each other and kept on going, even though they were working with something no one else could bear to think about. That afternoon, when he had found him hanging from the beam, he had thought just that, repeated his dad's mantra to himself over and over again, and it had worked. He had been able to lift him down, hold him, maybe it wasn't suicide, maybe it was just Dad's way of showing that it was he who decided, even over his own death.

The hours had passed. The pictures that stuck with him and the loneliness that assailed him, gone.

A new year.

Snow had been falling all night and the air was clear. He breathed lightly and listened to the crunching under his feet. It was still early when he left his home in Marcusville, still dark when he got into his car and took the detour down Mern Riffe Drive, the same ritual, always, since he was a teenager, stolen glances at the Finnigans' large house as he passed. The light was on in the kitchen and the living room, and the same thing that always struck him when he saw Alice inside: a feeling that was often yearning, sometimes grief, sometimes gratitude for having been close to a woman at least for a while.

He had thought they'd promised each other eternity, he'd been nineteen and didn't want to understand what she later told him when she left him during those strange weeks after cancer had taken his mother, and then a rope over a beam had taken his father.

The overwhelming emptiness that had suddenly engulfed him, drowned him.

He drove on toward Indian Drive and picked up Ruben Frey, who was ready and waiting on the veranda, the door already locked. They kept their overcoats on, the heating in the car hadn't been working well this winter. He ought to get it looked at but it was expensive and he had postponed it week after week and now it was only a couple of months more, then spring would be here.

They sat in silence in the front seats as he drove toward Route 23 and the first miles north toward Columbus. They had known each other for years, initially in the way that you knew everyone in Marcusville, a chat in the shop, a few words when you met on the street. Then came the day when all hell broke loose, when Elizabeth Finnigan was found shot on the floor of her home with John Meyer Frey's sperm inside her, and their relationship had rapidly changed. Vernon was the senior corrections officer on Death Row in the East Block of the prison and Ruben was the father of a seventeen-year-old boy who spent the first nights locked up there.

For some years, Ruben had avoided going into town as much as possible, and if he did occasionally venture out and they happened to meet, he looked away—shame makes people do that.

One morning at Sofio's they had sat, each at their own table, eating blueberry pancakes and reading the *Portsmouth Daily Times* before looking up at each other after a while, a faint smile, then Ruben Frey had put his hand on the empty chair next to him, *come over, come over so we can talk again.*

Vernon kept his focus on the road, the headlights like two big eyes in the dense dark. The heat gradually filled the damp air around them and he felt himself relaxing, his hands a touch looser on the wheel. Somewhere around Piketon he accelerated, sixty-five more miles to Columbus, they should be there in an hour or so.

"I'm never going to take part in an execution again. Have I told you that?"

Ruben Frey turned toward Vernon, shook his head.

"No, not in so many words. But I knew."

"I was young and on a training course in Florida the first time. There were twelve officers and the thirty-year-old man was also called John. He'd been found guilty of murder too. My job was to strap him to the chair with one of the other guards. Then I was just to watch and learn."

Vernon Eriksen swallowed as he changed gear on a sharp bend; he was back there again, in the room where he'd seen retribution for the first time.

"But the first shock, two thousand volts, burnt out the electrode on his leg. It just fell off. The officer who was supposed to shave his right leg had obviously done a bad job. So *I* had to shave it again. And I did it properly, held the mauled leg while someone else found a new electrode."

Vernon glanced over at his passenger. Ruben said nothing, just looked straight ahead, into the dark.

"The next shock lasted for three minutes. I'll never forget that image. The sinews in his neck were standing right out. His hands turned red before turning white. Fingers, toes, legs, everything was twisted, and the noise, the fucking noise, as if someone was frying meat. You get it? His eyes, he had a hood on but that didn't help, his eyes burst out and hung down his cheeks. He shat himself. He slobbered. He puked blood."

The bend that had become another bend now became a straight stretch and he changed gear and accelerated again.

"The third shock, Ruben, he was on fire. We put out the flames that leapt from his body. But most of all, it's so hard to explain, most of all it was the smell. Sweet. Burning flesh. Like a barbecue on a summer's night, you know. The smell that hangs like a cloud over every garden in Marcusville in the evening."

Ruben Frey listened as dawn tentatively allowed the light to slip in outside the car, the day taking its place. He saw his son in front of him. The long dark corridor with rows of cells. John sat there waiting every day, every week, every month, to stop living, for his death that was rapidly approaching.

"I decided already back then. The first time. That that was enough, not to be able to decide over life and death yourself, I couldn't do it anymore. So I was sick on the day of the next execution, and I've done the same ever since whenever I can."

They drove the last miles through the dawning day, caught the contours of Columbus early. Somewhere between half a million and a million inhabitants, Ohio's largest city, a state center that offered work; a good many folk commuted the hundred miles or so to and from Marcusville every day.

The parking lot outside Doctors Hospital was already full. Vernon circled around a couple of times before he saw a woman walking slowly toward a car and driving off shortly after. He moved as fast as he could and got to the empty space at the same time as a huge jeep. They stood hood to hood and Vernon stared furiously until the other driver backed down, gave him the finger and drove off.

"All these years, Ruben, all the murderers, I've met all sorts."

They were still sitting in the car. Vernon wanted to tell him, and he was sure that Ruben would listen.

"I know what they look like. I know how they behave, how they think. How the ones who are guilty *look* at you."

"I know that John is innocent."

"Ruben, I'm absolutely certain of it. Otherwise I wouldn't be here today."

Vernon had been there several times before. Without hesitation, he walked through the door that was the main entrance to the hospital and past the information desk, toward the elevators that connected the ninth floor with the rest of the building. They stood side by side in front of the large mirrors that you couldn't avoid. Vernon, who was tall with his thin hair in a comb-over, Ruben, who was short and about seventy pounds overweight.

"The truth is, Ruben, that several studies from all over the world have shown that somewhere around two, maybe even three percent of all people in prison have been wrongly convicted. Either they've been sentenced for the wrong crime or they're innocent. Some criminologists claim that it's even more. And John, your John, I'm as convinced as you are, he's one of them."

The short, fat man in the mirror put a hand to his face. If anyone had looked closely they would have seen that he was crying.

"That two percent, Ruben, some of that is here with me. On Death Row. Waiting to die. And it's us, the state, that kills them."

Vernon looked in the mirror at the image of the man who stood hunched forward, put his arm around the real thing.

"That's what makes it so impossible. At least in my world."

The prayer room was some way down the corridor on the ninth floor.

Two white candles stood lit on what Vernon had always assumed was the altar.

Some chairs farther back, a table had been carried in and put down in front of them.

The priest was there, Father Jennings, and both the doctors; the younger one was named Lawrence Greenwood and the older was named Bridget Burk. Vernon greeted them, then introduced Ruben, and they shook his hand, said that he was welcome, that together they would make sure that his son did not die.

february

IT WAS ALREADY THE THIRD WEEK IN FEBRUARY WHEN THE FIRST execution for several years took place at Southern Ohio Correctional Facility, in Marcusville, on behalf of the state of Ohio. Edward Finnigan watched from the green plastic flooring that was called the witness area. He had for a few minutes stood transfixed, and together with around twenty other people stared at a circular iron cage, painted the same green color as the floor, with large windows on all sides that looked out in every direction like a compound eye. He was lying in there. A man in his forties who had been waiting to die on Death Row for exactly ten years. A man by the name of Berry, who had been found guilty of armed robbery and the murder of a fifty-three-year-old man: thirty-three dollars and a bullet through the head by the cash register at a bakery counter.

It was as if Berry was sleeping now. His head to one side, eyes shut, two heavy-duty belts the length of his body and six across, he had been firmly strapped in for his death, on the white bench that had thick padding and looked quite soft.

An officer in prison uniform opened the door to the chamber and walked over to the man who had just died. He was careful, the guard, when he lifted the dead man's arms and pulled out the first cannula of three.

Edward Finnigan couldn't move.

He was looking at someone who was no longer breathing. He glanced over at the victim's sister and brother-in-law, who were standing in front of someone they hated, who were crying with grief and relief. The member of their family had not been returned but the person who had thought it his right to take him away forever was dead now too—had also been taken away; he had gotten his punishment and the family their retribution.

Now they could move on.

When this was over.

Move on. *Move on.*

Finnigan shook himself and felt his body start to move again without him

131

being able to control it. He had been waiting as long. Ten years. For ten years his daughter's murderer had been sitting not far away, in another part of the large building, and had just gone on and on living. Twice, the damned campaigners and lawyers had managed to stay all executions here. Not any longer. Not anymore. From this day on, executions were once more a fact in the state of Ohio. Soon it would be their turn. His and Alice's turn. To find that peace. To have their retribution. To be able to move on, *move on*.

The boy—and he had been a boy then—who had taken their daughter from them was now going to pay.

Soon he would be lying there, in the chamber, three needles in his body while his heart stopped.

Finnigan waited as he always did. When the others had seen enough, cried and cursed, then they would leave, while he remained, slow steps past the three windows. He wanted to see the ones who had to die, *life for life*, and he spat on the glass, the ones who would never be able to take anything away again.

He had settled with the warden and warned the main security desk in East Block that he would go through Death Row afterward. It was a long time since he'd been there. He just wanted to see what he looked like, if he had changed, if death had started to eat away at him.

The air was damp. It always was. He had time to forget between visits, how stuffy it was in the corridor lined with cells.

He stopped a couple of feet away. The bastard didn't know. A few long strides, then he stood in front of the metal bars that were Cell 8.

"It'll be you next. After the summer."

John Meyer Frey was lying with his face to the far wall. He wasn't asleep, not really, more dozing.

"Go away."

He heard the voice again, the one he'd learned to try and block out.

"It's been a long time, Frey."

"Just go away."

"I just saw one of your friends. He doesn't exist anymore. And in the autumn, you won't exist anymore either, Frey. No number of appeals will help this time."

"I haven't got any friends."

John Meyer Frey had just turned twenty-eight. He had been seventeen the day he came here. Didn't understand much. Everything had just happened, suddenly he was sitting here, waiting.

"Your sperm. Inside."

"I loved her."

"You killed her."

"You know that it wasn't me."

John looked at the man with the mustache and greased-back hair, at his eyes—he had never seen eyes like them before, not even here, with the madmen.

"It's a few years now since I last read for you."

The book in Finnigan's hands, the red cover, the gold on the edge of the pages.

"The Book of Numbers today, chapter thirty-five, verses sixteen to nineteen. I just don't want you to forget, Frey."

John didn't say anything. He couldn't face it.

But if he strikes him with an iron implement, so that he dies, he is a murderer; the murderer shall surely be put to death . . ."

Finnigan's voice, strained; he forced out what he carried with him.

"The avenger of blood himself shall put the murderer to death; when he meets him, he shall put him to death."

He snapped the book shut, an echo that grew in the desolate corridor.

"After the summer, Frey. These are new times in Ohio. After the summer, the campaigners can ask for all the damn respites they like. I work where I work. I know what I know. After the summer I'll read to you for the third time, the last thing you'll ever hear."

"My death won't bring Elizabeth back."

Finnigan took a final step forward, he could touch the metal bars. He spat into the cell.

"But *I* can move on. *Alice* can move on! And all the others—they'll read, they'll listen, learn that he who takes must also give."

John didn't move.

"Look around you, Finnigan. Why do you think it's so full in here? Because they've *learned*?"

"You're going to die! She was our only child."

"It wasn't me."

It was windy outside. There was no weather on Death Row, nothing that anyone could see. But you could hear it. After a while, anyone sitting waiting realized that you could hear the wind and occasionally the pattering rain. John even thought he could hear the snow sometimes, falling on the roof. That's what it sounded like now. When Finnigan began taunting him. Like it was snow.

"I know all the sentences that have been given to people like you, Frey!"

Finnigan ran down the middle of the corridor, punching the air at each cell as he passed, at each person who was locked up inside and who now turned toward the man who could no longer contain himself.

"Here, Frey, here! Savage, the guy in there, *sentenced for the murder of a minor!* And he maintained his innocence throughout the entire trial, the entire damn trial."

Edward Finnigan darted back and forth, pointing at the men behind bars and he didn't hear the sound in the distance, the sound that was made by the security door opening and three uniforms hurrying down the concrete corridor.

"And here, Frey! Here. That tall black bastard standing there, he's called Jackson. *Done for aggravated rape and murder!* According to forensics, he'd sodomized the corpse. And you know what! You know what, Frey? He *also* maintained his innocence throughout the whole damn trial."

The three officers moved swiftly and surrounded the haranguing Finnigan, their white gloves on his body, the long key chains swinging against their thighs as they held him tight and marched him toward the exit. None of them said anything about the hands that shot out from each cell as they passed, the middle finger upright and indignant.

John was tired.

Elizabeth's father's hate always took more out of him than he liked to admit, even to himself. And the last few visits, Finnigan's threats that it was time, that the likelihood of another postponement was as good as nothing, were probably more than arbitrary rants intended to hurt. Of course John knew that time was running out. That he was about to lose.

He lay down on the bunk again.

He listened. He could hear it.

Even though there had already been a lot in February, it continued, and it was normally around this time in the evening that he heard it: the sound that was probably snow.

march

IT WAS THE LAST FEW DAYS OF MARCH, AND VERNON ERIKSEN HAD FOR the eighth time in just under three months driven the distance between his home in Marcusville and Doctors Hospital in Columbus, with Ruben Frey sitting beside him in the passenger seat. Ruben seemed to have shrunk a little with each trip; the heavy man was still rotund but it was as if he had deflated, as you do when your expectations fade.

It was close now. He was sure of it.

There were plenty of parking spaces today, and even the elevator that went to the ninth floor was empty. The door to the prayer room was open, Father Jennings standing there waiting as he usually did, Drs. Lawrence Greenwood and Bridget Burk beside him. And farther back in the room, two new faces, lawyers; Anna Mosley and Marie Morehouse were young women with whom Vernon and Ruben shook hands and thanked for coming.

When Wilford Berry had been executed for the murder of a fifty-three-year-old baker one month earlier, it looked like their work together over the past few years had been in vain. It had been a long time since an execution had been carried out in Ohio, as if finally there had been room for other ideas, as if finally the argument against the death penalty had gotten the upper hand.

A four-page statement from the governor had put a stop to all that.

Lawyers' legal objections were thrown out. People's civil objections were rejected. Doctors' medical objections and the church's ethical objections—with references to Jesus blessing the murderers who hung on the crosses beside him—were discarded.

Ohio's governor had rejected all of it with his four-page statement. He had run an election campaign on the promise of reinstating the death penalty and now he was delivering it. The poison that had been injected into Berry's body was his virgin shot and it declared his power. Afterward he wanted more, in the way that someone who injects always wants more. It was no great secret that now the state of Ohio had reinstated executions, it would continue—there would be more. Vernon realized this. Ruben Frey realized this. From now on, those who had been sentenced to death would be taken one by one from Death Row to the Death House, to injections that kept power happy.

The people now present looked at each other and then sat down around the table in front of the prayer room altar: Jennings and the doctors and the lawyers and Vernon and Ruben, a small number of the group that called itself the Ohio Coalition to Abolish the Death Penalty.

They knew that there wasn't much time.

Wilford Berry had waited ten years for his death sentence to be carried out.

John Meyer Frey, who was still waiting in a cell on the same corridor that Wilford Berry had just left, had received his sentence the same year, a couple of months later.

april

IT WAS IN MID-APRIL THAT THE EXECUTION OF WILFORD BERRY STARTED to have a serious impact in Ohio. When activity in the murderer's heart had been stopped by 100 milliequivalents of potassium chloride two months earlier, it had been a symbolic act that once again opened the gulf between supporters of the death penalty and those who opposed it; the argument *against* the state's right to terminate a person's life was obliterated by the argument *for* the right to retribution for the victim's family. The value of implementing crime prevention measures was given less attention than the value of execution as a deterrent.

After years without anyone in the two cells of the Death House, the majority of Ohio's inhabitants now wanted to see death again.

And the line was long.

At night, the screams of the inmates on Death Row in Marcusville got louder—they were counting the days again.

John Meyer Frey was in Cell 8.

He knew that when the governor had declared the state's right to kill again, the end was nigh.

And when the wind was strong and blowing in the right direction, he could hear the clamor.

The noise that found its way in through the narrow windows up close to the ceiling, shouts that intensified and jostled at the gate on the other side of the wall, from the pro-campaigners outside whose ranks had swelled day by day.

He recognized the voice.

He knew that Edward Finnigan was at the forefront and that he was the one shouting loudest. *Burn, John, burn.*

IT WAS A BEAUTIFUL DAY, SPRING AND GREEN AND FULL OF HOPE, THE first week in May. And everything was about to go into free fall.

Vernon Eriksen had gotten up early, having decided late last night that he would go to Columbus again, to the hospital where Greenwood and Burk were both working that day. They couldn't wait any longer. Time was running out as they watched, they should be chasing the minutes. John Meyer Frey had become a matter of policy and prestige in the governor of Ohio's office. He was going to die. That was what the authorities wanted. His death would be another symbolic victory for the supporters of the death penalty and the start of Edward Finnigan's retribution, and the state was therefore prepared to take the life of someone who Vernon knew was innocent.

Ruben Frey had knocked on his door just before midnight and stood waiting on the veranda; Vernon had opened the door and pulled him in, quickly covering his mouth with both hands. He had been forced to explain to John's dad for a second time that he could not, under any circumstances, openly show that he had anything to do with the inmates' families; that his house was presumably tapped and regularly checked like those of his colleagues; that in order to work as senior corrections officer at Marcusville he had of course to appear to be wholeheartedly in favor of the death penalty.

He hadn't been able to get through to Ruben Frey and Vernon had slapped him hard in the face—he didn't have any choice. Then he had pulled down the blinds and they had sat by the kitchen table, each with a glass of Canadian whisky, maybe half an hour's silence, before Frey could even talk again.

His voice, rusty and tense.

I believe in the death penalty, he had almost whispered. I always have. You do understand that, don't you, Vernon?

No.

I believe that when you take a life you have to give a life.

It's not that simple, Ruben.

That is why—look at me Vernon!—*if* John had been guilty, *if* he had killed Elizabeth Finnigan, then he could have burned in hell as far as I'm concerned.

Ruben Frey had emptied the small glass before Vernon had even lifted his. He had pointed to the empty glass, Vernon had nodded and filled it again.

But I know he didn't do it!

He had tried to take hold of Vernon's hand but couldn't reach, or perhaps Vernon had pulled it back, he had maybe been too close.

They can't damn well take him if he's done nothing! Vernon! If he's done nothing, you hear, if he's . . .

The round man with the kind eyes had never finished the sentence, he had collapsed on one of Vernon Eriksen's chairs, his head hitting the table hard.

Vernon had at first thought it was a heart attack.

That Frey had died in front of him.

He had lost consciousness for a while, sweated profusely. Vernon had helped him up and supported him as they had made their way slowly upstairs and to the bedroom. He had gently laid him down in his clothes on the only bed in the house, a blanket over his trembling body. He had sat beside him until he fell asleep and then gone down into the kitchen again, to the whiskey that was waiting, to a long night.

That was when he made up his mind.

Alone in the dark and with Ruben's muffled snores vibrating through the whole house.

John Meyer Frey would not die strapped to a gurney with needles in his arms.

He had left Marcusville while it was still dark, as he normally did, and despite the slight mist had sped through a considerable part of Ohio. He had stopped at a gas station after he had driven some distance, borrowed a phone that was presumably not tapped, and let the two doctors know he was on his way. They were both working in the ER and had a lot to do that morning: two accidents involving buses on the roads outside Columbus a few hours earlier in the dark. But they agreed that he should come to the hospital all the same. There was always an empty room somewhere, always some time to spare between preliminary diagnosis and emergency treatment.

He had made one more phone call.

A confused Ruben Frey had answered, still sleepy and in Vernon Eriksen's bed. Vernon had asked him to contact a branch of Ohio Savings Bank in Columbus, the one on West Henderson Road, in order to arrange a mortgage on Frey's house. Just as they had agreed earlier; bank staff outside Marcusville would ask fewer questions and the money was prerequisite for them to take the next step.

As usual, Vernon walked briskly through the entrance to the Doctors Hospital, but this time turned immediately to the right, down a long corridor. A couple of hundred yards straight and far too bright, then some thick red metal doors.

He had opened the last door and continued on. The ER reception looked like a war zone. Conscious and unconscious people on beds spilling out into the corridor. Relatives who were crying or waiting or arguing loudly. Doctors and nurses and ambulance men in white and green and orange uniforms. First he spotted Greenwood, then a few minutes later Burk. They didn't see him, they were running between patients and examination rooms and he sat himself down on a hard, pine bench. He would have to wait a while, until the corridor was less full, until the people who were bleeding had been tended to.

An hour and a half later they sat down in the only empty receiving room in the ER, Lawrence Greenwood's young face sweaty, Bridget Burk with large damp patches under her arms. Vernon asked them to wait and then went out into the coincidently almost deserted waiting hall and over to the drinks machine that stood in the corner by a shelf of children's books and well-thumbed gossip mags. A dollar fifty later he carried back a cup of coffee for each of them with both hands, but they were hotter than he'd expected, burning against his palms.

They each sat on a chair with the coffee on the empty bed between them. They took a sip, the heat slowly making its way through their bodies.

The decision they were about to make would change the course of their lives forever.

It was not a matter of *what* they were going to do. They already knew that. They had met together on several previous occasions and worked out step-by-step what they deemed to be the last resort.

It was more a question of *whether* they would do it.

Vernon finished the last of his coffee and then looked at them. He was the one to summarize all the appeals that had failed; the lawyers', doctors', and church's joint appeals for humanity—that a state should not take life—had all been assigned to the trash can, again. The governor of Ohio had decided. There would be no more mercy, no more delays. It was May now, the date had already been set, John Meyer Frey was to be executed by lethal injection on the sixth of October at 2100 hours.

They had five months.

"Mr. Eriksen?"

"Yes?"

"This is important for you."

"Yes."

"How important?"

Vernon wasn't sure that the doctors with their spouses and children would be able to understand.

"Well, it's like this . . . this is what I think. I don't want to watch when a friend ceases to exist. Not another one. That's just the way it is. They're kind of my family . . . I don't really have anyone else. It might be difficult to understand. For you, I mean. But that's how it is."

Lawrence Greenwood moved his head slowly up and down in something that resembled a nod.

"That's heartbreaking."

Vernon Eriksen was breathing heavily.

"*I'm* the one who's there, watching over them. The people that society demands retribution from. That society wants to take revenge on. Murder. Every day I watch over them. And I somehow become . . . physically involved. I'm there when it's carried out. The murder. Do you understand?"

He opened out his hands.

"But it's not *my* revenge. I don't believe in damn retribution anymore, in revenge, in a society that takes life. And John . . . I am sure of it, John is innocent."

Vernon looked at both the silent doctors, asked them to think about it for a few minutes while he went out into the waiting hall again and got three more cups.

When he came back they had decided.

He could tell by looking at them. They never actually said anything to confirm it, just leaned in toward each other and repeated what they had already gone through.

Lawrence Greenwood and Bridget Burk would that very afternoon apply for the vacant position at the prison in Marcusville, one of the jobs that had been advertised in the spring without anyone taking it. They would both apply for a part-time position, motivated by the fact that they both wanted to keep a part-time position at the hospital in Columbus as well, and they would offer to start as early as the first of June.

Vernon would continue to crush haloperidol and ipecacuanha in his office, then sprinkle it over John's food, as he had been doing since the beginning of the year.

Once they started in their new job, Greenwood and Burk would immediately examine the inmate in Cell 8 on Death Row, who, after several months of haloperidol and ipecac, and without himself knowing why, had complained about feeling poorly and sick. They would give a speculative diagnosis of cardiomyopathy, soon to be backed up by X-rays already stored in a bank safety deposit box, and explain that John's heart muscle was not functioning as it should, that his heart was slowly growing bigger and bigger.

They would then wait until late summer, until sometime in the middle of August. That was when they would do it. What they had gone through together a long time ago, every step, every tiny detail, second by second, minute by minute.

John Meyer Frey would do what no one else had done before.

He would escape from Death Row.

He would die so that he didn't need to die.

PART III

wednesday

EWERT GRENS WAS FAIRLY CERTAIN HE'D SLEPT FOR AN HOUR, BETWEEN five and six, squashed onto the cramped sofa in his office. Klövje had run back and forth with a pile of faxes through the evening and early part of the night, which now lay scattered all over the floor; the autopsy report, patrol reports, and forensic records, upside down and in the wrong order— he was glad that they were numbered.

The printout of an inquiry concerning an inmate at a prison in southern Ohio still lying on his stomach, crumpled and with grease stains on most of the pages.

He remembered the loud-ass cat.

Just as he'd tried to get to sleep, it sat down in one of the empty parking spaces and made a hell of a racket in the courtyard. Whether it was in heat or angry or just lonely he didn't know and didn't particularly care either, it had screeched as only cats can and he remembered vaguely getting out his gun at one point and, in line with regulations, firing a couple of warning shots, deliberately high but close enough to shut the beast up for a few minutes. Then it had started again, of course, and he'd considered firing another shot, this time aiming and firing with intent, but had refrained, and it had eventually stopped of its own accord or he'd just stopped hearing it, drifted off to sleep.

Grens got up.

It was as if he had a hole in his back.

He looked at the alarm clock that stood on the edge of the desk. It had been late when he called Sven and Hermansson and Ågestam, but they had understood and in one hour, at seven, they would be sitting here in his office listening to his long night of faxed papers, telling a story unlike anything he'd come across before.

They were all early.

Ewert Grens looked at them with satisfaction when they were all seated. Their eyes were tired, their skin paler than usual, and Ågestam, who had come first and normally had an immaculate side parting, was a bit disheveled.

Grens spoke quietly.

"John Schwarz."

His only words. It was such a good story. Almost as if he wanted to string it out as long as possible.

"He's dead."

Their faces, Grens enjoyed their confusion—were they going to shout or was he putting them on, or were they just still tired and didn't understand?

"But yesterday, Ewert, I saw . . ."

Ewert Grens waved his hand at Sven and asked him to sit down again, to listen.

"He's still lying in his cell over at Kronoberg detention center."

Grens pointed to the wall behind his back, at the facility.

"And you might even say that he's doing very well. Given that he died over six years ago."

"Grens, what's this all about?"

The public prosecutor, Lars Ågestam, stood up, his thin legs restless.

"You too, Ågestam. Sit down."

"Not before you've explained yourself."

"When you sit down."

Ewert smiled. And waited.

"When you sit down, I'll explain to you why it may be a good thing to consider personal reasons when prioritizing."

Ågestam looked around the room, then made a great fuss of sitting down again.

"John Schwarz died while awaiting execution at a prison in Marcusville, some dump in south Ohio."

Their faces again. Equally uncomprehending.

"His name was John Meyer Frey back then. He had been on Death Row for more than ten years, convicted of the murder of a sixteen-year-old girl. He died in his cell of something that I think is pronounced *cardio-myopathy*."

Grens shrugged.

"Something to do with the heart growing so big that it finally quits."

He leaned over to pick up the glass of water that was standing by the alarm clock on his desk. He drank, filled the glass again, emptied the rather filthy jug.

"Does anyone else want some?"

They all shook their heads.

He took another drink, three sips, then he was finished.

"John Schwarz, who is John Doe, is in fact John Meyer Frey. A dead American citizen."

He smiled.

"My friends. We have, in other words, done something extraordinary."

His smile was even broader.

"We've imprisoned a corpse."

THE CLOCK ON TOP OF THE HEDVIG ELEONORA CHURCH HAD JUST STRUCK
seven when Thorulf Winge opened the main door to his building on
Nybrogatan and went out into the slight, but cold, wind. As always, he
crossed the street, holding a freshly squeezed orange juice in a paper cup
from the early morning café that already smelled of cinnamon buns and
the big brown ones with a gooey center.

It had been one hell of a morning already.

At half past four, he had finished an urgent call from Washington that
had been redirected to his home via the foreign ministry. The state
secretary for foreign affairs had gotten used to it over the years; it wasn't
unusual for the odd night to turn out like this, questions that needed
immediate answers, statements that had to be formulated before daylight
got the upper hand.

But he had never been involved in anything like this before.

An American prisoner who had died while awaiting execution on Death
Row. Who had been dead and buried for over six years. And was now
being held in custody in Stockholm.

Thorulf Winge walked from Nybrogatan on Östermalm toward the city,
Gustaf Adolfs Torg and the Ministry of Foreign Affairs. He was in good
shape despite the fact that he'd turned sixty a couple of years ago, slim,
straight backed, his hair still thick and dark. He worked more or less
continuously, but was different from the others, those who slowly burned
out when there was no rest and recuperation; the long hours, the very air
that he breathed, were *precisely* what kept him young and alert, there wasn't
much else.

He drank the juice full of pulp and filled his lungs with winter as he
mulled over the long conversation, the astonishing information, and
worked on a solution that was taking shape in his mind. This was what he
did; threw himself into looking for solutions the moment a crisis erupted.
It was what he was good at, as both he and the people around him knew.

This, this could have been another fairly straightforward case.

A prisoner who disappears, a criminal who escapes his punishment and lives the life of Riley in freedom and is then returned to his cell and the penalty.

But this was something else.

It was a matter of prestige, principle.

Crime and punishment and the victim's right to retribution held a unique position in American society. All those new prisons recently, even longer sentences, and governors and senators and congressmen who had won elections on the promise of tougher measures, of breaking the escalating cycle of crime. This person who was now sitting locked up in a Swedish prison would be a serious and dangerous headline for politicians who wanted to be reelected. They would get him back at all costs, he would be returned to his cell and he would be executed to the applause of the people and the authorities, *an eye for an eye*, that was the law of the land.

The United States would definitely demand his return.

Sweden, a little country in northern Europe, would be expected to comply.

But in recent years, the Swedish Ministry of Justice and the Ministry of Foreign Affairs had, in connection with negotiations on the extradition agreement between the EU and the United States, time and again explained that *no* EU country would *ever* extradite *anyone* with a death sentence.

Thorulf Winge looked appreciatively at his surroundings as he crossed the roundabout in front of the Ministry of Foreign Affairs, the building that was called the Hereditary Prince's Palace. It was still very quiet, not much traffic, only a handful of people to be seen in the corridor of power that ran from here to the parliament and government offices at Rosenbad.

He opened the door and walked into the impressive building.

He needed time.

He needed peace.

He needed complete latitude, and the longer it was until anyone else knew, the better.

Ewert Grens had looked at them, he had dazzled them with a broad grin. He was enjoying the situation, Lars Ågestam was sure of it. Once he had explained what had happened, let the statement *we have imprisoned a corpse* settle in the room, it was as if he quickened, his tired body and bitter face had radiated energy, something awful and awkward had happened and Grens lit up in the way that those who had worked with him before said he did, when he was at his best.

Ågestam sat still. This whole thing was something he'd never encountered before and he was just about to ask one of the many questions dancing around in his head when his phone rang. He put his hand into the inner pocket of his jacket, apologized, ignored Grens's irritated expression, left the detective superintendent's office and went out into the corridor that smelled of dust and something else.

He knew who it was.

But had never spoken to him before.

"Good morning. My name is Thorulf Winge, the state secretary for foreign affairs."

Lars Ågestam didn't really need much more than that. He had understood what it was about, even before Winge continued.

"I just want to confirm that the information I have is correct, that you are leading a preliminary investigation in connection with a certain John Schwarz who was recently detained."

"Why?"

"Don't bullshit me."

"You know that confidentiality prevents me from discussing who has been held in custody and who hasn't."

"And don't fucking tell me what I already know."

Ågestam saw some policemen coming down the corridor who were either about to start their day or had worked the night shift and were on their way home. He moved farther away so no one would overhear.

"What you're implying, what you're getting at, could be interpreted as unconstitutional ministerial rule."

He heard Winge take a deep breath, that he was preparing to raise his voice.

"The John Schwarz case doesn't officially exist. You will therefore, under no circumstances, answer any questions about the detainee. Keep a lid on it, Ågestam. Keep a lid on it!"

Lars Ågestam swallowed, in anger and surprise.

"Am I to understand the state secretary's . . . words as . . . well, let's just say that the blackout is a directive straight from . . . the minister of foreign affairs?"

"You little smart-ass . . . just wait five minutes. And then take the call."

Ågestam stood by the coffee machine. The weak disgusting coffee that Grens normally ran around with. He read the square buttons and then pushed one of them. It didn't look particularly nice. But he took the cup that had just been filled and drank it, as he needed something.

Exactly five minutes later his phone rang again.

The voice was more familiar. The chief prosecutor. His direct boss.

The conversation was brief.

The preliminary investigation into a case involving a man called John Schwarz, who was being held in detention, was now subject to total confidentiality.

Ågestam loitered in the corridor, finished the coffee that tasted of nothing. He tried to gather his thoughts. He had received a direct order. Totally incorrect, but an order all the same. He didn't like the earlier tone of voice, the state secretary's hiss; it smelled of old men, the tone that old men resorted to, old men who had lived with power for so long that they no longer noticed it, took it for granted.

He stood outside the closed door, looked at the handle, took a deep breath, opened it.

Grens was still standing up, holding some reports in his hand, quoting from one of them. Sundkvist and Hermansson were both sitting nearby listening and seemed to be unsettled by what they heard. They all looked at Ågestam, who walked over to the chair he had left twenty minutes ago.

"Well? What was it that was so much more important than our meeting?"

Ewert Grens waved the handful of papers at the young prosecutor.

"It *was* very important."

Grens was impatient, waved his pile up and down several times.

"Well?"

"This case. John Schwarz. From now on the preliminary investigation is subject to total confidentiality. We can't talk about it with anyone, at all."

"What the hell do you mean?"

Grens threw down the papers he'd been holding. They floated around the room, big white leaves on their way to the floor.

"It's an order."

"For Christ's sake, Ågestam, you'd better run along and comb your hair. Maybe you should *open* a preliminary inquiry first, before you make it confidential! The only preliminary investigation regarding John Schwarz that I'm aware of is in connection with a suspected act of aggression on the Finland ferry. And why should I keep quiet about that?"

Hermansson turned to look at Sven. She'd heard people talk about Ewert Grens's temper. But even though she'd been with the City Police for a good six months now, she had yet to see it this bad. Sven just shook his head discreetly and she realized that the force of the anger that was now bouncing off the walls couldn't be stopped.

"What I want to know, Ågestam, is where an order like that might come from?"

"My boss."

"Your boss? The chief prosecutor?"

"Yes."

"And when did you last suck him off?"

"I didn't hear that."

"The chief prosecutor! That ass kisser! Then it must come from even higher up. Because he's a spineless bastard like you, Ågestam, the sort that's well groomed and diligent and kindly passes the buck."

Hermansson couldn't bear it any longer. Ewert, who was about to lose his dignity, Ågestam, who looked like he was about to throw a punch, Sven, who just sat there and took it all in. She got up, looked each of them in the eye, and said in a quiet voice, almost a whisper: "That's enough."

If she had tried to raise her voice the sound would just have been drowned out by more of the same, but that was now interrupted as she forced them to listen.

"I want you to stop. I am not going to watch two grown men beating their chests. I appreciate that this investigation is difficult. I mean, if it really is true, if he really has been on Death Row and managed to escape and we're going be involved with sending him back to a death penalty we don't believe in, I mean, obviously that's going to be hard and we'd far rather just stand here and take it out on each other. But we don't have time. From above. The order came from above. Do you understand? This will require even more energy. So let's save it. Try to work together."

She lowered her voice even more, she was whispering now.

"Otherwise . . . I think everything will just fall apart."

VERNON ERIKSEN WAS SURPRISED AT HOW CALM HE FELT.

I should run.

I should hide.

My heart should be confused, beating wildly. I've been carrying this lie around for so long, so many times I've thought that today, today it will erupt, it's over, *I* am over now.

And yet I'm standing here. In the corridor between the cells on Death Row.

I can hear them sleeping, I walk up to Cell 8, which is empty, I do all this and yet I feel . . . calm.

It was half past one, U.S. time, on Wednesday morning in the correctional institution in Marcusville. Nearly twenty-four hours since he'd been called in to the warden, fruit and after-dinner mints in the big room that had a red carpet on the floor and a chandelier on the ceiling, nearly twenty-four hours since John had been taken into custody somewhere in northern Europe, therefore making a death in a cell in Ohio more than six years ago now very puzzling indeed—it demanded attention again.

You died here.

I helped you to die.

You carried on living.

I helped you to live.

Vernon stood, as he often did, a bit too long outside the abandoned cell. Their plan had worked. So much that could have gone wrong, but they had nothing to lose, not with John, not when the execution was only a few weeks away.

He hadn't known a thing.

That was the main premise. That John didn't know. For months he would feel sick and out of sorts because of the haloperidol and ipecacuanha, they wanted him to be as scared as he was when he found out

163

about the cardiomyopathy; he would need treatment, and the doctors, two new doctors who shared a full-time position, would visit him regularly and provide medication for the nonexistent illness that had to exist if the rest of the plan was going to work.

Vernon smiled.

John had really died.

That morning, John had been worse than usual; it was that morning. On Greenwood's request, Vernon had as usual sprinkled haloperidol and ipecacuanha over John Meyer Frey's food, but this time had also added a large dose of beta blockers, just as finely crushed and sprinkled, and John had felt dizzy, his blood pressure dropped and he had collapsed in his cell, just as intended, in the half hour when Greenwood and Burk were both on duty in East Block.

Vernon stepped forward and gripped two of the metal bars on the cell door with his hands, looking for traces inside, traces that were never left.

Each of the medicines had worked perfectly.

Bridget Burk had come to the cell first, she had knelt down on the floor beside John, who was sweating and clutching his stomach with both arms. She had explained as loudly as she could that it was his heart, cardiomyopathy, that he had to be treated.

She had given him the first medicine. A benzodiazepine. He mustn't remember. If he woke up suddenly, he mustn't remember. She pulled down his orange overalls, diazepam enema up his rectum; she had explained before: for this to work he had to be drowsy.

Lawrence Greenwood had run down from another part of the building. As he passed he had looked at Vernon, who was standing outside the cell with three other officers. He had glanced over and their eyes had locked for a split second; they had both known but shown nothing. Burk had informed Greenwood briefly about what he already knew she had done, what they had planned together several months ago, and in the meantime had taken out something that worked fast, that triggered amnesia, and that also affected the patient's memory—pure morphine caused not only amnesia but also slowed the breathing.

John had lain there in a daze, his pants down. Syringe in one hand, Greenwood had grabbed hold of his penis with the other and he had injected intravenously into one of the veins on his organ. Pavulon, a preparation similar to curare, totally paralyzing. He had explained to Vernon at their last meeting a couple of days earlier that he could inject in the inner arm or the groin or the neck but that he preferred the penis, erectile tissue, he wanted to leave as few marks as possible.

John was now in hell.

He hadn't known about anything, so the fear of death had engulfed him, he was the living dead.

Conscious and paralyzed.

His muscles totally flaccid, he couldn't move at all, he couldn't even breathe.

Vernon had remained outside for the minutes this took and looked on, but not really watched.

He couldn't bear it.

The boy who was lying on the floor had right then been close to death, for real, and he had just stood and watched.

They were aware that it could end like this, they had discussed it at length, that this was a risk they had to take, they only had a few minutes, no more.

Burk had also taken out a small bottle of eyedrops.

Atropine to provoke dull, dilated pupils.

A dead person's pupils.

Vernon remembered how it had felt to stand there and watch while the young man he had come to like so much, whom he knew was innocent, had in effect died in front of him. That was exactly how it looked. He hadn't moved, seeing those awful eyes that just stared; it had been hard not to forget what they were doing, not to leap toward the door and rush in.

The pulse had been the only thing they couldn't do anything about.

They couldn't stop it in any medical way that was plausible. Greenwood had used a morphine derivative that had slowed his pulse dramatically, but for the rest they just had to cross their fingers. Both doctors had taken turns to cover up a reduced but still working pulse—it was a case of acting as convincingly as possible and continuing to do so.

They had a maximum of eight minutes.

They had to ventilate him every second minute, their own breath in John's lungs.

It should work. But only if the process was started within eight minutes. Longer than that . . . his brain would be damaged, severely, perhaps forever.

Greenwood had stood up, turned toward Vernon and his three colleagues. He had spoken clearly to them, and to the prisoners who had followed the drama from their cells. Vernon could still recall at will, how Greenwood had almost screamed *he's dead*.

A quarter to two, the night outside was alive, the wind howled as always. Vernon looked up at the rectangular window just under the ceiling—should get it fixed, the noise was annoying.

He left Cell 8, walked down the row of locked cells toward the door that led out to the office block.

It would be madness to risk anything. But suddenly he realized there wasn't much time, that he should already have given warning, that it was his duty to do it. He went into one of the rooms in administration, one of the secretaries' offices—it was unlikely that anyone had the time to tap a phone in here in the middle of the night.

He had learned their numbers by heart.

First he phoned Austria. He had no idea what time it was there, and it didn't really matter, she would answer; if she saw this number, she would answer.

The conversation with Bridget Burk lasted no more than a minute.

He put down the receiver, then called Denver, Colorado. Lawrence Greenwood didn't say much, listened, and thanked him.

They both had new identities, new CVs, new doctors' licenses, new lives, six years ago now.

They existed, and yet they didn't.

MARIANA HERMANSSON WAS STILL UNCERTAIN ABOUT WHAT TO MAKE of the angry outburst her boss, Ewert Grens, had had just over an hour ago. It had seemed so . . . unnecessary. Of course she recognized the absurdity of a blackout, the probable disregard of ethical principles in the case of John Schwarz. But the rage he had unleashed, the aggression that he obviously carried around with him and let loose on anyone who happened to cross him, that frightened others and apparently had done so for many years, it bothered her, she was bewildered, almost sad.

She knew what aggression was. She had grown up with it.

But this, she didn't understand.

She had a Swedish mother and a Romanian father and had spent her formative years with a mix of around a hundred nationalities in an area of Skåne called Rosengård, part of Malmö where the politicians seemed to have no influence; an immigrant community that many people disliked, others were ashamed of, but that had its own energy and life and a lot of aggression that ran around sparking fires.

But it was just that. Aggression. That flared up and died down just as fast.

But this sort, Ewert's heavy anger that seemed to hang over him and cling to him and hurt, she found it harder to deal with, to accept, it was ugly and intrusive. She would talk to him about it later when there was time. She wanted to know where it came from, if he was aware of it himself, if it could ever be controlled.

She had worked in Stockholm for six months before her short-term contract was made permanent. Not very long, but she had already been in the detention center at Kronoberg several times. Sven Sundkvist was with her, he hadn't said very much since they left Ewert's room either. She realized that he was used to it and wondered whether he'd maybe given up. Or whether after ten years as a close working partner, it still bewildered him, if that was what he was thinking about, withdrawn from any conversation, barely there.

Schwarz was in the cell at the far end of the corridor. Or Frey, as he was apparently called. But here, he was still John Schwarz. She looked at the sign beside the cell door, his name and, underneath, the instruction, *full restrictions*.

She read it again, pointed at what was written and tried to bring Sven out of his stupor.

"What do you say to that?"

"Schwarz?"

"Full restrictions."

Sundkvist shrugged.

"I know what you mean. But I'm not surprised."

She was impatient, took hold of the sign and pulled it off.

"I don't. Understand, that is. Why has Ågestam given Schwarz full restrictions? Schwarz can't possibly influence the investigation in his condition. What difference would it make if he was to see his wife and son?"

"I hear what you're saying. And I agree. But like I said, it doesn't surprise me."

Hermansson put the sign back—it was crumpled and the tape wasn't very sticky anymore.

"In principle, I promised him. When we questioned him."

"You can try. If it would benefit the investigation, Ågestam might, I think, make concessions. Because that's what it's all about. Investigation strategy. Nothing else. Ågestam doesn't think for a moment that full restrictions make any difference. He knows, like we do, that Schwarz hasn't got much to give even if he wanted to. But he's trying to force him to talk by imposing restrictions. They often do that, prosecutors. Make it difficult, make threats to get the questioning moving and force an admission. You'd never get anyone to admit to it, but that's how it works."

Hermansson stood in front of the locked door. She didn't really know who he was, the man inside. But he had been imprisoned for aggravated assault, he had admitted to the actual circumstances and he was now not allowed to read newspapers, listen to the radio, watch TV, write letters, receive letters, wasn't allowed to see anyone other than his lawyer, the prison priest, the detention officers, and a few others such as herself, investigators. She was convinced that it was unreasonable.

One of the officers had come up to them. He looked through the peephole in the middle of the door, was satisfied with what he saw, and unlocked the cell.

John Schwarz, who was John Meyer Frey, was pale.

He sat on the floor and looked at them with empty eyes.

"John."

He didn't answer.

"We want to talk to you, John."

Hermansson went into the cell and stood in front of him, put a hand on his shoulder.

"We'll wait while you put on your shoes and get ready."

He stayed sitting where he was, shrugged.

"Why?"

"We've got a whole lot of new questions to ask you."

"Now?"

"Now."

They walked out of the cell and left the door open. They waited—he took his time, but he did come, and dragged his feet to the interview room that was a bit farther down the corridor, where Grens and Ågestam were sitting waiting.

He stopped by the door and looked around, as if he had counted them and then decided that four people were too many.

"Hello, John, come on in."

He hesitated.

"Now, John. Come in and sit yourself down."

Ewert Grens was irritated and didn't try to hide it.

"This isn't a formal interview. As we're not going to talk about the assault on the Finnish ferry at all."

John sat down on the only empty chair in the cold room. The others sat opposite him: three police officers and a prosecutor studying his face, his reactions.

"You have given and been living under a false identity. And we're trying to understand why. So that we're as clued in as we can be. So we need . . . let's say we need some information from you. Now, John, a lawyer—would you like one to be present?"

A lonely window with bars on the far wall. Otherwise nothing.

"No."

"No lawyer?"

John gave an exasperated shake of the head.

"How many times do I have to say no?"

"OK."

Grens looked at the thin man in oversized clothes. A short pause, then he continued.

"First of all, I wonder . . . just a simple question. You do know, John, that you're dead?"

It was as silent in the room as it had been before they'd all come in. John sat motionless on his chair. Ewert Grens wore a wide grin. Ågestam glared at the self-satisfied detective superintendent, Hermansson felt her discomfort grow and seep into every nook and cranny, and Sven Sundkvist looked down at the floor, didn't want to see the man in front of him disappear into another time.

The young male doctor stands next to me.

He stands there and says that I'm dead.

He declares me dead, says that John Meyer Frey died . . .

. . . that I died at zero nine thirteen at Southern Ohio Correctional Facility in Marcusville.

But I'm lying here.

Grens had hoped for a reaction, anything, something that showed that the little shit had understood that this was serious.

Nothing.

He just sat there, didn't even blink.

"I'm not dead. You can see that, you can all see that I'm alive."

Grens stood up abruptly. The lightweight chair tipped back and fell over when he tried to lean on it for support.

"Yesterday evening and through the night we've been in touch with Interpol in Washington and the FBI in both Washington and Cincinnati. Their documents show—and I want you to listen fucking closely here—that you are identical to one John Meyer Frey."

The thin, pale man on the chair in front of them trembled, not much, but enough for them to notice.

That name . . . he hadn't heard it . . . no one had said it for over six years.

"So, *Frey*, according to the same documents, you died in a cell in Marcusville, convicted of capital murder—the first-degree murder of a sixteen-year-old girl. You fucked her first, then put several bullets through her body. She was found dying on the floor of her parents' home."

John was no longer trembling, he was shaking now, as if his body was in spasm. He whispered.

"I loved her."

"You were stupid enough to leave the house when your sperm was deep inside her."

"We'd had sex. Because we loved each other. I would never . . ."

"According to the FBI, you died in your cell only months before you were due to be executed. I have to say, Frey, I'm quite impressed."

John got up from his chair, sat down on the dirty floor and leaned back against the wall, his face in his hands.

"Your father, he's called Ruben Frey, isn't he?"

He curled up even more. It was cold on the floor, a draft from somewhere; John was colder than he'd ever been before, but that wasn't why.

"It's only a few hours since the FBI in Cincinnati had their first interview with him. He states clearly that he has no idea what you are doing here. He claims that you're dead. That you are buried in the cemetery in Otway, about twenty miles west of Marcusville, the same cemetery where your mother is buried. He says he knows that it's true because he arranged and paid for the funeral. He says he knows that it's true because he was there himself, because he saw your coffin being lowered into the ground, because he said farewell to you in the company of around twenty other people."

His voice.

I haven't heard his voice for over six years.

"But your father can claim whatever he likes. The identification of you is one hundred percent."

I know that he was involved.

Not how, he never said, but his face was there in the backseat of the car, I can picture it whenever I want.

"Do you have anything you would like to say at this point?"

He was always so careful, about justice, with the authorities.

Now he's being questioned by the FBI again.

For me!

For my sake.

Hermansson had been sitting next to Grens, listening. She had eventually managed to repress the discomfort that was suffocating her, she was present again, she was a policewoman, she was the one who had first questioned the man she had arrested in his home on suspicion of aggravated assault, it was she who had offered him a cigarette, and something to drink, and fed him the promise that she would almost certainly be able to arrange for him to meet his family, she was the one who had been closest to winning the suspect's trust.

She put a hand on Ewert's shoulder, asked him to swallow his next question, indicated that she wanted to ask it.

Ewert Grens nodded.

"John."

She went over to him, sat down close to him, leaned back against the cold wall as well.

"Things are the way they are. We know what we've just been told. There's not much we can do about it right now. But you *have to cooperate* with us. For your own sake."

She took out a pack of cigarettes from her inside pocket, shook it until one came out.

"Cigarette?"

He looked at it.

"Yes."

She gave it to him, lit it for him, waited while he smoked, the minutes it took until it was finished.

"I want to talk to my wife first. She doesn't know anything. She has the right to hear it, from me."

Hermansson gave him another cigarette, then turned to the others and looked at Ågestam.

"Well?"

"No go."

"What do you mean?"

"There's a blackout. That's what I mean. That includes wives."

She didn't take her eyes off him.

"I would ask you to reconsider. How can she affect the investigation? And we need to know what this is about."

"No."

"Can I talk to you alone for a minute?"

Hermansson pointed to the door. Ågestam shrugged.

"Sure."

They left the room, Lars Ågestam first, Hermansson behind him; she avoided looking at the others as she shut the door.

She knew that she was right. But she also knew that the likelihood of her being proven right would increase if she didn't embarrass the public prosecutor in front of the others.

She looked at him, her voice was steady.

"We simply do it at the same time. He tells us. But she's there when he does it. She listens at the same time. All he's asking is that she hears it from him. What do you think?"

The public prosecutor said nothing.

"Ågestam, I think you also realize that it's in the best interests of the investigation. The only purpose of this investigation is to clarify the facts."

Lars Ågestam ran a hand through his hair, pushing his fringe farther to the side it was already lying on.

He realized that what she was saying was logical. It wasn't according to the book, and it was far from in line with the order of full restrictions, but it might undeniably be the step forward that the investigation so badly needed.

He sighed, turned around, and opened the door again.

"We'll interrupt this informal interview for a while. And bring in the wife. If that's what it takes to make a dead man talk."

KEVIN HUTTON SHOULD PERHAPS HAVE GONE TO BED. IT WAS THREE IN the morning, local time, and he felt his eyes straining as he drove along the wide, dark, and almost deserted highway between Cincinnati and Columbus.

But it wasn't possible to stop.

He had to know where all this weirdness led, what it was that had happened, if the friend from his teenage years whom he'd grieved for, whose funeral he'd attended, was alive, if he had in some way managed to get out of one of the country's top security prisons, if he had in some fucking way succeeded in escaping from the prison's Death Row a couple of months before he was due to be executed.

A hundred miles, about an hour to go. He had stopped at an all-night food place and bought a hotdog in an artificial, slightly yellow bun and some of those energy drinks based on caffeine and chemicals. He wasn't actually that tired, but the snow and the dark and encounters with headlights on the wrong setting had irritated his eyes and minced his mind, and he had felt dizzy for a while. Some air, some food, some sugar; he was feeling better already.

Ruben Frey was still in Cincinnati. They had questioned him for a good hour in the FBI's office; then they had sat long into the night, looking out over the darkened city, while they re-questioned him, a father who consistently claimed that his son was dead, that that was all he knew, that he was still grieving six years later.

He hadn't been able to give a satisfactory explanation as to why he had remortgaged his house for one hundred and fifty thousand dollars with a branch of the Ohio Savings Bank in Columbus five months before John's death, and when they continued to press him without getting an answer, he had after a while started to cry and begged them to stop scratching at the wounds that had slowly started to heal.

Frey was now asleep at the state's expense in a bed on the outskirts of town—unnecessarily expensive given what an average hotel it was.

Benjamin Clark was in the room next door, not that it felt like there was any risk that Ruben would open the door and run, but Kevin Hutton wanted to do this right—after all, he'd never come across a case like this in more than ten years' service with the FBI.

He'd never heard anyone talk about someone escaping from Death Row in any prison anywhere, ever.

Nor had he ever had anything to do with a dead person who was alive.

And he had never previously been involved in investigating a person who had been so close.

They had been there for each other for as long as he could remember. They had been neighbors in Marcusville; had played together with their red fire engines in the sandpit in the local playground; been in the same class, shoulder to shoulder to and from school every day; had played soccer together on Marcusville's various youth teams when they were deemed too weak for football; they had longed for girlfriends together, sat and jerked off together in the cellar room every time they found old man Richards's porn magazines in the trash—they had figured out when he chucked them, once every two weeks when a new one was issued.

They had lost contact a bit toward the end; John had met Elizabeth and screwed for real and had done two stints in a juvenile correction institution, for aggravated assault both times.

They had felt it even then, by the time they turned seventeen, that they were headed in different directions.

Kevin had become a special agent with the FBI.

John had been sentenced to death for murder.

But he had never really understood *what* actually happened. Sure, John was volatile, pigheaded at times, he seemed to seek out conflict and enjoy it, but he wasn't the sort of person who would first sleep with his girlfriend and then shoot her before calmly walking away.

He had visited him in prison several times in the first few years, decided to do it as a friend, a private individual, nothing to do with his rights as a federal agent, but all the procedures he had to go through as a result every time he wanted to go there—the hysterical security checks and feeling that you could never say anything without someone sitting there listening and taking note—made him lose the will, so he went less and less frequently and not at all in the last year.

Then suddenly John was dead.

Kevin had thought about visiting, of course he had, before he was due to be executed. He had followed Ruben's and the lawyers' appeals in the papers and realized that the governor was not going to postpone it any longer. John was not going to be granted clemency, he was going to be killed by lethal injection, confirmation that Ohio would once again be included in the statistics for completed executions.

Then he died in his cell.

Kevin gripped the wheel even harder, finished what was left of the energy drinks.

It had been hell.

He had undoubtedly undervalued their friendship, fooled himself into thinking that these were new times, that they didn't mean so much to each other anymore, that the fact that he didn't go to see him anymore was proof that what they'd once shared had faded, gone.

He still felt it.

He'd stood there in the cemetery and listened to the priest and the few people who had said something and he'd understood that a part of him had ceased to be, that part of him was being buried there as he watched.

Twenty-five miles left. He accelerated.

He didn't want to be late.

He was sitting in the front of his car and suddenly heard his own laughter—he was driving at seventy miles an hour in the middle of the night and laughing with nobody and without feeling happy.

"I should be ecstatic," he said out loud.

If it's true that you're alive.

But it doesn't work like that. Do you understand?

An animal darted along the side of the road in the headlights. He jumped, waited until what was a rather large rabbit had disappeared, and then accelerated again.

Jesus, John, you were convicted of murder!

You took a life.

So you owe one.

He had called Lyndon Robbins earlier that evening, as soon as they'd left for Marcusville to pick up Ruben Frey. Robbins had worked as the head doctor at Marcusville at the time of John's death but was now in Columbus, head doctor at Ohio State University Hospital somewhere on Tenth Avenue.

They were going to meet at the hospital at four o'clock. Robbins had asked if it could wait until the morning, or even better late morning, but

Kevin Hutton had cut short any discussion, had just explained that he expected Robbins to be at the entrance at 0400 hours precisely.

Lyndon Robbins was a big man, considerably taller than Kevin's average height, and he was also solid. Kevin estimated that the doctor who was waiting outside the hospital entrance must weigh at least two hundred and twenty pounds.

They shook hands, his eyes were tired, hair uncombed, but he looked friendly, patient somehow. They went into the large hospital, Robbins pointed down a never-ending corridor and they walked along it for a while, then through a door, two flights of stairs and another door.

Robbins's office was cramped, an oversized desk and piles of boxes, and as he closed the door behind them, Kevin looked around without success for somewhere to sit. It was a room that couldn't hold much more than Robbins, as if his large frame took up any remaining space and he wore the walls. He pointed to a stool in amongst all the mess in the corner under the only window. Kevin leaned forward, got hold of it, and sat down.

Lyndon Robbins was breathing heavily, the walk and the stairs had made him sweat, despite the January cold.

"Kevin Hutton, special agent in charge, is that right?"

"Yes, that's right."

"How can I help you?"

He didn't sound nervous. Nor did he seem to be trying to stay calm in order to hide the fact that he was.

Kevin could usually tell straightaway if there was something else, an unease, something that couldn't be heard. That wasn't the case here. Lyndon Robbins wiped his forehead with a handkerchief, he smiled, he sincerely meant what he said, that he wanted to help.

"Yes, you can perhaps help. With this."

Kevin Hutton had a thin briefcase with him. He picked it up from the floor, opened it, and took out an envelope with a single sheet of paper in it.

"A death certificate. Just over six years old. An inmate who was named John Meyer Frey and who died in prison in Marcusville."

Robbins searched around for his glasses and found them in the outer pocket of his jacket. He took the sheet that Kevin was holding out to him and read it.

"Yes. It's a death certificate. Is that why we're sitting here in the middle of the night?"

"Is that your signature?"

"Yes."

"Then that's why we're sitting here in the middle of the night."

Robbins read over the page again and threw up his hands.

"I don't understand. I was the head doctor at the corrections facility in Marcusville. If someone died, then I had to sign. What's the problem?"

"The problem? The problem is that the person there, the one who is deceased, is right now sitting in a cell in a detention center in Stockholm."

The large man looked at Kevin, at the paper he was still holding in his hand, then at Kevin again.

"Now I really don't understand."

"Well, he's alive. John Meyer Frey is alive. Despite the fact that you signed his death certificate a number of years ago."

"How do you mean, alive?"

"How do I mean? He's alive, simple."

Kevin Hutton took the paper that was starting to crease in Robbins's clutch. He put it back in the file and the briefcase.

"I'm going to have to ask you some questions. And I want you to answer them. Every single one."

Lyndon Robbins nodded.

"I'll answer."

Kevin made himself comfortable on the hard stool, studied Robbins's confused face.

"That's good."

"By the way, Hutton, is this some kind of formal questioning?"

"Not yet. For the moment we can say it's for information purposes."

Robbins wiped his brow again.

"I *know* that he's dead."

His eyes were empty, he was looking at something, on the wall perhaps, looking without seeing.

"You see, I worked at the prison in Marcusville for six years. And only a couple of people died during that time. Even though many of them were quite old, and even though many of them had been there for a long time. But *no one else*, I can assure you, died on Death Row. Which is why, Mr. Hutton, I remember it so clearly. I remember him. John Meyer Frey. And I remember the day he died."

HELENA SCHWARZ WAS LIKE A BIRD, THIN, FRAGILE, A BIG SWEATER AND pants that were so wide that her body lacked contours. But it was her face that made Ewert Grens think of birds. Her eyes that darted anxiously around the interview room, her jaw that she touched all the time, her mouth already formed into a warning cry, high-pitched desperation.

When she suddenly appeared at the door and looked tentatively in, John had bolted up, shouted something, and then run straight across the room. Ågestam had been about to stop him, but Ewert had stood in his way and together with Hermansson got him to sit back down—if husband and wife wanted to hug each other before all hell let loose, then they could.

They had stood just inside the door, foreheads touching, crying quietly, kissed each other's cheeks, sought each other's hands. Ågestam and Hermansson and Ewert and Sven had all tried to keep themselves busy, looked at the floor, or for some papers, or anything that had meant not staring curiously, to make room for private moments in here as well.

Grens had then approached them, asked John to return to his seat and Helena Schwarz to sit on a chair that had just been carried in and placed against the far wall.

It was stuffy, the air was heavy, a small room that was meant for two, maybe three people, and now there were six, so there wasn't much oxygen to share.

"John."

Ewert Grens leaned forward with his elbows on the bare table and turned toward the corner where John was sitting, red eyed, his focus on Helena.

"We made an agreement, didn't we? We would make sure you got to see your wife, despite having full restrictions. And you, John, you would tell us what this is all about."

John heard him and perhaps tried to talk, but he said nothing.

"Isn't that right, John?"

Helena Schwarz wasn't sitting down anymore, she was on her way across the open floor when Sven stopped her.

"I don't understand! What is this? He's kicked someone, I haven't even grasped that yet, my John doesn't kick—but this, locked up and I'm not allowed any contact and this room and now you want him to tell you something . . . God, what the hell are you up to?"

She hit Sven, a fist against his chest and one against his arm. She shouted, and Sven held her firmly until she calmed down, and then guided her back to her chair with determined steps.

Grens looked at John, then at Helena, his voice perhaps unnecessarily sharp.

"One more time. One more time and you'll be taken home in a police car just as quickly as you were brought here. You are here because John *asked* for you to be here. Now, sit down and keep quiet. Understand?"

Helena Schwarz sat with her head bowed, a slight nod.

"Good."

Ewert Grens turned to John again, small irritated movements, sufficient for the person who was supposed to be giving new information to notice.

"OK, let's start again, John."

The thin man with the pale face and great dark bags under his eyes swallowed nervously, licked his lips, breathed out through his nose.

"Helena."

His eyes sought her out.

"Helena, I want you to look at me."

She raised her head and squinted across the room.

"My love."

He breathed out, and started.

"My sweet love, there is so much you don't know. That no one knows. And I should have said. I should at least have told you."

Another deep breath, another long expiration.

"So this is it. Listen, Helena. Are you listening?"

He sighed.

"Helena . . . I am *not* John Schwarz. I . . . I *wasn't* born in Halifax in Canada. And I *didn't* come to Sweden because I'd met a woman and fallen in love."

He looked at her, she was looking at him.

"I'm . . . actually . . . I'm actually John Meyer Frey. I was born in a small town called Marcusville in Ohio. I have never known anyone named Schwarz. I had no idea where Sweden was. I came here because the man who was prepared to sell his identity and past had permanent residency here and I was on the run as I'd been in prison, I'd been on Death Row for over ten years."

Tears in his eyes, the harsh light reflected in them.

"Helena, I was sentenced to death. Do you understand? I was waiting to be executed. And I escaped. I still don't really know how; I have vague memories of a boat from Cleveland, a plane from Detroit to Moscow, another one to Stockholm."

He cleared his throat several times.

"I was convicted of a murder I hadn't committed. Listen to me, Helena! I was seventeen and convicted of a murder I had nothing to do with! I was going to die, Helena! A court had decided *exactly* when I was going to die."

He got up, the ill-fitting prison-issue shirt to his face as he dried his falling tears.

"I didn't die. I didn't die! I'm sitting here, I've got you, I've got Oscar, and I didn't die!"

Ewert Grens had seen it a few times before. He'd even been there himself.

How a person could suddenly become someone else. How a person's entire life could be wiped out with only a few sentences. A shared past, what had been a shared life, was no more. Only a lie, nothing else, just a big fat lie.

Of course there was no fixed pattern. But Helena Schwarz reacted in much the same way as all the others.

Forlorn, fooled, frightened, and so totally trampled on.

Of course she cried, of course she shouted and they let her do it. They didn't react quickly enough, though, when she suddenly leapt up and ran across the room again and started to hit him, hard slaps to his face with her open hand.

He didn't try to move.

He didn't hold up his hands for protection, he didn't bend forward, he let her hit him.

She turned to Grens, shouted at him, *well, say something, then!*, he didn't answer, didn't move, she screamed again, *and you believe this!*, he shrugged, *I don't believe anything*, she stared at him, turned back, and continued to hit the person she used to know, *I don't believe you!*, her voice was hoarse, *you're lying, you bastard, I don't believe you!*

LYNDON ROBBINS'S BIG BODY SAT QUIETLY ON THE CHAIR IN THE CRAMPED office. He had tried to answer the FBI agent's questions about a person who should be dead. He had explained that he'd been twenty-eight when he first went to Marcusville and was promoted to head doctor within three years. He didn't think it was as striking as it sounded, as the posts were often vacant there—a doctor who chose to work in a prison certainly wasn't doing it for status, because there wasn't any; it was either a desire to help those who were weakest, who in terms of hierarchy were without doubt at the bottom of the social ladder, or quite simply it was somewhere to begin, where you could gain the experience required for more attractive positions in more attractive hospitals. In his case, it had probably been a bit of both. He had been young and newly qualified and grateful for his first job, but he had also harbored something that was sincere and that had later been eroded, a wish to give which had slowly withered when he so seldom got anything back.

Kevin Hutton listened, but gradually started to feel the lack of sleep, and he had to stifle a few yawns. He excused himself and left the room, found a couple of vending machines in the corridor, and came back with two cans of seltzer water and a plastic-wrapped Danish each.

Half a can, half a Danish, then he continued asking questions and Robbins continued giving answers.

"Cardiomyopathy?"

"That's what it's called."

"Explain."

"Enlargement of the heart muscle. His heart quite simply grew too big. It's not usual, but it does happen."

Kevin Hutton broke a piece off the half of the Danish that was left, dunked the dry edges in what remained of the seltzer water.

"I've known John Meyer Frey for a long time. And I can't recall anyone ever talking about him having something wrong with his heart."

"That doesn't mean to say that it wasn't the case."

"What I mean is—"

"Cardiomyopathy often occurs later in life. And very often it's discovered too late. In Frey's case, I seem to remember it was only three or four months before he died."

Hutton took a notepad out of his briefcase, started to write down the medical knowledge that he lacked.

"How is it discovered? In Frey's case, for example?"

"Several different symptoms. Frey was like many others. He felt out of sorts, tired, no energy. But he was young, so his heart wasn't the first thing you'd think of."

"Well?"

"So it was only when Greenwood and Burk had his heart X-rayed that we realized what it was. An X-ray was all that was needed."

Hutton added the two names to his brief notes about the medical condition.

"Greenwood and Burk?"

"Lawrence Greenwood and Bridget Burk. The two were newly employed at the time, but good doctors who shared a post and otherwise worked at Doctors Hospital, which is here in Columbus."

"Good, you say?"

"Better and with more experience than most of the doctors who work in prisons in this country."

"So they couldn't have been mistaken? With regard to the size of the heart?"

"I saw the X-rays myself. Indisputable."

Hutton put the notepad to one side, reached for the phone that was a bit farther back on the desk.

"Can I use it? I need to make a call before we continue."

Lyndon Robbins nodded, and for a moment leaned back and closed his eyes. He heard Kevin Hutton dial a number, and several rings that woke a colleague called Clark, and Hutton asking the drowsy Clark to search for two doctors called Greenwood and Burk on his computer.

Hutton put the receiver down and they looked at each other.

"The autopsy report."

"Yes?"

"Do you have any idea where it is?"

Robbins shook his head.

"It should be there. In his file. With the other information."

183

"It should. But it isn't."

Lyndon Robbins sighed loudly.

"Jesus, what the hell is this?"

Kevin Hutton picked up his notebook again, turned some pages and then started to write.

"What exactly do you know about the postmortem?"

"What do I know? Not much. No more than that I had two extremely competent doctors whom I trusted, probably more competent than I was, and that they saw to the dead man and together with one of the prison officers transported the body to the pathologist for the autopsy."

Robbins had left his Danish to one side for a while now, he had said thank you but explained that he needed to watch his weight, that he was trying to eat properly and avoid things like that with icing.

Now he sighed again, wiped his brow with the handkerchief for the third time, and then picked up the soft Danish and in a single bite ate it.

"When I get stressed. Every time."

Kevin Hutton shrugged.

"I bite my nails myself. When things get a little frantic, don't even notice that I'm doing it, just do. But now I want to know everything you know about the results of the autopsy."

A few crumbs around his mouth. He brushed them away before he answered.

"To be honest, Hutton, I know absolutely nothing. He was dead. Wasn't he? And I had so many other things to do in Marcusville, you see, you were always trying to catch up, chasing time. Frey was deceased, we knew why he'd died, and two of my doctors looked after the body. That's all there was to it. So no, I in fact know nothing. I didn't have any reason or the time to give more thought to someone who was already dead."

"But maybe it was your responsibility. To know."

"I would have made the same assessment today, if the situation arose. And you would too."

It was twenty to five on Wednesday morning. It was dark outside, a winter night with a late dawn. Kevin Hutton realized that they were done, that his first impressions had been correct, that Lyndon Robbins had no intention of telling him anything other than the truth and that he had had no idea that John's death might be anything other than what it seemed.

Kevin was about to thank Robbins for giving him the time, for his honest answers, when a telephone rang somewhere in his briefcase, five long rings before he found it.

It was Benjamin Clark.

He said that he couldn't find them.

Lawrence Greenwood and Bridget Burk didn't exist anymore.

EWERT GRENS AND LARS ÅGESTAM HAD AGREED TO STOP THE INFORMAL interview temporarily. Helena Schwarz had been allowed to hit her hands against her husband's body until she was spent. He had stood there motionless and accepted the frustration that was also his own. She had shouted and they had both cried and Sven had encouraged Ewert, Ågestam, and Hermansson to follow him out into the corridor for a while, to leave them in peace for as long as they needed.

They had waited an hour, the clock struck twelve in Kungsholmen Church. They were all hungry, so had walked down to Hantverkargatan and the relatively expensive place with palm trees in the window. They had eaten in silence—not the sort that was uncomfortable, just a peaceful break, the kind you get when there is an unspoken agreement that everyone is allowed to have their own thoughts for a while. Then they got up and were about to leave when Sven Sundkvist went over to the register and paid for two salads of the day. He asked to have them in plastic containers with plastic cutlery to take away; he knew that they'd both need it, John and Helena Schwarz, something to eat, as their energy had run out a long time ago.

They were sitting in the middle of the floor.

John's arms around her birdlike body, cheek to cheek, hands intertwined.

Sven looked at the woman when he walked in and wondered if she had truly understood, or if she was in fact maybe someone who knew how to forgive.

Lars Ågestam came in, leaned forward, and squatted down while he explained that they should eat their food, that they would need it, and that John, when he was ready, should make sure to go up for some fresh January air in the net-covered cage on the detention center roof; Ågestam had just arranged for him to have a few minutes extra.

Helena Schwarz sat on a chair in the corridor of the jail and waited while John was escorted by an officer to the cage on the roof. She had asked if she could smoke, Ewert Grens, who was standing closest, had shrugged, which she took for a yes, and so rummaged around in her coat pocket for some menthol cigarettes.

"I haven't smoked for five years."

She lit up, inhaled greedily as if she was in a rush.

"What do you think?"

She was shaking a bit when she said it. Ewert didn't want to, but answered all the same.

"I don't think anything. I said that before."

"Is he telling the truth?"

"I don't know. You know him better than we do."

"Obviously not."

Two guards were on the move at the far end of the corridor, a cleaner scrubbing the floor nearby.

"Has he been in prison?"

"According to the American authorities, he has."

"For ten years?"

"Yes."

"Sentenced to death?"

"Yes."

She was crying, quietly.

"So he's taken someone's life."

"We don't know that."

"He's been convicted of murder."

"Yes. And he's probably guilty as hell. But at the same time, all the rest, what he said about his name, the sentence, the escape, that's true. So who knows, he *could* be telling the truth as well when he says that he's innocent."

He handed her a handkerchief that he always kept in a trouser pocket. She took it, dried her eyes, nose, and looked at him again.

"Does that happen?"

"That innocent people are convicted?"

"Yes."

"Not so often that it's a problem."

He had damp hair when he came back; his pale cheeks were red. It was cold outside and it was snowing, the winter hell continued.

The others were waiting when he came in.

The three police officers, the prosecutor, Helena.

They all looked at him, followed each step he took toward the chair where he would continue to talk.

"It's great when it's cold. I like it when it's windy, when you're freezing, when you come in again and get warm."

He met their eyes.

"That's how it was. That's how it felt. Where I grew up in Ohio."

Hermansson had for a long time sat quietly. She had known that her turn would come. It was her turn now.

"John, we're listening. And your wife—Helena—is listening."

It was she who had started the dialogue with him some days earlier, it was she who would finish it.

"But, John, we're all thinking, all of us, what do we believe? Is he telling the truth? And if so, why, why is he doing it *now*?"

John nodded.

"You can believe what you like. What I'm telling you *now*, is what I *know*."

Hermansson waited, then with her arm indicated, *on you go.*

A clock on the wall behind him, irritating, clocks—he still hated them.

"*I know* that I was a bastard. Out of order, volatile, I lashed out at everything and everyone. Twice I was sent to a reform school, and I deserved it, I deserved every single minute."

He turned and looked at the clock, a red plastic one.

"Can I take that down?"

Hermansson weathered his tense look.

"Of course. Take it down."

John got up, lifted down both the clock and the hook that it hung on, walked toward the door, opened it and put the clock down outside, then closed it again.

"*I know* that when I was sixteen I met the only woman, apart from you, Helena, who I've ever loved."

He looked at her, for a long time, then down at the floor, which was plastic, a green color.

"*I know* that one afternoon she was found dead on the floor of her parents' bedroom. Finnigan. That's what they were named. *I know* that she had my sperm inside her, my fingerprints all over her body and all over the house. We'd been dating for more than a year, for Christ's sake! *I know* that the trial was one long circus, journalists and politicians jostling outside the courtroom—she was a minor, she was beautiful, she was the daughter of a man who worked in the governor's office. *I know* that they wanted someone they could hate, someone who would die, like she had died. *I know* that I was convicted of murder. *I know* that I was seventeen years old and utterly terrified when I was led to a cell on Death Row in Marcusville. *I know* that I sat there and waited for ten years. And *I know* that one day I suddenly woke up in a big car on the road between Columbus and Cleveland."

He brought his hands up to his chest, hit it lightly.

"That's all. That's all I know."

Hermansson stood up, looked at the people sitting in the room, and then pointed to the door.

"It's really stuffy in here. Does anyone want anything to drink? I certainly need something. And you, John, you sound like you need something as well."

She came back with six cups of coffee, each one different, with milk and without milk, and with sugar, and with sugar and milk, and . . . She balanced their orders in a cardboard box for photocopy paper. They all drank in silence for a while, waiting for John to continue.

"The other part . . . how I got away . . . I don't know. I *don't* know."

He shook his head.

"It was mostly just noises. Some smells. Grainy images. Dark sometimes. Light. And then dark again."

Hermansson drank her coffee, the one with milk and a little sugar.

"Try. There's more. We want to know, we *have* to know, what more there is."

He was sweating in the stuffy room that lacked ventilation, told them about a heart that was no longer healthy, about how he had felt out of sorts for some months and that that day he'd been worse than before.

"Then one of the guards, I think it was the senior officer himself, Vernon he was named, suddenly opened the cell and walked in. Some other officers behind him. I was to be handcuffed. It was always like that. If someone came into your cell, or if you were going to be taken anywhere, handcuffs on and several guards behind."

"Do you want more?"

Hermansson lifted a hand toward his empty coffee cup.

"Thank you. In a while."

"Just let me know when."

Most of the time, John looked at the floor. He glanced up every so often, looked at his wife, at her eyes, no doubt wondering if she was taking in what he was saying.

"A doctor came in. She asked me to take off my pants. A pipette. I think that's what they're called. She had one in her hand and then she pushed it up here, and injected something in."

He pointed to his behind.

"The tiredness . . . but even worse somehow . . . I don't know if I've ever felt so . . . drowsy. And I think that another doctor came in. I'm not sure, maybe I was dreaming, but I think it was a man, younger than the woman, he had some tablets with him, I know that I swallowed something."

Ewert Grens fidgeted on his chair, it was uncomfortable and his damn back was sore as well. He glanced over at Sundkvist and Ågestam and Hermansson, who were sitting alongside, tried to change position without disturbing the bizarre story that was being unfolded before them.

"I lay on the floor, I don't really know why, I just lay there and . . . couldn't face getting up. Then . . . I felt something prick, exactly here. Do you understand? I was given an injection, I'm almost certain of it, one of them injected something into my penis."

He put his hand to his forehead and kept it there. He started to cry. Not loudly, not desperately, but tears that have to come out, bit by bit.

"I could count time. Every second ticked inside me. That was what we did. Counted down. But then . . . after the injection . . . I don't understand. If it was immediately, or much later. I couldn't breathe. I couldn't move. I couldn't blink, couldn't feel my heart, paralyzed— conscious but completely paralyzed!"

Hermansson took his empty cup and disappeared out into the corridor. John wasn't crying anymore when she got back. He took the coffee, drank half of it, leaned forward again.

"I died. I was absolutely sure of it. I died! Someone lifted my eyelids and put some drops in my eyes. I wanted to ask why, but I couldn't move . . . like I didn't exist. Do you understand? Do you understand! What you feel, when you're going to die, that fucking power that turns you inside out. Someone shouted it. *He's dying!* And I think . . . I think I was given another injection. In the heart. And something in my throat, someone who breathed for me. I must have fallen asleep. Or disappeared. Sometimes I think that I died for a while, and someone shouted that as well, *he's dead!* I was conscious, I was lying on the cell floor, and heard them pronounce me dead! The exact time, my name, I heard it. Do you understand? I heard it!"

His last words hurtled around the interview room, bouncing between them until he took them back.

"I was dead. I was sure of it. When I woke . . . when I saw . . . I knew it, that I wasn't alive. It was so cold. I was lying in a room that felt like a fridge and with someone else beside me, completely white, he was lying like me on a stretcher with his face to the ceiling. I couldn't understand it. How could I see, how could I be cold, when I was dead?"

He had another drink, finished the cup.

"I disappeared. Just disappeared. And after . . . I'm sure I lay in a sack afterward. Plastic. Plastic rustles. You know . . . you know that when you try to fight yourself free with handcuffs on, it doesn't work. You can't get your hands any farther than half a foot apart. And when you try to hit . . . it kind of comes to nothing."

Ågestam and Hermansson looked at each other, they were in agreement. They would stop now. He couldn't take any more. They would continue later, when the afternoon was older, when he'd had a chance to lie down in his cell for a while.

"Just one question before we take a break."

Ågestam had turned toward John.

"I just wondered, you said earlier that you *know* that you woke up in a car on the road somewhere between Columbus and Cleveland?"

"Yes, I *know* that."

"Well, John, then I want you to tell us who was driving the car. And if there was anyone else there, in the seat beside you."

John shook his head.

"No. Not yet."

"Not yet?"

"I won't talk about that now."

The two guards who were waiting outside escorted John back to his cell. He turned around several times, Helena Schwarz was still standing by the door—their eyes met. Ågestam and Hermansson beside her, they were talking about something, gesticulating a lot.

Ewert Grens looked at them, Frey, who had been sentenced to death, and his wife, who had had no idea, Hermansson, who conducted the interview with such calm, Ågestam, who for a moment seemed almost wise.

What he had recognized early on as a diplomatic bombshell was no less complicated now. Not for the bureaucrats who would try to assert the EU extradition agreement when John Meyer Frey's home country came and demanded him back.

They would demand their right to execute him properly.

It was all about keeping the confidence of people who voted for security and hard measures and the ability to act.

He turned to Sven Sundkvist, who still hadn't left the room.

"What do you think?"

Sundkvist pulled a face.

"This job never ceases to surprise me."

Ewert waited until they were alongside each other and then lowered his voice.

"I need your help."

"Of course."

"I want you to take the on-duty doctor at the detention center, whoever that is right now, to one side for a moment and tell him a bit about what we think we know. And I want him to examine Frey. I want to know what kind of state his heart's in. If it was just part of the escape. Or if he needs due care. And I want you to report to me as soon as you have an answer."

"I'll see to it."

Sven was already on his way down the corridor when Ewert called after him.

"Because we don't want him to lie down and die in his cell, do we? It might become a habit."

IT WAS STILL EARLY MORNING IN OHIO, THE WEDNESDAY THAT WAS already afternoon in Stockholm was about to take form, be lived. Vernon Eriksen had just hung his senior corrections officer uniform in his locker. He had finished his night shift, the last for this rotation, grateful that he would be working days over the weekend.

When he worked nights it was more obvious how life just slipped away.

He wasn't one for friends really, not one for going out at all; being awake all night and sleeping all day, he was constantly tired and never met anyone from the other reality, the one outside the walls.

He opened the door to the yard and walked toward the main entrance. He had phoned Greenwood and Burk. Neither of them had sounded distressed or frightened. It was as if they had both been waiting as well, had figured that it would happen, and had prepared themselves, maybe it was even a relief when the message finally came, time to stop hoping for one more day, and another after that.

Vernon went out through the gate that was opened by central security and he felt the relief.

Both doctors had known what it was about.

At their meetings, they had rattled off lists of medicines and diagnoses and possible actions, cardiomyopathy and benzodiazepine and haloperidol and Pavulon and morphine derivatives and . . . their hope to temporarily kill a person, to move him from a cell on Death Row to a morgue, to a body bag, to pathology transport, to a car heading north . . . it had worked, it had worked on every point. Afterward, they had stayed on in their posts for a few more months—to resign immediately would have aroused suspicion, but with such a high staff turnover, no one later asked why or how. John had long since been buried when Lawrence Greenwood and Bridget Burk handed in their white coats and took the bus from Marcusville to Columbus and then on to separate destinations with new IDs and doctors' licenses in their bags.

It was snowing lightly. Vernon looked up at the sky, big snowflakes drifting through the air and making the ground soft. He was approaching the town itself, Marcusville, where he knew every street, every tree; after all, he'd lived here for as long as he could remember.

They had tried to resuscitate him, at least they had *acted* so that it looked as if they were doing just that.

No one who had seen what they did at close hand would later be able to say anything other than that the medical team had done everything they should to save a person's life.

Greenwood had intubated John, who was then given the amount of oxygen he needed, at the same time that Burk had started CPR.

One of them had then called for a defibrillator and an officer had come running with the box under his arm; John's heart needed a high-voltage shock.

They had talked a lot about minimizing the shock, that they would give him only a single shock and then confirm no rhythm and point to the flat line on the ECG recorder.

The final injection had been done straight into his heart, exactly where it should, but filled with table salt rather than adrenaline.

In the middle of it all—it felt almost unreal even though he had been standing right beside them—Vernon felt a strange kind of pride that made him embarrassed.

Manipulating the ECG recorder had been his medical contribution.

And he had managed this with a couple of pieces of ordinary plastic film.

The evening before, he had cut the thin, transparent plastic to exactly the same size as the machine's electrodes. It had been that simple; to attach the plastic to the underside of each electrode and create an invisible membrane to fool the measuring instrument, and when it was put on naked skin, to prevent it from recognizing the heartbeat of a dead person.

Marcusville had just woken up, and as Vernon walked down the small streets in the falling snow, he saw families sitting around the kitchen table, candlesticks still in the window despite the fact that Christmas was long past. It was breakfast time and everyone was hurrying to finish their cereal, parents running around trying to put clothes on themselves and their children. He looked into the small houses with the small lawns and for a moment, only for a moment, he felt removed, that he wasn't part of anything; he had no family—at least, *outside* the walls.

John had died there on the cell floor. Anyone who didn't know the truth would not have thought otherwise. They had pronounced him dead.

Greenwood had spoken clearly, *John Meyer Frey died at zero nine thirteen at Southern Ohio Correctional Facility in Marcusville*, and Burk who was standing beside him had nodded slowly, looked just as dejected as they had agreed she should.

They had had eight minutes.

If they had taken any longer, John's brain—the damage would have been serious.

In their report later, they explained that the unfortunate incident had caused considerable agitation among the other inmates and they hadn't wanted to contribute to it anymore, they had feared that an event like this might spark and encourage disturbances; that it was always hard to predict how people who have witnessed a sudden death might react, there in particular, with people who were themselves waiting to die.

So they had hastily transported him away from Cell 8 and the inmates who had been sentenced to death in East Block.

As they walked along the prison corridors, Burk had bent down over the stretcher at two-minute intervals. Her mouth over John's, she had discreetly ventilated his lungs, which were still totally paralyzed, when they were certain that no one could see.

A strange feeling then to leave him in the morgue.

But they didn't have any choice. John had been forced to lie there, in the cold air. Greenwood and Burk had explained that they had to reduce his *metabolism* fast, his body's oxygen consumption.

Vernon had stood in the doorway to the morgue for as long as he could.

So many years since he had stood here for the first time. Every dead person he had known and looked after in the section had ended up here, empty shells—he'd always thought that there should be another room, for the souls.

He had stood there and looked at the immobile body that was drifting in and out of consciousness, that couldn't move and couldn't comprehend what had actually happened. The fear, the three of them could only imagine the sheer terror that would take hold of him when they shut the door: to wake up after a while alone in the freezing cold, not knowing whether he was dead or alive, gradually to remember bits of what had happened and still not understand.

He stopped and knocked his shoes on the edge of the sidewalk to dislodge some of the snow, waited for a moment, then continued on, the final steps.

Mern Riffe Drive looked like all the other streets in Marcusville.

Even though it was so close, he had in fact not come here very often, just got into the habit of looking into their house as he passed. He lived on the other side of town himself, the houses here were a bit more expensive, a bit bigger; even in a small community like this there was a place for people who were that little bit better off.

The Finnigans' house was at the end of the street, the last house on the left-hand side. He had known Edward Finnigan all his life—there weren't many years between them and they had gone to school at the same time—but they didn't really *know* each other, they didn't have anything in common other than a lifetime and a love for the same woman in a small town in Ohio.

He had avoided visiting this place; that's what had happened, he didn't have the strength to see her in a home that wasn't his.

He tried to remember as he opened the gate in the picket fence. Twice. He had lived in the town for fifty years and he had come to this house only twice. The first time when Edward got his job with the governor in Columbus and had invited everyone who was anyone to a kind of cocktail party one Friday afternoon. Vernon, the senior corrections officer at Marcusville's most dominant workplace, was obviously one of them, people who in Finnigan's eyes were important. He had been reluctant to go, uncomfortable as he was with parties that breathed emptiness, but he had eventually gone and given his congratulations on the new job and had a few sweet drinks and then sneaked off as fast as he could. The second time was when Elizabeth had been found murdered, he had gone the next day to offer his sincere condolences. He had watched her grow up, a beautiful, happy, and outgoing girl, and he had understood their loss.

The white snow was falling thicker. He knocked on the door.

It was Alice who opened it.

"Vernon. Come in."

She was an exceptional woman, Alice. Overshadowed by her dominant husband, but whenever he met her in town, in the shop or the post office, she had always been as easy to talk to as he remembered. And then she was beautiful, like before, she could smile, even laugh—he had never seen her do that in her husband's presence.

Edward Finnigan wasn't just a bad person; he was a bad husband.

Now they looked at each other—she had tired but friendly eyes. Vernon wondered if she ever thought about the past, that she had made the wrong choice, about how things could have been.

"Take off your coat. I was just making some tea."

"I won't stay long. I'm sorry that I called so early, but I knew that you'd want to hear what I have to say, both of you."

"I'm sure we've got time for a cup of tea. Come on in and sit yourself down."

Vernon looked around at the large hall and the rest of the house. Just as he remembered it. The wallpaper, the furniture, the thick carpets on the floor, they hadn't changed anything. Eighteen years since the last time. They had found her on the floor and like a reflex he looked into the room, as if she were still lying there. Their grief hadn't diminished; if anything it was maybe even greater now. It certainly felt like that—he went in and it was impossible not to feel it thrust in your face.

He stopped in the doorway to the kitchen.

"Is Edward at home?"

"In the cellar. You remember that he likes shooting?"

"He showed me the range the first time I came here."

"He normally does."

It smelled of cinnamon tea and some sort of pie, maybe apple. Vernon caught a glimpse of the large porcelain dish through the glass window of the oven.

"I'll go and get him, if you like. And have a look, for the second time."

He smiled at her, she smiled back. It wasn't difficult to see that she hated the cellar and the shooting range down there.

He opened the cellar door, a faint smell of damp, of enclosed air that should be let out. The corridor was about sixty-five feet long and wide enough to be able to walk down it while someone else stood and fired. At the far end, a target, five holes with frayed edges close to the middle. Finnigan was about to fire five more, stood completely still, took a deep breath each time he fired the pistol. Vernon watched: it was a good series, ten hits close to each other.

Finnigan had realized that he had a visitor now and signaled to him to wait a moment, then pressed a red button at shoulder height on the light concrete wall. The target ran on a wire, a quiet squeak. He unhooked it with one hand, looked at it, added up.

Vernon studied his satisfied face.

"You shoot well."

"Particularly in the mornings. If I concentrate. If I come straight down here after a long night and imagine Frey's face, if I picture it then fire at the target."

His eyes. Vernon worked with psychos and people who'd been sentenced to death, but it wasn't often that he saw eyes with so much hate.

"I wanted to speak to you and Alice."

"We've never really spoken much, you and me. What's it about?"

"I'd rather tell you upstairs. When you're both listening."

Finnigan nodded, took the magazine out of the pistol, and did a recoil operation to remove the last bullet. He went over to the gun safe that was screwed to the wall.

Vernon looked at him. All these guns, he thought, semiautomatics and automatics and pistols of various sizes, all the weapons in all the guns safes in this country. And that pistol there that he was locking in behind the glass, it had his fingerprints on it.

Finnigan turned toward Vernon, he was ready, folded the target into his pocket, pointed up and they walked together toward the stairs.

To begin with there was the kind of awkward silence that sometimes occurs. Each with a cup of tea, a piece of the warm apple pie, a bit too sweet for this time in the morning, but Vernon ate it, it felt best to.

One hundred fifty thousand dollars it had cost. To escape his death.

He looked at them, their faces.

The Finnigans didn't know that.

Nor did they know that there was still a man somewhere in Canada who regularly received payment for a passport and a past.

They chatted: a little about the snow that kept falling, a little about the new café by the post office with the rather odd Mexican decor, a little about the neighbors next door who had a great black dog that barked at everything and everyone who happened to pass.

The Finnigans were both waiting to find out why he'd actually come.

It had taken four months to find Schwarz.

He looked at their faces again.

A person who was roughly the same age as John, with permanent residency in two countries and who was willing to hand over his passport, his history, his life, for one hundred and fifty thousand dollars.

He couldn't draw it out any longer, couldn't worry about how to say it and how they would react.

He put down his cup and waited until they had done the same.

"John Meyer Frey."

He looked at them, first one then the other, and then revealed a truth that was more than six years old.

"John Meyer Frey is alive. Right now he's sitting in a cell awaiting trial in Stockholm, the capital of Sweden. He's been in custody for a few days now under a false identity."

They waited for him to continue.

"And it's been confirmed. It *is* him."

He then explained what little was known. Frey had died, Frey had been buried, and even so, earlier that week he had been arrested and detained following an aggravated assault on a ferry crossing from Finland to Sweden. It had taken a few days to determine his identity with the help of Interpol and the FBI. A dead man. Who was alive. Vernon saw their distressed faces and then fielded all the questions he couldn't answer, about how and when and why, that was all they knew right now, that John Meyer Frey was alive.

It's strange how ugly people can become. Vernon had seen it before in connection with executions, how the victim's family seemed to relish the fact that yet another person was going to die, that they would get their revenge and that the death would be settled—one all. He had seen it and reflected on the fact that their bodies, the way they moved, that everything that was part of them could change and quite simply become ugly.

Edward Finnigan sitting to his left, apple pie on his chin, had after a while understood what it was that Vernon was trying to tell them. The inconceivable had gradually become conceivable and now he stood up, ran toward the living room and a glass cabinet there, a bottle of cognac in one hand and three glasses in the other. Such light steps, bubbling from his chest the kind of joy that only someone who is about to kill can feel.

"That bastard, so he's alive!"

He put the glasses down on the table, one behind each teacup, and filled them.

"So I'm going to be able to watch him die!"

Vernon lifted a hand, he didn't want any. Alice glanced at him and did the same. Edward Finnigan shook his head and mumbled something that Vernon thought sounded like *pussies*, he wasn't quite sure, but Finnigan immediately emptied his own glass, took another one, and then slammed his hand down on the table.

"Eighteen years! I've waited eighteen years for that miserable creep to die while I watch! My retribution! Now, you see, it's time now!"

He spun around with his arms raised, that gurgling sound again. He took the bottle and poured another glass, drank, drank and continued to spin.

Vernon watched Alice, who sat with her head down, looking at the table, at the pie crumbs that had hardened on the porcelain plate. He wondered whether she was thinking about retribution, words like the ones that Edward Finnigan used instead of revenge. In her eyes were tears, and it felt like they'd spoken about this many times before.

"I'm going upstairs to lie down. I don't want to sit here anymore."

She looked at her husband.

"Are you satisfied now, Edward? Will it stop now? Edward, will it stop?"

She rushed toward the stairs and the second floor. Eighteen years of grief permeating every word, every thought.

Vernon remained seated, cleared his throat.

A bad taste.

He tried to swallow it, but it lay there, obstructive, choking.

EWERT GRENS SHUT THE DOOR TO HIS OFFICE AND SAT DOWN AT HIS DESK. He closed his eyes, listened to her voice—they were alone for a while, Siw and him, the past that found its way through the investigation files. With each verse he went back a few years, to a time when he and Anni were two young police officers who had started to discover each other, his first nervous, mumbled sentences, the very first time he held her hand, so new and so long ago, a whole adult lifetime ago.

He turned to the very large cassette player, increased the volume until it couldn't get any louder.

Tweedlee dee tweedlee dee—give it up give it up, give your love to me

Tweedlee do tweedlee dot—gimme gimme gimme gimme gimme all the love you got

Her voice, her version of "Tweedlee Dee," recorded 1955, was so fresh, so young, maybe the first song she ever recorded, he wasn't sure but nodded in rhythm, Anni's hand in his, everything that was about to start, everything that never had the time to get started.

He listened, two minutes and forty-five seconds, he knew exactly how long it was, then turned around again and lowered the volume a touch. Back. But to only thirty minutes earlier. He thought about Schwarz, so close to falling to pieces when he looked at his wife, who had known nothing, as if they would both burst. Grens had doubted the wife's claimed ignorance to begin with, it had seemed incredible that she didn't know, how could someone live so intimately with another person without knowing such a dark secret? He didn't doubt it anymore. She *hadn't* known. That thin bastard, who had managed to hide an entire life from her, must have done a lot of acting and suppressed the rest; Ewert Grens, if anyone, knew that it was possible.

He snorted loudly into the room.

After over thirty years in the police force, he'd thought he'd heard it all. But even he couldn't have made this story up, and it seemed to get better by the day. Grens knew now that it was true, every word was true; Schwarz really had done what no one else had come close to before. He had escaped from his own execution, locked up on Death Row in one of the most heavily guarded prisons in the United States. Damn, that wasn't half bad! The little bugger had managed to fool them all! Grens was positively amused—to stick your tongue out at a system that was building itself into the ground with all its new prisons and that was totally convinced that long sentences were the primary solution to escalating violence, that was good, that was really fucking good.

He heard the knock on the door.

"Am I disturbing you?"

"Not if you let me finish listening."

They all sounded the same, all Grens's lala songs. But it was quite sweet really, when he sat there with his eyes closed, his big body moving to the beat.

Hermansson waited, as she had learned to do.

"Did you want something?"

The music had finished and Grens was back in the present.

"Yes, I thought that maybe you and I could go dancing."

Grens was taken aback.

"You did, did you?"

He remembered her question the day before, about how long it had been, about why. He remembered his answer. *You can see how I look. With a limp and a neck that won't move.*

"What do you want?"

She looked toward the door.

"Helena Schwarz. She'll be here soon. I asked her to come."

"Right?"

"We have to talk to her. You saw for yourself that she's about to fall to pieces. It's our responsibility to keep her together as far as we can."

"I'm not sure about that."

"But he'll talk more then. If she's there. I'm convinced that that's needed if we want him to continue."

Grens stroked his thinning hair over his pate, picking up his eyebrows on the way. She was right, of course she was right.

"You did well, just now. In the interview room. You got him to calm down, to trust you. And someone who trusts you will also let you know what you want to know."

"Thank you."

"No flattery intended. Just an honest description of what happened."

"Shall we dance?"

She made him feel uncertain. Almost shy. He raised his voice, as he always did, to mask it.

"What the hell are you talking about?"

"Twenty-five years, Ewert. You said that you hadn't danced for twenty-five years. That's my whole life! And you're always sitting here, listening, marking the beat. You want to dance, that's not hard to see."

"Hermansson."

"I'm asking you out. Tonight. A place where they play your kind of music. I'll decide where, all you need to do is come."

He was still embarrassed.

"Hermansson, it's not possible. I can't dance anymore. And what's more, even *if* I could, even *if* I wanted to—I'm your boss."

"And?"

"It's not appropriate."

"If *you* were to ask me out. But it's *me* asking you. As a friend, not as an employee. I think we can keep the two things separate."

Grens put his hand to his head again.

"It's not just that. Hermansson, for Christ's sake, are you putting me on? You're a young, beautiful woman and I'm an ugly old man. Even if we were to go out as friends, I would still feel . . . I've always despised older men who run around pawing young women."

She got up from the visitor's chair, held out her hands.

"I promise, I feel perfectly OK about this. You're not exactly the sort who paws. It would just be fun. I want to see what you look like when you laugh."

Grens was just about to answer when Sven appeared in the doorway with Helena Schwarz by his side.

"I promised to bring her here."

Ewert nodded to him.

"Can you stay? I'd like you to listen."

Helena Schwarz hesitated before entering the room, her eyes anxiously scanning the walls. She was still a bird. The big, knitted sweater with overly long arms and a thick polo neck that swallowed up her throat, baggy jeans that looked like they'd been bought for someone considerably bigger, clumps of cropped hair that stood straight out. She was on her guard, ready to fly away; if she could have walked to the window and flown out, she would have.

"You can sit down there."

Grens pointed to the chair beside Hermansson. Helena Schwarz crept over, sat down without saying anything, staring straight ahead.

"Why doesn't he have a lawyer?"

She tried to look at him, her anxious eyes every which way.

"A public defense counselor, Kristina Björnsson, has been appointed, but he didn't want a lawyer present for the interview."

"Why not?"

"How the hell do I know? You'll have to ask him yourself."

Ewert Grens made a sweep with his arm toward the detention corridor.

"I understand that you're distressed. I've never heard anything like it either. But I believe him. Unfortunately. I believe that he's telling the truth, that he was sentenced to death for the murder of a girl his own age."

Helena Schwarz winced, as if he'd hit her.

"But you should know that there's more. And for you, some of it might be positive."

Her voice was as weak as it had been earlier in the interview room, but those sitting around her heard the slight shift, a nuance that hadn't been there before.

"Positive? Jesus Christ."

Ewert Grens pretended not to hear her sarcasm.

"First of all: Ylikoski woke up a while ago. He's now fully conscious and according to his neurologist doesn't appear to have sustained any chronic injuries from John's kick to his head."

She didn't react—at least, she didn't show anything. Grens wondered if she understood just how important what he had just said was. She probably didn't, not right now.

He continued.

"Second, there is someone John didn't mention in there. Someone I am sure he's protecting."

"I see."

"You perhaps recall that we asked him who else was in the getaway car? And that he refused to answer."

She pulled at her sweater, the green knitted arms got even longer.

"Don't ask me. You may have noticed there's an awful lot I don't seem to know."

"I'm not asking. I think I know who it is."

He looked at her.

"His name is Ruben Frey. And right now he's being questioned in the FBI's local office in Cincinnati. I think that's who John hoped he could avoid talking about."

"Frey?"

"John's father."

Helena Schwarz groaned, not long, and not particularly loud, but enough for the sound to rumble uncomfortably around the closed room.

"I don't understand."

"Ruben Frey is John's dad. Your father-in-law."

"He's dead."

"Hardly."

"John said his parents were dead."

"His mother died when he was young, if I've understood correctly. But his father is still just as alive as you and I."

Hermansson put her arm around Helena Schwarz's narrow shoulders. Sven left the room briefly, came back with a glass of water and gave it to her. She drank, all of it, five large gulps before she leaned forward.

"Ruben Frey?"

"Ruben Meyer Frey."

She swallowed, paused, swallowed again, as if she had decided not to cry anymore.

"So I have a father-in-law?"

Her face had got some color for the first time since she came into the room, something more than the previous near-white paleness.

"I have to meet him."

Her cheeks got even redder, her eyes more alert, before she continued.

"And my son, Oscar. *He* has to meet him. After all, I mean, he would be . . . his grandfather."

EDWARD FINNIGAN HAD SAT ON HIS OWN IN THE KITCHEN ONCE VERNON Eriksen said that he needed to go home and sleep after a long night at the prison. A couple more glasses of cognac and Finnigan stretched himself. He found it hard to sit still with the bubbling in his chest, he didn't know what to do with all the unfamiliar energy. He wanted to run, jump, even make love, it was years now since he and Alice had even embraced, he hadn't been able to touch her, he hadn't wanted her, and suddenly he felt desire, he was hard, he longed for her breasts, her bottom, her sex, he wanted to sink into her and have her all around him; this was a morning like no other.

He undressed by the kitchen table, walked naked through the hall, up the stairs, and over to the guest room door she had closed half an hour earlier.

He had forgotten about it.

Her soft body. How he used to brush his hand over her skin, he could almost remember how it felt.

He opened the door.

"Alice?"

"Edward, leave me alone."

"Alice . . . I need you."

The silence that was at first expectation and heavy breathing slowly became one filled with awkwardness, the feeling of being rejected. For a moment he was a little boy again, an uncertain boy trying to be seen.

"Alice? What's wrong with you?"

She was lying with a blanket pulled right up to her ears, her head turned away, the light from the window on the small area of her face that was visible. He went in, his short, overweight body was winter white.

"Don't you understand, Alice, the release, he exists, he can die, we can watch him die, for Elizabeth's sake! It's over! We can move on from all this. Don't you understand? We can find peace and quiet in our home once more. It will be our home again, not that bastard's, he's going to die and we can watch while he does it!"

He sat down on the edge of the bed and put his hand on her feet.

She pulled them to her, as if it had hurt.

"I don't understand, Alice, what's the matter with you?"

He knelt down on the floor, forced her to look at him.

"Alice, it'll soon be over."

She shook her head.

"Never."

"Never? What do you mean?"

"It won't make a scrap of difference. You're filled with hate. You don't listen. Edward, when the boy is dead, when you've had your revenge, it will still continue."

He was freezing. His erection gone. It was cold in the room, they didn't use much heating up here, and winter had its way.

"It *will* be over. For God's sake, it's what we've been waiting for!"

She looked at him and demonstratively pulled the blanket over her head. And when she spoke, he wasn't able to see her.

"You'll still be full of hate. Haven't you understood that? Edward, you'll still hate, only you won't have anyone to kill anymore. Your hate, your damn hate has taken everything, everything! It's sat down there on a chair in our kitchen and mocked us, ruled us, it's ruled everything. It will always be there, Edward. And he can only die once."

Edward Finnigan was naked when he sat down at the kitchen table again. The energy that danced inside him and demanded his attention would not subside. He took the telephone that hung on the wall by the stove hood and called his boss and line manager, the governor of the state of Ohio. It took a matter of minutes to explain what had happened and the governor's astonishment quickly translated into action—he realized what it entailed to have someone who had been sentenced to death running around in Europe giving the finger to him and the entire American legal system on which he'd based his election campaign. He asked Finnigan to hang up, he was going to call Washington, the U.S. Department of State, he knew whom he had to talk to and he wasn't going to give up until an extradition warrant had been issued. The bastard was going to come back here. He was going to be escorted home again, to Ohio, to the prison in Marcusville, to the execution that had never taken place.

THEY WALKED TOGETHER THROUGH THE POLICE HEADQUARTERS TO THE interview room in the detention center. Hermansson had asked Helena Schwarz several times if she wanted to continue listening and she had received a determined look in return every time. It was her life as much as his, his life-lie included her and their son, whether she wanted it to or not, and she was going to listen for as long as John told what was perhaps the truth.

Ewert Grens held the door open while Sven and Hermansson and Helena Schwarz filed in. John was already sitting there, as was Ågestam, they were talking quietly together about something, a conversation that stopped as soon as they had all found their seats, the same places as a couple of hours ago.

Grens sent a questioning glance to Ågestam, *what were you talking about*, but the young prosecutor just shrugged, *nothing, the weather and the long winter, just trying to get him to relax.*

John Schwarz looked tired.

It had drained him; it was probably the first time he had spoken about what had happened, a pretend death that he had believed was real. He had told them about how he had died in a cell, woken up temporarily in what he later realized must have been a morgue, woken up again in a car, driving away.

Surely it will be easier now, he thought. To continue. The great wall of fear had been smashed, and the rest is just that, the rest.

"I was lying in the backseat. I remember thinking that it was dark outside. That it was night and that the streetlights looked strange when you passed them lying down."

It *was* easier now. He knew that this had happened. He had been awake, conscious, real, it had to be, everything had been real.

"I was so . . . tired. Sick. Like I needed to throw up the whole time. I asked where we were. They said that we were on our way north, to Cleveland, that we'd just passed Columbus."

"They?"

Hermansson tried to catch his eye.

"It's not important."

"Who else was in the car? Who was sitting beside you? And who was driving?"

"This is about me."

John closed his eyes, for a moment in his own world where no one could get at him.

"We stopped at a bar near Cleveland and bought some food, then kept on going, toward a smaller town that I think is called Erie."

Ågestam was impatient. He took off his jacket, he was warm, sweating in the confined room.

"We? Who is 'we'?"

"I'm not going to say. Not to you, not to her."

John looked at Ågestam and pointed at Hermansson. Ågestam spoke in a low voice.

"Of course. Please continue."

Helena.

You're sitting there silent in front of me. Do you believe me?

You're the only one who knows me in this fucking room. I don't care about the others. But do *you* believe what I'm saying?

"I was awake. But still . . . muddled, not really with it. I think that we stopped for a while outside Erie, on a private beach with a private pier and the great dark water stretched as far as I could see. There was a boat there. I don't know much about boats, but I realized it was a powerful one, fast."

Helena.

I wish you would say something. Even during the murder trial there were people who were close to me who believed me, what I was saying.

Do *you*, now?

"I've no idea how long we were on the water. I think I slept a bit. But we came to a beautiful place, Long Point it was called, a peninsula on the Canadian side, a nice little town near St. Thomas. There was a car waiting there. Keys in the ignition. Three hours to Toronto, it started to get light early, as it does in summer."

Lars Ågestam had gone over to the back wall as John spoke. He pushed and pulled at what should be a fan, the ventilation as nonexistent as the oxygen.

"You'll have to excuse me, this stuffy heat, I need some air."

John took the chance to stand up, he straightened his back and bent to each side with his hands on his hips, stretched a couple of times. On the other side of the room, Ågestam hit a duct a couple of times, then gave up and sat down and raised his hand to John to continue.

"We waited at Toronto airport for a few hours, I think. I'd been given new ID documents in the car, I looked at the name, John Schwarz. There was a person somewhere, I'd understood that much, whose name and past I'd taken over."

He continued.

"Eight, maybe nine hours to Moscow with United Airlines, don't know why I remember that. Then a few hours of waiting and another flight to Stockholm."

Ågestam was still sweating, he wiped his hairline.

"Who flew with you?"

John gave a scornful laugh, shook his head.

"OK, what about Stockholm, then? When you got here? Someone must have helped you."

"All that's of no interest. I'm sitting here now. And I've done what you asked me to. I've told you who I am, where I come from, how I got here. I'd like to talk to Helena now, if that's OK."

"No."

Ågestam was abrupt; he didn't want any more questions.

"You can't talk to her on your own."

"I can't?"

"Absolutely not."

"Then I want to go back. To my cell."

John stood up and turned toward the door, as if he couldn't get out of there fast enough.

"I want you to wait a bit. Sit down."

Ewert Grens had remained silent throughout the informal interview. He had consciously let Hermansson and Ågestam ask the questions, the fewer people who made the suspect feel uncomfortable the better. But he couldn't wait any longer.

"There's one thing I don't understand, Schwarz or Frey or whatever you want to be called."

The obstreperous detective changed his position and stretched out his long legs.

"I can understand that you could pretend to die in the cell. Very talented,

210

I have to admit. A couple of doctors can, of course, in medical terms, make it *seem* like someone is dead. And if those same doctors happen to work in a prison and have decided to help one of the inmates escape from his cell, dead, well then he'd get out. And I understand all that with the car and the boat and inheriting another person's life with a false ID and the flight to Sweden via Moscow. A few good contacts in the underworld, a competent tour guide and plenty of money, then everything's possible."

Ewert Grens waved his hands around in the air, awkward gestures as he spoke.

"But what I don't understand, Schwarz, is how the hell you got from the morgue to the car. Out through the gates, from one of the America's maximum security prisons."

Grens's eyes met John's, he demanded an answer, this wasn't a formal interview, but all the same, he wasn't going to let him go until he had one.

John shrugged.

"I don't know."

Grens wasn't going to give up.

"You don't know?"

"No."

"Schwarz, I now understand even less."

The pale man in prison-issue clothes that were too big took a deep breath.

"All that I remember, all that I know . . . that I came to in what I later realized must be a morgue. And then . . . the car. The rest . . . I *don't* know."

"And you didn't ask?"

"No. I didn't. I had just died. Or at least thought that I had. There were other questions that were more pressing then. And suddenly, after having been in prison for ten years, I was on a plane to Europe. Of course I've wondered, in retrospect, but there's no one to ask."

Grens put no more pressure on him.

It was true. He could feel it. Schwarz had no idea how it had happened. They had been careful, didn't let him know, that in itself must have been a prerequisite for them to succeed.

Grens sighed.

The way they'd done it, the mock death and then not a trace. It was fucking obvious that the American authorities would start to put on the pressure. Prestige and power could be tarnished by people on the run from a death penalty.

IT HAD BEEN A LONG DAY, AND EVEN THOUGH THE AFTERNOON HAD slipped into evening some time ago, he knew that he still had several more hours to go before he could turn off the light on his desk, leave the office in the Ministry for Foreign Affairs, and walk through the city back to Nybrogatan.

The state secretary for foreign affairs, Thorulf Winge, had been woken at half past four in the morning by an urgent phone call from Washington and had since devoted the day to canceling all the meetings he could, in order to try to understand the circumstances surrounding an American, with a false Canadian passport, who had been sentenced to death but was now locked up in a holding cell at Kronoberg. Thorulf Winge wasn't tired and he didn't complain, he almost relished it, he was good at dealing with madness and diplomatic wrangling, and those around him had absolute faith that he would come up with the solution that was now taking shape. He was prepared, he had gone through two different scenarios and knew what advice to give the foreign minister, regardless of the position that official American channels might choose to take. He had, what's more, managed to silence the cocky young prosecutor—John Schwarz would not become a Swedish concern publicly until, and unless, the ministry so desired.

When the phone rang, it was sooner than he'd anticipated. He had known that the call would come, but it was only twelve hours since the news had reached, and been forwarded by, Washington.

The secretary at the American embassy explained briefly that the ambassador would appreciate an informal meeting as soon as possible, whenever it suited the state secretary.

Winge was in no doubt as to what the purpose of the proposed meeting was and replied equally tersely that anytime that evening would be fine.

He must have been waiting outside.

Winge studied the American ambassador as he came through the door into the large office. Precisely fifteen minutes had passed from the time that he received the phone call to security announcing his arrival. Leonardo Stevens was a nice enough man; Winge had had quite a lot to do with him in recent years. The September 11 tragedy had opened the way for closer contact and at times had even forced it, not just here but between most American embassies and their host countries throughout the world. An attractive man in a slightly old-fashioned way, gray well-groomed hair, clean features that turned your mind to aging actors. Winge had often thought that it felt as though the American ambassador had just stepped off the silver screen, even the way he moved and talked: his deep voice with what Winge presumed was an East Coast accent.

It was a short meeting, steeped in the ritualistic correctness and politeness that diplomacy is built on.

Stevens explained that the State Department in Washington would very shortly issue a formal request that the American citizen identified as John Meyer Frey be extradited from Sweden.

The request would be issued directly to the Swedish government, in accordance with the Agreement on Extradition between the European Union and the United States of America, which states that *all EU member states must cooperate in connection with the extradition of suspected criminals to the United States of America.* Stevens did not bother to mention Article 13 of the Agreement, which states that *any EU nation can refuse extradition if the criminal has been accused of a crime for which the penalty is death.*

Instead, the ambassador went on to extol, for a bit too long and a bit too openly, the good relations enjoyed by the two countries in recent years, the considerable mutual goodwill, how important it was in today's big world to have precisely the sort of understanding that the American and Swedish governments were so keen to demonstrate and, he assumed, had every intention of maintaining.

Thorulf Winge didn't need any help translating diplomatic bullshit.

He spoke it fluently, had used it himself for the greater part of his life.

The ambassador had just made it clear that the United States would not accept anything other than the extradition of John Schwarz alias John Meyer Frey, that he was to be returned to Death Row to await his execution.

He had prepared strategies for two different scenarios.

This was the worst one, the one he had hoped to avoid.

THEY HAD AGREED TO MEET IN FRONT OF THE HOT-DOG STAND IN Björns Trädgård, a small public park opposite Medborgarplatsen. Ewert Grens had got there early, as was his wont, and was walking around, almost nervous, back and forth on the asphalt, waiting. It had been tricky to decide what to wear. All his suits were over ten years old, the shoulders on the jackets had been white with dust when he took them out of the closet and laid them in a row on the bed. Seven of them; the entire color spectrum from summer-evening white to a funeral black. He had tried them all, very pleased that they still fit. After three quarters of an hour he had whittled it down to two: a dark gray slightly shiny one, and a light gray linen one that he had bought for the last office party he'd been to—a totally tragic affair with colleagues who had found each other after a few glasses of wine, their husbands and wives at home, and he had decided never to waste his free time with the idiots again. He had eventually gone for the gray slightly shiny one; after all, it was winter, and the darker shade made him look slimmer.

Some junkies were hanging on to each other on the steps near the playground, farther away a couple of small-time criminals he'd known for years, a prostitute here and there, freezing in short dresses and thin boots, panic-stricken eyes when the cash wasn't enough for their next fix. Same as it always was. All these years since he'd driven the police van, even longer since he been on the beat, and it was still just as wretched, nothing had changed.

Some colleagues in a car creeping along Tjärhovsgatan amongst all the Wednesday night riffraff—they waved and he raised his hand in greeting.

She turned up at half past eight on the dot, as agreed. She'd come on the metro and crossed the street from the station, weaving between men who turned and looked at her as she passed. She waved to him when she got to the old hotel entrance and he waved back. She looked happy, and it made him happy to see her.

"This might sound . . . damn, this is what I said I was afraid of . . . it sounds a bit like a lecherous old man, but . . . you look lovely."

Hermansson smiled, almost embarrassed.

"Thank you. And you, let me have a look, you've got a suit on, Ewert. I didn't think you even owned one."

They were in no rush and walked slowly around Medborgarplatsen, which was more or less deserted. An elderly couple looking for somewhere to eat, the odd group of teenagers who probably had no idea of where and why, and otherwise the usual tired souls trying to gather strength for the next day's exertions. Grens was glad that she had been so fucking stubborn—he had hidden and kept out of her way and made excuses until he didn't have any left. He remembered that only a few hours ago when he'd finally said yes, she had rushed out to buy a paper to see what was open, explained to him that she was looking for somewhere suitable for gentlemen who listened to Siw and needed to dance.

The wind blew cold over the open square and they were huddled close when Ewert pointed in the direction they were heading, his voice quiet.

"Göta Källare. I've never been there before."

She could see that he was tense; his authority, so evident as he moved around the police headquarters that anyone walking beside him kept their distance as a mark of respect, was not evident here. Ewert Grens was another person in his suit and tie and on his way to a dance with a woman for the first time in twenty-five years. She could see it and tried to help him to hold his head high here too, to look people in the eye.

They left their coats in the cloakroom. He commented again, almost bashfully, on how beautiful she looked, and she made him blush when she took him by the arm and said that he was very elegant in a suit.

It was a Wednesday evening in a tired week in January, a long time to payday and still in debt from Christmas and New Year's, but the place was nearly full all the same. Hermansson studied the people, who on average were nearly twice her age, with curiosity and surprise. On the dance floor, by the bar, sitting at tables with entrecôte steaks, they all looked so happy, full of expectation, they had come here because they wanted to laugh and to hold someone and to sweat to a four-beat, so that just for a while life would be simple.

The band and the dancers were thronged together under the strong spotlights at the far end of the expansive wooden dance floor. Ewert recognized the music—"Oh Carol," he'd heard it on the radio—and for a moment, so brief that he almost didn't catch it, but yet very real, that feeling in his tummy, like a butterfly, that he recognized as joy. He took a step—his limp meant that he rolled, as if he were about to start dancing.

"Already, Ewert?"

Hermansson laughed, Grens shrugged and kept walking. *Oh Carol I am but a fool.* They got to the bar and for a while squeezed in between those who had been there for slightly too long. Grens ordered a beer for both of them and tried to balance the glasses as he wove his way through the tight crush of bodies to an empty table.

"They've been around since the end of the sixties. I've danced to them quite a few times in the past."

Grens pointed to the band. Five elderly men in black suits, wide shirt collars on the lapel. He noticed that they seemed to be having a good time, that they were grinning up there on the stage. How the hell could they do that night after night, the same chords, the same lyrics?

"Tonix. That's what they're called. Ten hits on the Swedish charts. Nineteen records. You see, Hermansson, they know what works."

They drank their beer, watched the people around them, looked at each other a few times. Suddenly it was difficult to think of anything to say. They couldn't just comment on the band and the other patrons forever, and when they weren't talking about work, it became painfully obvious how little they knew each other and how many years there were between them.

"Do you want to dance, Ewert?"

She really did want to dance; she smiled, already starting to stand up.

"I don't know. No. Not yet."

They drank some more beer, looked at some more people, and then she asked gingerly who it was he was grieving for, because she'd realized that he was mourning a woman, that much was obvious.

He held back. But then started to talk and it struck him once he'd started that this was the first time. He talked about a woman who was roughly the same age as Hermansson was now. She had been his colleague and they had gradually grown together, everything had been so simple, so clear, then it was all shattered.

He fell silent and she didn't ask anything more.

They emptied their glasses and Ewert was about to go up and buy another when his mobile phone rang. He mouthed *Sven* and she nodded. A couple of minutes later the conversation was over.

"The doctor on duty at Kronoberg has been in touch. He's examined

Schwarz and also sent him for X-rays at St. Göran's. And as I thought, the bastard's got nothing wrong with his heart. Young and healthy. Not a trace of any cardiomyopathy."

Hermansson pulled her chair closer to the table when a large man holding hands with an equally large woman tried to squeeze past onto the dance floor. She followed them with her eyes, inquisitive, waited until they had their arms around each other in a slow dance.

"So the diagnosis was wrong."

"If his story is true, I'll bet my bottom dollar that the diagnosis was wrong *on purpose*. They'd given him medicine to make him ill. So that they could later confirm that he was. And have a plausible explanation as to why a young person should suddenly die on the floor of his cell."

The slow song blended into another equally slow one. Grens was now also watching the couple who had just squeezed by and still had their arms around each other.

"He said that if we were in any doubt, if we wanted to be absolutely certain, he could do another test, something that's apparently called a myocardial biopsy. But he also explained there are some risks involved. I asked Sven to say that it wasn't necessary."

He gave a short laugh.

"Jesus, Hermansson, they were thorough. Even planning a serious illness several months in advance, even that."

They sat together in silence for the time it took for the second slow dance to finish. Then Hermansson stood up abruptly and hurried toward the dance floor, between the patrons standing two by two waiting for the next song. Grens saw her talking to one of the men onstage, the one who sang and played the guitar and had fair, slightly too long hair, before she came back and stood in front of him.

"Now we're going to dance, Ewert."

He was about to protest when he heard what they had started to play. Siw. "Everybody's Somebody's Fool." The one he liked best of all.

He looked at her, shook his head and laughed, loud and booming, and she thought to herself that it was the first time she had heard him do that, with feeling, for real, from his belly with joy.

She held his hand on the way to the dance floor—he was still laughing, as if he would never stop.

He knew every word, every pause, both key changes. *I couldn't bring myself to say good-bye.* It was comfortable, he knew that he could move in rhythm and that it wouldn't look clumsy, limping or not. So long since he'd stood like this, in a crowd of people who seemed to be happy, so long since he'd touched a woman who wasn't a suspect or lying dead on a metal table in forensics. He looked at Hermansson, at her face, for a moment thirty years back, with another woman looking at him, he was holding her, leading her while the band played.

They danced for two more songs. A slower one that he'd never heard before, and a faster one that sounded like American sixties.

He raised a hand to the band in thanks for Siw; the singer with the guitar and the long blond hair smiled and stuck his thumb in the air. They went back to the table where they'd been sitting, two glasses half full of lager where they'd left them.

It was warm and they emptied their glasses.

"Still thirsty? Shall I get another?"

"Ewert, I can manage to buy one myself."

"You forced me here. And I'm grateful for it. You've done enough."

He waited for her to make her mind up.

"A Coke, maybe. It's an early start tomorrow."

"I'll get us both one."

He turned and walked toward the bar. She followed him, it was getting late and she didn't want to be a woman sitting on her own at a table and saying no to anyone who asked her to dance.

It was still just as full as before, so they waited at one end of the bar so as to avoid being crushed with the most thirsty. They had been waiting for a couple of minutes when Grens felt someone tap him on the shoulder.

"Hey, how old are you?"

The man in front of him was quite tall, a dark mustache that looked as dyed as his hair. He was in his forties and he reeked of booze.

Ewert Grens looked at him and turned back around.

Fingers prodding his shoulder again.

"You, I'm talking to you. I want to know how old you are."

Grens swallowed what was now anger.

"That's none of your business."

"What about her, then? How old is she?"

The drunk with the dyed mustache came a step closer. He pointed at Hermansson, his finger no more than a couple of inches from her eyes.

It wasn't possible.

He couldn't stop it, the rage that now thumped in his chest.

"I suggest that you leave us alone."

He stood there in front of them laughing.

"I'm not going anywhere. I just want to know how much you paid. For your bit of foreign fluff, that is."

Hermansson saw it flash in Ewert's eyes. The sudden rage, and it turned him into someone else, or maybe that was who he was; the suit became creased, his body straightened out, he got bigger and was back in the corridors of the police headquarters.

His voice, she'd never heard it like that before.

"Now you listen really fucking carefully to me, because I'm only going to say it once. I didn't hear what you said. Because you are just about to leave."

The mustache sneered with laughter.

"Well, if you didn't hear it, I'll say it again. I wondered how much that bit of foreign fluff you've dragged in here cost you?"

Hermansson was sure she could feel Ewert's fury and knew that she had to get there before him.

She raised her hand and hit the drunk man in the face, a hard slap on the cheek. He staggered, caught hold of the bar while she looked for her ID in one of the pockets of her wallet.

Then she held it up to his face, as close as he'd held his finger to her eyes, explained that the woman he had just called a bit of foreign fluff was in fact named Mariana Hermansson and was a detective sergeant with City Police, and that if he repeated what he had said again, his evening would continue in an interview room at Kronoberg.

They had danced again.

As if to get rid of the man.

When the two doormen in green uniforms who approached saw the two police IDs, they had escorted the drunken jerk-off out. But it wasn't enough, he was still there, his words splattered around the sweaty hall and no band music in the world could undo them.

When they left the dance hall, the cold January air felt almost pleasant.

They didn't say much as they walked, past Slussen, over Skeppsbron and past the palace, over the bridge to Gustav Adolfs Torg, pausing there amongst all the prestigious buildings: the opera house behind them and the Ministry of Foreign Affairs in front.

She lived on Kungsholmen, by Västerbron, he on Sveavägen, by the crossroads with Odengatan. They couldn't walk in the same direction any farther and were already going their separate ways.

Ewert Grens watched her back as she slowly disappeared. He stood at a loss for a couple of minutes. He didn't want to go home.

He held his face up to the sky for a while, to the light snow that fell on his skin. Until he felt cold and his cheeks were red; then he spun around and looked at the Ministry of Foreign Affairs, the window up there on the second floor that was still lit.

He thought he could see the outline of a person.

Someone standing looking out over the city.

No doubt some bureaucrat or other who was sitting there struggling with the John Schwarz case and the diplomatic pitfalls it entailed.

And good luck to them.

Half an hour until midnight. State Secretary Thorulf Winge stood by the window in the Ministry of Foreign Affairs, looking out at Gustav Adolfs Torg, not concentrating. An older man and a young woman down there, the woman kissed the man on the cheek and then they parted.

Thorulf Winge yawned, stretched his arms up above his head and turned back into the room.

He was starting to get tired. The long day had become even longer a few hours ago. A formal request for the extradition of John Meyer Frey had arrived by fax as soon as Leonardo Stevens had politely wished Winge good night and gone down the steps to the black car that would drive him to the residency at Gärdet.

But this was what he lived for.

Diplomatic sparring with no onlookers other than power.

He had been in contact with the foreign minister several times that day. Twice with the prime minister. And for the past three hours he had been locked up in his office together with two civil servants, going through every sentence of the extradition agreement between the EU and the United States in detail, looking at different solutions and the consequences that a refusal to extradite might have on relations between the two countries, trying to predict how the press and the public would react if the extradition case became known.

He stretched again, leaned forward, then back, as his physiotherapist had taught him. He got some warm water and put some fresh tea in the strainers in their cups.

Still a few hours of night left.

By dawn they would have a proposal regarding John Meyer Frey's future, and how to ensure it caused as little damage as possible.

EWERT GRENS WALKED THROUGH THE COLD AND ALMOST SILENT Stockholm night. He had tried to get her to take a taxi, it wasn't entirely without risk for a beautiful girl dressed up for dancing to walk alone through the city, but she had insisted, got him to cancel the reservation and trust that she could look after herself. He was in no doubt about that, of course, she could look after herself perfectly well. But he still wasn't happy about it and made her promise to keep her phone at hand with his number at the ready, just the press of a button away.

She had kissed him on the cheek and thanked him for a lovely evening, and when she left he had felt happier and lonelier than he had for years.

Now, with the front door to his large, empty apartment open in front of him, he felt the waste like a hand around his throat. He wandered in and out of the rooms that all looked the same as when he'd left them.

He drank some ice-cold water straight from the tap in the kitchen.

He leafed through a book that lay half-read on the table in his study.

He even switched on the TV and watched part of an episode of some police series that he'd watched a few years ago on a different channel, the sort where everything moves fast to monotone music and the cops always hold their guns with two hands when they fire.

Ewert Grens didn't want to be there.

He put his coat on again, called a cab, and hurried down to the entrance.

He would go back to Kronoberg, to his office and Siw Malmkvist and the Schwarz investigation; the night seemed shorter there, among things that he recognized.

thursday

WHEN THE COFFEE CUP SLIPPED OUT OF SVEN SUNDKVIST'S HAND IT WAS about the last thing he needed. He swore so loudly that it echoed down the deserted corridor, and he kicked the panel at the bottom of the machine before bending down to wipe away as much of the brownish liquid as possible with his hand.

It was six in the morning and he was tired, irritated, and far from being the policeman who normally radiated calm and thoughtfulness.

He longed to be at home, in his bed.

For the second night in succession, Ewert Grens had phoned and woken him. For the second night in succession, Grens had said there was an early meeting in connection with the Schwarz investigation.

And as if that wasn't enough, Ewert had then started to talk uncontrollably, first about John Schwarz and other things connected to their police work, and then after a while about everything else, about life, about things he generally never spoke about. In the end, Sven had asked if he was tipsy and Ewert had admitted that he'd had a couple of beers but that had been hours ago and why was he asking, anyway?

Sven had put down the receiver, pulled out the plug, and sworn that he would not head for the city any earlier than he'd promised Anita.

He walked down the dark corridor with a fresh cup of coffee in his hand, on his way to Ewert's office, but stopped abruptly on the threshold. There was someone in there already. Someone with his back to the door, bending over slightly, in a very expensive gray suit. Sven Sundkvist took a step to the side and decided to wait outside until the meeting was over.

"Sven, for God's sake, where do you think you're going?"

Sven went back to the door. He looked at the man in the gray suit. Ewert's voice. But no more than that.

"What the hell's wrong with you, boy?"

"Ewert?"

"Yes. Hello?"

"What do you look like?"

Ewert Grens danced toward the door and Sundkvist.

"Like a hunk."

"Like a what?"

"A hunk. Jesus, Sven, have you never seen a hunk before?"

"I don't think so."

"A good-looking guy. A hunk. I went out dancing with Hermansson last night. That's what she called me. The sort of thing young people say. Hunk, Sven, damn it!"

Sven was a few minutes early and sat down on the sofa that had once been dark brown corduroy, with distinct wales. Ewert stood in front of him in his new clothes, looking for all the world like a bureaucrat. Sven studied his face as he talked and saw a kind of relief there; Ewert told him about his first dance steps for twenty-five years, about how scared he'd been, that Hermansson had got the band to play "Everybody's Somebody's Fool" and that he'd laughed, an unexpected sound from his belly that had bubbled up and out and surprised him.

Lars Ågestam arrived at six o'clock sharp, Hermansson three minutes later.

They both looked surprisingly fresh and Sven suddenly felt even more tired, leaned back into the sofa and noticed that Hermansson gave an amused smile when she saw that her boss was still wearing last night's suit.

"Do you believe in capital punishment, Ågestam?"

Grens was searching through the piles of paper that lay strewn across the floor when he asked the question.

"You know that I don't."

"Sven?"

"No."

"Hermansson?"

"No."

Ewert Grens squatted down, picked out a sheet of paper here and there, and put them to one side.

"I guessed as much. And as I don't either, well, we may have a problem."

He had now gathered a smaller pile, ten to fifteen typed documents, and stood up. Sven watched the large man lumbering toward him, as did the others, and he couldn't stop thinking about the suit, and how incredibly different such an ordinary and accepted item of clothing could look on a person whose clothes were normally wrinkled, shabby, slightly too short or too big.

"I've talked to a number of people during the night."

No one who was sitting in the room questioned that.

"They're very busy now. The ass kissers who ordered the blackout via Ågestam."

Lars Ågestam was red in the face, about to stand up, but then decided not to. The bitter shit would never understand.

Ewert Grens recounted in minute detail each of the late-night phone calls, explained that the activity in both countries' foreign ministries was now focused on a person who was being held in custody a few floors up, who was under investigation by City Police for aggravated assault. The risk of extradition was starting to be more than a risk and he had no fucking idea how to prevent it.

He handed the pile of papers that he'd picked up from the floor to Sven.

"I want you to read this again. Everything we've got on Schwarz from the United States. You see, potentially we could be changing the sentencing framework in this country. We are in the process of imposing the death sentence on a man who possibly is guilty of aggravated assault."

United Airlines flight UA9358 from Chicago landed at Arlanda outside Stockholm at 0645 hours, fifteen minutes earlier than scheduled. The pilot, who spoke with an accent that Ruben Frey didn't recognize, had announced over the PA system that this was thanks to a strong tailwind, and when Ruben asked the man who was sitting next to him, who looked like a seasoned traveler, what that meant, he had been given a long and complicated answer that sounded knowledgeable but that he promptly forgot.

Ruben Frey had never been to Europe before. In fact, he had never flown before. The state of Ohio was large enough for him, and his regular trips from Marcusville to Columbus, or even as far as Cleveland, held about as much excitement as he needed from life. The day had started early in Marcusville. He had driven his second-hand Mercedes, a car that he'd owned for almost twenty years, from his home westward through the dawn to the airport in Cincinnati. He had checked in two hours before departure, just as he was requested to do on the ticket, and then eaten an expensive lunch in a chaotic restaurant for people with hand luggage who were on their way somewhere. A short flight from Cincinnati to Chicago, they were barely up in the air before they started the descent to a two-hour wait in an airport as big as Scioto County. It had taken considerably longer between Chicago and Stockholm, and even though the air hostesses had been friendly and the film that was shown on the small screens that hung down between the seats had been an OK comedy, once he was home he would never venture beyond Ohio's state lines again.

It was colder in Stockholm than in Marcusville; the snow lay deep along the roadside as he sat in a taxi from Arlanda airport into Stockholm. The driver spoke reasonable English and gave him a detailed report of the weather forecast that was for more snow and even lower temperatures over the coming days.

Ruben Frey had a pain in his chest.

The last few days were not something he ever wanted to experience again. It was eighteen years since the Finnigan girl had been murdered and his son had been accused, prosecuted, and convicted. Eighteen years and it was still going on.

It had been hard to deny it when he knew the truth so well. The interviews in Cincinnati had been horrible, he felt uncomfortable lying to the boy Hutton and his colleague, and several times he had been close to admitting what he mustn't. It had been even harder to pretend to be as happy and thankful as a father should be when he's told that his only son, whom he had buried, has now been found alive. Ruben gave a loud sigh and the driver glanced at him in the rearview mirror. He had been close to breaking, he assumed that it was pure luck that he hadn't been detained by the FBI and he wondered how much it had to do with the fact that it had been Kevin Hutton sitting on the other side of the desk.

It took a good half hour to get to Bergsgatan and Kronoberg. He had asked about Stockholm on the plane and been told that it was a beautiful capital, lots of water, parts of the city built on islands and an endless archipelago strewn out in the sea toward Finland.

It was undoubtedly beautiful. But he didn't see anything. To be honest, he didn't give a damn. He wasn't here to sightsee. He was here to rescue his son from death, for the second time.

He paid and got out. It was still early and the main entrance was locked.

He knew who he was looking for.

When Ruben Frey left the final interview, Kevin Hutton had pulled out and shown him one paper too many. He had put it down on the desk in front of Ruben, then turned to look out of the window as if something had caught his eye, and had waited long enough for Ruben to read it, before turning back again and picking it up.

It was a request for legal assistance in connection with the questioning of Ruben Frey.

The request had been faxed from Sweden, a formal request from the Swedish Ministry of Foreign Affairs, with a note that it had been copied to a detective superintendent called Ewert Grens.

Sven Sundkvist weighed the pile of paper in his hand for a while, distracted, then put it down on his knee while he looked at Ewert, who was standing choosing between two cassettes from the shelf behind his desk.

"A doctor can't participate in an execution. Did you know that?"

Ewert didn't answer, nor did Ågestam or Hermansson, as they hadn't heard it as a question.

"The Hippocratic oath they have to take, and the medical ethics they promise to respect, don't allow them to be present when society takes a life. On the other hand, and this is what's interesting, they are liable and responsible for the procurement of the drugs that are used for executions."

Sundkvist didn't expect a response. He wasn't even sure if the others had heard what he said. Ewert was still choosing between Siw and Siw, and Ågestam and Hermansson were reading the documents they'd been asked to read. It didn't matter. The irritation that had been buzzing around his head like an angry fly had gone, and the tiredness from a night of unwanted wakefulness was retreating. Ewert and his suit and talk of being a hunk, Hermansson and Ågestam in a good mood, the unlikely story they held in their hands and the realization of how serious it could become— Sven Sundkvist no longer had anything against sitting there on the worn sofa as the dark dissolved outside the window.

"He was seventeen years old."

Ågestam shook his head and looked at the others.

"Do you have any idea of how rare it is to impose the death sentence on a minor? Schwarz, or maybe we should call him Frey, was obviously considered to be and judged as an adult. Seventeen years old and such a serious penalty—that takes one hell of a lot."

He heard that Grens had put on his stupid music again, low; it provided an awkward backdrop when he continued.

"This is how it works in the United States: jurors serving on a case where the crime might lead to a death penalty are only selected if they are not opposed to capital punishment. You see? Right from the start the selected jury is made up of people who *support* the death penalty. And when the pro-death jury has decided that someone, in this case Frey, *is* guilty of a capital crime, in other words, that the crime might result in a death sentence, then it has to be decided whether to impose *life imprisonment with the possibility of parole after twenty-five or thirty years, life imprisonment with no possibility of parole,* or the third alternative, *the death penalty.*"

Ewert Grens nudged up the volume on the Siw Malmkvist tape, the calm that helped him to think, but he also listened with interest to the prosecutor, who had knowledge that he lacked. Ågestam looked at Grens and his music machine in irritation, but Grens just flapped his hands, *go on, I'm listening.*

"They choose to find him guilty, and they pick the third choice, the death penalty. Yes, his fingerprints were found everywhere in the house. Yes, it probably was his sperm inside her, according to the blood-group determination that seems highly likely. But good God, several witnesses have confirmed that the two had had sexual relations for over a year! Of course his fingerprints would be there, then, of course the pathologist could find traces of his sperm. It shouldn't take a jury long to work that out."

Lars Ågestam's face was getting redder, his thin body more agitated. He had stood up and was walking around the room as he talked.

"I'm not saying that it *wasn't* him. It *might possibly* have been. All I'm saying is that it's remarkably weak evidence to base a conviction on, and what's more, to then impose a death sentence on a seventeen-year-old boy. The prosecutor who succeeded in that did a damn good job. I would never have managed that. I don't even know if I would have started a prosecution with so little to go on."

He looked around the room with something close to anger, raised his voice without being aware of it.

"No one saw him there at the time of the murder. No blood belonging to him was found at the scene of the crime. Not a single sentence to say that traces of gunpowder were found on him or his clothes. All that we have, all that the jury had, is the sperm and fingerprints of a boyfriend who had frequented the house and had regular sex with the girl for a year. We also have a record of his background: he'd resorted to violence on previous occasions, and in two cases spent some months in a juvenile correctional institution. John Meyer Frey doesn't appear to have been a very nice young man. But that doesn't make him a murderer. Not even with a flimsy chain of circumstantial evidence."

Ruben Frey presented himself at the counter, showed his ID, and asked to talk to a Detective Superintendent Ewert Grens. He made great efforts to speak clearly and to sound as calm as he was not. The security guard was wearing a green uniform and sitting behind a glass wall, surrounded by a number of monitors that showed black-and-white images from different parts of the building's exterior, and he spoke English in the same correct, but rather stiff way that the taxi driver had, recommended brusquely that the visitor should sit down and wait on one of the three chairs that were lined up in the small reception area.

The lack of sleep was catching up with him. He had tried, but the hum of passengers talking incessantly and the sharp lights on the ceiling of the cabin had made it impossible. Ruben rubbed his itching eyes, he yawned twice, he leafed absentmindedly through a magazine that he didn't understand a word of but recognized in a way: photos of celebrities posing in pairs on a red carpet that led the way into some important cultural premiere. The same sort of gossip magazine that he would pick up at the barber's in Marcusville or in the newspaper rack at Sofio's restaurant; another language and different people, but the same content.

After a quarter of an hour he heard the green-clad guard call out his name and he hurried over, the clumsy brown travel bag in his hand. He was introduced to a woman wearing the same green uniform—she used her whole hand to indicate which direction to go in. Her English was considerably better than her colleague's, she didn't say much but when she did it was without hesitation. A couple of grim corridors and a couple of locked doors, then they stopped outside an office where the door was ajar and the music playing inside was slightly too loud.

The female guard knocked on the door and a voice shouted something like *come in.*

It was quite a large office, much bigger than the FBI room in Cincinnati where he'd sat answering questions for several hours the day before. The man who was standing in the middle of the room and who had asked them in a loud voice to come in was big, dressed in a rather fine gray suit and, Ruben guessed, about the same age as himself. Farther in, in front of a window that lacked curtains, three more people—a woman and two men—were sitting on a brown sofa.

He took another step into the room and put down his voluminous bag.

"My name is Ruben Meyer Frey."

He assumed that they understood and spoke English, everyone in this country seemed to. They stared at him, said nothing at all, waiting for the short, overweight American with red cheeks and tired eyes to continue.

"I'm here to talk to Yoo-ert Grens."

The big man in the suit winced a little, but nodded.

"That's me. Ewert. And what is it you think I can help you with?"

Ruben Frey tried to smile as he pointed toward the cassette player.

"I recognize that. Connie Francis. 'Everybody's Somebody's Fool.' Though I've never heard it in another language before."

"*Tunna skivor.*"

"Excuse me?"

"That's what it's called. In Swedish. Siw Malmkvist."

Ruben felt as if he'd got something that at least resembled a smile in return. He took a photograph out from his shirt pocket. It wasn't a particularly good one, the person in the picture was fuzzy and the sun was too strong for the real colors to come through. The grainy person was sitting on a stone, he had a bare chest and was pretending to tense his muscles for the photograph. A young boy, a teenager, long dark hair over his eyes and tied in a braid down his back, acne on both cheeks, a sparse mustache on his upper lip.

"This is my son. John. Many years ago. It's him that I want to talk to you about. Alone, if that's possible."

A person who knew Connie Francis and "Everybody's Somebody's Fool" had already by virtue of that won a little respect from Ewert Grens. No more than half an hour later the two men were sitting on either side of the detective superintendent's desk and that respect seemed to have grown on both sides.

Ruben Frey had quite quickly decided to be as honest, as open as possible. Everything that he hadn't been the day before. He quite simply had no choice. Ewert Grens had also emphasized that the presumed crime they were going to talk about had taken place in the United States and was therefore well beyond his jurisdiction, which meant that even if he had wanted to, there wasn't much he could do.

It was blowing hard outside the window, early morning fast turning into midmorning as the wind pounded regularly against the glass, dull explosions, a force that made them fall silent a couple of times and turn around to check that it hadn't smashed.

Ruben Frey declined the offer of coffee, mineral water perhaps, and

Ewert Grens had pressed a can for each of them out of the machine in the corridor that swallowed ten-kronor coins and always had a note taped to the front, in scrawled handwriting by whoever it was who was sick of a machine eating their money without giving anything in return and now demanded their money back, always with a telephone extension at the bottom. Ewert Grens often wondered why they bothered, or if any of them had ever been contacted by the machine owner and had, with an apology, been able to hold the swallowed ten-kronor coin in their hand again.

Frey drank directly from the can, a couple of mouthfuls and then it was empty.

"Do you have children?"

He was serious when he asked the question and Grens suddenly looked down at the desk.

"No."

"Why not?"

"With all due respect, that's none of your business."

Ruben rubbed a hand against his smooth, round cheeks and Ewert mused that it wasn't fair that some people didn't get wrinkles.

"OK. I'll put it differently. Can you understand how it feels to be about to lose your only child?"

Ewert Grens thought about another father, the father of the five-year-old girl who had been sexually assaulted and murdered two years ago. He remembered how terrible his face had been, the pain that was impossible to avoid.

"No. As I don't have any. But I've been faced with parents' grief, I've seen it and I could certainly feel the grief eating them up inside."

"Can you then understand how far a parent is prepared to go to avoid that?"

The mourning father had in that case sought out and shot to death the man who had taken his daughter's life, and Ewert had discovered in the course of the investigation that he didn't think that was entirely wrong.

"Yes. I think I can."

Ruben Frey rummaged for something in one of his trouser pockets. A pack of cigarettes. A red pack, a brand you couldn't buy in Sweden.

"Is it OK if I smoke?"

"Not in this fucking building. But I have no intention of arresting you if you do."

Frey smiled and lit up a cigarette. He leaned back, tried to relax, took a couple of drags and blew the smoke out in front of him in small grayish white puffs.

"I believe in the death penalty. I've voted for every governor who's campaigned for it. If my son, if John had been guilty, he would have deserved to die. I believe in an eye for an eye. But you see . . . John *is not* a murderer. A fucking troublemaker, true. Low impulse control is what the psychologists called it. A couple of them tried to link it to the loss of his mother, who died early, that his grief for Antonia triggered it. I don't believe that for a moment, all these quasi-hypotheses that in some way absolve the individual of responsibility. He was difficult, Superintendent Grens, but he *was not* a murderer."

From then on, for about half an hour, Grens did not need to ask a single question. Ruben Frey smoked and talked without interruption. He described the bitter atmosphere that was whipped up when the Finnigan girl was found dead. The sort of murder that the press decides to serialize and turn into a matter of principle, and Elizabeth Finnigan obviously sold well in the greater part of the state of Ohio. The public's demands to find a culprit and then have that person punished with the strictest possible penalty grew louder as the days passed, with each article that was published. The murder became public property and ignited public grief, and above all, politics. No bastard in Ohio was going to be able to take the life of a beautiful young woman with everything before her and get away with it. Ruben Frey was quite calm, collected, as he told the story chronologically; calm and collected when he spoke of the day that John was arrested and the hate they were confronted with from then until the jury announced their fucking verdict in the courtroom.

He told a story he had perhaps never told before. His cheeks were flushed, his brow shiny, he hadn't changed clothes since leaving home in Marcusville and he was starting to smell—sweat and something else—not that it bothered Grens but he noticed it and he asked Frey if he'd like to wash away his journey in one of the City Police showers once they had finished talking. Frey thanked him and apologized for the fact that he wasn't as clean as he might be, it had been a long day.

The strong wind continued to pound against the window with even greater force. The snow swirled outside, whirling up as much as falling down, old loose snow being harried to life again. Ewert Grens went over to the window and looked out at the whiteness. He waited. Frey was clearly tired but there was more.

"And his escape?"

"What do you mean?"

"What do you know about that?"

Ruben Frey had known that the question would come. He looked for yet another cigarette in the pack that was empty.

"Is this conversation strictly between you and me?"

"I don't see anyone else here."

"Do I have your word when I ask that it stays between us?"

"Yes. You have my word. I don't report to anyone."

Frey scrunched up the cigarette pack with the red symbol on it, took aim at the wastepaper basket under Grens's desk—he wasn't even close. He bent his bulky body forward and got hold of the crumpled cardboard, threw it again. Even farther away.

He shrugged, left it lying on the floor.

"Everything."

"Everything?"

"I knew everything. I was there, all the way. Until the airplane took off in Toronto and disappeared in the clouds heading for Moscow. A detour, but people we trusted often used that route. It was my money that financed every stage of the escape."

He sighed.

"That was six years ago. I haven't seen him since then, and I don't know if you understand, but each day that has passed without me hearing anything, each silent day, has been a good day."

By the time that Ruben Frey undressed and stepped into a shower at City Police, he had explained in detail the escape that his son had already described parts of. There had been several gaps in John's story, but everything he'd told of what he remembered was confirmed by his father in a closed room. Ewert Grens decided to believe what he had heard; Ruben Frey, a prison officer called Vernon Eriksen, and two doctors who had subsequently changed their identities and lives had together planned and implemented the escape of a person they believed was innocent.

The blue shirt with white stripes was now a white shirt with blue stripes and the black leather vest had changed to mocha brown. His hair was wet and you could smell the aftershave as soon as the door opened. Ruben looked clean, his eyes less tired. He put down his large travel bag where it had previously stood and asked where he could get something to eat. Grens pointed out into the corridor and Frey took a few steps before he turned around.

"I have *one* more question."

"I don't have much time. But ask away and I'll see if I can answer."

Ruben Frey put a hand to his wet hair, he straightened his pants and the waistband that had somehow got caught under his large belly.

It was still windy out there, they could both hear it.

"Six years. I've thought about him every day, every waking hour. I would dearly love to see him. Could you arrange that?"

Twenty minutes later, Ewert Grens walked beside him down one of the detention center corridors. There were restrictions, but there was also a way around restrictions. Grens accompanied the unauthorized visitor into the cell and then stood in front of the window from where they could be observed, without taking up room. They cried as they embraced each other, not sobbing, but quiet, almost mindful, the tears people cry after many years of loss.

EWERT GRENS DROVE AT GREAT SPEED AND ON AT LEAST TWO OCCASIONS against the traffic down a one-way street. He was late and had no intention of being even later.

It had been hard to get Ruben Frey to let go of his son.

It hadn't been easy to have to say that the informal visit was over, that they had to leave, John's drawn face and Ruben's round cheeks pressed together as they stood there, close, so close, and talked quietly about something that Grens neither could hear nor wanted to hear. He had arranged for Ruben Frey to be driven to Hotel Continental on Vasagatan and had given him a business card with all his work numbers on it, and his home number scrawled by hand on the back.

He glanced at the clock on the dashboard. Two minutes past eleven. The boat left from Gåshaga dock at seventeen minutes past. He could still make it.

It was only three days since he'd stood beside her at the window and she had raised her hand and waved.

He had seen it.

He was convinced that that was what she'd done when the white boat blew its horn down on the water, on Höggarnsfjärden. And then the staff had explained to him that it was neurologically impossible. What did that mean? A wave was a wave and he had seen what he'd seen. He didn't care if it was impossible or not.

Three days, no more, and yet it felt like an age ago. He should have thought about her more. Anni had always lain like a film over everything he did, everything he breathed, she had been with him every step he'd taken and he'd come to appreciate it, he was totally dependent on it.

But it was as if he hadn't had time in the past few days. He had tried several times when he suddenly realized that he'd lost her for a while: he started to think about her face again and her room and that he missed her, but it had been hard—forced thoughts that demanded an energy that for the first time wasn't there.

Grens crossed Lidingö Bridge, over the speed limit as always, then another three or four miles to the east of the large island, where property prices were so high that all you could do was laugh. He had never understood why it was so fucking fantastic to live there. He had thought at the time it was a good environment for Anni—the peace, the water, plus it was easy for him to visit—but good God, that was twenty-five years ago now, when house prices had been very different.

He looked at the clock again, four minutes left when he parked the car and got out. Some people were waiting, and farther down the dock, a cab closed its doors and drove off. He went down the slope, into the cold wind that rasped against his face.

It was a simple dock, from this distance it basically looked like a large lump of concrete that someone had poured into the water. The ice lay thick and hard around it, as if everything had been welded together; it was hard to tell under the layer of snow where the dock ended and the ice began. A channel of open water led up to the dock, it wasn't very wide and he wondered that there was enough room for a boat that size.

She was sitting in her wheelchair, a great white hat on her head and a thick coat with a brown fur collar that he'd given her two Christmases ago around her thin body. He got that feeling in his stomach, the same as always. The tenderness when he saw her, for a while he was at peace, didn't need to hurry anywhere. He said nothing to her when he got there, just stroked her cheek, it was red and chilly, and she leaned in toward his hand.

She had seen it.

In the distance, and slightly late, the white ferry sailing toward Gåshaga. According to the timetable, it should be alongside the dock at seventeen minutes past eleven, champing at the bit for the time it took for the new passengers to board.

Anni had seen it and her eyes didn't leave it. Ewert Grens kept on stroking her cheek, he was sure she was as happy as she looked.

He said hello to Susann, the medical student who worked extra shifts at the nursing home and whom he'd asked to go with them—he was paying her for the day from his own money. She was about Hermansson's age, slightly taller, more solid, blond rather than dark, they weren't at all like each other and yet they were similar, the way they talked, their self-confidence and authority. He wondered if all young women were like that and he just hadn't noticed.

An older couple standing over by the edge of the dock, a man in a black leather jacket and sneakers sitting on his own on a bench covered in snow, two girls standing a few feet away, giggling hysterically, glancing over at them when they thought no one would see. They were all waiting, checked their watches now and then, stamped their feet in the snow to keep warm.

The boat was getting closer, a dot that quickly grew bigger as it approached. When it was still some way off, the horn blew twice, Anni jumped and then made her sound, the one that he always heard as laughter, a gurgling, wheezing sound that came from somewhere at the base of her throat.

MS *Söderarm*. The boat she had waved to.

And now she was going to sail with her, she wanted to—she had shown him, after all.

The boat was bigger than he'd thought. One hundred thirty feet, two stories, shining white with a blue and yellow funnel, a long wire tied from stem to stern with colorful flags that fluttered in the gusty wind and every now and then made a loud slapping noise. He pushed her wheelchair in front of him. The small wheels got caught on the gangway and he had to struggle to get her free and then onboard. They went into the lower lounge, which was warm, where there were some empty wooden benches and a strong smell of coffee from the kiosk at the back.

Susann took off Anni's hat and unbuttoned her winter coat. Her hair was tousled and Ewert looked for his comb, a steel comb with wide gaps between the teeth, and he pulled it through the knots with great care until her hair hung straight again.

"Coffee?"

Ewert looked at Susann, who was straightening up the wheelchair. She pushed it back and forth with vigor until she found a position at the short end of the table that was good.

"No, thanks."

"I'll pay."

"I don't want one."

"I insist. It's important for me that you're here today."

She still didn't look up; she was bending down to lock the wheels.

"If you insist."

Grens walked down the narrow aisle, countering the boat's tendency to roll. MS *Söderarm*. He liked the name. One that he'd heard for years mumbled in a monotone on the shipping forecast on Sveriges Radio: *Söderarm, southwesterly, twenty-six feet per second, visibility good.* He had also been there a few times, at the far end of the archipelago, when as a boy he sailed there with his father. He couldn't remember that they'd done much together, but those sailing trips, he remembered them, Tjärven lighthouse that flashed and swooped and the sea and the sky that blended together in the same color blue . . . it had been deserted out there, nature was naked, not much life, barren rocks and endless sea.

"She's called *Söderarm*, the boat."

The boy, because he was just a kid, who was standing behind the brown wooden counter pouring three cups of coffee, looked at him in surprise.

"Yes. Would you like anything else?"

"Why's she called that?"

The spotty face and stressed eyes tried to avoid his odd questions.

"I don't know. I'm new. Can I get you anything else?"

"Three Danishes, with cheese."

They drank the coffee and ate the Danishes and looked out of the window as the boat cut through the water that still came in waves, despite the fact that there was only a narrow channel through the ice. The boat journey would take forty minutes. At eleven fifty-seven they would disembark at Vaxholm and have a seafood lunch at Vaxholm Hotel—Ewert had reserved a table for three by the window with a view of the sea.

He wound down. He felt calm. But all the same, fucking Schwarz forced his way in. Despite all the water out there, the ice, the archipelago. He just needed a few hours of peace! He would have the strength to face this story and get to the bottom of it if he could only have these measly few hours to forget it! Grens closed his eyes and forced himself to think of something other than Schwarz. For a few minutes, maybe a couple, then Ruben Frey was there again, asking how far Ewert would be prepared to go to save his children.

I don't have any damn children. We never had damn children. We didn't get the time. Anni, we didn't get the time.

But if we had. For example, Hermansson. If we'd had a daughter like Hermansson.

But we don't. But if we had had, Anni, you know that I would go to any lengths to protect her.

Ewert leaned forward over the table and wiped the crumbs away from her chin with a red Christmas napkin. Then he asked if they wanted to go out. He thought that Anni would maybe like to feel the wind, the sea, the long days cooped up in her room and the hours spent looking out of the window at a world that she couldn't be part of, she had to take the opportunity, she had waved.

They weren't going particularly fast. He didn't know much about speeds at sea, but the pimply boy in the kiosk knew that the maximum speed was twelve knots and that certainly didn't sound far wrong. He carried Anni up the stairs, held her in his arms and rolled up the stairs as his limp compensated for the sea, Susann a few steps behind him with the wheelchair that she had folded up for the moment to get it through the door onto the deck.

The wind was even stronger out here. It was hard to stand still, and they both helped to hold Anni's wheelchair. The odd drop of saltwater on their cheeks when the waves were big, but it felt good, like the shiver of a slightly too cold shower in the morning. He looked at Anni, who was sitting by the railing, her chin just reaching over it, so she could be part of something that lived its own life. The happiness that she sometimes gave him washed over him again, simply by showing herself that *she* was happy.

"I know what you're hoping for. And I think it's good what you're doing, what you're giving her, but I don't want you to hope for *too much*."

"Call me Ewert."

"I mean, because then it could really hurt when it doesn't happen."

"She waved."

The medical student called Susann had one hand on Anni's shoulder, the other still around the handle of the wheelchair. She didn't look at him when she said all this, her eyes fixed on Vaxholm, which was expanding on the port side of the boat.

"I know that that's what you think you saw. I also know that it's impossible, in neurological terms. A reflex. I think it was a reflex movement. That's all."

"I know exactly what the hell I saw."

She turned toward him.

"I don't want to upset you. But you will be, you'll get hurt if you invest too much hope in this. That's all. I mean, you should take her out like this, I think it's fantastic for her, and maybe that's enough, isn't it? To know that, I mean."

He didn't really know what he'd actually thought. That when she saw the boat, she'd wave again? That she'd show the bastards, convince them? They ate in silence, the fish was as good as he'd heard it was, but there wasn't much more to talk about. Anni had a good appetite, she ate and she dribbled and spilled on herself, and he and Susann raced to be the first to clean her up. He'd arranged for a cab to come at half past one and it arrived on time, and an hour or so later they parted at Gåshaga dock. He kissed Anni on the forehead and promised to come and see her, on Monday at the latest. He managed to get through the city pretty quickly as the rush-hour traffic hadn't built up yet, so he could concentrate on making a call to Sven Sundkvist from the car to get an update on what had happened in the past few hours, and to Ruben Frey at Hotel Continental— he wanted to talk to the poor man, he wanted to warn him that perhaps he shouldn't hope for *too much*.

THE PAST TWENTY-FOUR HOURS WERE UNLIKE ANYTHING HE HAD experienced before. Not even that day eighteen years ago when his only child had been found dying on his own bedroom floor. He had been emotionally more open then, easier to touch. He had really internalized her death, he had felt it and understood that it was real, and on several occasions had been close to taking his own life, as there was nothing left to live for. He had become more closed since then. He had, apart from the time when they desperately tried to have another child, not been able to touch Alice, not at all; he had been as good as the living dead.

Edward Finnigan was sitting in his car driving north along Route 23. He had worked as the governor's adviser for as long as they could remember, since they met when studying law at Ohio State University two decades before Robert was elected. And then when the long campaign that they had fought together for all those years finally resulted in a governor post, they had simply moved their work to the office on South High Street in Columbus, all their efforts and strategic planning had finally paid off, he was the governor's closest partner and the one who dealt with everything that officially and unofficially passed through Ohio's center of power.

It was as if Elizabeth's death had made him even more efficient. He worked even harder so he didn't have to feel, and somewhere, somehow, hoped the victory in his working life would translate into solace in his private life. He wound down the window on the driver's side and spat angrily into the cold air. How incredibly naive he had been.

He had realized this in the hours that had passed since the prison's senior corrections officer, Vernon Eriksen, had come to visit them early in the morning the day before. Suddenly, after all these years, it was as if he could feel again. When Eriksen had told what he'd come to tell them, when he had explained that Frey was alive, that he was being held behind bars in a city in northern Europe, it was as if someone had pummeled Finnigan hard with a fist again and again until they were certain that he

243

could really feel the blows. He was alive. That meant he could die. Edward Finnigan had stripped when Eriksen left, crying out for her skin again, his erection as hard as it had been long ago, and she hadn't understood, she'd asked him to leave.

Of course he'd phoned. And Robert had understood and immediately contacted Washington. They would get Frey at any cost. They perhaps didn't have the same motivation, Finnigan who wanted revenge and the governor who wanted to be reelected, but that didn't matter: the bastard was coming back and they would stand together and watch his execution.

It was only seventy-four miles between Marcusville and Columbus and he drove his year-old Ford there and back several times a week. He did have an apartment he could use only a hundred yards from the office, at the top of a beautiful building and with an interior that was professionally designed at the state's expense, but he wasn't comfortable there. The small rooms reeked of loneliness, and strangely enough, despite having closed down, he didn't want to feel lonely, so he commuted every day, there and back, and if he left early and drove slightly too fast, he could avoid most of the traffic and do it in just under an hour.

It was quite icy and he had driven more slowly than usual, the dark was deceptive and he had already veered too close to the shoulder on two occasions. As he approached what was the geographical and political heart of Ohio—around eight hundred thousand people with a considerably higher than average wage, education, and living standard than the population of Marcusville—he phoned and asked the governor for an early morning meeting in his office. He wanted to know what was happening with the Frey case. Or rather, why nothing at all seemed to have happened in the past twenty-four hours.

The office was on the thirteenth floor, 77 South High Street. It wasn't particularly impressive, and the few friends who had dropped by to say hello over the years had tried hard to hide their disappointment when the office of the governor's adviser turned out be pretty much like any other office in any other company, for any level of management—Edward Finnigan had made a point of it. To be fair, his bright office had a view over half of Columbus, but the exterior was modest and the interior simple and functional, thus communicating cost-effectiveness and moderation, which were important in a state that regularly battled threats of tax hikes.

Robert was already sitting in the visitor's chair when he came in. Two sticky doughnuts on a plate on the desk. He looked healthy following a short break, skiing in Telluride, about as high as you could go in Colorado and the Rocky Mountains. He was tall and fit, with a tanned face and fair hair parted in the middle, and he looked young, certainly much younger than Edward. There was only a month between them, and no one who saw them, absolutely no one, would ever believe anyone who told them that. Lean versus lumpy, a mane of hair versus balding, suntanned versus pasty, but for the most part it was the sorrow that had weathered him, for each year that had passed since Elizabeth was taken away, Edward Finnigan had lived two.

"Edward, if I'm going to be honest, you look terrible."

Finnigan walked into the room, a few hurried steps across the soft carpet to the window. The sun that shone in the distance behind the high-rise blocks was strong and he didn't want all that damn light. The blinds were dark and he adjusted them so that it was impossible to see the day outside that wanted attention.

"Bob, I want to know why nothing's happening."

The governor took one of the doughnuts, ate half of the sticky treat and kept the rest in his hand.

"You've been waiting eighteen years. Eighteen years, Edward! I, if anyone, know how you feel, and what you want, but just let the wheels of bureaucracy turn for a while, be patient, you've already waited so long. He's coming back here. He's going to sit on Death Row again, in Marcusville prison, and he's going to be executed. Every time that you and Alice get ready to go for a walk in town, I assure you, every time you see that great ugly wall you will know that he sat inside there, that it was there he ceased to be."

Edward Finnigan snorted. He couldn't remember that he'd ever done that to his oldest friend. He looked in the briefcase he had with him—the envelope had slipped in between two plastic files and he swore loudly before he found it. He emptied the contents onto the desk and asked the governor to look at it.

A photograph. A man in a dark shirt who seemed to want to avoid the camera.

"Do you know who that is?"

"I can guess."

"I hate him!"

"And you're sure that it's him?"

"He's cut his hair, he's thinner, his eyes are somehow darker, more wrinkles. But it's him. I've known him since he started primary school. It's him, Bob!"

The governor picked up the photograph, held it under the desk lamp so he could see better in the dark room.

"You don't need to worry. He'll be coming back."

"I can't wait any longer!"

Finnigan paced restlessly around the room, his voice was too loud and the governor didn't like it.

"Edward, if you'd like me to stay, I want you to sit here and calm down. We've gone through this far too many times before. I'm your friend. And I think of you as mine. I watched your daughter grow up. You know that I would happily administrate his execution. And we will. If you don't lose your head now."

They'd both thought about it, were forced to every now and then when they worked side by side over a long period of time. Even from their student days it had been obvious: Robert had been the politician candidate and Edward his trusted adviser. It wasn't anything they'd decided, it had just turned out like that, they had found their roles and were happy with them. They seldom, or rather never, responded hierarchically, they were friends and friends didn't shout at each other, so the fact that Robert had now raised his voice and demonstrated his irritation was so unusual that they were both startled for a moment. Edward took a step forward and pulled the photograph from his grasp.

"For six years, I've thought he was dead! He tried to trick me from my legal right to revenge. And then I find out that he's alive in goddamn Sweden! I want to see him here. Now! I won't wait any longer."

The governor had been particular when he made sure that the door to Finnigan's office was closed. He had then pulled up the blinds, despite Edward's protests, and let in the light that would give them energy. He had even opened a window wide, allowing the rumble of the traffic to find its way up and into the room to compete with their raised voices.

They had then shouted at each other as they had never done before.

For all these years, they had consciously avoided confrontation. They had built a relationship that was uneasily protected from strong words and had feared the day that would inevitably come. Now it was here and it was almost a relief to get rid of everything, to shout until they were hoarse, to not give a damn for once whether the staff were listening outside, and if they were, what they were thinking.

Their argument came to a violent end after about twenty minutes.

In a fury, Robert had pushed his friend up against the wall and with his mouth close to his ear lowered his voice and pointed out that if Edward wanted to succeed in this, it was fucking important that no one could interpret it as a personal vendetta, that they had to make it political and use political arguments, just like the last time, that they would get the journalists to write about men who killed women and then ran around making a joke of the American legal system.

He had stood there with a firm grip on his adviser's collar.

Suddenly, Finnigan had twisted himself free, and struck him to the floor with his fist, then turned, picked up a penholder and thrown it in his face.

The governor had started to bleed profusely from a cut on his forehead, and heard his best friend tell him to go to hell as he flung open the door and stormed out.

IT WAS AFTERNOON IN STOCKHOLM. STILL COLD, STILL WINDY, AND SPRING seemed more distant than ever. State Secretary Thorulf Winge had just replaced lunch with a cup of Earl Grey and a dry cinnamon bun that had been lying on the table since the late meeting the evening before. He had dipped it in the hot liquid and it hadn't really tasted of anything, but for a moment had resembled something like nourishment. On days like this, there simply wasn't the time, and that was that.

He walked the short distance from the Ministry of Foreign Affairs to the government offices in Rosenbad. Head down, eyes focused on the icy asphalt, he looked like all the other people trying to escape the cold that assailed your face in January. He walked along the water beside the parliament—this was where he existed, amongst the corridors of power, and it was to these corridors that he had given most of his life.

He nodded to the security guard who was sitting behind the glass wall, in a light uniform shirt and brown beret with a brass badge on the front. The guard, an older man who had been there almost as long as Winge, nodded in recognition and pressed the button that opened the main door.

He was well prepared. The meeting with the prime minister and minister of foreign affairs was their first concerning John Meyer Frey, squeezed into the prime minister's already full schedule.

Thorulf Winge took a deep breath and looked at the clock on the wall.

He had exactly fifteen minutes to explain why they would be forced to hand over the detained American citizen to the United States as early as tomorrow morning.

EDWARD FINNIGAN'S FACE GLEAMED WITH SWEAT IN THE REFLECTION IN the rectangular mirror in the elevator. His breathing was still labored, raising his voice against Robert, struggling free from his grip and then throwing that stupid penholder in his face, it was as if he'd been running for hours. The physical strain had perhaps not been so great, but he was tired to the point of exhaustion. People got in and out of the elevator on the way down, but he barely registered them. Someone was standing in his way, a fifty-five-year-old man who stared back at him in confusion from the mirror and wondered what the hell to do now.

He was frightened.

He didn't regret that he'd shouted and fought. But he suddenly felt the fear when he realized what he was capable of. An act of violence. He who had never fought before. Uncontrolled anger that he had let loose, here, in an environment where he'd always been in control.

The man in the mirror continued to stare.

He had been dreading this confrontation for a long time. Just as he was sure that Robert had dreaded it. Thirty years together without ever clearing the air, as if their friendship was so fragile that they had both consciously avoided situations that might destroy the trust. Now he felt uncertain, he was filled with anxiety. An anxiety about the consequences that rattled in his chest, that as a result of the shouting and the fight he risked losing the support, the support of power, when he most needed it.

He got out of the elevator on the ground floor. It was freezing out there; people seemed to huddle against the wind and cold. He loitered by reception for a while, nodded at the ubiquitous man who stood there every morning in his uniform and smiled at everyone who came in, who didn't seem to have much more to do than that, other than put out the yellow plastic signs to warn that the marble floor was wet and slippery and people walked there at their own peril. Finnigan had always been irritated by the warnings that had no other function than *to have been there* in the event that someone did slip and then decided to go to a lawyer with their foot in a cast and file a suit against the owner of the property for not looking after the floor properly. Too much of the legal system was clogged up by ridiculous cases that were of little importance, and this morning he really wanted to kick the sign in front of him to bits.

He waited in the warmth until he had decided what he was going to do.

He didn't kick anything, he left the yellow plastic sign standing there when he hurried out to the car that was illegally parked right in front of the building.

It wasn't far to Port Columbus International and he pulled his phone out of his coat pocket as he drove, phoned direct to the ticket desk and booked a seat on the United Airlines flight that was due to depart at twenty-nine minutes past ten.

An hour's flight later and he could see Washington Dulles International from the air. A few minutes ago, the pilot had started to prepare for landing, which was scheduled for eleven thirty-five. Edward Finnigan had traveled this route more times than he could remember in recent years, just enough time to read *USA Today* and the *New York Times*, have a beer and a sandwich, then a taxi and today's *Washington Post* before he arrived at the center of the capital.

You give and you get.

He had learned the golden rule of power a long, long time ago.

He asked to be dropped off some way down D Street. The Monocle on Capitol Hill was a lunch restaurant that was in no way as good as its reputation, but he didn't go there for the food. They had met at a table at the back of the beautiful restaurant several times before when they had passed on information and promised support in exchange for support.

You give and you get.

He liked the tables with the red-and-white checked tablecloths, well-done pieces of tender meat, salads that tasted fresh. He even liked the bustling waiter who could sniff out tips. But most of all, he liked the open-plan design that made it easy to see who was coming and going, when you should lower your voice without it appearing to be evasive.

Norman Hill was about fifteen years older than him. A nice, softly spoken gentleman who seemed to have been born to this. The sort of person who was pointed out in primary school as a potential senator. He was thin, even thinner than Finnigan remembered, and several times he was about to ask if he was ill but refrained; Hill's eyes and face radiated the same energy that he always did, he was the kind of man you listened to, had confidence in. Authority, Edward Finnigan thought to himself, had nothing to do with physical weight.

At some point in the middle of their conversation, Finnigan started to smile. For the first time since Vernon Eriksen's visit, he relaxed, felt his shoulders fall, the tension around the back of his neck let go. There was something so familiar about all this, secure even. They had sat like this eighteen years ago, in another restaurant a couple of hundred yards away, and Finnigan had appealed to him to apply political pressure that would result in media pressure—back then it involved a seventeen-year-old boy who had taken the life of a schoolgirl a year younger than him—to stoke public opinion in support of the severest legal penalty, even though the murderer was a minor. Senator Hill had then pressed all the buttons he could: ones that Finnigan had heard about and ones that you got to know only when your whole world was the blocks between the Potomac and Pennsylvania Avenue.

Edward Finnigan actually didn't need to say much. He ate his pink beef and drank the beer with a European label while Hill picked at a Caesar salad and ordered more mineral water. Finnigan had prepared a long speech on the plane about maintaining confidence in the American legal system, about the party's credibility, about a continued focus on the death penalty as a deterrent and preventative measure. It wasn't necessary. It didn't take more than a couple of minutes for him to recount the tale of John Meyer Frey's death and resurrection. Norman Hill had interrupted him, a thin hand in the air and then those eyes. Not even the promise of a favor in return. The slight senator had thanked him for the lunch, held Finnigan's hand in both of his, and said that he didn't need to worry about all this.

Twenty-five minutes later, he ordered two double espressos at the Starbucks farther down Pennsylvania Avenue. The congresswoman was named Jane Ketterer and she had aged with dignity. Edward Finnigan didn't remember ever thinking that she was beautiful before, but he did now. When she smiled he felt the desire that Alice had rejected, he wanted to hold her and touch the skin under her long skirt, but he was there to talk about the same thing he just had, and she listened and nodded and was indignant. He desired her even more when they emptied their coffee cups and parted a while later, leaving the place with a few minutes between them.

He took a taxi to Mr. Henry's. It was on the same street, but there was quite a distance between numbers 237 and 601. He had once some years earlier walked the whole length of Pennsylvania Avenue and he would never do it again, he had been considerably younger, but his black shoes had rubbed his feet raw in several places and it had still been painful to walk a week later.

Mr. Henry's was one of the few bars in Washington that he always went back to. Hushed conversations, a bartender who didn't try to be funny, it was discreet, away from the louts who wanted cheap beer and to get drunk quick.

Jonathan Apanovitch was much younger than he was, he guessed no more than forty. He was tall and fair with eyes that resembled Norman Hill's and he had worked as a journalist for the *Washington Post* for nearly half his life. Edward Finnigan had done a quick count while he waited; this was the twelfth time they had met here over the years and they were both happy with their agreement. Finnigan had a channel for the information he wanted to plant and Apanovitch strengthened his position as an investigative journalist with a nose for news.

This time the story was so good that Finnigan drew it out for as long as he could; he knew that what he felt was absurd, but it was real and he accepted it, his daughter's death, the greatest loss of his life, was for a while a triumph, something that made his knowledge desirable, perhaps the only way to cope with it.

He gave Apanovitch the names of two people that he knew would be able to comment on his story, a senator called Norman Hill and a congresswoman called Jane Ketterer.

He had one condition. It had to happen fast. The story about an American who was due to be executed and had managed to escape from Death Row by faking his own death and was now alive and being held in a European prison had to be published the following day.

You give and you get.

Jonathan Apanovitch thanked him for the beer that he hadn't finished and then disappeared out toward the car that he had parked, as agreed, a block away.

IT WAS LATE AND THE CLOCK ON THE CHURCH THAT HE COULDN'T remember the name of in Gamla Stan struck twelve. The red building that housed the government offices emerged from the dark as he got closer. Thorulf Winge had walked for the second time that day from the Ministry of Foreign Affairs to Rosenbad. The afternoon and the greater part of the evening had passed since he had been given fifteen minutes in the prime minister's office to explain why John Meyer Frey would, in a few hours' time, have to be deported out of the country, to the other side of the border.

He was cold. The expensive coat over his suit gave no more protection than paper. It was a long time since the sun had gone down and the beautiful clear night spread cold like an aggressive cancer, constantly dividing in order to reach farther and drain people of energy until they fell; minus seventeen was more than he could stand.

The older man who recognized him had gone home and a young woman was now sitting in the security post. Winge had never seen her before, nor she him. He showed his ID and she checked his details on the computer screen, followed up by a phone call, and he had drummed his fingers on the metal strip for a bit too long when she finally opened the big glass door and he could go in.

In the course of the allotted fifteen minutes, Thorulf Winge had got both the minister of foreign affairs and the prime minister to accept that it was reasonable to extradite Frey in line with the requests submitted by the American ambassador and direct from Washington. All three had agreed that a little shit who murdered young girls and kicked Finnish ferry passengers in the face should under no circumstances be allowed to jeopardize the good relations that had been nurtured with great care since Prime Minister Palme's day; following his vociferous contempt for the Americans in Vietnam, the Swedish government had slowly, step by step, developed an entente with the only superpower that was left, and to aggravate this relationship for a prisoner who had been convicted of murder was not in the interests of their political work, nor the political visions of either party.

He had got them to understand *why*.

But not how.

He had asked for more time and had finally been given it once the fully booked day was over, which in this case was twenty past midnight in the dark between a freezing cold Thursday and Friday.

There was a thermos of coffee on the table, another of tea, a couple of bottles of mineral water, and in the middle some cans of a fizzy drink that tasted like Coke. They were all used to long days, to the constant need to have ready-made answers on all sorts of issues and to be questioned if there was even the slightest doubt, to be put under a magnifying glass when answers were not foolproof and to expect calls for their resignation when they made an error of judgment. They were tired, wanted to go home, but the matter at hand had to be resolved by dawn.

Thorulf Winge poured a cup of tea for the minister of foreign affairs and the prime minister and a black coffee for himself; he had long since given up the idea of sleeping before the night was over.

It was a beautiful room with a high ceiling, exclusively Swedish-designed furniture, spacious, airy, even the lighting was pleasant. It struck Winge that you would appreciate that only when your eyes were tired from a day of too much and too harsh light.

He looked at the men, each sitting on a generous wooden chair covered in soft red fabric, silk perhaps, he wasn't sure, something that would be delightful against your cheek should you decide to lean your head on it.

There wasn't time for chitchat. They knew why they were there.

And they looked at Winge, so he started to speak.

"This is going to be published in the *Washington Post* tomorrow."

He had copied and enlarged the fax he had received an hour earlier. Part of an article that would dominate the front page of the newspaper in America's capital. He put two copies down on the table, one in front of each of the ministers.

"The reporter, someone called Apanovitch, sent this to us asking if someone could comment."

Both men fumbled with hard black spectacle cases, the paper copies rustled in their hands as they read carefully and in silence. A story about an American citizen who had been sentenced to death and who, several years after dying in his cell on Death Row, was now very much alive and being held in custody in a Swedish jail. A background about Frey's crime and judgment, two photographs, one of a boy in a courtroom wearing orange prison overalls, one of a considerably older man, short hair, thin, taken in a photo booth, glued into a false Canadian passport. Then a correct description of events, that he was suspected of aggravated assault and had been arrested four days ago by the Swedish police, taken into custody, and presented for pre-trial proceedings in the Swedish capital. Apanovitch referred to several anonymous sources and closed with indignant comments from a Senator Hill and Congresswoman Ketterer.

Winge studied both his colleagues as they read. Overweight, gray hair, suits that were both expensive and elegant, but never quite fitted properly. He had known them since they were young men. They had met and worked together in the party's youth organization, they trusted each other and they had made decisions in private together before.

"Describe Hill."

Senator Norman Hill had chosen formulations that were clear and unimpeachable. He led the reader to understand that a country that was barely visible on the map would not be permitted to obstruct the American legal system's right to impose the death penalty, but he said it in different words, eloquent and experienced, balancing diplomacy outward with authority on the home front.

Winge looked at his ultimate boss.

"Hill is sixty-eight years old. He has been a senator for a good number of these years. He has political responsibility, is the unofficial campaign manager for the Republicans' presidential candidate in the upcoming election. He stays well in the background but is generally recognized to be one of the most influential people in the party."

Car horns blared somewhere in the distance, someone shouted something, sounds outside the window that were muffled by the wind and cold. The Stockholm night was as alive as it always was, people moving around in a capital that gave them space. The location of the government offices, in the city in amongst all the bars and homeless people and tourists, was symbolic, power in the midst of life, but also ironic; out there someone was getting drunk on cheap wine and pissing against the walls, in here the most powerful people in the country sat and decided between life and death.

Thorulf Winge poured himself some more black coffee, held the thermos up and looked questioningly at the others, who shook their heads.

He took a sip and turned to his bosses. He wanted to continue, raise the bar.

"They're not going to give in. We can decide to resolve it now. Or, we can draw out the process, get egg on our faces, and *then* still be forced into the same solution. They've already got the lethal injection in their hand."

The minister of foreign affairs ran his hands through his gray hair, as he often did, always when he was thinking, when he felt pressured.

"Political suicide."

"The ambassador and Washington have both pointed out that Sweden is obligated to extradite suspected criminals to the States, that is, insofar as they are not Swedish citizens. And Frey is American, even if he has been declared dead."

"Political suicide. If it becomes public knowledge."

Winge was waiting for a response from the prime minister, who had chosen to remain silent until now. They had both been in Luxembourg a few years ago and taken part in the negotiations between the EU member states and the United States regarding a new extradition agreement between the two centers of power. An initiative proposed by the American government following the terrorist attack on September 11, 2001. Now he stood up, took off his glasses, hung his jacket over the back of the chair covered in soft red fabric.

"Thorulf, we were both there. And we both remember the issues, don't we? I certainly remember that, on your advice, I smiled when I spoke about our concern that there should be sufficient guarantees that those who are extradited would be given a fair trial and would *never* be sentenced to death."

"I also recall the discussion. *It is incontrovertible that any EU member state will refuse to extradite someone who is at risk of being sentenced to death.* But don't you understand? We won't be doing that. John Meyer Frey does not *risk* being sentenced to death. He *is already* sentenced to death."

The prime minister was a tall man, and when he stood under the chandelier, the glittering cut glass hung like a hat over his sweating brow. His tired eyes roamed the room, he put a nervous hand to his nose, smacked his lips without being aware of it.

"I know that you have a proposal. And I will listen to it. As I always do. Then I want to take a break. It's late. I want to phone home to say it will be even later. And when I've had my break, I'll make a decision. Thorulf, please."

They had realized *that* some time ago. Now they would understand *how.*

"I don't want any more articles like that one."

Winge pointed to the copies of the faxed front page of the *Washington Post* for the following day, which was still lying on the table amongst all the cups.

"I think we all agree on that. Please continue."

The prime minister showed his irritation, which was unnecessary, and Thorulf Winge for a moment considered whether to comment, but held back. They were all tired, they all knew that no matter what the solution was and whether it was best for the country or not, they would still be accused of double standards, and none of them was without standards.

"I have a suggestion as to how this can be resolved."

The prime minister, who was standing under the chandelier, and the minister of foreign affairs, who was sitting smoothing down his hair, listened.

"We know that Frey came here via Canada and Russia. He flew from Toronto to Moscow to Stockholm. We don't know the reason for this route, and right now that's not important. What is important is that Russia can be seen as a transit country. We can deport him back *there.* And he will not be executed *there.*"

The prime minister stood immobile.

"What the hell are you saying?"

"I said that Frey came via—"

"I heard what you said. But hoped that I'd heard wrong. *If* we were to send him back to Moscow, he would immediately be sent to the United States from there."

"We know nothing about that."

"To Death Row."

"Speculation. That is not something we can be certain of."

"To his death."

"With all due respect, that is not our problem. And formally, we have not done anything that we can't defend. *We* have not extradited him to the United States."

Winge looked at the gilt clock that hung above the sofa. Three minutes to one. They would need this break. They would need to digest what he had just explained in order to realize that it was the only possible solution. He opened his black briefcase again, put some new papers on top of the faxed article.

"And then there's this, before we take a break."

The prime minister waved at him.

"Just tell us what it is."

Winge lifted up the two pages.

"Deportation papers. From the Migration Board. I received them earlier this evening. *If* we decide to let him leave the country, that is. Then we have this, his deportation papers here, in writing."

He smiled for the first time since he'd gotten there.

"To Russia."

IT WAS ONE OF THOSE NIGHTS.

Ewert Grens prowled around in his big apartment, restless and fighting the emptiness that insisted on taking up occupancy whenever he relaxed. He should have stayed on the sofa in his office in Kronoberg. He usually managed to get at least a few hours' sleep there, even when his head was sore from thinking. It was impossible here. The building was so damn quiet that each step echoed, his right foot falling harder on the parquet and the sound bouncing around until it hit him on the neck. He had been close to calling both Hermansson and Anni—he had stood with the receiver in his hand and had even dialed the numbers only then to put the receiver down before it had started to ring. He had never been particularly bothered by loneliness, he held it at arm's length, and on the occasions that it came to visit, he regarded it as a temporary guest. But now, it was as if the contrast had made it so obvious, the hours with Hermansson on the dance floor and with Anni on a boat on Höggarnsfjärden, so much life compared to all his unlived-in rooms.

He went into the kitchen, consumed two pieces of bread with expensive liver pâté and half a liter of orange juice. He ate too much on sleepless nights but had long since stopped caring about how it affected his appearance. When after a while the silence was concentrated on his chewing, he reached out for the transistor radio that stood at the far end of the kitchen table. He had got used to listening to P3's night shows, the soothing voices and music, no hysterical jingles and no stupid jokers, worthy of those who for whatever reason were awake while others slept.

The sound of the phone ringing was therefore striking.

It mixed with the silence and a slow jazz piece but soon dominated as it stubbornly persisted.

"Hello."

"Ewert Grens?"

"Depends on who I'm talking to."

"We've met a couple of times before. My name is Thorulf Winge, state secretary with the Ministry of Foreign Affairs."

Grens stretched over to the transistor radio and turned down the volume as a velvet female voice announced the next record. He couldn't remember the man who claimed he was a state secretary.

"If you say so."

"Would you like to call me back to check?"

"I'm more interested in how you managed to get my number."

"Would you like to call me back?"

"Just say what you've got to say and then we can hang up."

He already felt uneasy. He didn't doubt that the man was who he said he was. But it was half past two in the morning and that always meant that something had gone seriously wrong.

"It's regarding someone you're holding in custody, and who you are investigating. A John Schwarz. Or to be more precise, John Meyer Frey."

"And I'll bet you're the bureaucrat who's been running around handing out directives about *blackouts* and other political nonsense."

"As I said, John Meyer Frey. I'm holding some papers here from the Migration Board. Deportation papers. Frey has to be on the other side of the border by seven o'clock this morning."

Grens was silent at first, but then started to talk furiously and very loudly.

"What the hell are you talking about?"

"The decision was made earlier this evening, at nineteen hundred hours, and has to be effective within twelve hours. I'm phoning you with a request for help in assisting his deportation."

He was clutching the receiver.

"How the hell did you manage to get all this through within twenty-four hours?"

Winge didn't for a moment lose his composure, he had been given a task and he was simply performing it.

"John Meyer Frey does not have a residence permit."

"You're sending him to his death."

"John Meyer Frey entered Sweden illegally via Russia."

"I will never contribute to a person who is being detained in Sweden being sent to his death."

"And when he is deported, according to the papers in my hand, it will be to Russia."

Sven Sundkvist should have been asleep. He seldom had difficulties in sleeping, with Anita's breathing close to his face and her warm skin next to his, the security that he needed to relax.

They had started to get ready for bed about four hours ago. He had lain there beside her and she had asked what was wrong. He had no idea what she meant.

You're different.

Am I?

I know that something's up.

He hadn't even noticed it himself. Not until Anita pointed it out. And then he had lain there and tried to find out what it was, why he wasn't there; in his thoughts, he had gone through various questions and come to the same conclusion each time.

Schwarz.

I don't understand, Sven. Schwarz?

I think it's him I'm preoccupied with.

From what you've said, it sounds terrible. But, sweetheart, do we need to take him to bed with us?

He had really wanted her to understand. It was because of Schwarz's son. When he realized that there was also a child involved, it suddenly became a different story. Because he had understood some time ago how it might end.

I'm not interested in whether he's guilty or not.

Well, you should be.

I'm just thinking about the child.

The child?

I mean, why should the authorities have the right to decide whether a child should grow up without one of his parents, by imposing the death penalty?

It's the law, Sven.

But I mean, the child, the child isn't guilty.

That's the system there.

Doesn't make it any more just.

The people have voted for it, democratically. Just like here. We have life sentences. Or other long prison terms with no release for years. You often talk about that, don't you?

It's not the same.

It's *exactly* the same. For the child. Death penalty or no contact for say . . . twenty years. What's the difference?

I don't know.

Nothing. There isn't one.

All I know, all I understand is that Schwarz's son, who's just turned five, risks losing one of his parents forever if we let his father be extradited. Don't you understand, Anita? It's always the family. It's always the ones who are closest that we punish the most.

They had lain there until the argument petered out; then both got up and went down to the kitchen table, where they looked at the crossword together, as they sometimes did. She had his big black sweater on and she had been so beautiful that sometime later, once they had finished the crossword and the conversation about Schwarz was over, they had gone up to the bedroom and held each other tight as they made love. She had fallen asleep afterward. Her breathing deepened into small snores, whereas he just lay there as awake as before.

Ewert Grens stood up with the receiver in his hand and didn't know whether to throw it at the cradle on the wall where it belonged, or smash it on the table until it broke. He didn't do either. He just dropped it and watched it land on the chair where he'd been sitting, then opened the door onto the balcony and walked out barefoot into the snow and ice and minus twenty. He heard the cars driving past down below on Sveavägen, one by one, as he roared *fucking shitbags* until he was spent.

His bare feet were red when he went in a few minutes later and hurried toward the hall and the mobile phone that was ringing in the pocket of his winter overcoat.

He didn't speak to his boss very often.

Grens had his own territory and worked harder and more effectively than most when left to his own devices, and over the years an unspoken agreement had gradually developed between him and the chief superintendent: you let me be and I'll let you be. And he certainly couldn't remember the last time they had spoken together at night.

"I talked to State Secretary Winge a short while ago, so I knew you were up."

Ewert Grens imagined his boss in front of him. Ten years younger than he was, always neat and tidy in a suit, he reminded him a bit of Ågestam, something about the way they were always so perfect that Ewert had recognized and learned to despise.

"Right."

"And as I understand it, you didn't fully comprehend your orders."

"You could put it that way. No damn wannabe politician is going to take my investigation abroad when there is a person in the hospital who not long ago was hovering between life and death."

"It was *me* who gave Winge your name. So *I* was the one who gave the orders. And . . ."

"Then you'll already know how much I think this whole thing stinks."

"And that is why *I* am now ordering you, on the part of City Police, to ensure that the deportation order is fulfilled."

"Have you got your pajamas on?"

Ewert wondered whether his boss was sitting on the edge of his bed in blue-and-white striped flannel. The asshole wasn't the type to stay up and wander around in his big house fully dressed in the middle of the night.

"Excuse me?"

"You see, it's not my job to carry out orders that come from corrupt cowards."

"I—"

"And what's more, you know as well as I do that deportation equals death for Frey."

The chief superintendent, whose name was Göransson, cleared his throat.

"He's going to Moscow. There's no risk of him being executed there."

"Even you're not that fucking stupid."

Göransson cleared his throat again, louder this time, his voice sharper.

"To be perfectly honest, you can think exactly what you like about all this, Ewert. When you are where you are now. At home. But when you're at work, you will follow orders. And I've never said this to you before. And I won't ever do it again. But if you don't follow my direct orders this time, Ewert, I would advise you to start looking for a new position tomorrow."

Grens threw down the dead telephone and went over to the balcony door, opened it, and went back out. It was just as cold as before, and he didn't notice it this time either. He sat down on one of the plastic chairs that had been left out there all autumn. Hard ice on the cushion, hard ice on the concrete floor. His bare feet almost stuck to it, his skin felt sticky against the otherwise smooth surface.

A clear, starry night.

The city lights meant that the sky was never truly dark, but tonight, it was as dark as it would ever be, every bright light in sharp contrast. It was beautiful and he rested his eyes on it for a few minutes. The sheet-metal roofs around him, cars in the distance, he realized that he didn't sit here often enough, and had probably never done it barefoot in winter before.

It was not difficult for him to lose his temper. The anger lurked there all day. But the feeling he had now wasn't like that, it wasn't as simple as rage. He was angry, frustrated, disturbed, saddened, panic-stricken, frightened, at a loss—all at once and in no particular order.

He sat out there without moving.

Until he knew what to do, at least for the moment.

He would spend the next few hours on the phone. He had to make some calls. As he dialed the first number, he looked down at his bare, red feet and discovered to his surprise that he wasn't cold.

It was nine o'clock on Thursday evening, U.S. time, when Edward Finnigan went down to the bar of the hotel in west Georgetown where he had checked in a few hours earlier. He had stayed there every time he was in town on business, and the woman with the beautiful eyes and Mona Lisa smile had nodded in recognition when he asked whether Room 504 was available.

Norman Hill was already at the table in the far corner, a glass of red wine in front of him. He was the sort who never drank a lot, always and only expensive wines, who knew all about the vintage and how it was stored, who talked about wine with the same passion as they might about lovers. Finnigan normally tasted it and asked polite questions but had never really understood what the fuss was all about. For him, alcohol was a way to relax, so who cared which grape it was that made it possible?

Hill ordered another glass of wine from the same bottle that he'd selected. Finnigan tasted it, made the sort of comment that he thought you were supposed to. He then looked at the copy of an article that was lying on the table and that was to be printed in the *Washington Post* in a few hours' time. A story by an investigative journalist about a prisoner on the run, who had been sentenced to death, and about the demands that were being made for him to be returned to the cell he had escaped from. Finnigan read it and then listened to Hill, who outlined their most recent communication with the Swedish government representatives and a resolution that guaranteed that Frey would be deported out of the country the next day.

"From one communist country to another."

"And then here?"

"Patience, Edward."

"When?"

"On a waiting plane."

Edward Finnigan stood up and went to the bar to buy a cigar. He promised Hill that he would drink the wine first; it was an Australian grape from a vineyard near Adelaide, and he had learned enough to know that wine experts didn't like to mix smells, or maybe it was tastes. Whatever, he would smoke it later, when their glasses were empty, maybe he'd even phone Alice—he longed for her.

Helena Schwarz had reacted in precisely the way Grens had feared. He had woken her and her son, he heard the boy's distressed and sleepy shouts in the background. He had of course realized that a phone call at half past three in the morning would do that but felt that there was no alternative. Outside on the balcony, in the cold, Ewert Grens had decided to ignore all the technicalities implied by the total confidence order imposed on the preliminary investigation. And Schwarz's wife, whom he realized he cared for in some way—her angry and alarmed reactions at the hearing that had been followed by composure appealed to him—was the first person he called.

She had alternately cried and shouted at him and he had let her do it. She understood precisely what he had understood: that John's deportation to Russia was just a political detour on his journey west. She had several times whispered *you can't do this* and had repeated that they had a son and that John had said he was innocent and that the extradition agreement didn't apply to anyone who had been sentenced to death and Grens had waited until she calmed down, until there was silence.

She had asked him to wait on the phone while she went to check on her son and to get a drink of water and they had then talked quietly together about something he couldn't remember until she had suddenly begged him to go too.

At first he hadn't understood.

Go too? Where?

And she had explained and wept and explained again.

If John really was going to leave . . . if it was going to happen, with or without the detective superintendent's intervention . . .

She begged Ewert Grens to be the one to go with him and that his colleagues should also be there: the other man who was slightly younger and seemed so kind, and the girl who her husband seemed to trust when he was being questioned.

If they were there, then at least he would have faces around him that he recognized.

The bar was still quite empty: a young couple holding hands two tables away, a man sitting on his own over by the window reading the newspaper while he waited for the chef's cheeseburger and potato wedges. Norman Hill had just left, his thin body hidden in a gray coat and a hat that was as high as it was wide. Edward Finnigan ordered a bottle of beer and sat with his mobile phone in his hand, hesitating, before he dialed.

He had punched his best friend to the ground and then thrown a penholder at him. They could talk about that later. He had something else he wanted to discuss.

Robert listened while Finnigan gave a summary of his meetings earlier in the day and the evening's final conversation with Hill. Neither of them mentioned the fact that the governor had asked his closest colleague only that morning when they'd argued to let the process run its course, to curb his hate and fervor and wait until everything was resolved.

The unease that had brewed in his chest and that he'd tried to get away from whenever it plagued him the most gradually evaporated until it was nothing, and nothing was not frightening. His voice, his punch, had not destroyed the support that he would soon need more than ever. Their friendship had survived their first confrontation, the one they had both dreaded for so long and had therefore always skirted around.

Robert was still there beside him, he would listen.

And Frey would be on his way in a matter of hours.

It was time for the governor of Ohio to contact the judge who once upon a time had sentenced Elizabeth Finnigan's murderer to death, to accelerate the process of fixing a new date for the execution.

Sven Sundkvist gave up. The night was already lost to him, so just to lie there and wait for sleep made his body ache with impatience. He slipped on a pair of brown slippers and a long-sleeved, polo-neck top. He walked slowly through the terraced house—soon they would have lived there for ten years, and he couldn't imagine them living and getting old anywhere else.

He stopped by the door to Jonas's room. Their little boy who was getting big. He had been less than a year old when they had gone to the town one hundred twenty-five miles west of Phnom Penh; he had been so beautiful, so calm, everything they had longed for. His eighth birthday was fast approaching, he was in second grade and even had homework for English and natural sciences. Sven thought about his discussion with Anita a few hours ago about the child not having any choice. Jonas had not chosen himself to lie snuffling and snoring in this particular house, and he hoped that his son would never hold him to account for it. But *if* he did, he would try to explain as best he could.

But if Schwarz's son wondered if it was true that *his* father had been extradited to face the death penalty, who would he then hold to account—who would have to stand there and explain?

Sven was just about to go in and kiss Jonas on the forehead as he so often did, when an irritated electronic buzz broke the silence. Jonas moaned and turned over in the bed in front of him and Sven sprinted back to the bedroom and the mobile phone that was in there. He sighed when he saw the number: Ewert, another ruined night.

Grens had phoned and quickly explained the situation to Sven Sundkvist, then Hermansson and then Ågestam.

He hadn't had time for questions, a brief conversation, enough to get Sven and Hermansson to understand that they had to be at Kronoberg by six o'clock, and prepared, if so required, to travel and be away longer than their prescribed working hours.

He stood in the kitchen, looked out of the window at the morning that was still some way off. He knew that there wasn't much time. And that he, for the second time in an hour, would ignore the total confidentiality stamp on the preliminary investigation.

Vincent Carlsson answered immediately.

His voice was chirpy, he was working nights, as Grens had hoped he was.

It took ten minutes to explain the whole story in a way that was clear and he could understand. Vincent Carlsson immediately realized who he was talking to and that this was seriously potent news that had just been released by the otherwise taciturn detective superintendent.

There was still plenty of time before the first news broadcast of the day.

And by then, the planned program schedule would have been cleared and replaced, every news item taken out except the one that would dominate. Not only today's news bulletins, but possibly all other bulletins for some days to come.

He looked at his watch, two minutes to four, then he called a meeting with the entire news-desk editorial team.

friday

IT WAS STILL DARK WHEN A CITY POLICE VAN DROVE TOWARD THE MAIN
terminal at Bromma Airport. The air was cold and clear; the vehicle's
headlamps sparkled in icy patches on the road and the exhaust from the
car in front hung in a compact cloud as it often does in extreme
temperatures.

Ewert Grens had left his apartment on Sveavägen two hours ago and
taken a taxi to Kronoberg. Helena Schwarz had phoned him twice in the
space of ten minutes and begged, as she had in their first phone call, that if
the decision to deport her husband was not overturned, then he and his
two colleagues would be the officers who accompanied him out of the
country.

And here he was, sitting in the back of the van, next to Hermansson. In
front of her, Sven with a handcuff around his right wrist, the partner of
which was attached to John Schwarz's left wrist. A young, rather large
police constable was driving, Grens didn't know his name and couldn't be
bothered to ask.

The last few hours had been dreadful.

He had woken everyone who had anything to do with the case, shouted
and told a lot of them to go to hell, and gradually come to accept that John
Schwarz was going to be deported, whether he liked it or not, that this was
politics and the powers that be had acted with greater alacrity than he
could have anticipated.

He hated journalists and normally wanted nothing to do with them and
had never made a secret of it, but the anger inside had driven him to
contact one for the first time in his police career. He had met Vincent
Carlsson two years earlier in connection with a sensational pedophile
murder. Carlsson had known the father, who had shot his daughter's
murderer, and unlike most other TV journalists seemed to be almost wise
and sensible. They had spoken together three times over the past few hours
and Carlsson was now at Hotel Continental in the room where Ruben Frey
had until recently been asleep, while his colleagues gathered and caused a

commotion outside Rosenbad and the Ministry of Foreign Affairs, demanding answers. Grens didn't imagine that it would make the slightest bit of difference, it was too late for that, but the media spotlight would at least blind the damned bureaucrats for a while and shine light on their shit.

He had also made a nighttime call to Kristina Björnsson, the public defense counselor whom John had refused to have present when he was questioned. She had been awake and Grens had for a moment wondered why, before briefing her about the deportation demand, then exhorting her to appeal the decision. She had taken a deep breath and been about to answer when he had continued, asking her to investigate the requirements for political asylum. When he then stopped talking, she had asked in a tired voice whether it was her turn now, and gone on to explain that John hadn't allowed her to entertain any such thoughts, he seemed to have given up, he had no hopes or desires, and besides, there wasn't time—she was nearly whispering when she said this—John would have landed in Moscow before the Migration Board even started its working day. Grens hadn't listened, or had refused to accept what she was saying, he had continued to exhort her, plead with her until he realized that she was right, that these were possibilities that would never be tried.

He turned and looked at him.

John Schwarz seemed to be smaller than ever.

Hunched up, head down, alarmingly loose at the neck, his pale face was gray, his eyes empty; he had closed himself off, was somewhere else. He hadn't said a word, hadn't showed any emotion when they opened the cell and asked him to get dressed in his own clothes and then come with them. Sven had several times tried to start a conversation, spoken about the wind and the weather, asked questions, made provocative claims, but had just been met with silence. Schwarz was unreachable.

They passed a long line of taxis that had already delivered passengers who had an early check-in for the first morning flights. Sleepy travelers had put their luggage down in the road while they got out, and the constable who was driving honked in irritation until they registered the marked vehicle and quickly moved up onto the sidewalk.

The van drove on a few hundred feet past the terminal building, pulled up in front of a wrought-iron gate in the fence, and waited there until it was opened by a man in Air Navigation Services coveralls. He turned when he was ready, nodded to the driver, and then without much success tried to peer into the van, curious to catch a momentary glimpse of the person he assumed was the reason for the secure transport.

There didn't seem to be any wind. But out on the airstrip it was blowing, not hard but enough; at close to minus twenty degrees even the slightest wind could flay any unprotected face in the short distance from the van to the plane.

Ewert Grens studied the government plane before starting to walk toward it.

It was a Gulfstream model, snow-white and a lot smaller than he'd imagined. It had been bought some years ago to shuttle important people between capitals, in advance of Sweden taking over presidency of the EU, and was officially owned by the air force. When it became public knowledge that it had cost two hundred and eighty million kronor, it caused a great deal of grumbling. Grens knew that it was used regularly by the government and the royal family but was certain that this was the first time the tank had been filled to ensure that a person who was suspected of aggravated assault left the country.

A few airport staff were moving about on the asphalt and the runway, others were loading luggage into the hold of Malmö Aviation's early morning flight south, otherwise no one else to be seen, or to see. But Sven still took off his thick winter coat and covered the handcuffs that linked him to Schwarz, the less attention the better.

It was surprisingly spacious inside. Room for fifteen passengers, with soft, white leather seats. They sat in the same positions as they had in the van. Sven with Schwarz beside him, Ewert and Hermansson behind them, with full overview. Four people sitting close together while they waited for a flight that was not going to be particularly long. The plane's fuel tank was large enough to cross the Atlantic, so there was hardly the need to stop before Moscow.

Grens leaned forward between the seats when the pilot started the engines—he tried to make contact with Schwarz, spoke to him without getting a response. The prisoner was still detached, his body language clear; a person retreating to a far-off place.

When Sveriges Television had broadcast a ten-minute report on the night's events at six o'clock in the morning, it was the start of a weeklong focus on John Meyer Frey, the person and the story in which he played the main part. Every news bulletin on all Swedish channels and radio stations, every edition of the Swedish newspapers, carried new information about the American prisoner who had been sentenced to death and escaped, but had then been arrested some years later for aggravated assault, and deported from the country to an impending execution with the Swedish government's consent.

The story had been released into the public sphere following a few brief conversations between a detective superintendent and a TV journalist, and was now subject to the scrutiny that a handful of decision makers had hoped to avoid.

Vincent Carlsson would soon celebrate his fiftieth birthday, which surprised everyone who met him, as he didn't seem to be a day over thirty-five, except for a few gray streaks in his otherwise dark hair; still a boy in an older man's body. When Ewert Grens had phoned him in the middle of the night, as they were preparing for the first news bulletin of the day, he had immediately understood that this conversation would make an impact. Detective Superintendent Grens normally snubbed the press, kept himself to himself until an investigation was over and then left it to a press officer to give succinct answers to any questions. So to call himself and give an anonymous tip, that was almost as unlikely as what he had then proceeded to tell.

Rosenbad had called a press conference for half past seven.

The demand for answers was so overwhelming from the start, the hordes of journalists crowded outside the Ministry of Foreign Affairs so large, that an open press conference was the only solution.

The big conference room in the government building was already full. Seventeen rows of journalists on folding chairs covered in blue fabric, at the front the photographers were focusing on the forest of microphones, at the back the soundmen were desperately trying to ensure that the reporters could hear their feeds properly but had to contend with the hum of one hundred and twenty people, the noise swirling around and ricocheting off the bare walls, dying out only once it reached the skylight forty feet up.

It was a long time since Vincent Carlsson had reported live from the scene, a couple of years working as news editor for the early morning news had meant better working hours and more money, but also being cut off from reality in a large newsroom lined with TV monitors.

Now he was back in the field for a few days, in the other world, the baiting and crush, and he loved it.

He took another step forward, had decided to lean against the wall at the side by the front row, when two men of roughly the same age and wearing similar suits sat down on the green podium at an oblique angle in front of him.

One of them was the minister of foreign affairs and the other looked like State Secretary Thorulf Winge.

It was going to be a nice day in Moscow. It was cold, quite bright, and the air was easy to breathe. It looked like it would be sunny, so the snow-covered surroundings would sparkle.

The most outlying terminal at Sheremetyevo International Airport was about half a mile north of the runway. A newly built smaller part of the huge Moscow airport, secluded from the scheduled flights that landed and took off every minute, to and from worlds outside Russia.

The two morning flights that were normally scheduled to take off from here had been relocated to another terminal earlier that morning. The vast expanses of asphalt were empty and waiting when a small troop of uniformed and armed Russian soldiers were given access.

It was hot in the large government conference room, almost unbearable.

"Why has a person, who was in custody for aggravated assault, been deported?"

Too many people in a closed space, too many lights to be able to adjust the brightness for live transmission, pants that were too heavy and sweaters that were too thick, designed to protect against the winter cold.

"Why was the Migration Board's decision subject to secrecy?"

Already after the minister's opening statement, sweat was trickling down foreheads and cheeks, skin itching with tension, anger, expectation.

"How did the government manage to secure the deportation papers within a couple of days?"

Vincent Carlsson was standing at the front, the cameraman beside him with his lights focused on the podium and the two spokesmen for the Ministry of Foreign Affairs. He had started to ask his questions as soon as the usual pleasantries were over, and the foreign minister had countered each one by referring to the ongoing investigation and national security and the obligation to refrain from commenting on individual cases.

Vincent listened impatiently to the empty platitudes, looked around the room.

His colleagues remained silent.

So it was still his story and he could keep asking questions for a while.

He smiled to himself. At a press conference like this, when the news reeked of something fishy, behavior could easily end up being infantile. He'd seen it so many times before. First they went out onto the savannah, males fighting for territory and the right to fill their bellies, and then they regressed to the sandpit: I had it first, no you didn't, I had it first.

He was glad he didn't have to deal with that aspect at the moment.

"I'm going to keep on asking questions until I get something that at least resembles an answer."

He took a step forward, the cameraman by his side; they were close, one person's face filled the screen.

"State Secretary Winge, can you please explain to us, and to the viewers who right now are waiting for a straight answer, how the government managed to secure the deportation papers in no more than a couple of days? We all know that decisions like that normally involve months of investigation."

Both men on the podium had been up all night. Their eyes were tired, their skin gray. One hundred and twenty journalists were waiting to dissect each and every word, to weigh every hesitation.

Thorulf Winge looked straight at the man who had asked the question and his camera.

"John Meyer Frey has been domiciled in Sweden illegally, without a residency permit, for six years. So the decision to deport him has not only taken 'a couple of days.' It has taken six years and a couple of days."

The state secretary had taken a good many classes in interview technique. He had decided what he would say and would say only that. There was no doubt there, his eyes didn't waver. He knew that each tiny movement was magnified by a camera lens, that any emphasis on a particular word was so much stronger when transmitted via a television screen.

He was slick, Vincent could tell.

"State Secretary Winge, Sweden has a long tradition of yielding to greater powers. It allowed Nazi transport to crisscross its neutrality, and today, we allow prisoners to be held illegally in Cuba while we look the other way. And this . . . well, it feels like we might be reinforcing the tradition here. Yielding, I mean."

"Is that a question?"

"Do you have an answer?"

"Deporting an illegal immigrant who has committed a serious crime in Sweden could hardly be described as yielding."

Vincent couldn't get any closer now, he leaned in toward the podium, his hand holding the microphone right in front of Winge's mouth as he adjusted his jacket: *it's so hot, the sweat is running down my back, irritating.*

"Extraditing someone who has been sentenced to death and risks execution, does that not contravene the extradition agreement between the EU and the USA?"

His eyes just as steady.

"I think you have misunderstood. John Meyer Frey is *not being extradited* to the United States. He is being *deported* to the country he entered from. To Russia."

Two hours and twelve minutes after taking off from Bromma Airport in Stockholm, the Swedish government Gulfstream jet landed at Sheremetyevo International Airport outside Moscow. It then rolled on across the airstrip, several hundred yards to a smaller terminal that was closed to the public for the morning.

John Schwarz had not spoken for the entire journey.

For the first hour, he had sat hunched forward, cradling his head in his free hand. Somewhere over Finland he had tried to stand up, Sven Sundkvist had at first resisted but then looked at Grens, who nodded. They had stood still, felt the plane rolling slightly, and when Schwarz had then started to wander around restlessly, Sven had obligingly stayed by his side in the open cabin until they had finally sat down again in a couple of empty seats toward the rear of the plane. And at roughly the same time, Schwarz had started to sing. Indistinct, quiet, but you could make out the occasional English word. The same monotonous verse without interruption for the rest of the journey.

He seemed to be calmer now, his eyes timidly taking things in, as if he had decided to take some tiny part in this world.

Ewert Grens had found it hard to relax. He was in the process of losing and it made him furious. There was so much in life that could not be predicted. How the hell were you supposed to prepare for something that could never happen? A prisoner who had been sentenced to death for years becomes the subject of one of your investigations and is detained on your order, only to be transported to his own death under your supervision a few days later. He had sworn at everything that could be sworn at during the night on the balcony and later at Kronoberg, holding the phone in his hand. There was nothing left, he was empty and exhausted and longed to be able to lean his head into Anni's, in silence. In her room, beside her, a hand on her cheek and then just sit there, trying to understand what she was looking at through the window out there, what he knew she had waved at.

There was silence when the plane came a halt and the pilot turned off the engines. They remained in their seats until the steps were in place. A time difference of two hours, bright, strong sunlight outside, the day had progressed further here.

When Vincent Carlsson suddenly stopped asking questions and instead asked Thorulf Winge to listen to a short, round man who was standing next to him, no one reacted. Because no one knew who he was. Until he started to speak loudly with Vincent's microphone in front of him, in English with an obvious American accent.

"My name is Ruben Frey. I have a son. Why do you want to kill him?"

After his conversation with Grens, Vincent had gone to Hotel Continental, woken Frey, and told him about the decision that had been made during the night and the early morning transportation. He had then asked him to get dressed and accompany him to a press conference, armed with the ID and accreditation of a producer the same age.

Frey's voice was deep and powerful and no one in the large room had any difficulty in hearing.

"Answer me! I want to know why you want to kill my son!"

This was beyond even the rules of the savannah. But Winge realized that with the camera rolling and the conference being broadcast live, there would be only one loser if he started to tell a desperate father that he couldn't ask questions about his son who risked execution. If he did that or left the premises in a rage, the clip would be shown triumphantly over and over again. He therefore looked calmly at the man who was about the same age as him, his face deep red with agitation and despair.

"Mr. Frey, with all due respect, your son has been convicted of murder in the United States and is on the run. *We* are not the ones who want to kill him. It's *your* country that applies the death penalty."

The small man turned to Vincent, as if looking for support, help in dealing with the civil servant in front of him. He felt a fear that then spilled over into anger, a helplessness that made him want to lash out.

"He faces execution in the United States. You *know* that!"

"Mr. Frey, Russia was a transit country for your son, when he—"

"Damn murderers!"

"—when he illegally entered Sweden. He has been deported back there by the Migration Board. Not by the Swedish government."

Ruben Frey's voice didn't hold any longer.

He clutched his chest as if in pain and wept, his face twisted, as he ran out.

According to the information they had received, the Russian officer was to be a high-ranking one. Ewert Grens checked the shoulders of his uniform, it was true.

He was waiting on the asphalt when they came down the steps, and Grens was struck by the thought that the man a few yards in front of him looked like a parody of every Russian soldier ever shown on film. Tall, abnormally straight backed, crew cut, a face that had forgotten how to laugh or even smile, deep creases in fair cheeks, tense jaw that jutted forward. He was backlit by the strong sun and it wasn't easy to see the six or seven armed men standing behind him.

They all wore uniforms.

And had what were probably Kalashnikovs in their hands.

Grens caught himself almost smiling for a moment at the stereotypical film image, even down to the type of gun.

But he didn't smile.

He greeted the Russian colonel and shook his hand and then waited in silence until Grens, much to his own surprise, suddenly pointed first to himself and then to John and stated that in his capacity as John Meyer Frey's authorized representative he was seeking political asylum in Russia on his behalf. They stared at each other as moment chased moment, strangers with an empty void between them and the constant drone of scheduled air traffic only a few hundred yards away; the officer first explained that he didn't understand Grens's school English, so Hermansson quickly made things clearer, and then he replied that it wasn't possible to give political asylum to someone who was dead, surely the Swedish policeman must understand that.

It was blowing. Ewert Grens felt the wind tugging at them in the open space, he saw the snow lift from the concrete and followed the solid flakes that danced across the airstrip.

He had the whole time been holding a plastic folder with some documents in his hand, it was light and the wind caught it, the papers were ready to fly when he reluctantly handed it over. The colonel read over every page, took out a pen and signed one after the other, still standing out in the open, in the strong wind and without anything to write against.

Grens looked at Hermansson, who was waiting to his left. Her face showed nothing. Behind her Sven, furrowed brow as always when he was stressed, but he still gave off an air of calm, and only someone who had known him well for many years could see that that wasn't the case. Schwarz, on the other hand—he was almost hanging from the handcuffs that were attached to Sven's wrist. The noise was still with him, like a song, monotonous and the same English word mumbled almost inaudibly over and over again.

Ruben Frey ran out of the conference room, down the short flight of white marble stairs and out through the glass doors of the main entrance. He had no overcoat, didn't know where he was going, just that he had to get away from the press conference where he couldn't breathe.

He was crying and two women coming in the opposite direction peered at him curiously, turned when he'd passed and watched him disappear toward Vasagatan.

His extra pounds weighed heavily on his knees and hips as always, and he soon stopped and leaned against a wall when the pain made it impossible to continue.

He didn't care about the passersby who looked for slightly too long at the man who was sweating despite the cold. He waited until his heart was no longer pounding, until he thought he could talk more or less normally. He took his mobile phone from the inner pocket of his jacket and dialed the number of the prison in Marcusville.

He then did what they had agreed. When he heard Vernon Eriksen's voice, he asked the senior corrections officer to call him back from another phone. Eriksen instructed him to wait fifteen minutes. They both knew that he would rush into town to Sofio's, where there was a pay phone, by the toilets, that they had used before.

When Sven Sundkvist unlocked the handcuffs and Schwarz was officially handed over to the colonel who had signed the documents in the plastic folder, the American citizen was promptly positioned in the middle of the formation of armed and alert soldiers.

He was taken away immediately. Six uniforms marching in front, beside, and behind the object they were to escort one thousand feet to the far corner of the newly built terminal.

The intense light made it difficult to see anything other than the outline of the waiting plane.

But the colors painted on the wings looked like they could be an American flag.

The Russian colonel was still standing with the three Swedish police officers, and he felt Grens glaring at him. His face was just as stern, his back just as straight, and he shrugged as he spoke English slowly, with a thick accent, for the second time.

"We're just doing the same as you."

Grens snorted, his English equally clumsy.

"What are you talking about?"

"That."

The officer pointed to Schwarz and his troop a couple of hundred yards away, and the airplane they were now approaching. It hadn't taken more than a couple of minutes to escort John there.

"You got rid of a problem in Sweden. We get rid of the same problem in Russia."

Vernon Eriksen sat down on the large brown leather armchair in the cloakroom at Sofio's with the pay phone receiver to his ear. Ruben Frey had sounded terrible and he had suspected he knew what it was about but still harbored a small hope, as you do until you know for certain.

Now he knew. He had gone to a phone that they guessed would not be tapped and called back. It had taken Ruben nearly ten minutes to summarize what had happened. A matter of days and the Swedish government had yielded. A tiny scrap of a country that pissed itself the moment the big boys so much as coughed. He could see John in front of him. Six years ago. He had hoped then that the past would stop here, on the far side of the Atlantic.

Ruben had found it difficult to talk, his voice had broken several times. Vernon had never had children himself, but in recent years he had made a concerted effort to try to understand and believed that he had come close to what Ruben was feeling, what it felt like to be a father who was about to lose his son.

He put the receiver down and looked around the twenty-four-hour diner.

A few guests sitting alone spread out among the empty tables, some with a sandwich and tepid whiskey in front of them, others with a beer in one hand and the evening news in the other, while a slow Miles Davis number played over the loudspeaker above the bar.

Vernon Eriksen knew that it was over.

It was far from over.

He didn't want to live in a society that murdered its own citizens. This time he would carry out his plan to the full. The one he had had from the start but had lacked the courage to complete once everything got going. Now it didn't matter a damn anymore. John was on his way toward death once again. There was nothing to lose.

Vernon listened to the haunting trumpet, looked out into the dark.

This time.

This time he had to dare to go the whole way.

Ewert Grens, Sven Sundkvist, and Hermansson had just sat down in the plane again when they saw the humiliation through the oval windows.

The light was filtered for a few minutes through some thin clouds and it was not difficult to see what was happening some way off.

Six armed uniforms deposited John at the bottom of the steps up to the American plane. To new guards. Dark suits, four, possibly five of them.

It didn't take long to cut up his clothes, it was cold and his thin, pale frame was shaking. He was body searched and then had to bend forward while a sedative was stuck up his anus.

The diaper they put on him was a plain white, the orange coveralls declared *DR* in big letters on his back and outside leg. No shoes, his bare feet on the asphalt.

Handcuffs around his wrists, leg irons around his ankles.

Short, shuffling steps as they led him onto the plane.

When Ruben Frey went to the reception of Hotel Continental to pick up his room key, a man dressed in a blue uniform waved to him from the back office. He was given his key by a young woman who smiled at him from behind the counter, then stood there waiting for the older man who had attracted his attention.

"Mr. Frey?"

"Yes?"

The man gave him a friendly, practiced smile, just like the girl behind reception who had given him the key.

"A woman called here looking for you. She seemed to be very keen to get hold of you, she didn't give in until I promised to pass on the message personally. Which I'm doing now. Here. She left her number."

"A woman?"

Ruben Frey thanked him and asked if he could use the phone in reception—he didn't particularly want to use his own and leave traces when he didn't know who would answer.

Her voice was high.

"Ruben Frey?"

She pronounced his name perfectly. And she was nervous, he could feel it.

"Who am I talking to?"

"My name is Helena Schwarz."

He felt winded, just under the ribs. As if someone had punched him where he was least protected.

"Hello?"

It was difficult to speak.

"Schwarz?"

"I took the name when I married John. Our son, Oscar, is also named Schwarz."

Ruben Frey sat down on a chair by the reception desk.

"I have to meet you."

"I didn't know that you existed. That I had a father-in-law. That Oscar had a grandfather."

"Where are you now?"

His breathing started to even out again and was almost regular by the time she answered.

"Turn around. The table by the window, about halfway down the big room."

They cried as they embraced. For several minutes they stood in the hotel dining room and held someone they had never met before, tight. He kissed her on the forehead and she stroked his cheeks, and she smiled when she loosened her grip and pulled back a bit so they could look at each other.

"There."

She pointed over his shoulder.

"Can you see him?"

At the back of the lobby there was something that looked like a children's corner. Colorful cardboard figures in a tepee, two tables beside it with books, paper, pens, and big multicolored Lego pieces. A boy was sitting at one of them, drawing with great concentration on a sheet of green paper. Ruben found it difficult to gauge his age, it was so long since he had had anything to do with small children, but he guessed around five or six.

"Five. The year after John came here. I must have got pregnant the first time we met."

She took Ruben by the hand and started to walk slowly toward the boy. They stopped just behind him, didn't move, and the boy, Oscar, didn't notice; all that existed for him was the big house that he was drawing with a red crayon.

Ruben had short, robust legs that normally stood solid. But now they were shaking and there was nothing he could do.

"Oscar."

Helena Schwarz had squatted down beside her son, one arm around his shoulders.

"There's someone here I'd like you to meet."

He hadn't finished the house. There should be some smoke coming out of the chimney, and a flowerpot in the window and the sun, half hidden, in the top right-hand corner.

"Nice house."

Ruben swallowed, felt stupid, he'd said it in English, as he couldn't speak a word of Swedish.

The house was finished and the boy turned toward the man who had just spoken.

"Thank you."

Oscar flashed a smile and then turned around again. Ruben looked at Helena, she laughed, the kind of uninhibited laughter that sometimes is surprisingly loud when in stark contrast to everything else.

"He's bilingual. I've always spoken Swedish to him, and John always spoke English. We thought that was the best way, to learn two languages naturally. Which means you can talk to each other."

Ruben Frey sat down at the low children's table in front of the colorful tepee and stayed there for the next two hours. To live six years in the remains of a morning was impossible, but they tried, and at times it was as painful as it then was easy to embrace a minute later. He glossed over the boy's questions that interrupted every now and then: did he know where his daddy was, when was Daddy coming back, why wasn't Daddy where he should be.

They ate lunch in the hotel restaurant and then went upstairs to his room. Oscar lay on the bed and watched cartoons on a children's channel with characters that all looked the same, so Ruben and Helena were able sit in the armchairs at the back of the room and speak together quietly.

Ruben Frey talked about his son who had grown up in Marcusville alone with his father, how things had gone wrong early on, an aggression that none of them could understand and two short stints in juvenile correctional institutions for convictions of assault. It hadn't been easy, and at times John had not been particularly lovable.

Ruben held his daughter-in-law's hands tight.

John's baggage, his dark past, had become his noose the day that the Finnigan girl was found dying in her parents' bedroom.

He is not a murderer.

Ruben had for a moment forgotten Oscar in front of the TV with the cartoon characters, and raised his voice.

He is not a murderer.

John had at times been a damn fool, he had undoubtedly had a relationship with Elizabeth Finnigan, and it had been proved that they'd had sex earlier that day, there were traces of him all over the house, *but that doesn't make him a murderer.*

Ruben Frey explained to his son's wife that he believed in capital punishment, that he had voted for it every time since he'd come of age, and that *if* John had been guilty, he would also have deserved to give up his life. But Ruben was certain, the lawyers who had gone through the judgment later had all supported him, there were flaws, a long chain of circumstantial evidence, but nothing else.

He told her about the escape.

Helena Schwarz listened and she realized that John's vague memories tallied with what she was hearing.

So he had been telling the truth in the interview room.

He had also said he was innocent.

She clutched the round man's hands, looked over at her son who was half asleep on the bedspread listening to the familiar sound of the TV, and she couldn't bear to think where her husband might be right now.

THE INTENTIONAL HUMILIATION OF JOHN SCHWARZ WAS POSSIBLY THE most offensive that Grens had ever seen. During his thirty-four years in the police he had investigated many acts that he didn't think living beings were capable of, met people who were so disturbed that he found it difficult to describe them as human. Only a couple of years earlier he had seen, on the autopsy table, what remained of a five-year-old girl's genitalia that had been shredded with a metal instrument, and he had been convinced that a person could never be abused in a more grotesque way.

But this, this was just as terrible.

Not the physical pain, not the physical consequences, not anything that could be seen externally; Schwarz had only had to stand naked in minus fifteen on the open airstrip and have a enema stuck up his anus before being pushed barefoot across the asphalt.

It was more a question of who the abuser was.

A person who stuck sharp metal objects up a little girl's vagina was a sick bastard who should be locked up, Grens was convinced of that, just as someone who raped another person should be locked up, or someone who assaulted another person should be locked up. Anyone who deliberately abused someone else should, in the world that Ewert Grens tried to inhabit, be penalized. So far, so simple. Even though it was not possible to understand the abuse, it was in certain cases possible to imagine that the sick people he encountered when they were arrested were capable of it.

But this.

These were presumably people who were healthy in body and mind, doing their job, carrying out a task as ordered by the authority that paid their salaries.

Humiliate.

As much as possible.

When we've got him again, he's to be undressed outside, his bare penis seen by everyone who's watching, make him bend over so we can shove a suppository up his ass and then put a diaper on him, let him know that we're watching, let him know that the state can violate you if it wants to.

Ewert Grens looked out of the window at the white fluffy clouds as they passed through them.

He had never experienced a humiliation that was so impossible to understand, an abuser who was so elusive. A state. An authority. This time it wasn't possible to explain it away with one-off, psychologically sick; this was a pact with the electorate, the people.

None of them said a word on the flight home.

They listened to music on their earphones and flicked through the morning papers that had been lying on the tables even before they left Sweden. Grens, Sundkvist, Hermansson—they tried not to look at each other, scared that they might then be expected to strike up a conversation.

They parted at Bromma Airport. Ewert Grens asked Sven and Hermansson to go directly home and take the rest of the day off, then use the weekend to forget, and to spend time with people they liked being with. Sven had muttered that with Grens as his boss, he knew how things usually turned out when he tried to take time off, and they had managed to muster a laugh before he got into a taxi, paid for by the City Police, that would take him all the way from the airport to his home in Gustavsberg.

It was a long time since he'd seen the terraced house in daylight on a weekday.

He'd phoned Anita and asked her to come home early, and Jonas to stay at home instead of just dumping his backpack and disappearing off with his skates to one of the local ice rinks. He wanted them to be a family this Friday. Together. The only one he had, the only people he needed.

It didn't go as planned.

He hugged them before taking off his coat. They were sitting at the kitchen table drinking orange soda and eating cinnamon buns, they looked at the class photographs that Jonas had brought home with him from school for approval, and laughed loudly when Sven went and got his old photos and compared. Jonas rolled around on the floor howling with laughter when he understood that the short boy with long blond hair on the far left was his dad when he was the same age as Jonas was now.

It didn't help.

Sven had felt the way things were going since the morning. When they'd finished laughing at the boy who refused to cut his hair, he couldn't hold it back any longer. He wept. Tears streaming down his cheeks and he didn't want to pretend.

"Why are you crying, Daddy?"

Anita looked at him. Jonas looked at him.

"I don't know."

"Why?"

"I can't explain."

"Why, Daddy?"

He looked at Anita. How can you explain something to a child that you don't understand as an adult? She shrugged. She didn't know. But didn't try to stop him.

"There's a little boy. That's why I'm sad. It's like that sometimes, when bad things happen, especially if you've got a little boy too."

"What boy?"

"A boy you don't know. His daddy might die soon."

"Do you know for certain?"

"No."

"I don't understand."

"He lives in a different country. The United States, you know. There are lots of people there who think that he killed another person. And there . . . they kill people who kill people."

Jonas sat down on the chair again. He drank what was left of his sweet, orange soda. He looked at his father, as children do when they're far from satisfied.

"I don't understand."

"Nor do I."

"I don't understand who kills someone."

Sven Sundkvist was proud of the questions he asked, to have a child who had learned to think for himself, but he was desperate for want of a reasonable answer.

"The state. The country. I can't explain it any better."

"Who decides that he's going to be killed? There must be someone who decides, isn't there?"

"A jury. And a judge. You know, in court, like you've seen on TV."

"A jury?"

"Yes."

"And a judge?"

"Yes."

"Are they people?"

"Yes, they're people. Ordinary people."

"Who's going to kill them, then?"

"They're not going to die."

"But if they decide that someone's going to die, then they're killing them. And then they have to die too. And who's going to do that, Dad? I don't understand."

Ewert Grens had gone straight from Bromma Airport to the police headquarters at Kronoberg, with Hermansson sitting beside him in the backseat of the waiting police van. He had had no idea what he was going to do there. He had eaten a vending machine lunch in his office, two Danishes and a square carton of orange juice, from one of the machines in one of the corridors that he passed on his way up. He had phoned the nursing home and spoken to a woman in reception who said that Anni was sleeping, that she had been tired after lunch and fallen asleep in her wheelchair. There was nothing wrong with her, she was well and looked peaceful with her head on her shoulder, gentle snores that could be heard through the door. He had then sat down behind a pile of ongoing investigations that had been pushed to one side for the past week, leafed through a couple of them: aggravated assault of a driver who had made an offensive hand gesture at another driver on Hamngatan in the middle of rush hour and then driven off; a murder in Vårberg with a Colombian necktie, witnesses who hadn't seen anything and a series of interviews using interpreters who hardly dared to translate. Cases that had been left too long and now smelled as bad as their chances of actually catching the perpetrator.

He should go home. There was only a gnawing unrest here. He did a circuit of the room, listened to his music. He wasn't going to go back.

Someone knocked on the door.

"I thought I sent you home."

Hermansson smiled at his angry voice, asked if she could come in and then did, without waiting for an answer.

"Yes, but there wasn't any point. I can't go home after all this. How would I deal with it at home? You can't just dump something like this in a tiny rented apartment."

She sat down where she normally sat, in the middle of his big but worn sofa. She looked tired, her young eyes had aged since the morning.

"What is it?"

She swallowed, looked at the floor, then up at her boss.

"You remember Ågestam's theory that two percent of everyone in prison is innocent or has been wrongly convicted?"

The young prat of a prosecutor. He was glad he hadn't had to deal with him today.

"Old truths."

"I checked with something called the Ohio Department of Rehabilitation and Correction. Just there, in the state of Ohio alone, there are one hundred and fifty-five people sitting on Death Row, awaiting execution. One hundred and fifty-four men and one woman. If the two percent theory applies there too, and why shouldn't it, that means that three of them will be executed without even being guilty. Ewert, look at me, do you realize what I'm saying? If it should ever be proven that someone who is innocent has been executed, then nothing can be done to right that wrong. Don't you understand?"

Grens looked at her, as she had asked him to do. She was upset, more sad than angry, a young person who had just started out, who still had so much crap to see and wade through. He was holding a newspaper in his hand, waved it at her.

"Do you want to go out for something to eat this evening? There's a show at Hamburger Börs. Siw Malmkvist. She sings while you eat. I haven't seen her live for thirty years."

"Ewert, what are you saying? I'm talking about people who are going to be executed."

He stopped waving the paper around and sat down, suddenly deflated; it was hard to look her in the eye.

"And I'm talking about the fact that you forced me to go out the other day when I wasn't aware that I needed it. Now I'm going to force you. I want you to think about something else."

"I don't know."

Again. He was going to bring himself to say it again, and look at her while she listened.

"I haven't asked a woman out . . . I don't know . . . it's so long ago. And I don't want you to think this is . . . well, you know . . . it would just be nice to return the invitation. No more than that."

The smell of grilled meat, flowery perfume, and sweat hit you as soon as you went in; the cloakroom was in the foyer and it cost twenty kronor to hang up your coat. Ewert Grens was wearing the same gray suit as a couple of nights ago. He smiled and tried to feel light, almost happy, a bubbling up from his belly through his body and out through his eyes that should shine. For a few hours he would force all the crap down where it couldn't be seen, he would forget the madmen and the humiliation, with a smart young woman by his side and Siw Malmkvist on the stage, good things in a crappy life that never ceased to amaze him.

Hermansson was wearing a beige dress with a sparkly top. She was beautiful and he bashfully told her so. She thanked him, put her arm through his and he felt proud as they walked side by side into the large venue with white tablecloths and shiny porcelain. He estimated there were about four hundred people, perhaps a few more, all there to eat and drink and chat and then drink a couple of glasses more while they waited for Siw.

He liked her a lot. The daughter he'd never had. She made him feel happy, needed, alive. He let it show and she registered it and he hoped that it didn't frighten her.

People everywhere were laughing loudly and ordering more wine, the background music was some smooth American sixties number, even the elderly man to Hermansson's right was excited and put down his cane and flirted wildly with her. She tried to laugh, he was sweet, probably in his eighties, but it didn't work after a while.

They were there to forget. That's what they had to do this evening.

"Do you know when Sweden abolished the death penalty?"

Hermansson had moved her plate and leaned over the table. Grens wasn't sure whether he'd heard her right.

"I'm sorry, Ewert. I can't do it. It won't go away. And you've got all dressed up and the food is good and Siw is about to sing. It doesn't help. I can't get away from this morning and Sheremetycvo."

Sometimes you can't push the crap down as far as you'd like.

The old man to her right tapped her on the shoulder, whispered something to her and expected her to laugh. She didn't.

"I'm sorry, but I'm talking to my companion here."

She turned back to Grens.

"Do you know, Ewert?"

"Hermansson."

"When Sweden abolished the death penalty?"

He sighed, emptied his glass of full-bodied red wine.

"No. I'm here for different reasons."

"Nineteen seventy-four."

He had decided not to listen but looked as astonished as he was.

"What did you just say?"

"The nineteen seventy-four amendment. Until then, we still had the death penalty. Even though the last execution was long before that."

A waiter hurried past behind him with some bottles on a silver tray. Grens called over and asked him to fill their empty glasses.

"Three years later, the first execution was carried out in the United States following the reintroduction of the death penalty. A firing squad in Salt Lake City that caused an international outcry in the media. The state of Utah shot the person, up and down, several times. And they're still doing it. The last one was only a year or so ago."

Grens lifted his glass and took a drink without tasting it.

"You've been reading up."

"When we got back from Bromma. I couldn't concentrate on anything useful."

When Siw Malmkvist came onto the stage ten rather quiet minutes later, only a few yards away from him, Grens felt how life can sometimes stop, a frozen moment, no yesterday, no tomorrow, just now, Siw in front of him and every lyric that was stored in his heart now made him fizz over as he sang along as loud as he dared to.

He remembered the first times he'd seen her onstage. Folkets Park in Kristianstad, he had even been able to get up close and take some black-and-white photos that he still sometimes took out and looked at. She had been so bold, so powerful, and he had fallen in love with the singer from a distance, despite Anni. He still felt the same. She was up there burning brightly, she wasn't young anymore, moved more slowly and had a deeper voice, but she was there for him and he was just as infatuated with her as back then.

It was in the middle of the chorus of the fifth song that his mobile phone interrupted the music with a shrill electric ring. "California, Here I Come," he remembered the cover, Siw's EP from Metronome, with the bright red scarf on her head and the same shade of lipstick, as she smiled at whoever was buying the record.

It rang three times before he managed to get it out of his trouser pocket, and a good many people turned around in irritation to see where the noise was coming from.

Helena Schwarz.

He couldn't hear what she was saying, as her voice was so high.

He was trying to get her to calm down when the music suddenly stopped at the end of the third verse. One of Stockholm's largest venues held its breath, four hundred stunned people, first looking up at the stage and the female artist who was standing there holding a microphone without making a sound, then at the large man in his fifties who was sitting at one of the front tables with a phone to his mouth whispering slightly too loud.

"Am I disturbing you?"

Siw Malmkvist had turned toward the table where they were sitting, toward him, her voice was friendly but the message clear.

"Please, don't mind me. Of course I'll wait. Until you've finished talking, that is."

The audience laughed. Jolly from the wine and full of good food, they admired the legend who tackled the embarrassing situation so well. Hermansson kept her eyes on the table while Ewert Grens stood up and mumbled something inaudible about being a policeman, then hurried out through the same door he had come in two hours earlier.

Helena Schwarz continued to speak too loudly until he was well out of the room and could therefore, in an equally loud voice, ask her to take a deep breath and calm down, to tell him what had happened in a normal voice.

She cried as she spoke.

She had just found out that a judge in Ohio had set the date for John Meyer Frey's execution.

Schwarz had barely left Sheremetyevo International Airport and Moscow when the process of setting an execution date, which was normally very protracted, was already complete.

Schwarz had not even landed in the country to which he was being transported by the time the court had processed his case and set the *exact* time of his death.

Ewert Grens listened to the wife's incoherent monologue for a few minutes and then asked her to hang up, he would call her back later, but he had a couple of things he needed to do first.

He then made a quick call to the duty security manager at the Ministry of Foreign Affairs and got the answer he wanted. When he opened the door back into the venue, Siw was singing her version of "Lucky Lips" and he stood swaying and smiling through half the old hit before once again walking through the room while the show was going on and drawing looks that quickly changed from enjoyment to irritation—a woman of around his age with fiery red hair set in a bun even shook her fist at him as he passed.

He stopped behind Hermansson, who pretended not to notice, bent forward and whispered in her ear that he had to leave, that she could of course stay if she wanted to, and if not he would pay for her taxi home.

She followed him out, trying to hide behind his broad back to avoid the contempt.

Her light-colored coat that looked new and his dark overcoat that once had been; the boy in the cloakroom put back the empty coat hangers with a look of surprise on his face as the whole house sang along.

"Ewert, what's going on?"

It was cold outside, just as it had been early in the morning, this day seemed like it would never fucking end.

"I'm going to the Ministry of Foreign Affairs. I have to talk to the people in charge. A person who called me at home in the middle of the night, less than twenty-four hours ago."

"I can tell that you're furious."

"That was Helena Schwarz on the phone. The date for the execution has already been set."

Grens had never seen Hermansson get really angry. Control, that was the word that popped up when he thought about how to describe her response to emotions. Now she turned her face up to the dark sky and struggled not to scream, not to cry.

"I'm coming with you."

"I'm going to do this alone."

"Ewert—"

"It's not up for discussion. I'll get you a taxi."

"*You* are not going to pay for *me* to get home."

Someone came out into the foyer behind them and they heard the applause that rushed out through the doors and windows. The audience was having a good time.

"Then I won't. But I do want you to take a car home. If nothing else, for the sake of an old-fashioned S.O.B."

Grens dialed the number for the police command post despite her protests and ordered a radio car to pick Detective Sergeant Hermansson up from Jakobs Torg and drive her home to Kungsholmen. Then he started to walk. The clock on Jakob's Church struck twice and he looked up at the illuminated face: half past ten. It wasn't more than a couple of hundred yards to the Ministry of Foreign Affairs, and the man with a limp, dressed in a smart suit, didn't meet anyone on his way there, so his face, flushed red with fury, did not draw any attention.

PART IV

two months later

tuesday evening, 2100 hours

twenty-four hours left

HE HAD LAIN ON THE BUNK FOR THE FIRST FOUR WEEKS. AS IF HE HAD already died. The green ceiling had been repainted, a shade of light blue. The smell had been the same. A single breath and the six years of freedom had never happened. He had tried not to gag but then had to throw up until he was empty and could smell that smell again and had to spew again. He had lain staring up at the light that was always on, didn't blink even though his eyes ached—it had been hard to see anything after a couple of days. He had not said a word. Not to the Mexican in the next cell, not to the guy with the German name on the other side. Not even to the senior corrections officer whom he knew so well; Vernon Eriksen had stood outside the cell and asked all sorts of friendly questions, but John hadn't even been able to get up, turn around, open his mouth.

The cold seeped in from the rectangular windows up under the ceiling in East Block. There was still some snow, as was usual in March, the last remnants before spring took over.

Ewert Grens had fallen asleep around midnight. He had curled up on the too-short sofa in his office at the City Police headquarters until his dreams had stopped hounding him. He sat up now, wide awake, his back aching, his neck stiffer than ever.

The investigation was closed and he had gone back to work. It was still unclear what exactly had happened two months earlier when he'd walked from a show in a restaurant, dressed in a suit, his breath smelling of alcohol, to the Ministry of Foreign Affairs, got past security, and forced his way into the state secretary's room. There were witness statements that spoke of arguments and someone who passed the office also thought they heard the detective superintendent shouting words that Thorulf Winge later claimed were unlawful threats when he reported the incident, statements that could not be proved.

Grens looked at the alarm clock that stood on his desk. Just after three, night in Stockholm, evening in Ohio.

Suddenly he realized why he'd woken up.

Exactly twenty-four hours until the execution.

He got up and left the room, wandered down one of the many dark corridors of the police headquarters. A coffee from the machine, a stale bun from a basket on a table in a staffroom, someone had obviously been celebrating and brought in coffee and cake and left what hadn't been eaten for others.

He had never been prevented from working before. A month without being allowed to come here. The investigation and suspension had transformed daily life into living hell, nowhere to go, nothing to do to while away the time. If it hadn't been clear before, it certainly was now, crystal clear, that there was nothing else.

The corridors echoed as he limped through the dark. He was at home here, sad or not, that was the truth and he hadn't thought of apologizing.

Twenty-four hours left. A person was going to be executed, a process that Grens himself had unwittingly started was now coming to a close; a person, maybe even an *innocent* person, was going to die in a nation-state's name. Grens would continue to pursue people who abused others forever and laugh every time they spat at him from behind bars. But death? If he had ever wondered what he really thought of the death sentence, he now knew.

Another bun from the basket on his way back to the office again, where he sat down at the desk.

He was going to make a phone call. He should have done it a long time ago.

Grens lifted the receiver, wished the switchboard lady good evening, and asked to be connected to a number in Ohio, in the United States. It felt good to hear Ruben Frey's surprised voice a few seconds later, and he explained that he just wanted to say to him and Helena Schwarz that he was thinking about them.

The warden of the Southern Ohio Correctional Facility looked at the telephone demanding attention on his desk. He turned around, let the ringing beat against the walls of his big office. He moved slowly from the desk to the group of sofas and a small dish of after-dinner mints, from there to the window with a view of the town that was waiting, a few miles away. He had taken the phone calls to begin with, explained to each journalist and anyone who was interested that he had set up an inquiry, that he, especially, was anxious to establish how, six years ago, an inmate had managed to escape his execution, from a prison from which it was impossible to escape.

He looked out into the dark, counted the streetlamps along the road that linked a wall with the rest of the world, balls of light that softened the night that was finally free of snow.

Eight weeks and still he knew nothing.

Frey had refused to talk, he had been questioned by the FBI and the prison's head of security. And all the others, the corrections officers and anyone who had ever had anything to do with Frey, which eventually was the greater part of Marcusville's inhabitants, all those interviews and still absolutely nothing.

It was evening outside, and he longed to be out there.

Twenty-four hours to go. He turned around and looked at the telephone that was now screaming for his attention, he would just let the noise echo around the room, it would soon be over. The investigation and interviews had led to nothing, but he didn't begrudge them—quite the opposite—there had been no revelations of any errors on the part of the prison at the time of John Meyer Frey's disappearance.

What had happened had happened.

The sooner the truth about the escape was forgotten both inside and outside the prison, the better.

He remembered the conversations with Marv. John missed having someone to talk to, about death, someone who knew, someone else who knew *exactly* when.

Marv had often spoken about a town.

About two hundred white people and one black man.

John knew all about that now. He'd been on his own in towns like that all his life. On the lawns of Marcusville as he grew up, a decade in the corridor in East Block, six years and two days in Sweden. He knew who the town's only black man was. That fucking veil all around him everywhere, he couldn't touch them, he could never reach out to them.

A couple of times he'd knocked on the wall and waited for Marv's answer. It had all felt so familiar, so easy to forget the years that had passed since they spoke to each other for the last time, before he was taken away.

Alice Finnigan was putting her clothes on the chair by her bed when she felt the hands stroking her back. They carried on up and grabbed her breasts from behind and held them like no one had held them for years. She heard her husband's warm breath on her neck. She didn't dare move at all, scared of doing something wrong, scared of feeling the wrong thing. Edward hadn't touched her for so long. Not even tried, apart from the day when they'd heard that John Meyer Frey was still alive and therefore could still be killed. She had rejected him then. She couldn't do it again. She felt the force of his erection push against her bottom and she turned around. His cheeks were red, his neck flushed, he held her so tight that it hurt when they lay down. His eyes were almost happy when he looked at her, and he moved back and forth with an energy she thought he no longer had, he was so fervent, he wanted to feel her around him.

She tried to suppress her revulsion when he wanted to lie close to her afterward, when his sticky penis nudged her thigh.

Sven sat on a chair in Jonas's room. Anita had been asleep for a few hours now in the room next door and his son was breathing deeply in the bed in front of him, the sleep of babes, free of worry. In the weeks that had passed since he broke down in tears in front of his family, they had spoken several times about the prisoner who Sven had accompanied out of the country and who was now going to die. Jonas had been actively interested in the at times intense media focus that was so evident on TV and in the papers. He had written an essay in school about people who had to be punished and die, in art he had drawn pictures of people lying in front of executioners with black hoods on their heads; a catalogue of execution methods from the mind of an eight-year-old.

Sven looked at his son, his small body that twitched every now and then under the covers and soft, fluffy animals. Perhaps it was good to talk to his son about life and death, he had thought about it many times. But not like this. He was certain that a child's reflections on death should not start with the question of a state's right to take life.

John Meyer Frey had been informed that Revised Code 2949.22 no longer gave every prisoner the right to choose his or her own method of execution, but the Ohio Department of Rehabilitation and Correction guaranteed that the execution would be carried out in a professional, humane, and dignified manner.

He had ironically asked for the firing squad—it had to be that quick—

but the warden who was standing in front of him waiting for his answer told him curtly that the state of Ohio wasn't allowed to shoot people to death.

He had asked to be hanged, as it meant that your neck was broken and you weren't slowly strangled, just a few seconds, alive one minute, dead the next—but the state of Ohio wasn't allowed to hang people.

He had asked for the electric chair, but the state of Ohio was no longer allowed to generate nine hundred to two thousand volts and pass them through a person's body.

His choice: lethal injection.

He had been dreaming a lot, last night as well.

Helena Schwarz stood in the hall of Ruben Frey's large house in Marcusville. She looked at her father-in-law's back, concentrated on the telephone conversation he was about to finish. She had listened to his responses and understood that it was someone calling to see how John was, how they all were, waiting. She wasn't sure, but it could be that middle-aged policeman from Stockholm—a few of the things that Ruben had said gave that impression. It was hard to understand, it had been so intense, but she hadn't thought about him or anyone else at all since she came here nearly six weeks ago now; the only things that mattered were here.

"Mr. Grens."

So it was him.

"What did he want?"

"Nothing, I don't think. Just to ask how we were."

Helena had been trying to put her son to bed since eight o'clock. It was now nearly half past nine. He could feel it, of course he could, something that was more important than sleep, that made his mother and grandfather anxious and sad, he had picked up on it and was therefore anxious and sad himself.

They couldn't pretend any longer.

Helena didn't try to avoid it, to hide away. She cried for the first time since they'd come to Ohio, while her son watched. Maybe it was his right to see, maybe she didn't care.

She sat on the flowery sofa in Ruben's sitting room and read a long and well-written article in the *Cincinnati Post* about how the twelve members of a special execution team at the Southern Ohio Correctional Facility had for the past month been preparing to carry out the execution of John Meyer

Frey at nine the following evening. She didn't know why she was reading it—she had previously avoided all information of this sort on purpose—but it felt like she'd given up now, as if he really was going to die, and if that was the case, she had to know, maybe for John's sake, maybe for her own.

The most difficult thing, according to the journalist who had drawn on research from several executions and had met all the members of the execution team, was getting the needles in the right veins. Since the first execution by lethal injection in nineteen eighty-two in Huntsville—a black man called Charles Brooks—several had turned into a shambles when the execution team couldn't find a usable vein. The journalist gave several examples where the convict was lying strapped to the bed while they tried to find a suitable vein for thirty-five minutes, forty-five minutes, in front of the waiting witnesses. In a couple of cases, the prisoner had a long history of drug abuse and had eventually offered and been allowed to identify a suitable vein. In another case, the execution quite simply had to be abandoned when the needles came loose and the shunts pumped chemicals out into the room and on to the glass window in front of the shocked viewers.

"Mommy?"

His pajamas were blue, different colored crocodiles in something that presumably was supposed to look like water.

"Yes?"

"I want to come too."

"Not this time. I'm going to meet Daddy by myself this evening."

"I want to."

"Tomorrow. You can come with me tomorrow."

He snuggled into her, curled up on a cushion. She stroked his cheek, his hair. One of the local channels—she could never differentiate between them—was on the TV. A reporter standing in front of the solid wall of Marcusville prison spoke excitedly about the fact that there were only twenty-four hours to go until Ohio's third execution of the year, about John Meyer Frey's escape and return, and the sentence that now, many years later, was about to be fulfilled. Then a short clip from a press conference with the governor of Ohio that was interrupted when a group of activists opposed to the death penalty had leapt onto the stage and handed over hundreds of letters of protest, long lists of names and signatures.

Helena Schwarz listened but wasn't sure that she'd understood.

That it was her husband they were talking about. That it was for real.

When a Catholic priest was interviewed and condemned the death penalty as a *barbaric relic in a modern society*, she looked at her son again, wondered whether he understood, if he knew that his father was going to die, that it was him who all these people they didn't know were talking about.

She watched him for a few minutes without saying anything, then stood, lifted up her son and held him in her arms, explained that she had to go, that Granddad was going to stay at home with him.

It was cold out, windy, and more snow.

She was on her way to the prison, she would soon see him alone for the last time, in a new cell and for two hours.

She knew that it was unusual to be allowed to go there at this time of night and she was grateful to Vernon Eriksen, who had made it possible, and yet she resented every step she took, wanted to turn around, go home, close her eyes, and wake up when it was all over.

John heard them before they'd even passed through central security. Not because they said anything—they weren't talking—not because their keys were rattling, it was the footsteps of the five men in the corridor, black boots with hard heels on dirty concrete. He was lying on the bunk with his face turned toward the bars and he waited until they were outside, until Vernon Eriksen cleared his throat and John felt the words on his skin.

"Are you ready, John?"

He stayed lying there for a few minutes longer, the newly painted ceiling, the light that was always on, the smell he couldn't bear to swallow anymore. He got up and looked at the senior corrections officer, whom he respected, at the four others standing a bit farther back, whom he didn't know.

"No."

"We have to go now, John."

"I'm not ready."

"You've even got someone waiting for you there."

Handcuffs, leg irons. He'd seen others being taken away. He knew what it looked like. They were on their way to the Death House, an even smaller cell with a red floor that sat next to the chamber where he would be strapped to a gurney twenty-four hours later, while people watched on the other side of the glass window.

wednesday morning, 0900 hours

twelve hours left

THE UNREST IN THE CORRIDORS OF MARCUSVILLE PRISON INCREASED during the night, loud cries for help, the uncontrollable fear that a long wait might stop; someone was going to be executed and every time that happened their own end came closer. It was not unexpected, the unrest was a malignant tumor that could never be removed, the prison staff had often experienced it since the state of Ohio had resumed capital punishment a few years back.

That was why none of them even questioned the prison management's decision to keep all cells in all corridors locked for twenty-four hours from nine o'clock that morning. The unrest could escalate into protests and riots, and keeping the doors locked until an execution was over and the anguish of the following night had eased was the simplest way to guarantee continued security.

John Meyer Frey sat on a stool in one of the cells of what was called the Death House. Even smaller than a normal cell, clean to the point of sterile, there was nothing personal here, there was no smell here, a stool and a washbasin and a pot to shit in, a red floor covering that did the hating for the prisoner who no longer had the energy to do that himself. He had been informed that the camera on the wall opposite was constantly on and the images were transmitted to a monitor in the observation room that was watched by no fewer than three people at any one time. With only twelve hours left to live, the likelihood of a breakdown was acute.

John had a piece of paper on his knee, a pen in his hand.

He had been trying to write the instructions for his funeral and a will for a couple of hours now, but found it impossible; he couldn't formulate the consequences of his own death.

He looked up at the camera, threw up his hands, asked in a too loud voice for those watching to come to the cell and take away the paper, to throw it away, things could run their own course.

Anna Mosley and Marie Morehouse had been two very young law school graduates when they had worked with Ruben Frey and Vernon Eriksen six years earlier in the Ohio Coalition to Abolish the Death Penalty, which had used the prayer room in a hospital in Columbus as its base. They were now partners in their own firm with an office on the ground floor of a dilapidated building on North Ninth Street.

They had been devastated the day that John was found dead on his cell floor.

They had for the past six years known absolutely nothing about the escape that a small part of the pressure group had planned and carried out.

They could therefore have been justifiably angry about not being told, but if they were, it was not something they showed. Since John had been returned to Marcusville prison, a great deal of their shared—and unpaid—work was dedicated to appealing for a reprieve, bombarding all legal institutions in Ohio with arguments for a stay of execution.

With only twelve hours to go, they were sitting close together in a large waiting room in central Columbus. They needed each other, as everyone needs someone when all they want to do is lie down and give up. They were tired, they had been working all night and knew that their chances of influencing the decision were as good as next to nothing; John Meyer Frey's execution was a matter of concern for the whole of Ohio, his death would mean that justice had been served.

They sat on a bench clutching a bundle of papers, almost alone in the imposing, over-the-top waiting room, green marble floor and something that resembled classical Greek pillars down the main aisle.

They hadn't given up.

They were prepared and would very soon make their last appeal to the Ohio Supreme Court. They would then jump in a car and drive to Cincinnati and the U.S. Court of Appeals for the Sixth Circuit. John Meyer Frey had already died once and survived, he could do it again.

It wasn't over. It was never over.

When John stood up and looked at the camera with his will in his hand, the observation group had alerted Vernon Eriksen. A prisoner who was about to be executed had to be healthy and uninjured, but death had already started to eat away at this one. Vernon had run down the bare corridors lined with all the locked doors and when he got to the Death House, he had asked one of the guards to let him into the cell, to the man who had only twelve hours left to live. He had sat down on a stool next to him and they had talked about everything except what was going to happen, their voices quiet, and Vernon had put his hand on John's shoulder several times.

All that the people watching them on the silent black-and-white monitor in the observation room saw was a senior corrections officer calming down a condemned man who was panicking. They couldn't feel their closeness, nor even register John's surprise when Vernon admitted the major role he had played in John's escape. It was therefore also impossible to hear the prisoner suddenly start to thank the man who was responsible for looking after him unto death, for the days that had passed and become six extra years, for what had been an extended life, all because a person who he didn't really know had risked everything to give him the opportunity to continue breathing.

Ewert Grens was not in the least bit tired. Sleep was overrated. He had continued to get cups of coffee as night lightened into dawn into morning, and his very being had been consumed by a restless energy that came from the anxiety and anger that he no longer had room for but had to go somewhere. He had picked up Sven, who had been drained by too many sleepless hours, and asked him to go with him to the County Communications Center: two months of intense media coverage of *a political decision to deport a person in custody with an impending execution for which the date had already been set* would culminate today. Great organized demonstrations and violent unorganized clashes thirsting for the attention of every extra police officer who had been called in. When he arrived, Grens offered to relieve one of the operators, and when the first call came from the American embassy, requesting police reinforcement to help control the swelling crowd that was about to break into embassy property, he picked up the receiver and calmly explained, *sorry, no cars available*. He ignored Sven Sundkvist's shocked face and went on to the next call, and when a frightened embassy official described the demonstrators as an increasing threat, he gave the same answer, *sorry, no cars available*. The third time, when the demonstrators' shouts could be heard on the receiver and the officer was hysterical and pleaded for help from the police, Ewert Grens smiled as he whispered, *then call in the marines*, and hung up.

Helena, her son, Oscar, and her father-in-law, Ruben, were given permission by Vernon Eriksen to see the waiting prisoner in his cell in the Death House for their last family visit. They could then see him sitting behind a wall of thin steel bars instead of the square of steel-wire-reinforced glass that visitors were normally shown to in the final twenty-four hours.

It was hard to make out from the closed-circuit camera why they didn't seem to be talking at all, they just seemed to be sitting there, John Meyer Frey with his stool on the inside of the locked cell, his family in the corridor outside, as if that was all they wanted, to be near each other, no more words when everything had been said.

Thorulf Winge had walked from his home on Nybrogatan to the Ministry of Foreign Affairs on Gustav Adolfs Torg long before dawn. Yet another long day, he'd understood that much, yet more cameras, yet more questions.

A day he had been looking forward to.

When it was over, when night and dark had fallen, the two months of hell would be behind them. He had spent all his adult life in the halls of power, he had fended off a good deal of stupidity, hidden dozens of scandals in the shadows of diplomacy, negotiated a way out of both national and international crises before they had had a chance to grow beyond the embryonic stage. But everything paled in comparison to this damn girl killer. Winge had sometimes wondered, when he was on his own in the evenings, when the hate had taken a break, whether he was getting tired, if he didn't have the energy anymore, he was perhaps just too old. Every day! New claims, interviews, opinion polls, demands for his resignation. All over the deportation of a criminal? The papers, the TV channels, they loved it. The readers, the viewers loved it. It went on and on, but maybe it would ease off once Frey was dead, maybe it wouldn't be as much fun then to be involved.

He heard the shouts from the demonstrators—*Sweden! Murderer!*—that filled the big square outside. They had been chanting without interruption—*Sweden! Murderer!*—since lunch, he wondered how they could be bothered, if they didn't have work to go to.

He left the window and went back to his desk. He wasn't going to answer any questions today, he would stay in his office in the ministry, wait them out and go home about the time that the execution was due to take place.

The three officers who were observing John Meyer Frey's cell in the Death House via a camera had just started to relax slightly when one of the three visitors, a child of five, pulled himself loose from his mother's arms and ran toward the wall of bars that separated him from his father. It was clear on the black-and-white monitor that the senior corrections officer rushed forward and tried to prevent the child from holding on to two of the bars, that he pulled at one of the child's hands and that the mother hurried forward and pulled at the other. The recordings were without sound and so it wasn't possible to hear the voices, but the boy screamed, his face twisted; it took two or three minutes before he let go and then curled up on the floor like a fetus.

wednesday afternoon, 1500 hours

six hours left

IT WAS TWO MONTHS SINCE HE HAD DISEMBARKED FROM THE FERRY together with all the other passengers carrying plastic bags full of duty-free Absolut vodka in one hand and shyly holding the hand of the person they'd met the night before in the other as they walked down the ramp. He had longed to be home, hurried down the sidewalk that smelled of damp and carbon dioxide until impatience got the better of him and he had hailed a taxi to take him back to the block at Alphyddevägen 43. He had lived there, with his wife and son, a life that could have continued.

They had eaten rice pudding and blueberry jam. Oscar's choice, Daddy had been away and was home again and now they were going to eat what he liked best in the world, together.

It was hard to swallow.

John sat with the plate in front of him, his spoon midair, the blue-and-white mass seemed to grow as it got closer to his mouth.

The last supper.

So absurd. A person who is going to be executed can choose six hours before his death what will be found in his belly if there is a postmortem. He didn't want anything, said that there was no point in eating when it would soon be over. But Vernon, the senior corrections officer, had insisted, it was important, if not for him then for his family to know that he was as well as could be expected, and that food was a more important signal than John perhaps appreciated.

He had chosen Oscar's rice pudding. And he really had tried. But when he swallowed, it was as if it got stuck in his throat, the esophagus pressed against the windpipe, he couldn't eat.

He'd asked Vernon to sit with him. He was wise, they'd had their first conversation the very day that he'd come to the prison and Death Row, when he was seventeen. John knew that this level of intimacy was not right for a corrections officer and they had never talked like that when other ears could hear. The people watching them in the cell via the camera saw a dedicated member of the staff who was doing everything he could to calm a prisoner down in advance of his execution, which had attracted considerable attention.

"I can't."

"At least you tried."

"I can't even swallow a mouthful. Could you ask for someone to come and take the tray?"

Vernon had nothing more to say, there wasn't much more that could be said, only a few formalities, he'd never been particularly good at giving comfort.

"I'm about to go. I'll take it with me."

John wanted to ask about the weather outside. There was no day in here, no weather. A cell without windows in a corridor without windows. Maybe it didn't matter. If it was snowing, if it was getting warmer.

"John, you haven't asked for any family members."

Vernon looked at the man who was twenty years younger than him and seemed to be shrinking with every minute that remained.

"You must."

John shook his head.

"No."

"There will be lots of people there. Who you don't know. Who you've never seen. You need to look into someone's eyes, eyes you trust."

"Helena is not going to watch. Dad is not going to watch. And Oscar . . . there is no one else."

"John, please think about it, that's all I'm asking. When you're lying there, much more will be going on inside than you can ever imagine."

John closed his eyes, shook his head.

"Not them. But maybe you? I'd like that. If *you* were there. The eyes I recognize and trust."

Ewert Grens found it harder and harder to deal with the restlessness with every hour that passed. When the demonstrations in town had grown far beyond what anyone had anticipated, he had asked Sven to stay at the communications center and had himself gone to the car and driven toward Djurgården and the American embassy, to get his own impression of what was happening.

There was a vast number of people. The traffic had come to a standstill already in Strandvägen as people ran across the road without bothering about cars or buses, on their way to join the hordes of people and chants that now surrounded the various buildings in the block that comprised the American embassy. Grens was in a hurry and had driven along sidewalks, park paths, and then stopped at a distance, laughed for a while at the fools who were sitting in there shitting themselves. Served them right, it wasn't much justice perhaps, but for a few hours at least, it was a finger up the wide ass of power.

He had then driven on and realized suddenly that he was crossing Lidingö Bridge, on his way to the nursing home on the other side of the water.

Now he was sitting here beside her, his hand in hers, looking out of the window.

He had needed her and she had listened. A long story about a person who was going to be executed in six hours, that maybe it was his fault, that even after thirty-four years in one profession it was still so hard to know which stones should be left unturned.

More saliva had dribbled than normal.

He hadn't liked it, it made him uneasy.

So he had left her alone for a while, hurried out into the hall back to reception, insisted on talking to another member of staff, someone older and more experienced.

The nurse had seen him and been unable to stifle a deep sigh when she followed him back. One look would have been enough. But she knew what it was usually like and had stayed a little longer. A hand on Anni's forehead, her pulse, her breathing, she had examined her for a couple of minutes and then confirmed that she was just as well today as she had been every other time Grens had come running in a panic.

Ewert looked at Anni again, her eyes gazing out of the window, she smiled and he kissed her cheek, his hand in hers again.

He said it as gently as he could, that she had to stop scaring him like that, that he wouldn't manage long without her.

When the answer came that the Ohio Supreme Court had unanimously voted no to any further consideration of a possible reprieve for John Meyer Frey, Anna Mosley and Marie Morehouse were in the car on the way back from Cincinnati. Anna Mosley immediately pulled in to the coffeehouse they were just passing; too upset to carry on driving, she needed a cup of hot tea and a cigarette to stop her from screaming with disappointment.

Ruben Frey's house smelled of chicken and curry. A blue-striped apron around his rotund body, he liked making food and he did it every day even though he always ate alone. Since John had been taken from his childhood room for questioning in connection with the murder of Elizabeth Finnigan nearly twenty years earlier, Ruben had lived on his own, eaten on his own, gone through life on his own.

And this was all so unfamiliar.

His son was going to be executed in a few hours' time, would cease to be, forever. And that was why Ruben Frey's life was now richer than it had been for a very long time. A five-year-old grandson had moved into John's old room and was sleeping in his old bed, a beautiful young woman who was his daughter-in-law now sat opposite him at the kitchen table at night and drank twelve-year-old whiskey with him and talked about John and herself and her son, gave Ruben a sense of belonging that he could never have dreamed of. It was a peculiar feeling, the joy he had found in the midst of everything, all thanks to a death sentence, and he didn't know how to handle it.

It was Helena who answered when Marie Morehouse called from some café along Interstate 71 from Cincinnati. Morehouse's disappointment was tangible, they had worked hard and eventually the Frey/Schwarz family had started to hope and even believe that the arguments of the two diligent young lawyers, couched in legal terms, would succeed.

Helena Schwarz didn't even have the energy to cry. Morehouse had explained that they were still waiting to hear from several other courts: they expected the final answer from the U.S. Court of Appeals for the Sixth Circuit in exactly three hours' time, and from a judge called Anthony Glenn Adams at the U.S. Supreme Court; courts that were in themselves powerful enough to stop and postpone the decision to carry out the execution at 2100 hours.

She had sat down at the kitchen table, eaten what had smelled of curry for a couple of hours now, and given answers to her son's persistent questions that she herself could not yet comprehend; that he couldn't see his dad again today, that that was just the way it was, that Daddy didn't want to live in the house behind the high walls that you could see from Granddad's bedroom, and of course he still cared about them, but he might not come home again even so.

Vernon Eriksen hadn't been prepared. The question was so out of the blue, he hadn't had time to think it through, he hadn't had time to formulate a nice way of saying no.

"I can't, John. I can't be there."

He took John's hand and squeezed it.

"I've avoided executions as much as possible for the past twenty years. And I won't ever take part in one again. I try to get sick leave, whenever I can, I stay at home when I know that someone I've looked after is about to leave us."

John stood up, tried to move in the tiny cell, but Vernon was there, so he couldn't. He leaned against the bars, held the metal the way he always had, his thumb and finger around their cold until they went white.

"Then I want you to be the one who tends to me."

"What do you mean?"

"When I'm dead."

He looked at the funeral director's son. They had both grown up in Marcusville where freedom was what it was when everyone knew everyone. John's only image of Vernon outside, he remembered it clearly from when he was little: four years old, hand in hand with his father Ruben—his mother had just died and they went to the funeral parlor. Vernon was still working at home then, it was the same year that the prison was built, and he had greeted them in a room full of coffins.

Vernon bent down and picked up the tray of untouched food. To tend to a person who was no longer alive. *As if I am the one who decides over life and death.* He looked at John, got ready to leave.

"Yes."

He knew that it wouldn't happen. That *if* John really was going to be executed, he wouldn't be there. But he said it all the same.

"Yes. I'll do that."

John's face, a hint of relief.

"And John . . ."

His fingers around the bars, even harder, in silence.

"I don't know if it makes any difference. But I know that you're innocent. I don't believe that you murdered the Finnigan girl. That was what I thought the first time that I spoke to you, and I still believe it now."

wednesday evening, 1800 hours
three hours left

IT WAS DARK OUTSIDE, HE COULDN'T SEE IT BUT HE KNEW IT, THAT DAY
had turned to evening in Marcusville. People were sitting in their kitchens
and eating supper together—most of them came home around now, not
many of them went to the two bars in town, it had never been that sort of
place. John remembered his early puberty, the energy that thumped in his
chest, when Marcusville had been like an enormous plastic bag that made
it impossible to breathe. He had longed to get away, just like all his peers;
life had been waiting far beyond the main road into this town.

Three hours.

John tried to catch a look at the left arm of the officer who was standing
closest, dark and hairy, with a watch in silver metal.

Three hours left.

They were waiting outside the cell. Black caps, peaks pulled down over
their eyes, dark green shirts and pants, black shiny boots. Keys hanging on
yard-long chains, every step, every movement rattling, four guards in
identical uniforms and barely fifty yards from the washroom that smelled
of old drains. Two of them walked half a step in front, two of them half a
step behind. None of them said a word, he wasn't sure that they were even
looking at him, almost as if he had already ceased to be.

He was allowed to shower for ten minutes. The water was hot and he
liked it, turned his face up and let it burn the thin skin. Once he was used
to it, he turned the heat up to the next level, welcoming the pain.

The diaper was important. He had to bend over, for a moment back at
Sheremetyevo airport in Moscow, different kind that had to be closed at
the hip but it felt more or less the same.

He hadn't asked any questions then, he didn't ask any now. He knew
why he was wearing it.

The dark blue trousers were recently washed, he recognized the smell of
the laundry detergent, but the red stripe down the leg was new, he hadn't
seen pants like that before. A white top, V-neck, short sleeves, bare skin
meant visible veins.

It was when they were on their way back that one of the guards, the one with the watch, leaned forward and whispered something. John didn't hear it at first, asked him to repeat.

Fifteen judges with a unanimous result.

He'd also gotten a no from the U.S. Court of Appeals for the Sixth Circuit.

wednesday evening, 2000 hours

one hour left

MOST OF ALL, HE THOUGHT ABOUT HER SMILE. ELIZABETH HAD ONE OF those smiles that made everyone who looked at her uncertain. Was it tenderness, scorn, insecurity—it was impossible to decide. John had longed for those smiling lips, for several years he had longed for them; they had gone to the same school and walked the same way there and back. He had been sixteen years old when she asked him to kiss them. Soft, that had been his first thought, so unbelievably soft.

Helena? Probably the way she held a glass. He would never be able to explain it to anyone. She held it so delicately, so hard. It didn't break.

He looked up at the camera on the wall. People who were sitting in another room watching another person's last minutes. Did they enjoy it? Or was it just work? Eight hours watching someone who was about to be executed, then home to make supper? Maybe they were playing cards. Watching a tennis match, one all and the final set, on a sports channel on another monitor.

He shouted loudly until one of the guards came running. He'd changed his mind. He wanted to exercise his right to use the telephone that stood on a trolley farther down the corridor, which you could call from if the recipient accepted the charge.

It would never be enough. He knew that.

But their voices, one more time.

wednesday evening, 2045 hours

fifteen minutes left

THE MESSAGE THAT JUDGE ANTHONY GLENN ADAMS OF THE U.S. SUPREME Court had rejected the appeal for a stay of execution never reached the prisoner who was sitting waiting in one of the two cells in the Death House. Adams, who had the authority to process cases that were urgent unilaterally, had done what he usually did when a case involved the death penalty: he'd left it to the court's nine members to reason and reach a decision together.

Their conclusion had been unanimous.

One of the three phones that hung on a simple wooden panel on the wall of the room behind the death chamber was therefore connected directly to the governor's office in Columbus.

The line would be held open until the execution had been completed.

Only a call from the governor of Ohio in the fifteen minutes that remained could now prevent the execution of John Meyer Frey from being carried out.

wednesday evening, 2050 hours
ten minutes left

"MR. FREY?"

"Yes?"

"My name is Rodney Wiley. I'm one of the nurses here at Marcusville. I'd like to ask you to sit down, please."

John had been standing in the cell when the small man in an oversized white coat had opened the door and held out a thin, sweaty hand. Less than fifteen minutes to go, maybe ten, he had his clock ticking inside, the one he had carried with him since he was seventeen and realized that the only thing left to do was to count down.

He'd never seen Rodney Wiley before, he didn't know him, and yet he would now be one of the last people he saw and spoke to.

"Completely still, please, Mr. Frey."

The liquid that the nurse doused some cotton wool with was pungent. A disinfectant, the thin hand dabbed it carefully on the bend in his arm, around and around with the soft cotton wad. Wiley was about to insert the cannula, and it had to be clean for that, he wanted to avoid infection, someone who was still alive should be seen and treated as such, as a living being.

"Heparin. Anticoagulant. That's what I'm about to give you. We don't want anything clogging up the system, do we, Mr. Frey?"

It sounded more absurd than intended and Wiley immediately regretted it. He was nervous, scared; every time was just as difficult and he still hadn't learned how to talk to someone whose death he was preparing.

A few seconds more, he tried to avoid the prisoner's eyes, concentrated like normal on the bare arms and on making sure he injected what he knew to be enough anticoagulant.

"That's me done, Mr. Frey. I'll go now. You won't see me again."

His thin hand once more, a feeble handshake and they held on until Wiley couldn't bear it any longer.

The four guards had been standing outside waiting. When the nurse hurried off they came forward, looked at John, and asked him to leave the cell himself. He didn't have to take many steps to get to the death chamber, but they watched every single one, people who are going to die often demand a lot of attention.

The room was hexagonal, not much more than forty square feet, the walls were actually just large glass panes through which the witnesses could watch. The gurney stretched from wall to wall and was covered in a thick white cloth that made a rasping sound when his body was secured with six separate straps, broad and black, four across and two the length of his body, the one over his rib cage pressed hardest against his skin.

The lines that would then be connected to the two cannulas were transparent, making it easy to see when the fluid was being pumped through.

wednesday evening, 2100 hours

HE RECOGNIZED SEVERAL OF THE FACES THAT LOOKED AT HIM FROM THE other side of the large glass wall and who had the right to be there, in compliance with what was called Administrative Code 2949.25.

Farthest to the left was Charles Hartnett, so much older than John remembered, now a retiree, but the policeman who had arrested him that morning in his room, seventeen years old and still not properly awake, the stranger who had ordered him to stand by the bed with his legs apart.

Beside him, Jacob Holt, head of the Ohio Department of Rehabilitation and Correction, or ODRC, who a few hours before every execution left his spacious office in central Columbus and traveled south to Marcusville, one of his duties, to watch people die.

Shoulder to shoulder with him, the warden of Marcusville, a tall dark man of John's age, the sort who tilted his head back when he looked at you, as if to be even more above you.

A long row of what he was certain were journalists.

A few suits that he had never seen before.

A priest, the man who many years before had visited Marvin Williams regularly, he had heard them talking in the next cell, praying together; Marv had always seemed lighter, almost absolved, afterward.

Four guards, half a step behind, the peaks of their caps even farther down over their eyes than before.

Only one woman.

He recognized her, knew her so well. Alice Finnigan. He had always liked her, she had been warm, welcoming, to the boy with a bad reputation who was courting her daughter.

He avoided looking at the father who was hate, at the red face that couldn't get close enough.

John had been requested to choose three witnesses of his own but had refrained from exercising this right.

He didn't want anyone he cared about to be there.

Total silence.

The four last minutes were one long wait for time to expire. They all looked at their watches and hoped that it would soon be over, it didn't seem that any of them were in the habit of counting down.

The telephone on the wooden panel on the wall. The only thing that still existed. A call from the governor and everything would stop.

You could almost hear it, the ring that was louder than any other, the ring that never came.

Forty-five seconds left, to be on the safe side of what was absolutely nothing.

Then the warden nodded to an older man with a gray, well-groomed beard. Patrick McCarthy, proud, straight back, the longest-serving corrections officer in Marcusville. He had been waiting beside the machine that was designed to supply the drugs and now nodded back as his finger pushed in the large white plastic switch.

Sodium thiopental, 5 grams, John yawned, lost consciousness.

Pancuronium bromide, 100 milligrams, his muscles were paralyzed, his breathing stopped.

Potassium chloride, 100 milliequivalents, heart attack.

wednesday evening, 2111 hours

WHEN THE PRISON DOCTOR EXAMINED THE BODY OF JOHN MEYER FREY and with a faint voice announced to the warden that the execution had been successful, it was as if life came back to the people who were standing close together in the witness area. The silence, the waiting, it was over, everything else could continue now. The warden did what he usually did, clapped his hands twice to get everyone's attention and announced that the prisoner had been proclaimed dead by the duty doctor at 21:10:07 hours.

Edward Finnigan took another step forward. He wanted to see the body that wasn't moving, feel the peace he so longed for. The agitation, the dark, the hate that Alice had accused him of, it should all be gone.

He looked at the face that was totally relaxed.

The hate.

It was still there.

Finnigan spat at the glass several times, at the body that was being removed from the gurney with a white sheet and black straps. Alice Finnigan surged forward and pounded her hands against her husband's back, she screamed that he should calm down, she cried and hit him until he left the room, without turning around.

thursday

IT WAS ONE OF THOSE COLD, CLOUDLESS MORNINGS, FULL OF AIR, WHEN winter is turning to spring.

Vernon Eriksen had woken up several hours earlier, agitated in the dark, the dream again: he was small and sitting looking down at his father from upstairs, the clothes and makeup that brought the dead back to life for a while, the grieving who were crying and waiting outside. He had gotten up, shaken off the night, warm milk and a sandwich at half past three. He had sat at his kitchen table and looked out over Marcusville's tired streets as they slowly came to life, the newspaper boy who cycled past, the odd bird that landed on the empty asphalt, neighbors in their pajamas and slippers shuffling out to get the morning paper to read with their cornflakes and vanilla yogurt. He still had a sick note, covering the whole day until six o'clock and the back shift, no one at the prison would miss him until then.

He knew what no one else knew. That he would never go back there again.

Vernon looked around. He liked his kitchen. His parents' home, he had always lived here. He had been nineteen when both of them had disappeared from his life without explaining why. He had then bought out his older sister; she had always been more restless, more curious than he was, and had moved to Cleveland some years before to study and had stayed there.

He had never gone anywhere.

His work as senior corrections officer on Death Row, occasional encounters with people who frightened him in their attempts to get close, a whole lot of books and long walks, the few months with Alice a long time ago, and following their breakup at the time of his parents' death, the endless emptiness, he had not really cared about much at all. Until his growing involvement with a group of activists who were opposed to the death penalty. He liked to think of it as an opposition movement, like a soldier, to feel that he was actively taking part in the fight against a society's old-fashioned values. Always in the background, always unofficial, he was aware that a prison guard could not be associated with things like that. And he needed his job, to be a friend to those who counted time, it felt right, and was perhaps as important as the meetings and protest lists and contact with lawyers who had to be persuaded to take an interest in the future of prisoners who had been sentenced to death, for next to no money.

Vernon waited until the clock by the oven turned eight. Then he lifted the telephone from its cradle on the wall, dialed the number for Marcusville's outpatient clinic, and asked for Nurse Alice Finnigan. When his call was connected and she answered, he put the phone down.

He had just wanted to hear her voice one more time.

The morning chill snapped at his cheeks, the light wind making it colder than he'd thought. He wasn't going particularly far, only a couple of minutes away, he was freezing but could cope.

There wasn't much he needed really. He'd organized the paper bag, white with the prison's green logo on it, the evening before. He was carrying it folded in one hand, it weighed nothing.

Finnigan's impressive house on Mern Riffe Drive in front of him. Two months since his last visit. He had told them about John, that he was alive, that he was living in a country in northern Europe. He remembered Edward Finnigan's reaction and it still made him feel sick. He had thought then how incredibly ugly people could become and that he had seen such ugliness when the dates for executions were set, when the victim's family delighted, the hate and revenge that made them feel alive. He also remembered Alice's sorrow, her shame and the distaste she had felt for her husband had been intense. Vernon had left, shaken by a married woman's unbelievable loneliness.

Not until he had rung the bell for the third time did he hear anyone moving about in the house.

Slow, heavy steps down the stairs, an inner door being opened, more steps, and then Edward Finnigan's blank face.

"Eriksen?"

Edward Finnigan's skin was white, dark circles under his eyes, a terry dressing gown around his corpulent frame.

"I should perhaps have called first."

Finnigan held the door half-open, his bare feet started to freeze.

"What do you want?"

"Can I come in?"

"It's not the best time. I've taken the day off."

"I know."

"You know?"

"I was told. Aren't you going to let me in?"

Finnigan made some coffee in a percolator that coughed loudly. He wasn't used to doing it, that was obvious, it was the sort of thing Alice normally did.

"Black?"

"A little milk."

They drank from white porcelain cups with an expensive stamp on the bottom and avoided looking at each other. Vernon had known Finnigan all his life, and yet he had no idea who he really was.

"What was it you wanted?"

"I want to talk about Elizabeth."

"Elizabeth?"

"Yes."

"Not today."

"Today."

Finnigan thumped his cup down, a big brown stain on the light tablecloth.

"Do you have any idea what happened yesterday?"

"Yes."

"Well, then you can damn well figure out that today of all days I have absolutely no wish to talk about my dead daughter to someone I don't really care about."

There was a clock in the large, elegant sitting room. The kind that ticked loudly, every second was a stroke of lightning. Vernon had always wondered how people could stand it, but right now the sound was comforting, it hid the intense silence.

"You can't possibly understand."

For the first time since they'd sat down, Finnigan looked straight at Vernon.

"You have no idea of what it's like to go around thinking about a person's death, every hour, every day for nearly twenty years. You have no fucking idea of how much you can hate when you have to."

Finnigan's eyes were red, shiny, the bitter man was close to tears.

"You don't get it! He's dead now! I saw him die! And it doesn't help!"

He put his hand to his eyes and rubbed hard.

"It doesn't help a fucking iota! She was right. Alice was right all along. Do you know how hard it is to accept that? That you can't hate a dead person. That it doesn't help. My daughter isn't here. She still isn't here!"

Edward Finnigan bent forward toward the coffee table, his face close to the top. So he didn't see Vernon's fleeting smile before he spoke.

"The toilet? Could I use it?"

Vernon went in the direction that Finnigan pointed, out through the kitchen, into the hall. But when he got to the toilet, he kept going, hasty steps down into the cellar and the shooting range where he had waited for Finnigan the last time. He stood in front of the gun cabinet that hung on the wall, put a plastic bag on his hand and opened it. The pistol he was looking for was at the back on the second shelf. He remembered that Finnigan had emptied it of ammunition and then put it back there. He carefully lifted it up, with the plastic bag still on his hand—he wanted to preserve the fingerprints that were already there.

It had taken a minute, no more.

He went up again, put the gun in the paper bag he had left on the hall carpet and then went into the toilet and flushed. Finnigan was still sitting where he'd left him, his empty eyes fixed on the tabletop.

"I'm here to talk about Elizabeth."

"So you said. And I said that today is not a good day."

"It is a good day. You'll think so too, afterward. But first, just a bit about John."

"Not a word about him in this house!"

He hit his hand on the table and a glass candlestick that had been standing close to the edge jumped onto the parquet and broke in two.

"Never again!"

Vernon was calm, his voice low.

"I'm not going to leave. Not until you listen to what I have to say."

It had nearly turned into a fight. They had stood facing each other, Finnigan's white face was now red and he was panting, but Vernon Eriksen was a big man and Finnigan had glared at him for a while before more or less collapsing onto the sofa.

Vernon watched him closely now, wanted to be absolutely sure he saw his reaction.

"I was responsible for John Meyer Frey's escape from Marcusville."

Edward Finnigan deflated as the senior corrections officer in front of him told the story of how a prisoner who had been sentenced to death, his daughter's murderer, had escaped from his cell on Death Row and then lived in freedom in another part of the world for six years. Eriksen took almost thirty minutes to describe the escape in detail, the medical preparations and drugs that were used to create the illusion of death and then the journey via Canada and Russia to the capital of Sweden. He spent considerable time describing the transport from the prison morgue to a car that was waiting outside, he liked that bit best, the actual escape from inside the prison walls was closer to his heart than medicines and false passports. He even smiled broadly when he described the body bag requested by the two doctors for transportation to the medical examiner in Columbus, no one would open it to look at a dead person, and when the van had been unloaded and was on its way back to Marcusville, it hadn't taken long to lift the body bag and put it in the back of the other car that was waiting farther along the same loading dock.

Finnigan didn't move. He didn't speak. Vernon looked at the man lying on the sofa with his hands clutching his belly and he felt a peace, all these years he had thought about this, he was finally there.

"But it wasn't John who took your daughter's life."

As if he had hit him.

"The person who was executed yesterday, as a result of the death penalty that you so firmly believe in, was innocent."

Finnigan tried to get up but fell back, as his arms lacked strength.

"You and Alice were seldom home before eight in the evening, Elizabeth usually had the house to herself until then. I saw John leaving, they held each other for a while at the front door over there, then he walked off."

Vernon was still watching Finnigan, he wanted to see his face, how it changed when he found out.

"I slipped in ten minutes after he'd gone. He'd held her, they'd had sex, they usually did before you came home. Didn't you know that? Fingerprints, sperm, he was all over her body. It only took a couple of minutes, no more, she was lying there on the floor when I shut the front door behind me."

Vernon kept on speaking until Finnigan leapt at him in a fury and tried to hit his face with clenched fists. That was exactly what he wanted. The bright red man screamed and hit and bit and Vernon let him until he was sure that they had exchanged enough blood and skin cells.

Then one hard blow to the point on Finnigan's chest that would hurl him into unconsciousness. He hurried out to the hall and the paper bag and took out a thin rag and a small bottle of ether.

He reckoned it was enough to make sure that Edward Finnigan would lie there unconscious for about an hour and a half, the time that he needed.

VERNON ERIKSEN HAD NEVER MET RICHARD HINES BEFORE. BUT HE HAD read his articles about the American legal system in the *Cincinnati Post* over the last ten years. He didn't always share the views of the reporter, but Vernon had appreciated his sharp wit, his choice of words, his precision; Hines's research was always correct, his claims might not be comfortable, but they were always correct.

They had arranged to meet in a small café near the main road into Marcusville, ten minutes' walk from the Finnigans' house. Vernon knew that the place was usually more or less empty at this time of the morning. One waitress, a few truck drivers, otherwise just crumbs on the table and tired music piped out through cheap loudspeakers.

Richard Hines was already there, a beer and a sandwich with something that looked like roast beef. He was smaller than Vernon had imagined, a slim man of no more than a hundred and thirty pounds or so, but his eyes were alert and his smile as wide as his face was narrow.

"Eriksen?"

Vernon nodded, looked at the waitress and pointed at Hines's beer bottle before sitting down opposite him.

"Thank you for coming."

Hines gave a wave of his hand.

"I wasn't going to at first. I have to admit that you did sound like just another nut. I get a lot of calls, litigious people who have read something and see me as their informal counsel. But I checked your employment details and I'd be an idiot if I didn't listen to a senior corrections officer on Death Row in one of the state's maximum security prisons when he calls and says he wants to meet twelve hours after a planned execution and claims that he has a scoop."

The waitress was a young woman, more of a girl really, with a life that had just begun. She came over with the beer and Vernon wondered why she was satisfied with this, some squalid café in a dump of a town, when the world was waiting out there.

"I'll give you some news, all right. I only have one condition. That it's printed no later than tomorrow."

Hines laughed, a hint of derision in his voice.

"*I'll* be the judge of that."

"Tomorrow."

"Let's get one thing straight before we start. *I'll* be the judge of the newsworthiness. If your story's good enough, I write it. If it's not, well, then we've just had a beer together."

"It's good enough."

The buzz of the background music was irritating. Vernon excused himself, went over to the waitress and asked her to turn down the volume, then sat down again at the compact pine table with four red plastic place mats.

"So now we can hear each other."

He looked at Hines and started to talk.

"I've worked at Marcusville prison all my adult life. I guess I've almost lived there, with the inmates, for over thirty years. I've seen all there is to see of criminality. All sorts of criminals, the consequences of all sorts of crimes. I believe in punishment. A society that penalizes is a society with norms."

A truck braked outside the window. A quick glance, they both saw the big man with a pigtail get out and head for the entrance.

"With one exception. The death penalty. A society with norms cannot have a state that takes life. It took me some years on Death Row to understand that. You see, every prison holds someone who is innocent or who has been convicted wrongly. I know that, anyone who works in a prison knows that. I'm sure that a couple of those I was responsible for fell into that category."

The truck driver sat down at a table at the opposite end of the café, Vernon had lowered his voice when he came in, but now raised it again.

"All it takes is for one innocent person to be executed. Just one, and the system fails! If it's discovered, afterward, it can never be undone. Can it? No amount of damages can bring back life."

He had been preparing what he was going to say for eighteen years. Now . . . it was suddenly hard to find the words.

"The victim's retribution . . . Hines, that's nothing more than revenge. All that stuff about justice. Rehabilitation. Do you believe it? It's not about that anymore. If it ever was. I see it every day. Revenge . . . that's the state's real driving force."

He finished his beer, glanced at Hines, who still looked interested.

"And sometimes . . . sometimes you have to take a life to save other lives. Did you know that, Hines? I chose Edward Finnigan. That's what I did, I *chose*. Finnigan is the sort of person people listen to. An outspoken proponent of the death penalty with considerable power in the state. Perfect. He had a daughter who he would mourn. The daughter had a boyfriend who was a troublemaker, so it would be easy to get him convicted. Two lives. That was all, Hines. I've sacrificed two lives so that a nation can understand how wrong the death penalty is. If those two lives get us to question a system that could take many more lives, then it was worth it."

Richard Hines sat completely still. He had stopped taking notes, unsure that he'd really understood what he'd just heard.

"I took Elizabeth Finnigan's life. I knew that John Meyer Frey would be sentenced to death because she was a minor. When he had been executed, then I would do this, what I'm doing now, stand up and say what actually happened."

Hines writhed in discomfort. A senior corrections officer was sitting opposite him and had just claimed that he was responsible for one of the state's most sensational murders in recent times.

He was human and wanted to run away and report the madman. But he was also a journalist and wanted to know more.

"Frey escaped. What you're saying . . . there's something that's not quite right."

"Something happened. Suddenly . . . I couldn't go through with what I'd planned so carefully. I . . . started to care about the boy. John was smart, vulnerable . . . I'd never gotten close to anyone like that before. The others, I don't know, every time one of the people I was responsible for in there died, it was like a family member had stopped breathing. And John—like a son, I can't explain it any better than that. I didn't have the courage to let him die. Do you understand?"

"No. I don't understand."

"For many years I've been involved with various networks that oppose the death penalty. I started to work with the group that was campaigning for John. And I started to plan his escape with a handful of key people."

He shrugged.

"And then . . . one mistake after six years of freedom! I knew immediately that everything would happen fast. It was a matter of prestige.

Finnigan's position. So I'm doing it now instead. Completing what I started a long time ago."

The last drops of beer had been warm for some time but he was thirsty and drank what he could of the foam at the bottom of the glass. He rummaged in his trouser pockets, found four one-dollar bills and left them beside the empty glass.

"Hines, I was the one who killed her. And John Meyer Frey was executed. A system based on the death penalty will never work. I know that you're going to write about this. Before tomorrow even. It's too good for you or anyone else not to. And when it becomes general knowledge, when people know . . . the system is done for."

Vernon had stood up, buttoned his coat, he was already on his way out of the deserted café.

"Sit down."

"I don't have time."

"We're not done yet. Assuming that you still want it to be printed?"

Vernon looked at his watch. Fifty-five minutes left. He sat down.

"This is all a bit too simple. It's a good story. But I need more. Things to *prove* that what you're saying is true."

"On your desk. When you get back. You'll find a package."

"A package?"

"The sort of thing that the person who killed Elizabeth Finnigan might have. Her bracelet, for example. The one she always had on. I haven't seen it mentioned in the investigation. Her parents will confirm that it's hers."

"Anything else?"

"The sort of thing that only someone who was responsible for John's escape would know. You've got an eight-page document which describes in detail how it was done. When you read it and compare it with the records about his . . . death, you'll understand."

"Or so you say."

"Pictures. You'll have pictures that only someone who was there could have taken. Of her body lying on the floor. Of John's body in the morgue, in the body bag and boarding a plane in Toronto."

Richard Hines turned his gaze to the window, wanted to get away, down the road that was behind the big truck.

"I've never heard anything like it. If you ask me . . . you're fucking sick."

"Sick? No. Anyone who thinks that a state can take life, that's sick. Trying to do away with the death penalty, what can be healthier than that?"

Hines shook his head.

"Thankfully, I don't need to be the judge of that. You'll be charged for this. You'll be convicted."

Vernon Eriksen smiled for the first time since they'd met, it was as if the nervousness slipped away, he was almost done and he had plenty of time.

"You know that I won't be. That would be as good as declaring the system was useless. The state of Ohio would never, *never*, admit to executing the wrong person. No prosecutor would take up the case again."

Vernon got up to leave for the second time. He didn't shake Hines's hand, just gave a friendly nod to the reporter who would immediately jump in his car and drive back to Cincinnati and write the most extraordinary article he had ever written.

"Thank you for coming. I'm going to go and see Edward Finnigan now. And I'm sure that he'll listen to me too."

HE LOOKED AT HIS WATCH. FORTY-FIVE MINUTES LEFT.

He'd manage it.

It was still cold, he did up the top button on his coat and pulled on his gloves. He walked toward Mern Riffe Drive, slowed down as he passed the Finnigans' big, silent house, if anyone had happened to look out the window they would later say that Vernon Eriksen had been there around that time.

He kept on walking for another half mile or so, along the path through the woods that started where Mern Riffe Drive ended. His regular walk, several times a week he breathed in the air that was trees and moss, and at the end of the path, a small lake. As a child he had cycled here in summer, the water was cold but clean, the bottom covered in sludge and sharp stones, but as long as you didn't put your feet down, the lake was a good place to swim, the only one in Marcusville.

Vernon stood still, looked at the mirrorlike surface of the water, at the trees that meant that no one could see, at the sky that was ice blue.

It was such a beautiful day.

He went over to the tree, the one that was biggest, about fifteen to twenty yards from the water. The rooks loved it. There were no leaves, just bare branches and bare twigs, but you couldn't see that, as hundreds of rooks sat there, made it darker, alive, as if they were replacing the great greenness.

He had Finnigan's gun in the paper bag. The ammunition, two bullets only, lay loose beside it. He loaded it and aimed in the air above the tree. The birds lifted as they normally did when he fired, cawing and squawking in confusion. But not for long. They circled up, then descended cautiously, and were back sitting on the tree within minutes.

Vernon felt nothing, realized that he had never been so empty before.

It had taken nearly twenty years and now he was here, only a couple of minutes to go, no more. *It's not God who decides over life and death*. It was this last bit that meant most. *I do*. He had always been convinced that two young people dying would be enough to get a state, perhaps even a whole

364

nation, that championed the death penalty, to think again. That process would start tomorrow morning when the *Cincinnati Post* carried an account of what *actually* happened. But this, this would take the question even further into people's homes, the discussions around the kitchen table would take on another dimension when the champion of the death penalty in Ohio, the father of the murdered girl himself, who had for all these years spoken about the victim's right to retribution and said that it was obvious that any society with morals had to offer an eye for an eye . . . when he was the one who was in the dock.

A couple of birds in the tree cackling, a light wind that rustled the reeds, otherwise silence.

He took out what was left in the bag. A thin hemp string. A small lump of tallow that had a powerful odor. A few steps toward the stony beach, he ripped the paper bag to pieces and threw them into the water before turning back.

He stopped beneath one of the tree's solid lower branches. He hunkered down and rubbed the smelly lump of tallow onto the hemp string, from one end to the other until it shone like silver. The rooks would see it. The rooks would smell it. He had tried it before and knew that it worked.

He would use his left hand. When he then fell, his left arm would end up in such a twisted position that it would be impossible for anyone to imagine it was suicide.

Every movement as he'd rehearsed it.

He tied one end of the sticky twine loosely around his left wrist, threw the rest over the branch and made sure that it would hang down near his head. He switched the gun from his right-hand coat pocket to his left hand, then, in the same hand, caught the end of the string that was hanging loose.

He had murdered Edward Finnigan's only child.

He had now made sure that a reporter knew that he was going to tell Edward Finnigan the truth today.

There was a motive.

A forensic investigation would later find traces of him in Edward Finnigan's house, confirm that the weapon that had been fired was registered to Edward Finnigan, and had his fingerprints on it, confirm that the traces of blood and skin found on him were those of Edward Finnigan.

It was hard to aim at his right temple with his left hand loosely tied in the string, but if he didn't blink, and if he turned his cheek just slightly closer, then he was sure he'd succeed.

The shot scared the hundred or so crows that were sitting in the tree above the person who fell to the ground. They lifted, circled, cawed in agitation, then returned after a couple of minutes. Whatever it was that was gleaming down there, and that smelled of tallow, had shortly after enticed all of them down to the ground. It took about half an hour, and when they had eaten the short, thin hemp string, they went back and sat on the leafless branches.

They weren't particularly bothered by the person who was lying there dead, shot in the head with a pistol that would later be found a few yards from his body.

some months later

IT WAS SUMMER OUT THERE, BUT IT COULDN'T BE SEEN FROM THE LONG corridor of cells on Death Row in Marcusville prison; the only visible sign was a strip of bright sunlight that found its way in through the narrow window up by the ceiling. Michael Oken had worked there for only nine weeks and had already gotten into the habit of walking down the hard concrete twice a day and looking carefully into each cell, to get to know who was where and to demonstrate that the change in senior corrections officer meant continued discipline, maintaining control.

He often stopped for a while in front of one of them, a cell that had once been empty for a long time, about halfway down. The prisoner on the bunk in the confined space was the only one he had never heard say a word; he was always lying down, always staring at the ceiling, and it was hard to tell whether he was awake or unconscious.

And today, just like any other. The large body on its back, face to the ceiling and slightly turned from the corridor. The orange coveralls with DR on the leg. Michael Oken looked at him for a while, wished that he would turn around and start to talk, there was so much that he wanted to know.

A deranged man who had killed Oken's predecessor, execution style, one bullet in the temple, who had also been the governor's closest adviser.

Michael Oken sighed, they all had their stories, but that one, he would love to hear that one.

FROM THE AUTHORS

CELL 8 IS A NOVEL.

The characters in the book are therefore fictitious.

Not even Ewert Grens, whom we like so much, is one of us. So how could any of the others be?

Marcusville doesn't exist either.

And we knowingly took certain liberties with the historical timeline and other facts in the service of the story. For instance, the state of Ohio is not responsible for two of the executions described in this book—one by electric chair and one by lethal injection—as neither John Meyer Frey nor his neighbor, Marv Williams, ever existed. Indeed, the last execution by electrocution in Ohio took place in 1963, decades before Marv was executed.

And all the stuff about *retribution*—the fact that Swedish and American, as well as other international politicians, might seek to limit the pursuit of a solution to increasingly serious crimes and clothe it with simple rhetoric about the victims' right to retribution—is possibly also just a figment of the authors' imagination.

A big thank-you to Johnnie, Tim, Cynth, Andy, and Ron for your indispensable help.

Black Bob, because you fooled them all.

Lasse Lagergren for your medical knowledge, Jan Stålhamre for your knowledge about police work, and Lars-Åke Pettersson for your knowledge about Kronoberg detention facility.

Fia Svensson for your countless hours on the first reading, proofreading, and all the other sorts of reading that we didn't know existed.

Niclas Breimar, Ewa Eiman, Mikael Nyman, and Vanja Svensson for particularly wise observations.

Our literary agent, Niclas Salomonsson, and his crew at Salomonsson Agency for always giving us energy.

And of course our UK editorial team, Georgina Difford, Liz Hatherell, Richard Arcus, Judith Colleran, and the rest of the Quercus family.

And a special thanks to Jon Riley, our publisher.

Anders Roslund and Börge Hellström
STOCKHOLM, 2011